P9-EMH-653

Titles by Kate Carlisle

Bibliophile Mysteries

Homicide in Hardcover

If Books Could Kill

The Lies That Bind

Murder Under Cover

Pages of Sin
(Novella: E-book Only)

One Book in the Grave

Peril in Paperback

A Cookbook Conspiracy

The Book Stops Here

Ripped from the Pages

Books of a Feather

Once Upon a Spine

Buried in Books

The Book Supremacy

The Grim Reader

Fixer-Upper Mysteries

A High-End Finish

This Old Homicide

Crowned and Moldering

Deck the Hallways

Eaves of Destruction

A Wrench in the Works

Shot Through the Hearth

Premeditated Mortar

THE GRIM READER

A Bibliophile Mystery

Kate Carlisle

BERKLEY PRIME CRIME
New York

BERKLEY PRIME CRIME
Published by Berkley
An imprint of Penguin Random House LLC
penguinrandomhouse.com

ISBN: 9780451491442

Berkley Prime Crime hardcover edition / June 2020
Berkley Prime Crime mass-market edition / April 2021

Printed in the United States of America
1 3 5 7 9 10 8 6 4 2

*This book is dedicated to my
beautiful Auntie Kay, with
all my love*

Chapter 1

"It's good to be back in Dharma," Derek said, breathing in the crisp fall air.

We stood on the balcony outside the master bedroom of the home we'd be living in for the next two weeks and took in the gorgeous scenery. I felt all of my stress dissipate as I gazed out at the green terraced hills. As far as the eye could see, thousands of sturdy grapevines grew tall and lush, their leaves turning golden brown in the autumn sun. Even from this far away, I could see the clusters of ripe fruit more than ready for the coming harvest.

"This view never gets old," I said with a happy sigh, smiling up at him.

Derek pulled me close and kissed my temple. "Beautiful."

"It's been way too long since we were here." I rested my head on my husband's shoulder. Actually, it had only been a few months, I realized with some amazement. But so much had happened in that time, it seemed longer. First I had attended a national librarians' convention and faced down a deadly librarian or two. Then Derek and I had gotten married and we'd flown off to honeymoon in Paris. It had been an incredibly romantic time. And then we had come home to find dangerous goons with guns, a vicious assassin, and more than one victim of cold-blooded murder.

Sudden shivers skittered across my shoulders at the memory. You would think I'd be used to finding dead bodies by now. But no, it shocked me to my very core every time.

With determination, I shook off the chills. We were in Dharma now. We could relax and enjoy our families and friends. This coming weekend was Dharma's first annual Book Festival and the following week we would stay to help with the grape harvest. I took a few more deep breaths to get rid of the last of those shivers. I didn't want anything to interfere with my excitement over the upcoming book festival. There would be books everywhere—and no dead bodies!

Yes, it was good to be back in Dharma with Derek. It was good to be back in this place where my family and I had lived since I was eight years old, before there was even a town called Dharma. Back then, there were only Airstream campers and tents and grapevines. I had been very unhappy that our parents had forced us to move from San Francisco out to the boondocks, until I climbed down from the family van and spotted a little dark-haired girl. She defiantly clutched her bald Barbie doll and looked just as pissed off as I felt. That was Robin. We clicked instantly and everything was okay after that.

Our parents were part of a group of Deadheads and seekers of wisdom who had followed their spiritual leader Avatar Robson Benedict—or Guru Bob, as my siblings and I called him—to the wilds of Sonoma

County, where they created the Fellowship for Spiritual Enlightenment and Higher Artistic Consciousness.

Now, of course, most members of the commune lived in beautiful homes that dotted the hills and valleys around Dharma. They worked for the wineries or in the vineyards or contributed in other ways to the busy, thriving community of shops, tech firms, and restaurants scattered around Dharma. Thanks to plenty of canny advice from Guru Bob and the lucrative profit-sharing plan that he'd established early on, his followers had learned to invest wisely. And now, twenty-five years later, our people were thriving and our town had become one of the most popular destination spots in wine country.

And lately some of Derek's family had bought homes in the area, so for me, Dharma kept getting better and better.

"Is everything out of the car?" I asked.

"Yes." Derek grinned. "Including all of your bookbinding supplies. And Charlie."

I reached out and squeezed his hand. "Thank you."

Just that morning Derek and I had driven here from San Francisco with our cat Charlie. The drive itself had only taken an hour, but it had taken even longer to move our clothes and essential items from the car into the house. Now it was time to take a minute and enjoy the quiet.

I felt a whisper of movement and glanced down to see Charlie winding herself around and between my legs, brushing her thick, creamy white tail against my ankles. "Well, look who ventured out of her crate."

After a few more sweeps of her tail, Charlie slinked over to Derek, who stooped down and picked her up in his arms. "We'll have to be extra cautious that she doesn't wander outside."

Despite being a mecca for sophisticated wine enthusiasts, Dharma was still rustic and woodsy, so there were plenty of hawks and coyotes to worry about. And even though Charlie was a full-grown cat now, I still imagined her to be a defenseless little kitten and would be heartbroken if anything happened to her.

"Yes, we will." I reached over to stroke Charlie's soft back and give her a scratch between her ears. "We don't want to lose you," I murmured. Our girl was an indoor cat, having spent most of her life inside our San Francisco apartment. I knew there were any number of wild animals out there looking for a tasty snack in the form of a fluffy, well-behaved housecat. I was always reading stories in the paper about small animals being carried off by red hawks or attacked by raccoons. Lately I had even seen reports of a mountain lion sighting nearby. I wasn't about to let Charlie roam outside with predators like that skulking around.

Derek led the way back inside and I carefully closed the door behind us. The cat was precious to both of us, ever since Derek had brought her home as a surprise for me.

Footsteps sounded from behind us and I turned to watch Annie walk into the master bedroom where we were standing.

I gave her shoulder a soft squeeze. "Thank you for letting us stay."

"It's your house, too," she said lightly.

It was a long story, but basically this house had once belonged to my old bookbinding mentor Abraham Karastovsky. He'd never known he had a daughter until the last few days of his life and he had been looking forward to getting to know her better after their first brief meeting. Sadly, he was killed before that could happen, and consequently, he left his entire estate to me, including his sumptuous Mediterranean-style house with its amazing views, along with the equally amazing, fully stocked bookbinding workshop out beyond the pool. Plus six million dollars, but that's a whole other story.

So legally the house belonged to me, but after my family and I got to know Annie—and after the required paternity test results came through proving that Annie was indeed Abraham's daughter—I asked the lawyers to write out a joint tenant agreement that gave half of the property to Annie. We also set up a trust that would pay Annie a generous allowance until she could determine what she wanted to do with the rest of her life.

Annie's mother—the woman who had never told Annie or Abraham about their connection to each other—had passed away during that same period. So with no more attachments, Annie moved to Dharma, where she was welcomed by my mother with open arms.

After a very short time, Annie figured out exactly what she wanted to do with the rest of her life. She had taken her money and opened a cute kitchenware shop on Dharma's fashionable shopping lane. Since then, she had become an integral member of Dharma's business community and now she was truly thriving. But I could still picture the grief-stricken Goth girl she had been when we first met.

"Does everything look okay?" she asked, giving the bedspread a minute tug to straighten it. "This room is pretty nice, isn't it?"

"It's fabulous," I said. "The whole house is amazing and the view from the balcony is wonderful."

Annie sighed and glanced around the master bedroom. "I could never bring myself to move into this room. I've replaced all the furniture and painted the walls, but it still reminds me of Abraham." Her eyes clouded, then she seemed to shake herself out of the mood. "Besides, I prefer staying on the first floor. It's easier and, you know, it suits me."

"It's kind of you to open up your home to us," Derek said.

"Oh. Gosh, Derek, it's really no problem." Her eyelashes fluttered and she gave him a sappy smile, clearly charmed. Derek had that effect on people, especially women. It might've been his elegant British accent that did it, or maybe it was his amazing good looks. Either way, I, too, found myself charmed daily.

"We really do appreciate you letting us stay here," I added.

"To be honest," she admitted, "having you here gives me a good excuse to stay with Presley for the next two weeks. We've been talking about moving in together so this'll either make us or break us."

I grinned. Annie's boyfriend Presley was the son of an old friend of my mother's. "In that case, we're happy to help you out."

"It's a win-win." Annie headed for the stairway. "I'm about to take off and leave you guys alone, but first I want to go over a few things in the kitchen."

"Sounds good."

Derek and I followed her downstairs, with Charlie keeping up alongside us.

Annie gave us quick lessons on using the coffeemaker and the toaster oven. "You're welcome to drink my coffee and eat anything you find in the pantry or the fridge. Oh, and I have an unopened package of English muffins in the freezer if you want any of those. And cupcakes. Help yourself."

"You're leaving cupcakes?" I said, my eyes lighting up.

"Presley won't eat them." Her frown was sorrowful. "He gives me grief whenever he sees me eating sweets."

I narrowed my eyes. "Hmm. You sure about this guy?"

"I know what you're thinking." She grinned. "But hey, he's cute."

"That makes all the difference," I said with a quick laugh. "But anything we eat, including the cupcakes, we'll be sure to replace."

"That works for me." She glanced across the room. "Oh, let me show you how to work the television."

"Good thinking." We tagged along and got the easy instructions for operating the remote control.

Heading back to the kitchen, Annie glanced down at the clear plastic crates I'd set on the floor near the door leading to the laundry room and into the garage. It was easy to see the stacks of books and papers inside. "Looks like you're ready for the book festival."

"As ready as I'll ever be, I guess." I snapped the lid off the top crate and surveyed the contents. "I brought along a few dozen demonstration books and a ton of bookbinding supplies, just in case."

I had thought about leaving these items at home because I had a complete bookbinding shop behind Abraham's house. His supplies were still stored there so why would I need to bring more? But I wanted my own things. I was comfortable with my tools. I would definitely make use of his supplies of bookbinding glue and his heavy-duty book press, but otherwise, I was happier with my stuff.

"Probably a good thing. Your mom says you've got back-to-back presentations lined up on all three days."

I rolled my eyes. "That's what happens when your mother is cochair of the festival committee."

She leaned against the kitchen counter, folded her arms across her chest, and smiled indulgently. "Your mom's really proud of you. And it doesn't hurt that you're the book guru of the Western world."

I chuckled. "Book guru. I like that."

"It suits you," Derek said with a grin.

The first annual Dharma Book Festival was the main reason we had moved in for the next two weeks. I'd been campaigning for years to have a book fair in Dharma, had taken time to visit every bookstore owner in wine country in hopes of convincing them to take part in the project, and now it was finally happening. It was my very own dream come true and I had big hopes that the festival would bring lots of smart new visitors to the area. You know, the kind of visitors who liked to read books.

And yes, my mother had signed me up for at least a dozen events on all three days of the festival, but it didn't bother me one bit. I'm a bookbinder specializing in rare-book restoration. Books are my life, so why would I mind?

When the idea of putting on a book festival first came up, Mom had researched the subject with single-minded determination. She signed up for extension classes at the local college and even took several online courses. She formulated a budget and obtained some big local sponsors including three popular radio stations, a number of the larger Dharma wineries, the Sonoma Institute of the Arts, the Friends of the County Library, and

four area bookstores. She established a working timeline and solicited an enthusiastic group of residents to
help form a committee.

The committee members divided up the responsibilities of contacting vendors and booking authors, pre-
senters, and other participants. There was someone
assigned to promotion and someone else working out an
elaborate schedule of events and activities. A beautiful
program was designed and posters were displayed in every
shop in town. Mom was relentless in her desire to put on
the best festival ever.

In her research, she had learned that the latest trend
with book festivals was to designate a classic novel as
the official "book of the festival." After a lot of wran-
gling, the Dharma Festival Committee had chosen *Little Women* to be that book. Apparently there had been
some serious arguments over the choice. Some of the
men on the committee balked at the "girlie" choice.
They wanted *Call of the Wild*, a more "manly" read. It
made some sense to choose that one because Jack London had lived in Sonoma County and his sprawling property in the hills above Glen Ellen was a famous historical
landmark. But seriously, was it important to choose a
"manly" book? Mom had pointed out that, statistically,
women bought more books and did more reading than
men, and it didn't hurt that the biggest proponent of *Little
Women* was Mom's *male* cochairman, Lawson Schmidt,
whose mother had been a big fan of the book. Ultimately
the decision came down to the fact that there were simply more women on the committee than men, so *Little Women* had won out in the end.

The entire town and anyone planning to attend had
been encouraged to read the book in anticipation of the

various events and workshops that would celebrate the story and the author. The committee had invited a Louisa May Alcott scholar to take part in several panel discussions. But the biggest and most exciting event of the entire festival promised to be the one-time performance of *Little Women*, The Musical.

A bunch of people we knew had signed up to work on the musical production and my family members were no exception. My youngest sister London had been pegged to be the director, which made sense because she was immensely talented in the arts and, frankly, she enjoyed telling people what to do. My sister China, a brilliant weaver, was making all the costumes—with help from some of the ladies in town. I figured my sister Savannah, a Michelin-starred chef in town, would help with the catering. And then Annie, of course, had one of the starring roles. She wasn't an official Wainwright daughter, but Mom treated her like one of her own anyway.

And by the way, if you've never heard of the musical version of *Little Women*, you are not alone. It had even been performed on Broadway, and yet it was still relatively obscure. I wasn't sure why. How bad could it be?

"We're looking forward to seeing you in the musical," Derek said. "Rebecca tells us you're the real star of the show."

Derek was one of the few people in the world who called my mother Rebecca. And after hearing Derek repeat Mom's compliment, Annie practically melted and pressed her hands against her chest. "Awwww, that's so sweet."

"It's true," I confirmed. "Mom said she was blown away when she heard you sing at one of the rehearsals."

Annie actually blushed, but then waved away the

compliment. "I just got lucky. They gave me a really pretty song to sing and then I get to die."

"It doesn't get better than that," I agreed.

"I know, right? But Shandi Patrick is playing Marmee, so she's the real star of the show."

I made a face. Shandi Patrick was a well-known Hollywood actress who had been living in Sonoma for a few years now and was part owner of a local winery. Many of the locals called her "the Diva." Not because of the Hollywood connection but because she could be a real pain in the butt. According to the town buzz, anyway. I had never met the woman.

Shandi hadn't made a movie or TV show in a long time, so I had to wonder if she could still be considered a *star*, except in her own mind. The few times I'd seen her walking along Shakespeare Lane (more casually known as the Lane), I'd noticed she'd been wearing a lot of spandex to accentuate her statuesque figure. Not that there was anything wrong with that. It was also a well-known fact that Shandi had a regular weekly appointment at Tangled, Dharma's premier hair salon, to touch up those gray roots of hers.

Doesn't that make me sound catty? I don't even know her, but I've paid attention to the gossip.

"I'll bet she hates playing the mom," I said with a smirk.

"She wanted to be Meg at first," Annie admitted.

"Seriously?" I rolled my eyes. The woman had to be at least fifty years old, probably older. What made her think she could play a teenager?

"Yeah, it was a stretch, for sure," Annie said. "And she doesn't have the soprano voice that the part calls for. London ended up giving the role to Sara Janz."

"Much more age-appropriate." Sara was a high school junior and the favorite babysitter for China's little girl, Hannah.

Annie nodded. "And Sara's good. Everyone is, really. Including Shandi. Despite the rumors about her, she's actually kind of . . . nice."

"I'm glad." I smiled. If Shandi was being nice to Annie, I might consider changing my opinion of her. "Sounds like you're having fun with the production."

"I am. It's a lot of hard work, but I love it."

"Well, we can't wait to see it," I said.

Annie glanced around the room for one last check, then grabbed her tote bag and purse. "I'd better get going. I'll probably see you around town, but definitely at the festival."

"Hopefully sooner," I said. "Maybe dinner at Mom's?"

"Sounds great."

"And I plan to come by your store to pick up some goodies."

"Anytime." She wiggled her eyebrows. "I'll give you the family discount."

"Awesome."

As soon as Annie left I checked my wristwatch. "I told Dad I might be able to pick up Mom from her committee meeting. I think it'll be fun to surprise her. Do you want to come with me or would you rather go visit your parents first?"

Derek's parents and mine had become such good friends that the Stones bought a home nearby. They planned to come out here twice a year and stay for a few months each time.

"We'll see my parents later," he said, wrapping his arms around me. "I'll come with you now."

"Good." I breathed him in for a long moment, then

gazed up into his dark blue eyes. "The committee is meeting at the town hall, so if you want, we can park at the far end of the Lane and take a nice walk, see what's new and exciting."

"Sounds like a plan."

We got Charlie settled, made sure she knew where her food bowls were, and showed her the powder room where Annie had suggested we put the cat box. Then I carried her over to the little cat bed and pointed out her mini jungle gym nearby. We wanted her to know the lay of the land and where she could sleep or play or eat or just chill, whatever she wanted to do while we were gone. Cats needed to have some fun, too, just like their humans.

"When did we become cat people?" Derek wondered aloud and grinned as we walked out to the car.

"I think it happened while we were sleeping."

We found a parking space on the Lane—a few blocks south of Arugula, my sister Savannah's gourmet veggie restaurant, and headed north toward the town hall. The weather had cooled off and I zipped up my jacket to stay cozy.

Derek reached over and pulled my arm through his. "Come over here and we'll keep each other warm."

"What a good idea."

"The Lane looks especially festive today," he remarked.

"People pull out all the stops for the Harvest. It's everyone's favorite season."

It was lovely to see the leaves changing colors on the trees that lined the Lane. Burnt oranges, dark reds, and golden browns mingled with the occasional stubborn green leaf that refused to accept the inevitable. A few yards ahead of us, one little girl dashed here and there, stooping down to collect the most beautiful leaves she could find to impress her mom and dad.

The shops and cafés had been festooned in their best fall colors. Wreaths, garlands, and tiny twinkle lights decorated doorways and the windows gleamed in the cool sunlight. It was nice to see so many people I recognized. Even the strangers we passed were friendly enough to nod a greeting.

And every single shop window displayed a poster for the upcoming book festival and the *Little Women* musical to be performed on the last evening.

When we reached the doorway of Warped, my sister China's yarn and weaving shop, Derek and I stopped and waved. The shop looked toasty, with beautiful wool hats and scarves and intricate wall weavings displayed on every surface. Baskets hanging from the ceiling held gorgeous shawls and blankets in every shade imaginable, and the cubbyholes that lined the back wall were bursting with yarns in all the colors of autumn, from warm gold to sage green to dark brown.

All of my brothers and sisters had various shades of blond hair like our parents, including Savannah, if she would only stop shaving her head every day. China wore her long shiny hair wrapped in a bun on top of her head and she managed to look sophisticated and artistic, while I was pretty sure I would've looked like a slob.

It only took a few seconds for China to notice us and she came running out to give us big hugs. She wore a gorgeous variegated sweater that she'd obviously knitted herself over slim jeans and lace-up boots. "Come inside."

I shook my head. "We're on our way to pick up Mom so we can't stay. But we'll see you in the next day or so."

"No problem," she said, and reached for the door handle. "Love you guys."

We waved and continued walking. "I'm so happy we're here," I said to Derek.

"I am as well," he said. "It's lovely to recognize more faces each time I return."

But as we started on the next block, I began to feel a chill that had nothing to do with the autumn weather. I realized we were approaching Turturino's Fish Market, a fabulous place where my parents and most of the town had shopped forever. My steps slowed and I almost stumbled as the flashback hit me. It was a day several years ago when our good friend Gabriel was shot in front of the fishmonger's shop. I remember Joey Turturino poking his head out from behind the screen door to see what was going on, then running back inside to call the police.

Gabriel lay on the ground, his head puddled in so much blood, I'd almost fainted.

Thankfully, Gabriel had survived and thrived, so I tried not to focus on that old memory but on all the happier ones that had followed.

I glanced up and saw the look on Derek's face. "You're remembering, too."

"Yes. I recall that I finally caught up with you at the hospital." He grimaced. "But that was after I'd seen all the blood on the sidewalk. Someone told me you had gone to the hospital and I thought you were the one who'd been injured. I've never driven so fast before or since."

I squeezed his arm and tried for lightness. "It was the beginning of a beautiful friendship, remember? Between you and Gabriel, I mean."

He laughed and we let go of that memory together.

"We'll have to invite Gabriel over for dinner," I said. "I've missed him."

"I spoke to him yesterday. He's already invited himself."

"He would." The thought of seeing Gabriel again cheered me right up. "He can bring the wine."

We continued chatting about this and that as we walked the rest of the way to the town hall.

I checked my watch as we entered the building. It was three forty-five. *Perfect timing*, I thought. Dad had mentioned that the festival committee meetings usually wrapped up by four o'clock, so Derek and I could sit in the back of the room and watch and listen to the conversation until Mom was ready to leave. I just hoped that, since we were planning to surprise Mom, she didn't interrupt the meeting to make a fuss over us.

We walked across the empty main hall. We had used this space last year for an unusual installation of photographs of art and artifacts found in one of our wine caves. Recently the photographs had been moved to a smaller space inside the town hall to make room for panel discussions with some of the book festival's biggest authors and their audience.

"I'm not sure which room the committee members are using," I said, my voice echoing in the large space. We entered the hallway that led to several meeting rooms and that's when we heard a loud argument.

"I believe we can figure this out," Derek murmured.

"Yeah, no kidding." But I frowned at the sound of a man's vitriolic tone, followed by my mother's quiet response. "That's definitely my mom."

Derek hustled us toward the door that was open a

crack and we slipped inside. Mom didn't even notice us as we sat down in two of the chairs that lined the back wall.

I took a quick glance at the conference table and recognized almost everyone sitting there. Mom held court at one end and Lawson Schmidt, her cochair, sat beside her. Saffron Bergeron sat opposite Lawson, wearing a burnt orange poncho and a permanent frown. There was Clyde Good, owner of the Good Book bookshop on the Lane, and next to him was Sue Flanders, an old Deadhead friend of Mom's and an eternal hippie with her long, curly gray hair, granny glasses, tie-dyed sweatshirt, jeans, and chunky work boots.

Winston Laurie, the thinnest man I knew, was there, too. He was a Fellowship member and good friend of our family. Jan Yarnell, my old school pal and spelling bee rival, sat next to him. Jan worked in the Dharma Winery with my brother Austin. He was also a booklover and president of the Friends of the Dharma Library.

I didn't recognize the cute younger man with the shaggy blond hair, but he was watching the argument with interest. He looked like the dictionary definition of *preppy* in khakis, a white button-down shirt, and a gray cardigan wrapped jauntily around his neck. There were five others at the table but I was distracted by the ongoing argument between Mom and a big guy who was standing right in front of her. His fist was raised and he was shouting at her.

"Who is that?" I stood and took one step forward, but Derek stopped me. "Wait."

"You incompetent twit," the big man bellowed. "This festival will be a complete failure and it'll be all your fault."

"What the hell?" I muttered, and shot a glance at Derek, who also stood. I read his body language easily: *Ready to kill.*

But Mom wasn't cowed.

"That's beyond ridiculous," she said, standing her ground. "This is going to be the most successful event the county's ever seen."

"Not if I can't be there." He was almost as tall as Derek but much bulkier, with a thick chest and a heavy stomach. He reminded me of an angry bull who was used to throwing his weight around. He was standing so close to Mom that I knew she could feel his breath. It made my skin crawl. "Don't you know how important I am? My company is on the verge of taking over this whole valley," he crowed. "I've already bought up six wineries and I'm not done yet."

"Well, you're done here," Mom said.

"The media will expect me to be there," he continued. "Everyone knows my name. You're a fool if you shut me out."

I didn't have a clue what this was all about, but I was seriously going to tackle that guy if he didn't back off. Nobody raises a fist to my mother and lives to talk about it. Sure, I knew she could handle whatever came her way, but she didn't have to handle it alone.

The man turned and glared at Lawson, the co-chairman of the committee. I'd known Lawson for years. "And you, Schmidt. You're nothing but a thief and a liar."

I blinked at his harsh words.

Lawson stood. He was almost as tall as the blowhard but thin enough that his trousers were hiked up almost to his chest. "Really, Mr. Banyan, you should go."

Banyan? I'd never heard of him. He was dressed like

a San Francisco banker, with a dark suit, a white shirt, and a bright red tie, but he still came across as a thug. Who was he?

The guy brushed off Lawson and turned back to my mother, wagging his finger in her face. "I know you're the real troublemaker here and I'll make sure you pay for this."

"Time for you to leave, Mr. Banyan."

"Oh, I will," he said, his tone threatening. "But don't try to cross me, lady. You've got a happy little family here. Be a real shame if something happened to one of them."

Mom gasped. "You're going to be sorry you said that."

The guy sounded like a mob boss! Incensed and ready to pounce, I took a step forward. Derek grabbed the back of my sweater to stop me. "Your mother is handling this berk just fine."

I turned on him. "Did you hear what that *berk* said?"

"Yes, love."

I was breathing fire, but Derek's sharp, steady gaze calmed me down. I also appreciated his use of British slang for twit or idiot. Banyan was both. So for Derek I compromised. I stayed right where I was and shouted at Banyan, "Get outta here, you jerk!"

Banyan whipped around and sneered at me, then glanced back at Mom. "Can't fight your own battles, I guess."

Mom ignored that comment. "If you threaten me or my family again, I'll have you arrested."

"Ooh," he taunted. "I'm so afraid of the Mayberry police force."

She fisted her hands on her hips. "Just leave, Mr. Banyan."

"Oh, I'm going." He scanned the room, eyeing everyone there. "But you won't stop me for long. I'll win this one."

Lawson bared his teeth, but didn't make eye contact. Under his breath, he muttered, "Over my dead body."

Banyan leaned in to Lawson and murmured softly, "Be careful what you wish for." Then he turned and stormed out of the room.

Chapter 2

"Oh, Lawson," Mom said, reaching into her tote bag. "You know better than to say things like that." She pulled out a clump of tightly wrapped white sage, quickly lit it with a Bic lighter, and then waved it around Lawson's head and torso. Every few seconds, she would blow on the tuft to send bits of smoke and ash his way. "Gotta get rid of those dark vibes ASAP."

Lawson collapsed in his chair. "Can't believe I said that out loud."

"You sure did," Mom said, and continued to flutter the smudge stick in the air.

"That's . . . okay, Becky." He blinked to keep the smoke from his eyes, then finally grabbed hold of Mom's wrist. "Thank you. I'll be fine."

"I think that helped. I'm feeling better, anyway." Mom held the sage low at her side, where the white smoke drifted skyward in a slender stream. Yes, she carried that stuff with her wherever she went because you just never knew when an opportunity would present itself to cleanse a room—or a cochairman—of bad juju.

And despite the fury I'd felt less than a minute ago, I had to admire my mother who, in the midst of all this drama, cared more about Lawson's welfare than her own.

The rest of the members were grumbling and mumbling to each other so Mom picked up a gavel and gently pounded it on the table to draw their attention back to her. "Let's take a five-minute coffee break to realign our chakras and do a little shake-shake-shake, shall we?" She made a "jazz hands" movement, smiled sweetly to the group, then dashed over to Derek and me.

Wrapping her arms around both of us, she whispered, "I'm so sorry you had to see that."

"I'm just sorry we can't watch you do the shake-shake-shake," I said.

She moved her shoulders up and down. "Sometimes you've got to loosen up, change the vibe, right?"

Derek wasn't smiling. "Rebecca, who is that man who threatened you?"

"Good question," I said. "I plan to hunt him down and kill him."

She pressed her forehead against mine. "Oh, sweetie, he's not worth one millisecond of your energy."

"But he was so hostile to you."

"Yes, and that wasn't the first time." She sighed. "His name is Jacob Banyan and he owns Raging Stallion Winery."

"I've never heard of it." I would've remembered such a ridiculous name. And I had to wonder: did he consider himself the raging stallion? Ugh. "Is the winery nearby?"

"Close enough," she grumbled. "They're right over the ridge near Glen Ellen."

"Why don't you want him at the book festival?" I asked. "Other than the fact that he's a bully and a blowhard."

"That's exactly what he is." She lowered her voice.

"Did you hear him say he's been buying up vineyards all over the valley?"

"Yeah."

"In some cases, he simply goes to the bank, pays off the second mortgage on the property, and kicks out the owners."

"That sounds downright criminal," I whispered.

"Apparently he's getting away with it."

"He's a dangerous man," Derek said, though his tone was mild.

Mom's lips were pressed in a stubborn line. "I'm not afraid of him."

"Perhaps you should be," he said. "I didn't care for the way he spoke to you."

"I appreciate that, sweetie," she said, patting his arm. "But that's just one of the many reasons why I won't allow him to be a part of the festival."

"Do we know any of the people who lost their land?" I asked.

"He took over Misty Vineyards, for one." She scowled. "Changed the name to Rowdy Acres."

"What a twit." Especially when it came to naming wineries. But the news about Misty really hurt. She was a longtime member of the Fellowship and a good friend of Mom's. "Didn't Misty win a bunch of awards at the Sonoma County Fair last year?"

"Yes. Her wines are outstanding. But as soon as Banyan took over, he began watering down what was left in Misty's barrels and turned it all into box wine."

My mouth gaped. "*Box* wine?"

"And he did the same thing to Dalrooney Cellars."

This couldn't be happening. "B-but Dalrooney is just up the road from Dharma."

"That's right. He's getting closer and closer."

"Oh my God. That's hideous."

She sniffed. "Thank you, sweetie."

"For what?"

"For your outrage."

"Of course I'm outraged! He's hurting good people." I took a breath. "Look, there's nothing wrong with a cheap box wine if you're going to an outdoor concert where you can't bring a glass bottle. But Dharma is known for its high-quality wines. If people get wind that box wine is being made here, it could literally destroy our economy."

She jabbed her finger toward me. "Exactly!"

"No wonder you're pissed off."

"You bet I am." Her fists bunched up and she let out a little shriek of frustration. "He's such a dipwad."

For all my mom's soft heart and tendency to forgive and forget and turn the other cheek . . . she had a do-not-cross line and I was pretty sure Banyan had crossed it.

I nodded. "He really is."

"Does everyone on the committee agree with your decision?" Derek asked.

She glanced around, scowled again, and lowered her voice even more. "No."

"You've got to be kidding," I said. "Why would any-one support this guy?"

She sighed a little, in exasperation and pure frustra-tion. "Because he's wealthy and powerful."

I exchanged a quick look with Derek. "Mom, in case you haven't noticed, you're wealthy and powerful, too."

She pondered that. "I guess I don't wear my power the same way he does."

"That's because you're not a dipwad," Derek said so-berly.

Mom and I both grinned. The word sounded unusually insulting when spoken with a distinguished English accent.

"Also," Mom added, "a few of the committee members aren't wine people, so they don't know the owners of the affected wineries. And they don't seem to care that he makes box wine."

"They should," I groused. "Whatever their business is, our local wine industry is what keeps them afloat."

"I agree."

I pondered her dilemma. "You could always quit the committee."

"If I quit, the committee will be taken over by dipwads like Banyan. No." She gritted her teeth. "I can't risk Banyan getting an even tighter grip on the local wine industry and what we do here. I'm very proud to be in charge of our first book festival. We've all worked really hard to make it happen and it's going to be awesome. And no dipwads are going to ruin it for the rest of us."

"Hear, hear," I said stoutly.

"I'm so glad you two are here." She glanced behind her as the rest of the committee returned to their seats. "I'd better get back to the meeting. Are you taking me home?"

"Yes," Derek said. "Whenever you're ready."

She glanced at her watch. "I'll wrap this up in about ten minutes."

"We'll be right here."

Derek and I sat down and watched Mom return to the table. He took hold of my hand. "I imagine the rest of the meeting will be pretty cut and dried."

Mom pounded the gavel. "Shall we move on to new business?"

"Not quite yet, Becky." Saffron Bergeron stood up. She owned the flower shop over on Montana Ridge

Road, and I'd known her for years and had never heard her say a nice word to anyone. I hated to admit it, but I just didn't like her. She was mean and sneaky. Yes, Dharma was all about love and peace, but Saffron had never caught on to that concept.

I watched Mom sigh. "Yes, Saffron. You have a point to make?"

"I wish to protest your exclusion of Jacob Banyan," she said. "He's a resident of the area, just like you and me."

"Yes, but unlike me, Jacob Banyan is a predator." Mom tugged on her ponytail, a sure sign of irritation. "He raids and destroys businesses without a single glance back. He's hurting our friends and neighbors. Stealing their life savings. He's not a nice person."

"You can say that again." Winston Laurie slapped his hand on the table. "Many of us will be taking turns serving wine in the Dharma Winery booth, and if Banyan does get a booth, I don't want him anywhere near us."

"Neither do I," said Jan Yarnell, glaring at Saffron. "If you want to give him a booth, you can sit right next to him and deal with his snotty attitude and rude comments."

"And his crappy box wine," Winston muttered.

"That's not the point," Saffron began.

"It's exactly the point," Mom insisted. "We have a responsibility to the other festival vendors as well. When ninety-nine percent of our vendors are upstanding members of our community who are bringing excellent products to our customers, I won't allow one percent to ruin it for everyone else.

"Half of our local vintners are scared to death that he'll drop a foreclosure notice on them and the other half are just afraid he'll mock them or call them names.

The man is like a dark cloud. He treats us all like we're chum and he's the shark in the water."

"Ooh," I whispered. "Good one, Mom."

Derek patted my knee. "She'll win this fight."

"Her metaphors are killing it." Despite my concerns, I had to smile. Mom had been a Deadhead, a farmer, a wife, and a mother. She had astral traveled with her spirit guide, Ramlar X, and was the current Grand Raven Mistress of her local druidic witch coven.

But now she was in corporate mode and I could honestly say that I'd never seen her like this before. She was in charge of an important event that promised to bring thousands of visitors to Dharma less than a week from now and she wasn't putting up with any nonsense. And dang, she had just totally *played* that shrew Saffron Bergeron.

But Saffron just rolled her eyes. "What's that supposed to mean, Becky?"

Jan fumed. "It means he thinks we're all idiots."

"It means he's trying to gobble us up," Sue added. "Like a shark. Get it?"

"Banyan's hurt too many people," Mom said. "I refuse to allow him to be a part of the book festival."

"*You* refuse?" Saffron mocked. "It's not your decision, Becky."

Mom shot a look at her cochairman. "The committee elected me and Lawson to make the tough decisions."

"Sounds like you're turning it into a dictatorship."

"Don't be melodramatic, Saffron," Lawson said wearily, staring at his hands. He looked defeated and I wondered if he was afraid to say anything more about Banyan in front of Saffron, who seemed to take Banyan's side of the issue.

Lawson was a nice man, but he was the last guy I'd turn to for any tough decisions.

"I agree with Becky," Clyde said. "Banyan is toxic."

Mom nodded. "And I'm doing exactly what the committee appointed me to do. Ensuring the success of the festival."

"Exactly," Lawson said.

"Naturally you would side with Becky," Saffron said sulkily. She turned to Mom. "Why don't you let the whole committee vote? See how the rest of us feel."

"All right." Mom stood, still holding her gavel. "All in favor of barring Jacob Banyan from the festival, raise your hands and say 'aye.'"

I quickly counted eight people who voted with Mom. "Those opposed?"

Four people waved their arms and shouted "nay." I tried to see who had voted against my mother. There was Saffron, of course, Professor Dinkins, and the cute blond guy. I couldn't tell who the fourth arm belonged to. A woman for sure, but it could've been either Penny Lewis, who owned the dry cleaners over on Montana Ridge Road, or the woman sitting next to her whose name I'd forgotten.

"That seems to settle it," Mom said, and pounded the gavel once. "Banyan's out."

Saffron snorted. "You've padded the committee with all of your cult members. I can't possibly win."

"Don't be insulting," Mom said. "First of all, people chose to join this committee because they live in Dharma, *not* because they're in the Fellowship. And more importantly, we're not a cult and you know it."

"Whatever," Saffron said with a disdainful flip of her hair. "Your little *fellowship*"—she used air quotes—"is nothing but a freak-filled secret society. Who knows what goes on in those clandestine meetings you have."

Mom looked completely stunned. "What is wrong with you?"

"She's just jealous," Clyde said, "because we don't invite her to our secret meetings." Clyde owned the most wonderful used bookshop in town and he had always been one of my favorite people.

Jan snorted. "Yeah, right. Secret meetings."

But Winston was frowning. "The book festival has nothing to do with the Fellowship."

"Of course not," Mom said. "And just because the majority of this committee voted to keep that offensive box-wine jerk from having a booth at the festival, you're now accusing us of being part of a secret cult? That's just stupid."

"Now I'm stupid!" Saffron was outraged at the implication but I couldn't figure out why. She'd surely heard it before.

Mom breathed in and out to calm herself. "I didn't call *you* stupid, Saffron. But your accusation was stupid."

"I'm not stupid," she snapped. "You're stupid."

"Enough!" Clyde shouted and stood up for emphasis. "Yes, Saffron, you're stupid if you think we're part of a cult. Why don't you just admit the truth? Jacob Banyan offered you money if you'd get him a booth."

"You . . . how . . . he did not!" she sputtered. "How dare you!"

"Is that true?" Mom asked.

She huffed. "Of course not!"

"The lady doth protest too much, methinks," Clyde said with a smirk.

Leave it to old Clyde to quote Shakespeare properly, I thought fondly. The guy was a world-class curmudgeon but smart as a whip and snarky to boot.

Saffron pushed away from the table, clearly affronted. "I didn't take any money, but even if I did, who cares? What matters is that you're blackballing him just because he isn't a member of your hoity-toity commune."

Now Mom stood. "That has nothing to do with our decision and you know it."

"I don't believe you."

"That's too bad," Mom said, taking a step toward Saffron. "The only reason that man isn't welcome at the festival is that he's vicious."

"He's a pillager," Winston cried.

"He's bent on destroying our community," Jan added.

"You're all being ridiculous," Saffron chided. "Jacob Banyan is a well-respected businessman, pure and simple. He's pumped plenty of money into our local economy, and even if you don't agree with the way he does business, that doesn't mean he should be shunned."

Sue sneered. "He might be a businessman, but he's not well respected."

"He destroyed Misty Vineyards!" Jan shouted. "Misty had to take a job as a barista at the Kaffe Klatch."

"Oh, cry me a river," Saffron snapped.

Mom pounded her gavel for order, then said, "Misty's not the only one. Dalrooney, Clearwater Winery, and Clayborn Cellars all went belly up, thanks to Banyan. And Oak Road Barrel Company just went out of business."

"It's not Banyan's fault the barrel company went under."

"Oh, Saffron." Mom's tone was pitying. "Being deliberately obtuse is just so unattractive. You know as well as I do that there is a clear correlation."

The good-looking preppy guy who'd voted "nay" stood up and coughed self-consciously. "Don't you think that's stretching it, Mrs. Wainwright?"

"Not really, Ryan," Mom explained. "Our community of winegrowers is like an ecosystem. Banyan's a predatory fungus that's killing off all the good wine to the point that eventually we won't need barrels anymore."

Okay, maybe she was stretching the theory a little, but I could see her point. Wooden barrels were used to store and age the wine, but wine destined for boxes—or cans—was rarely barreled. If the box wine trend were to continue unabated, nobody would need barrels anymore.

"Look, Banyan's not welcome at the festival," Mom said. "The ayes have it. We won't reward predatory behavior. That's my final word."

She blew out a breath, sat up straight, and rolled her shoulders slowly. I recognized her attempt to realign her chakras and I had to give her props. She was hanging in there in the face of all that negativity, mostly coming from Saffron Bergeron, one of my *least* favorite people ever.

For someone who worked with beautiful flowers, Saffron Bergeron had a downright ugly disposition. She was desperate, sneaky, and suspicious, always thought the worst of people, and clearly hung out with the wrong crowd. She had lived in the area for nearly as long as we had, but she'd never been friendly or neighborly. She had always reminded me of the Wicked Witch of the West in *The Wizard of Oz*. I didn't know what her problem was, but I'd had it up to *here* with her verbal abuse of my mom.

"Any other comments before we adjourn for the day?" Mom asked calmly.

"What's the use?" Saffron whined. "You don't listen to anyone else's opinions."

"On the contrary, Saffron," Mom said on a sigh, "we've all listened to far too many of your opinions today."

"Don't be a whiner, Saffron," Jan murmured.

Winston shook his head. "Poor loser."

Saffron didn't respond, but she looked furious enough to rip the skin off both of their faces.

Mom ignored Saffron as she checked her notes. "We just have one more item to mention, and it's good news. Lawson will tell us all about it."

She nodded to her cochair who pushed back his chair and stood. "I'm pleased to announce that Bettina Trimble, our Louisa May Alcott scholar, will be here in a few days. She and I have had several delightful conversations and I can't wait for you all to meet her. She's a lovely woman and a true academic. We're planning a nice reception with tea and pastries and I hope you will all attend."

"Wonderful," Mom said, smiling at Lawson. Her cochair was a real fanboy. "Won't that be exciting?"

"Whoop-de-do," one of the "nay" men said sarcastically. It was Mr. Dinkins, a professor at the Sonoma Institute of the Arts. I'd thought he was an okay guy when I met him a few years ago while teaching a bookbinding class at the Institute. I wondered what his problem was now. Maybe he had voted against the "girlie" *Little Women* and wasn't taking the defeat well.

Mom ignored him, smiled sweetly, and pounded her gavel. "Meeting adjourned."

*   *   *

Most of the committee members had left the room and Mom was slipping her clipboard into her tote bag when Lawson began a quick, hushed discussion with her. We couldn't hear what they were saying, but when they were finished, Mom patted his shoulder and said, "I'll be fine. You take care of yourself, won't you?"

"I will." But he didn't look happy as he strode out of the room.

He must be concerned about Banyan confronting my mother, I thought. But leave it to Mom to be more concerned about someone else's problems than her own. With the way tempers were flaring, though, I was right there with Lawson. I couldn't help but worry about her safety. And the fact that I needed to worry was really unsettling. Up until a few years ago, Dharma had always been a refuge from the ugliness of the outside world. Seeing that ugliness creeping in here was discomforting. And extremely disappointing.

Everyone else was gone by the time Mom walked toward us. "I think we can go now."

Derek met her halfway. "Let me carry that for you," he said, and reached for her tote bag.

"Oh, thank you, sweetie, but I'm just going to tuck it inside my cubby." She walked to the far wall where a dozen square cubicles and shelves held various items of clothing, books, and notepads. Setting her tote bag into one of them, she explained, "Some of us leave our notes and things here between meetings instead of carting them back and forth from home every day. And we keep the door locked so nobody will take anything."

"As long as it's safe," I said.

"Safe as can be." She pulled her smaller handbag from the tote. "But I keep my personal stuff with me."

"Good," I said. "You ready to go?"

She took a deep breath and let it out slowly. She looked exhausted. "I'm ready."

I walked over and slipped my arm through hers. "We thought we'd show up and surprise you, Mom. But this probably wasn't the happiest moment to sneak in here."

"Don't worry," she said, waving her hand dismissively. "We'll all be friends again tomorrow."

Of course my mother would believe that, but I doubted it. Still, I smiled encouragingly. "I hope so. But Mr. Dinkins sounded really angry."

"He'll snap out of it," she said sharply.

"Ooo-kay." I cast a quick glance at Derek, who flanked Mom's other side and wrapped his arm around her shoulders.

"Let's get you home, Rebecca."

Usually when someone called her Rebecca, Mom would tell them to call her Becky. But when Derek said it, she purred like a happy kitten. I couldn't blame her.

She leaned her head against his chest. "I'm so glad to see you."

"It's lovely to see you, too."

Mom lifted her head and glanced at me. "I should apologize for all the ugly vibes circulating around here today."

"Not your fault, Mom. Let's go home and have a glass of wine."

"Now you're talking."

Feeling the need to protect my mother from those vibes she mentioned, Derek and I stuck close to her all the way out to the sidewalk along Berkeley Circle. I observed a few of the committee members talking together in small groups and hoped they weren't planning a coup.

Mom didn't need that aggravation. I waved to Clyde but he was talking to Lawson and didn't notice me.

Mom looked around. "Where did you park?"

"It's such a nice day," I said, "we parked a few blocks away and walked. But if you'd rather . . ."

Derek caught my glance. "Why don't you two wait here and I'll go get the car."

Mom patted his arm. "No, no. The walk will do me good. Calm my nerves."

Derek stared into her eyes. "If you're sure."

"Absolutely."

"All right, then."

With Derek and me still flanking Mom, we strolled around the curve of Berkeley Circle to the Lane and headed south toward the car.

I finally had to say what I was thinking. "I can't understand why anyone would want that Banyan guy to take part in the festival."

Mom shrugged. "For one thing, most of the members who voted 'nay' don't own wineries. And not that it matters, but since they're not commune members, they don't think they have a stake in Dharma's future."

"But that's ridiculous. We're a community like any other in the country."

"I've tried to tell them." Mom sighed. "I mean, Saffron owns a business in town and half of her customers are Fellowship members. Nobody boycotts her simply because she's not a member. Why would she pick a fight over a nonexistent issue?"

"I think Clyde had it right," I mused. "Jacob Banyan is paying her to do his dirty work."

"Apparently that's true, even though she tried to deny it." Mom shook her head. "It's kind of sad."

I squeezed Mom's arm. "I would feel a lot more sympathetic, but she's such a grinch."

"She can't help it, poor thing," Mom admitted. "Her aura is positively gray. And her complaints are completely unfounded. It's just not fair. I didn't try to stack the committee with Fellowship members. There are just more of us than anyone else in Dharma because, you know, we built the town. And we tend to take an interest in what's going on in our town because, well, it's ours. Robson instilled that sense of community in all of us from the very beginning."

"That's true, Mom." Guru Bob had always led by example. He was committed to living a life of quality, kindness, and service. My mom and dad and the rest of his followers had strived to do the same, and those lessons had been drummed into their children's psyches from an early age.

Mom thought about it for a long moment. "What I'm trying to say is that even though Saffron and others like her have lived here a long time, they've never once tried to learn our history or our philosophy. They don't understand that part of our culture is to welcome everyone. We make a big deal about *not* being, you know, an exclusive club. A cult. A secret society. Any of those silly things."

"You've always bent over backward to avoid giving that impression." And maybe, I couldn't help thinking, that hadn't always been the best way. If they'd been more careful in who they'd allowed to move into town, they wouldn't be dealing with Saffron and her allies now. But that just wasn't the commune's way. And to be honest, I wouldn't want it to be.

"It's their loss, Rebecca," Derek said. "Your generosity is overflowing and I, for one, feel very fortunate to be a part of your family and your life."

Mom beamed at Derek and then flashed me a smile. "Have I told you lately how much I love this guy?"

"Yeah." I grinned. "Me, too."

As we approached Warped, Mom said, "Did you get a chance to talk to China earlier?"

"Yes, briefly. But we can stop if you want to talk to her."

"No, we don't have to stop," Mom said. "We'll just wave as we pass by."

"Okay."

We stopped in front of China's shop window and waved. She saw us and waved back. Then we all laughed at ourselves and the three of us continued our walk.

"That was fun," Mom said, clearly feeling better.

As we passed the Good Book, Clyde stepped outside the shop. "Brooklyn, hold on."

I turned. "Hey, Clyde." With a grin, I grabbed him in a hug. "It's great to see you."

He patted my shoulder, then stepped back and scratched his head self-consciously. "Saw you at the committee meeting but couldn't stop to chat. I had to get the hell out of there."

"I don't blame you. The meeting seemed to get a little tense."

"Ya think?" Clyde rolled his eyes. "Anyway, I'm glad I caught you."

"Me, too."

Mom touched Derek's arm. "You remember Brooklyn's husband Derek."

"Sure do. You're a lucky man," Clyde said gruffly, shaking Derek's hand.

"I'm well aware," Derek said with a smile.

"Good." Not one to dawdle, Clyde turned and yanked the shop door open. "Come in here. I've got a book for you."

I glanced at Mom and we both raised our eyebrows. "I can't wait to see it."

I walked in and was instantly enveloped by the intoxicating scent of books. Call me a weirdo, but I could get high off that heady combination of pulpy vellum and aged leather, along with the slightest hint of cinnamon. It was a trick used by savvy booklovers to treat their wooden bookshelves with cinnamon oil in order to ward off the infestation of silverfish and other annoying paper-loving insects.

"I know it's a bit late to ask," Clyde explained, "but I just came across this little gem yesterday." He reached behind the counter, pulled out a small package wrapped in brown paper, and handed it to me. "If you have time to fix it, great. If not, I'll understand."

I carefully unwrapped the paper and stared at the book inside. "*Little Women*," I said, smiling. "How perfect." I noted that the poor book had been handled badly, but underneath the scruffiness was a beautiful treasure waiting to be rediscovered. "Where did you find it?"

"Uh, just around," Clyde muttered.

"Wow, lucky find."

"Yeah, sure. I, uh, found it in a used bookstore. Yeah, over in Grass Valley." He cleared his throat nervously. "Paid almost nothing for it, but I thought it could be worth some money if it got fixed up."

"Definitely," I said, immediately wondering why Clyde sounded nervous.

"It's kind of a mess," he continued, his voice stronger

now. "But the paper's good and the cover's pretty decent. Just need you to resew it and glue it and, you know, do all that other magical stuff you do."

I turned the book to study it from different angles. On the front cover, a vibrant color illustration showed the backs of four young women walking arm in arm through a tree-lined park. Each of them wore a long skirt and petticoat in the style of the 1860s and a different colorful shawl across her shoulders.

I could tell that the book's spine, though worn and faded and coming loose, had once been a pretty shade of blue.

Both back and front covers of the book were dangling by a few threads. Most of the signatures—those folded pages that are sewn together to make up the textblock— had come apart completely. As a whole, the book *was* a mess, but its individual parts were outstanding.

I had my work cut out for me.

"Do you plan to sell it during the festival?" I asked.

"That was the original plan. But if you can get the work done in time, I was thinking of entering it in the silent auction. That way, all the money will go to charity."

The silent auction was part of the Saturday-night festivities and the proceeds would be donated to an adult-literacy organization.

"That's a lovely idea, Clyde," Mom said.

As a book nerd, I had to agree.

Clyde coughed again, but this time I knew it was because he tended to feel awkward when anyone tried to pay him a compliment. This was part of his curmudgeonly charm, as far as I was concerned. "Huh," he muttered, then looked at me. "Well, do you think you can finish it in time?"

"Of course I can." I almost laughed. Clyde knew me

too well, knew that as soon as I saw this jewel of a book, I would be itching to start work on it.

"I'll pay you, of course."

I gave him a long look. "How about if you take the money you'd normally pay me and put it toward the charity."

He didn't smile exactly, but gazed at me with something that might've been pride. "You're a good girl, Brooklyn."

"She sure is," Mom said sweetly, giving my arm a squeeze.

"I should be able to finish it by the end of the week," I said.

"Perfect." He gave me a curt nod. "Thanks."

Now that our business was completed, I took a moment or two to check out the bookstore. Sadly, I hadn't visited Clyde's shop in more than a year. But growing up, I used to stop in at least once a week. I adored this little shop with its narrow aisles and its rolling library ladder. I loved its mix of new bestsellers, classic used books, fascinating how-tos, and the rack of comics by the front desk.

The most surprising aspect of the shop was its cleanliness. I had been in hundreds of used bookshops in dozens of cities all over the world. And while I loved them all in different ways, I could admit that, in general, every one of them could use some serious housecleaning at least once a year or so.

But Clyde's shop was nearly spotless and virtually dust-free. I knew he had been inspired to overhaul the entire space from top to bottom soon after his grandkids began visiting the store and picking out their own books. It turned out that his youngest granddaughter was allergic to everything and would start sneezing as soon as she walked inside. The dust in the shop triggered her asthma, Clyde had explained, so he took action.

In each of the four corners there was a comfortable chair for reading. In the middle of the shop was a round reading table large enough to seat eight people.

Once a month Clyde held a "Meet the Author" event where he would invite a famous author to visit. He served wine and cookies, and generally attracted a good crowd. The one unusual aspect of the event was that the authors were always dead. So basically, Clyde held a séance once a month.

My mother was a regular attendee and a big fan of all the dead authors. And now with Derek's mother Meg visiting Dharma on a regular basis, the two of them attended the events together as often as possible.

I gave Clyde another hug. "I'll have to come back and browse when I have more time."

"You're welcome anytime, as always."

"And I'll have the book back to you by Friday."

"That'll do it."

We left the store and continued walking down the Lane toward the car. When we were a block away, I heard footsteps pounding on the sidewalk behind us and turned around.

"Oh my God," I cried.

"What is it, dear?" Mom asked, then turned and gasped.

Derek had already whipped around and moved in front of Mom to protect her from Jacob Banyan.

I felt every muscle in my body tense up in alarm.

Mom touched Derek's back. "It's all right, Derek. I'm sure Mr. Banyan just wanted to say hello."

"I very much doubt that," Derek said, his laser-like gaze focused on Banyan.

"What do you want, Banyan?" I asked.

Banyan curled his lip in disgust. "Quite the little army you've got here, Becky. They won't always be around to protect you, though."

"I don't need protection from you, Banyan."

"Want to bet?" he murmured, his tone menacing.

Derek leaned closer. "You should think twice about threatening people, Banyan. It could get you into trouble."

"From you?" He scoffed. "*That* sounds like a threat to me. I'm just trying to live my life here."

"Then go do that," Derek said quietly. "Walk away. Now."

Banyan bared his teeth. "I don't follow orders from you, pretty boy."

Good grief, I thought again. I hoped for Banyan's sake that he wouldn't find out what a big mistake he was making.

Derek just laughed. "You have no idea what you're doing, do you?"

"I know exactly what I'm doing. And you'll be sorry if you get in my way."

And then he actually tried to shove Derek aside. Derek didn't budge an inch and Banyan scowled. He leaned to his left to make eye contact with Mom, but Derek took a step in that direction and blocked his view.

"For goodness' sake, Jacob." Mom was clearly fed up. She patted Derek's back and stepped around him to confront Banyan. "What do you want?"

Banyan gripped Mom's arm. "I heard what you said about me after I left the meeting."

"Looks like you have your own little army reporting back to you then," Mom said, mocking him. "Isn't that special?"

He might've squeezed her arm tighter, but in a lightning-fast move, Derek grabbed Banyan's arm and wrenched it behind his back.

"Ow! Ow! Ow!" Banyan howled, arching his back to try and relieve the pain.

"I warned you," Derek said, his voice deadly calm.

"Let go of me!"

Derek released him suddenly and Banyan almost fell over.

Rubbing his shoulder, Banyan muttered, "I'll kill you for that."

Derek made a *tsking* sound. "Sounds like another threat."

Banyan's nostrils flared like those of an angry bull, but he was smart enough to leave Derek alone. Instead, he jabbed his finger in Mom's direction. "Don't try to blackball me, you witch."

"But I'm a good witch," Mom said saucily.

Unlike Saffron Bergeron, I thought, but kept silent.

"Think you're real funny, don't you?" He bared his teeth. "One of these days I'll find you all alone and wipe that smile off your pretty little face."

Mom gave him a cool stare. "That's enough. You're boring me, Banyan. Now get out of my way."

"I'll go when I'm good and ready." But he was still rubbing his shoulder. "Just remember this. You try to keep me out of the festival and I'll make sure you don't live to see another day."

Chapter 3

We walked the rest of the way in silence, deep in our own thoughts, until I couldn't take it anymore. "He's horrible!"

Derek nodded. "Yes, and dangerous."

"Why does he care about the festival so much?" I wondered out loud.

"I think he's trying to gain respectability," Mom said with a shrug. "He thought that buying up wineries would do it, but that's turned into a disaster. So now he's looking to the book festival to raise his social standing."

"It's not working," I muttered.

"No, indeed," Derek said.

"I've been putting up with him for months now," Mom said, waving one hand as if wiping away our concerns. "I mostly try to ignore it because nobody around here will do anything about him. They're all afraid of him."

"Robson isn't afraid of him," I said.

"Neither am I," Mom responded quickly. "Besides, I don't want to have to depend on Robson every time I have a run-in with someone."

I frowned. "Mom, you never have run-ins with any-one."

"And this was hardly a simple run-in," Derek said. "The man just threatened you with murder. I suggest you don't go anywhere alone while we're here."

"Oh, Derek dear, don't worry so much."

"I'll talk to Robson myself," I vowed.

"There's no need for that," Mom said. "This will all blow over in a few days. You'll see. When Banyan figures out that he's not going to get what he wants, he'll crawl back under his rock and leave us alone."

"It won't be that easy," I said.

"Positive thinking is what is required here," she said, though she was starting to sound fed up with the whole situation. "However, I admit that Banyan tasks my abilities to smile through trials and tribulations."

One thing Mom hadn't talked about was my father's response to all of this. I couldn't imagine he was taking it well. "What does Dad think? Why wasn't he at the meeting?"

Clearly insulted, Mom gave me a head shake. "Your father knows very well that I can take care of myself."

I wasn't fooled. "Uh-huh. So he doesn't know what's going on?"

She sighed. "Not everything, no."

"Mom . . ."

"Rebecca, he should know," Derek said. "Everyone should know. Including Robson and the local police."

"Oh, I think that's a little much."

Derek smiled at her. "I don't."

"I suppose not," she said.

Derek pressed a button on his key fob to unlock his car. He held the front passenger door open for Mom.

"I'll get in the back," I said, stopping her before she could try to climb inside. "You sit up front with Derek."

"Oh, honey. That's not right."

I chuckled as I sat down in the very comfortable back seat of Derek's Bentley. "It's just a short ride up the hill. I can survive without Derek next to me for at least five minutes."

"Funny girl," she said, and managed a smile as she took the front seat. She waited until Derek was in the car before she said, "I know you're both going to lecture me, and that's fine. But first I need to ask you not to mention anything to your father. I don't want to upset him. That's why I haven't told him."

"Come on, Mom. You know that's crazy. Dad needs to know."

Derek started the car, then turned to face Mom. "Jim will be far more upset if he finds out that we were keeping this from him."

Realizing Derek and I were a united front and she would not win this fight, Mom slumped in her seat. "Okay, fine. I know you're right. But I hate having your father think he's got to fight my battles for me."

I reached up and squeezed her arm. "But you'd do the same for him, wouldn't you?"

She grumbled under her breath.

"And by the way, Mom," I continued. "It won't be just Dad fighting this battle, but all of us. We're all going after this slimy snake."

"I love doing things as a family," she said wryly, "but this is ridiculous."

"Now who's the funny one?" I said.

Derek eased away from the curb and as soon as we were out of range of the tourist traffic pouring into town, he took hold of Mom's hand. "Don't underestimate the danger here, Rebecca. You've made a formidable enemy of Banyan and his threat is quite credible."

"I suppose you're right," she muttered, and stewed in silence for a few minutes. "I'm not sure why I'm suddenly the target. There were eight other votes against him."

"You're the chair of the committee."

"Cochair."

I snorted. "Lawson Schmidt has never taken a firm stand against anything."

"Oh, but he's a nice man."

"He's nice enough," I allowed, but I recalled Banyan getting in Lawson's face. *You're nothing but a thief and a liar.* I wondered what he meant. "Banyan's comment to Lawson seemed to hit awfully close to home. Lawson looked really upset."

"He did indeed," Derek murmured.

"Lawson's in charge of the festival funds, so that's why Banyan was taunting him." Mom shrugged. "It didn't mean anything. The truth is, Lawson is amazing with money. We put him in charge of the finances because he's obsessive about it. He loves to count our money over and over."

That seemed a little weird, but who was I to judge? Lawson did come across as nervous most of the time, but that didn't make him a thief. So why did Banyan attack him on such a personal level?

Derek's gaze met mine in the rearview mirror and I saw the concern in his eyes. We needed to nip this Banyan conflict in the bud before the festival itself turned into an armed camp.

As Derek eased onto Vivaldi Way and maneuvered the car up the winding hill toward my parents' house, Mom suddenly turned in her seat to face both of us, her eyes narrowed and her jaw clenched in resolve. It was as if she had suddenly found the fire within. "Jacob Ban-yan overplayed his hand today and you were there to witness it."

"Yeah, and it wasn't pretty."

"I'm just glad you're both on my side in case we have to deal with him again."

"Of course we're on your side," I said, pleased to see that Mom had regained her fighting spirit.

"Good. I'll wager my army can wipe out his any day of the week."

"I wouldn't bet against you," Derek said with a firm nod. A moment later we reached the top of the hill and Derek swung the car into my parents' driveway.

Dad came out of the house wearing his usual work uniform of blue jeans, plaid flannel shirt, and boots. He grinned with delight and wrapped his arms around me. "Hey, kiddo. How's my beautiful girl?"

"I'm great, Dad." I inhaled deeply and smiled at the familiar scents of Old Spice and Juicy Fruit gum. "It's so good to see you."

"You, too, honey." He turned and grabbed Derek in a man-hug, thumping his back. "Come on in." He reached for Mom's hand and led the way back into the house.

Once inside, he pulled Mom into his arms for a warm hug. "How was your meeting, babe? Did they beat you up again?"

"A little," Mom whispered. "I'll survive." But she stayed in his arms for another long moment before step-ping back. "Is there wine?"

"We ran out," he said, and then laughed at Mom's shocked expression. "Baby, we own a vineyard. We'll never run out."

"Oh, thank heaven." She was still clearly discombobulated from the angry confrontation she'd experienced only a few minutes ago.

"I'll take some of that wine," I said.

Dad winked at me. "That's my girl. I've got a bottle of our new Chardonnay chilling. After that, we can move on to the estate Pinot Noir."

"Sounds wonderful." Then I caught Derek's glance. "Oh, but you know, we should drive the car back to Abraham's and check on Charlie first."

"Good idea, love," Derek said, taking my hand. "That'll give your mother and father a few minutes to talk by themselves."

"We'll be back soon," I promised, giving my mother a steely look. I wanted to make sure she knew that if she didn't tell Dad what was going on, then we would do it when we returned. "Feel free to start without us if you want."

"Take your time, sweetie," Mom said.

"We'll wait for you," Dad assured us, and we took off.

We walked into the kitchen of our home away from home and I set my purse on the counter. Clyde's book was sticking out of the top and I reached for it. I'd been so distracted by Jacob Banyan accosting my mother that I'd forgotten all about the book. But now I carefully unwrapped the brown paper and took another look at it, mentally tallying the work I would have to do to get it back into beautiful shape for the silent auction.

Unfortunately, I was still distracted by that maniac's assault and couldn't concentrate, so I wrapped up the book and then began to pace the length of the kitchen. I punched my palm with my fist as I moved, even angrier than I'd been when we confronted Banyan on the Lane.

"I want to hunt that big creep down and put the fear of God into him."

"I feel the same way, darling," Derek said. Stopping me mid-pace, he rubbed my shoulders. "But in my experience, men like Jacob Banyan are too stupid to fear God. They have much too high an opinion of themselves."

"You're right." I scowled in frustration. "I've met a few of those types in my life."

"Don't I know it," he murmured.

Of course he knew. We'd both confronted egocentric men—and a couple of women—over the past few years. Occasionally they wanted to kill me, which indicated that they just might be psychopaths.

With a sigh, I let him go and sat at the kitchen table. Derek leaned against the counter and we gazed at each other. "So do you think she's telling him?" he asked.

"I hope so. That's why I wanted to leave them alone for a few minutes. On the other hand, she might wait for us to return first, knowing Dad will go ballistic when he hears what Banyan did. Probably thinks we can help hold him back from killing the guy with his bare hands."

"I've never actually seen your father lose his temper," Derek mused. "I've seen him get angry, but I don't believe he's ever gone ballistic in my presence."

"It's a rare sight," I admitted. "And it's only happened when one of us was being threatened." My father, the original Deadhead, always said he was mellow to the marrow. And it was true. He was a lover, not a fighter. But that philosophy was about to be put to the test.

I was ridiculously pleased when Charlie hopped up on my lap. "Hello, sweet kitty," I murmured, petting her soft fur and listening to her contented purring. "I think she had an okay day. She seems happy."

"I'm quite certain she is." He leaned forward and scratched Charlie's chin. Her eyes closed and she purred even louder.

"Who wouldn't be happy with all of her favorite things around her?" I scratched her ears and hugged her, then set her down on the floor. With a heavy sigh, I stood. "Are you ready to go back to Mom's?"

"Yes." He wrapped his arms around me for one long moment. "I know you're upset about this, and so am I. But there's no question that your father should be told about Banyan's threats."

"Oh, absolutely. In fact, I think I'll call Robin and ask her and Austin to stop by. Safety in numbers, right?"

"Yes. Everyone in the family should hear about this and realize that your mother will need protection for the next few days, at least. I'll call Gabriel and ask him to join us at your parents' house."

"Sounds like a party." But we both looked pretty grim as we locked the door and hiked back up the hill, holding hands. On the way, I called Robin. With no hesitation, she said that she and Austin would come by in a little while.

Then Derek pressed Gabriel's number and spoke to him for less than a minute.

"He's on his way."

"Good. Do you think we should call the police?"

He twisted his lips in a frown. "I'll talk to Gabriel about it."

All three of my sisters were working, but I'd be calling them later, too. It made me smile to know that our friends and family would be there at a moment's notice if we needed them.

When we reached the edge of my parents' property, I hesitated.

Derek stopped and turned. "What is it, love?"

"I'm just so bummed," I admitted. "I was hoping we would be able to relax and enjoy the week leading up to the festival, but now I'm so stressed out and worried about Mom, I don't know what to do."

"*We're* doing it," he assured me. "With all of our family and friends aware of the situation, your mother will be perfectly safe."

"Yes, she will. Even if we have to lock her in a closet to guarantee it." I leaned against him for sheer comfort and sighed. "I love you so much."

"I love you right back." He grinned and grabbed my hand. "Come on now. Let's go inside and get a glass of wine."

"There's a good idea."

We climbed the steps and pushed open the front door. I could tell the minute we walked inside that Mom hadn't said a word to Dad about Banyan's threat.

"Here you go," Dad said cheerfully, handing us each a glass of chilled white wine. He and Mom already had theirs and we all clinked our glasses together.

"Cheers," Dad and Mom said in unison.

"Thanks, Dad." I took a sip. "Delicious."

"This was the first Chardonnay to age in our new concrete tanks."

"Is that what gives it the mineral tones?" Derek asked.

Dad grinned. "Actually, that mineral taste is the true essence of the grape and the vine and the earth. It happens when the wine doesn't spend as much time in oak barrels."

"So the oak tends to overpower everything else?" Derek said.

"You got it." Dad grinned and took another sip. "I'm digging these new tanks."

I sipped, too, and then stared at the color of the wine. "I love the earthiness, Dad."

"Thanks, honey. Me, too."

"I hope you guys don't mind, but I invited Robin and Austin to join us. And Gabriel's going to show up, too."

Mom's eyes grew wide with suspicion while Dad just said, "Yeah! Better open another bottle."

When Dad jogged into the kitchen, Mom moved in on us. "Why are they coming?"

"They're family," I said lightly.

"That's not why you invited them, Brooklyn."

"Yes, it is. They need to know. So do Savannah and China and London." Then I repeated what I'd said to Derek a few minutes ago. "There's safety in numbers, Mom."

She rolled her eyes. "We're making a mountain out of a molehill."

"That guy is no molehill," I whispered. "He's vicious and I won't allow him to threaten you or anyone else I care about. So suck it up, buttercup."

She cocked her head and stared at me. "Did you just say 'suck it up, buttercup' to me?"

"Yeah." I sounded a little defensive.

She stared for another few seconds, then nodded. "I like it."

"It's yours." I laughed ruefully, then gave her a hug.

She patted my back, rocked back and forth, and cooed softly as though I were the one that needed a hug. Maybe I was. The thought of that nasty bully attacking my mom was just too gruesome to consider.

Dad wheeled a liquor cart into the living room. There were several bottles of wine standing on the top shelf and a dozen or so wineglasses hanging underneath.

"Wow, that's a cool new thing," I said.

"I know. Check it out." He pointed out the features. "There's room to store ten bottles on the bottom level and at least sixteen glasses above that. And this little contraption on the side holds all your tools, like your wine opener and a knife and stuff. It's got an ice bucket, too. And there's a cutting board for your limes when you're hankering for a shot of tequila."

"Very nice," I said, happy to see that the cart was made of hardwood and steel instead of one of those fancy gold carts with mirrors and curlicues everywhere. This one had a modern industrial feel to it and suited Dad perfectly.

"Your father loves it," Mom said.

"Where'd you find it?" I asked.

Mom smiled. "Robin and Austin brought it over one day, for no reason."

"Yup, out of the blue," Dad said.

"They are such suck-ups," I muttered. Now I was going to have to put some serious thought into how I could one-up my best friend and my brother.

Mom and Dad both laughed, thank goodness. Dad was in such a good mood that it was once again clear to me that Mom hadn't said anything yet. I hated to be the dark cloud that destroyed his happy mood, but it had to be done. I would blame it on Jacob Banyan.

As if on cue, the door opened.

"It's only us," Robin said, smiling as she and Austin walked into the house. She wore an adorable red plaid jacket with skinny jeans and knee-high boots. I smiled and thought about how we'd always been such opposites. She was short with dark curly hair and loved to dress up and party. I was tall with straight blond hair and loved to curl up with an old book. How we ever became friends was a question for the ages.

I grabbed her and hugged her tightly, holding on for an extra few seconds.

Robin had been my best friend since we were eight years old and I missed her a lot, ever since she had moved back to Dharma and married my brother Austin. Those two had been in love since third grade and I knew they were deliriously happy to be together.

Sometimes it was a little overwhelming to realize how far we'd come since our two little eight-year-old selves had played with our Barbie dolls together.

"You okay, girl?" Robin asked, staring into my face and rubbing my shoulders.

I took a deep breath and exhaled. "I'm just happy to see you."

"Yeah. Me, too. Let's try to do lunch sometime this week."

"I'd love to."

"Here you go, sweetheart," Dad said, handing a glass of wine to Robin.

"Thanks, Dad."

It touched my heart that she called him Dad. Her mom had traveled so much when she was young that she used to spend weeks and sometimes months at my house. I knew my folks had been much better parents to her than her own mother had ever been.

When everyone had a glass in their hand, Austin cleared his throat and said, "I want to propose a toast."

We all held our glasses up and Austin said, "A toast to my beautiful wife, the love of my life, who's pregnant with our first child."

Mom gasped and burst into tears.

I was close to it. "Oh my God, oh my God." I had to take a bunch of deep breaths to keep from losing it totally.

"Congratulations, love," Derek said, when it was his turn to hug Robin.

"Thank you, Derek," she whispered.

Dad slapped Austin on the back, then yanked him into his arms. "So proud of you, son."

"Me?" Austin said. "Robin's doing all the heavy lifting."

"I'm proud of you for choosing the right woman."

"Thank you, Dad," Robin said, grinning. She set down her wineglass—which I noticed she'd left untouched—and hugged Dad, then turned to Mom, who was blowing her nose and still sobbing.

"They're happy tears," Mom insisted, fanning herself with her hands.

"I hope so." Robin grinned. "I thought you might be weeping at the thought of having to babysit for us."

"I can't wait." She hugged her again, then grabbed Austin and simply buried her face in his chest. Austin was grinning like a loon as he rubbed her back.

"You've made me so happy," Mom said. She grabbed both Austin's and Robin's hands and clutched them to her heart. "After all the crap I've been through, you two have really turned my day around."

I choked on a laugh. "That's so touching, Mom."

She waved her hands. "Oh, you know what I mean."

"I do." I gave her a meaningful glance.

"What do you mean, Becky?" Robin asked, her tone wary, and I was reminded that even though Robin called my father Dad, she had always called my mother Becky. I think she avoided saying the word *Mom* because she didn't want to be reminded that her own mother had been less than nurturing, to say the least.

Dad was frowning. "Yeah. What kind of crap?"

The doorbell rang.

"Saved by the bell," Mom muttered.

Gabriel opened the door without waiting for an invitation and walked in.

There were more hugs and Robin handed him her wineglass. "I can't drink this so why don't you take it?"

"You sick, babe?"

"No, I'm pregnant."

He stared at her in shock, then quickly grabbed her in a hug. "Wow! That's fantastic. Congrats, honey."

"Thank you, Gabriel."

Gabriel held up the wineglass and pointed at Austin. "You, too, buddy."

Austin was beaming like a fool. "Thanks, man."

I was blinking back fresh tears. It was lovely to see everyone so happy.

"Here, sweetie," Mom said, handing Robin a glass of sparkling water with a chunk of lime.

"Thanks, Becky." She took a quick sip. "Now let's get back to all that crap you've been through. What happened?"

Mom dragged her feet, but slowly the story came out. I filled in some blanks, but then Mom kicked into gear and gave us an earful about what had been going on from day one when the festival committee was first formed. I was shocked to hear that Banyan had been such a jackass early on.

"If he'd been a little nicer, he might've gotten everything he wanted."

"But no." Austin scowled. "Once a putz, always a putz."

"You know him?" I asked.

"Oh yeah," he muttered.

Dad's jaw tightened and I could see his anger growing. But Mom didn't seem to notice as she started in on another horror story about Banyan's spitefulness. I kept an eye on Dad as she revealed the many confrontations she'd had with the big jerk. By the time she finished, Dad's teeth were bared and I thought he might start chewing the walls. And was that smoke coming out of his ears?

"I hate that guy," Robin said, before Dad could say a word.

"Yup." Austin nodded. "He really pissed off Robin."

Instantly concerned, I asked, "How? When?"

"In the supermarket," Austin said. "Just last week."

"That's right." Robin sat on the end of the couch. "I still can't believe it."

"What happened?"

"Well, first of all," she began, "he struts around like he owns the place. It's so gross. And then he actually pushed me out of the way so he could get a package of ground beef."

"Ground beef?" I shook my head. "Was it the last package left in the store?"

"No. There were a few dozen packages left and they weren't even on sale. He just wants what he wants when he wants it and has no regard for anyone but himself. He makes me sick."

"Everyone I know has had a run-in with him," Austin said. "The guy's got a screw loose."

"Maybe I do, too," Robin admitted, "because I was so angry, I kicked him."

"Yay, Robin!" I cheered.

"Well, he just made me so mad. I told him I was here first, and he said, 'Who cares?'"

"Oh my God," Mom murmured. "He's so awful."

"Yeah. So I kicked him and he freaked out. I told him he deserved it. I said, 'You're a bully and a toad, and you need to be taught a lesson.' And then I strutted away."

I chuckled at her words, although I was scared to death for my friend. And I realized that Dad's gentle hands had turned into raging fists. I could tell he was ready to go after Jacob Banyan, and I couldn't blame him.

"And then he started to follow me around the store," Robin continued. "I told him more than once to leave me alone or I'd kick him again, but that only seemed to make him madder. When I left, he followed me out to the parking lot."

"Robin, what did you do?" Mom asked.

"I got in my car, locked the doors, and called Austin. I wasn't going to have Banyan follow me home and try something there. He didn't budge, just stood there and watched me, trying to intimidate me as I sat in my car and waited for Austin to show up."

"I think I broke the speed limit trying to get there."

She smiled at him. "You were there in less than ten minutes."

"Pretty good timing," Gabriel said.

Austin and Robin lived at the top of Red Mountain on the other side of the Dharma Winery. It was more than a ten-minute ride, for sure.

"I walked right up to Banyan and stared at him," Austin said. "After what felt like a long minute, I said, 'Are you trying to threaten my wife? Why are you staring at her?' His eyes got real big and round, and he mumbled something stupid and ran off to his car."

"Good," Mom said.

"Sounds like you scared him silly," Dad said. "Good job."

"He's just a big bully," I said in disgust. "Which makes him nothing but a coward."

"A dangerous, vicious coward," Derek added with emphasis.

"Exactly," Robin said.

Gabriel leaned against the mantel and looked thoughtful as he reached for his wineglass. "One of these days he'll pick on the wrong person and get himself killed."

Chapter 4

Mom invited us all to stay for dinner and we enthusiastically agreed. Not only was she a great cook, but she'd cleverly revealed that she still had a bunch of leftover fried chicken she'd made for a recent Fellowship event. Mom's fried chicken was amazing.

I was grateful that Austin and Derek took Dad outside to the terrace to talk through the problem of Jacob Banyan. I had watched Dad growing angrier by the second and it was a rare and scary sight to see.

In the kitchen, Robin and I put together a big green salad while Mom cooked a potful of rice. I set the table and then watched Mom pull a homemade lasagna out of the refrigerator and pop it into the oven. Because who didn't have an extra dish of homemade lasagna hanging around, just in case? And sure enough, she took out a plastic container of her amazing fried chicken and popped it into the microwave.

I stopped for a moment and gazed at Robin. "I still can't believe that the scrawny little girl I've known since we were eight years old is pregnant."

"I've never been scrawny, but it's crazy, isn't it?" Robin said with a soft smile.

"Totally." I shook my head in wonder. "I'm going to need another glass of wine."

"You always were a mean girl," she grumbled.

"Hey, I'm drinking for two." I laughed and gave her a noisy kiss on the cheek. "Besides, you know you'd do the same for me."

"True enough."

We were deliberately not talking about Banyan. It was as if bringing him up right now would taint the celebration for Robin and Austin. But later, I told myself, we would be looking at what to do about the miserable man who'd actually threatened my mother.

A few minutes before dinner was ready, Robin and I worked out a schedule of our availability over the next week to drive Mom wherever she needed to go. Because of Robin's run-in with Banyan and in light of her current pregnant state, she wouldn't be part of Mom's protection squad. But I could do it and I volunteered Derek in case I was stuck somewhere else. Robin volunteered Austin. I knew Gabriel would step in if necessary as well, and Dad was usually available at a moment's notice.

"Derek's parents just arrived a few days ago," I said. "Meg and John will probably be happy to drive you anywhere you'd like to go, too, Mom."

"That's a good idea, Brooklyn," Mom said, no longer pooh-poohing our insistence that she take precautions.

It was Robin's story of encountering Jacob Banyan at the supermarket that had finally changed Mom's mind. She was now convinced that she needed to take someone with her over the next few days, at least until the book festival was over.

"Banyan doesn't even know you," Mom said, clutching Robin's hand. "And yet he decided to terrorize you.

The man is clearly unbalanced. This is what happens when you neglect your chakras. You turn on people, even strangers, because your own body is fighting your better impulses."

I thought she was being a little too understanding of the old creep, but that was Mom for you.

"Well, I did kick him in the shin," Robin reminded everyone.

"After he shoved you out of the way and almost knocked you over," I countered.

She nodded. "True."

"The man needs more than a chakra tune-up," I grumbled. "He's a psycho nutball." And I hated that this brute had scared the heck out of both Robin and Mom.

Mom winced. "Robin might've been minding her own business, but I have been actively working against him for weeks now. I practically threw him out of the meeting this afternoon."

"And now he's threatened you twice, Mom." I was glad I'd kept up with my friend Alex's Krav Maga classes because I was so ready to take him down. Not that I could actually do that, but I did have a few defensive moves I'd been working on so I might be able to hurt him a little. Hopefully it wouldn't come to that because I still had a tendency to freeze up when actually confronted with danger. I mentally brushed that acknowledgment aside. "We can't let him get close enough to do it again."

"Thank you, sweetie." Mom rubbed her arms. "Right now I'm more worried about Robin than me. The thought of him stalking you up and down the supermarket aisles is giving me shivers."

Robin could see Mom's growing concern and she gave her a hug. Then she turned and gave me a warning look. "Let's put it out of our minds for now and enjoy a beautiful dinner."

"Great idea," I said. It was definitely time to change the subject. I especially didn't want to get Dad all heated up again. Mom arranged the fried chicken on a big platter and we carried everything out to the table.

My parents' house was the center for all of us. The furniture and paint colors might change, depending on their moods at the time, but it was always our home, the place where we had gathered for the important events in our lives. We'd all grown up here—and I include Robin in that because she was in and out of our house just like the rest of us.

There had been battles between the siblings until one or both of our parents had sat us down to remind us that we were a family, and that we should let our love for each other overcome our petty differences. We'd had parties in this house that all the neighbors had attended. We'd cried with those same neighbors after funerals. This house, these walls, were a comfort that we drew on even when we didn't know we needed it.

And the heart of this house was Mom and Dad.

We all sat down to eat, and rather than continuing the ugly subject of Jacob Banyan, we all began to ask Robin questions about the baby and about her health and her diet, and whether they knew if it was a girl or a boy, and whether she would have a C-section or natural birth, and every invasive thing we could think of until she finally begged us to stop.

With a laugh, I said, "Okay, let's move on to another topic. I want to know why Saffron Bergeron is such a nasty, mean-spirited crank."

"Good question," Robin muttered.

"She really is nasty," Mom admitted with reluctance.

"And I don't know why. She's so rude to me and I've always tried to be nice to her."

"Maybe that's why," Gabriel suggested with a shrug. "She's naturally an unpleasant woman, so having you be nice to her only underlines her own lack of compassion."

Mom stared at him, then nodded. "That's very deep, dear. I think you may have a point."

I ducked my head to hide a smile, then forked up a tender morsel of chicken, ready to pop it in my mouth. But then I stopped when I thought of another point to make. "What I didn't like was the way she went on and on about the Fellowship. How we're a *cult* and we have *clandestine* meetings, blah-blah-blah." I scowled. "That whole cult thing really bugs me. She's lived here long enough to know it's not true."

"Oh, honey," Mom said kindly. "We've been putting up with that nonsense since the day we moved to Sonoma. Don't let it bother you."

I set down my fork. "What bothers me is that she did it to *you*, Mom. As you say, you're always nice to her. You're nice to everybody. You go out of your way to help people. And so does Guru Bob, for that matter. So it's really annoying to hear people like Saffron Bergeron spout that bogus crap as though it's a well-known fact."

"Some people are just stupid," Robin said philosophically.

I smiled wryly and pointed my fork at her. "That's the answer, right there."

Mom was right. Ever since we had moved to Sonoma more than twenty-five years ago, the "cult" thing had been an issue. Not constantly, but every so often. It usually happened when some ambitious journalist would drive up to Dharma, anxious to capture the "real story" of the Fellowship. Invariably he or she had heard rumors that a bunch of hippie-dippie types had formed a commune and were trying to start their own winery. And ooh, they followed some holy guy. Must be a cult!

But we were never a cult. We were never actually a commune, for that matter. We didn't share our belongings with each other or grow vegetables for the good of the group. In Israel we might've been known as a kibbutz, but even that term didn't describe the Fellowship. We lived in our own homes and our families went their own ways in terms of employment and income and schools. But we supported each other in other ways and we all contributed to the winery and the vineyards and the other common buildings like the town hall and the theater and exhibit center. And my parents tried to live by the teachings and philosophy of Robson Benedict.

That ambitious journalist undoubtedly dreamed of winning the Pulitzer Prize for the big exposé they would write about Guru Bob and his followers, including my parents and all of our friends and how we were living off the land, bilking our neighbors, and running around naked under the harvest moon. Or something along those lines.

It was insulting and stupid and completely false, which every journalist was forced, in the end, to admit. Mom was right, we'd grown used to it over the years. But that didn't mean I would forgive and forget.

Early on, my parents had schooled us on what to say if we were ever approached by a writer or a reporter. We would simply be friendly and tell the truth. What else could we do? The writer would draw his or her own conclusions, no matter what we said. Many of them would end up basing their story on gossip they picked up from people like Saffron Bergeron and her ilk. We had been dealing with that kind of ignorance for many years.

"Saffron's just a miserable person," I said.

Robin set down her fork. "And that's why she hates your mom. It's like Gabriel said. Becky is a naturally happy person and Saffron can't stand it."

I sighed. "All Guru Bob wants is for everyone to live in peace and be happy." It was the reason he'd eventually opened Dharma to people outside the Fellowship, to own property and live.

"That's totally true," Dad said, then grinned. "Guess it's no wonder Saffron hates the Fellowship."

"That's completely twisted," I said, shaking my head. "But since we're talking about Saffron, it makes perfect sense."

"This chicken is delicious, Rebecca," Derek said, and patted his mouth with the napkin. He could tell I was annoyed and was trying to change the subject.

I flashed him an appreciative smile.

"Thank you, Derek," Mom said. "You're so sweet."

"He speaks the truth," Dad declared, and reached for another piece. "Becky's always had a way with chicken."

Austin grinned. "Every kid in school wanted to come home with us on fried chicken day."

"And the lasagna was awesome," I added.

Mom beamed. There was nothing she liked better than having her family around her and all of the compliments were really making her shine.

I took a sip of wine. "Mom, I meant to ask you. Who's that young guy on your committee? Blond hair, preppy looking, one of the 'nay' votes."

"That's Ryan." She smiled wistfully. "He's a sweet boy, but he doesn't have much of a personality and he's not very, um, creative. He's Shandi Patrick's personal assistant and he only joined the committee in order to make sure we do everything we can to support her."

"Seriously?"

"Yes." Mom wore a look of frustration. "When he first joined, I was encouraged that someone young and new to Dharma would be interested in helping with the book festival. It gave me some hope."

"I get that," Robin said. "You want some fresh blood."

"That's one way to put it," Mom said. "He's quite interesting on paper. He served in the military, and besides being her assistant, he's also her bodyguard and in-house chef."

"Wow, I want one of those," Robin said.

Mom sighed. "But I've been so disappointed in him. I hate to say it, but Ryan seems very dull. He has no opinion on anything. He only tells us what Shandi wants. It's as if he lives his life through her."

I shrugged. "I guess that makes him a good assistant. But why did he vote 'nay'?"

Now she scowled. "Probably because Shandi and Jacob were friends." Mom used air quotes when she said the word *friends*.

I stared at her. "You said they *were* friends. Are they still?"

Mom held up both hands. "It's complicated. A few months ago, Shandi started talking up Jacob's company."

"Shandi Patrick is hawking box wine?" Robin said. "Doesn't that go against the reputation she's tried to create for herself?"

"What do you mean?" I asked.

Robin frowned. "When she first moved here, everyone made a big deal about her investing in Glenmaron Winery."

"For good reason," Austin said, taking up the story. "Glenmaron is one of the premier wineries in Sonoma County. They consistently get high ratings in all the trade magazines. So when the Hollywood press found out about Shandi's new venture with Glenmaron, the news hounds converged on Dharma and interviewed anyone who would talk to them about Shandi. Everyone raved about her good taste and business acumen."

"Hmm," Gabriel said. "Wonder how the Hollywood elite would react to the box wine news."

"Good question," Dad said. "I'm guessing they would tear her reputation to shreds."

"But the Hollywood press hasn't come around yet," Robin said.

"Are people around town talking about it?" I asked.

"Something else is going on," Mom said cryptically.

We all stared at her for a long moment.

"Well, don't just sit there, spill," I demanded, sitting on the edge of my seat.

"Late this afternoon Shandi was seen storming into the bank after Jacob Banyan," Mom revealed. "They had a big argument and then walked out together. Or rather, she dragged him out of there."

There was silence again, then I asked, "How do you hear about these things?"

She gazed at me. "Remember my friend Benny?"

"Of course." I blinked at the realization. "He works at the bank."

"Exactly. Well, Benny called me this afternoon, right after you two dropped me off and went home."

"I was wondering who that call was from," Dad said.

"I was going to tell you," she explained, "but the kids came back just then."

We were only gone a few minutes, I thought. *Bad timing.* "Mom, why did he call you?"

She lifted her shoulders in a defensive move. "Because he's my friend and he knows about my problems with Jacob Banyan. If Banyan's trying to destroy Glenmaron along with all the other wineries, that's one more reason to keep him out of the festival."

My head was spinning with this news so I had to think fast. "If that happened late this afternoon, it was probably around the same time that your committee was voting whether to include Banyan in the festival or not. So Ryan wouldn't have known that Shandi was angry with Banyan."

"So he voted nay in support of Banyan," Derek said. "It starts to makes sense."

I frowned at Dad. "Would Banyan actually try to foreclose on Shandi's winery?"

"It would be a fool's move," Dad said.

"Well, he *is* a big fool," Mom muttered.

"Dad, do you really think Glenmaron is in trouble?"

"I would probably have heard if they were in deep financial trouble and I've heard nothing." He swirled his wine and gazed at the way the liquid coated the inside of the glass. "But even if they were, Shandi's partners at Glenmaron are more powerful than the other owners that Banyan has foreclosed on. And Shandi is a force to be reckoned with on her own. He wouldn't have a chance."

Mom nodded. "It's complicated by the fact that the last thing Shandi wants is for people to find out that Glenmaron might be in trouble. She just can't afford to have that happen."

"Why?" Robin asked.

Mom took a deep breath. "Benny said she's been trying to raise enough capital to finance a movie and make a Hollywood comeback."

"Seriously?" I shook my head.

Robin frowned. "I wonder why she came here in the first place if she just wants to go back to Hollywood."

Dad shrugged. "A lot of people around here think that she only bought into Glenmaron Winery for the résumé."

That was fairly common. Plenty of people only got into the wine business to impress others. These types had very little interest in actually growing grapes and learning about the art and craft and science of winemaking. They couldn't care less about things like terroir, meteorological data, or soil type. They didn't give a hoot about oak barrels versus concrete tanks, or plastic corks versus real corks. They just wanted to be able to say they owned a winery. Maybe they liked to drink wine, but they didn't actually want to *make* wine.

They just wanted to add it to their *résumé*.

"You know how I feel about those résumé types," Mom said. "There are just too many of them in the wine country. So it would be a real shame if Shandi turned out to be one of them. Maybe it wouldn't affect her Hollywood reputation, but it would certainly damage her status around here."

Robin sipped her water. "So what happens if she moves back to Hollywood? Will she have to admit that she's simply been dabbling in the wine business or will she pretend that she wants to do both?"

It's hard to feel sympathy for a rich poser, I thought. *But since I've never met the woman, I suppose it would be fair to withhold judgment. But when has that ever been my style?* I grinned at my thoughts.

"Good question," Mom said. "If she moves back to Hollywood, we might not ever see her again. And that's why I don't trust Shandi Patrick."

Austin gave her a long look. "You've given this a lot of thought."

Mom blew out a breath, then took in another one and I knew she was trying to center herself. "I've been working with these people for a year now. That's a lot of time to get to know their foibles."

She sat back in her chair, closed her eyes, and did some more deep breathing. "When this is over I'm going to need a full-tilt Panchakarma cleansing and a detoxification session at the Laughing Goat sweat lodge."

"Maybe Robin can join you," I suggested.

"What? Wait. Whoa," Austin sputtered. "That can't be good for the baby."

I laughed until my sides hurt. Panchakarma was an Ayurvedic cleansing treatment that often included purging and high colonics. It was said to be the best way to clean out every orifice and purify the body of toxins.

Or you could just eat twelve chili dogs.

Robin patted Austin's arm, Mom chuckled at her son's horrified expression, and I couldn't help laughing all over again. Derek winked at me and I reached out to squeeze his hand.

I finally sighed. "It feels good to laugh."

"At my expense," Robin said, elbowing me. But she was grinning, too.

When the doorbell rang, instead of being exasperated with the interruption, Mom looked relieved. "It's about time."

I looked at Derek. "About time for what?"

"No idea."

I looked at my mother. "Mom? What's going on?"

"You'll see."

Dad pushed away from the table and went to answer the door. "Hey, come on in."

"Are we late?"

"Right on time," Dad said, and walked with the new arrivals to the dining room. "Look who's here!"

"It's Meg and John." I jumped up from the table and turned to Mom. "You knew they were coming?"

"Of course."

She was already hugging Meg when Derek stood up and grabbed his father in a big hug.

"Hello, son," John Stone said, grinning broadly. He was as tall and handsome as Derek, with streaks of gray hair along his temples that only made him look more distinguished.

"Dad, it's so good to see you," Derek said.

"You, too."

Then John embraced me warmly and Derek pulled his mother into his arms. "Hello, Mum."

"Darling son," she whispered, and held him tightly for a long moment. Then she leaned back, reached up, and pressed her hand to his cheek. "Oh, it's so good to be here with all of you. We haven't seen you since your wedding."

"I'm so glad to see you both," Derek said. "And as always, you look beautiful."

"Oh, you're silly," she demurred. "But I love you for saying so."

"I'm never silly," Derek said soberly, then grinned at her.

"Derek's right," I said, when it was my turn to give Meg a hug. Much like my own mother, the woman didn't seem to age. She had clear blue eyes, a wonderful smile, and she wore her platinum gray hair in a chic bob. She was almost as tall as me, which meant she was around five foot seven. "You look fabulous."

"And so do you, you sweet thing." Meg glanced around the table and waved everyone back. "Now, we can have a gabfest later, but right now you should all sit and finish your dinner. We'll be here on the sidelines, kibitzing."

"We're practically finished," I said, brushing off her concerns. "I'll start clearing the table so you can join us."

"I'll help you, love," Derek said.

"Oh, you stay and chat with your parents. This will only take a minute or two."

I began collecting the serving platters and salad bowl.

"I've got coffee brewing," Mom said. "Unless you'd like tea."

"I'll fix the tea," Meg said. "John, you sit and relax with Jim and the boys."

I smiled at Derek. He and Austin were the boys, I guess.

It was great that our families had connected as well as they had. Our parents had become good friends and I couldn't think of anything better than having Derek's folks living half the year here in Dharma.

Meg was obviously familiar with and comfortable in my parents' home, and that made me happy. Meg and my mom had clicked from the first time they met a few months ago, just before our wedding. They were like sisters separated at birth, their interests and feelings were so similar. They loved books and cooking and traveling and music, and they both had big, loving families. And both women considered themselves psychic, which was just plain scary, but entertaining as heck.

I gazed at Mom as I came back for more dishes. "So you decided to surprise us with Meg and John?"

She smiled. "They already had plans for dinner tonight at Arugula with Dalton but said they might stop by afterwards."

Dalton was Derek's younger brother, the last of five sons. He had met and fallen in love with my sister Savannah a year or so ago and now he lived with her in Dharma. So Meg and John had even more reason to own a house here as well as their place in England.

Austin brought two more chairs to the table and John had a seat while Meg finished making tea.

Dad handed John a glass of wine. "This is the new Pinot I was telling you about."

"It's marvelous," he said after taking a sip. Glancing around, he added, "Now what were you all talking about before we so rudely interrupted your dinner?"

I wasn't about to bring up the subject of cults or psychopaths again. Instead Robin said, "We're going to have a baby."

"That's wonderful!" John cried, and raised his glass in a toast. "Congratulations."

Meg came running in from the kitchen. "Oh, what happy news! I'm so pleased for both of you."

"Thanks, Meg," Austin said, grinning as he kissed Robin's hand. "We're very excited."

"Of course you are," she said, and leaned down to capture Robin's face between her hands before kissing her forehead. "I'll make you a cup of my special sweet tea. Becky has all the ingredients I'll need. I drank it through every one of my pregnancies. It's very soothing, if you know what I mean."

She rubbed her stomach and gave Robin a meaningful look. I assumed she meant morning sickness.

"Sounds perfect," Robin said, with a grateful smile. "Thank you, Meg."

Dad opened a fresh bottle of Pinot Noir and winked at Robin. "I'm saving a bottle of this just for you, sweetheart."

She beamed at him. "Thanks, Dad. You're the best."

With Meg and John here, we all had a lot to say. We stayed around the table and chatted for another hour, catching up with Derek's parents and talking about the book festival. Meg was thrilled to be sharing a booth with Mom in which she would do palm readings while Mom would give magic spells and incantations to anyone who requested help. They would both do Tarot readings. I had no doubt that theirs would be the most popular booth at the festival.

When Robin began to yawn, Austin announced that it was time to go home.

Meg and John decided they would stay and hang out with my parents for a little while longer. Derek and I headed for home after promising to visit his folks in their new house tomorrow. *It's great to be back in Dharma*, I thought, *with the people we love*.

As we got into bed, I sighed. "I still can't believe Robin's going to have a baby."

"It's lovely news," Derek said. "They'll be excellent parents."

"Oh, absolutely." But then I frowned. "I just hope I don't dream about pregnant women being chased up and down the supermarket aisles by a psychopath."

"Thanks very much," he groused. "Now that you've planted the seed, we're both going to have that dream."

"Sorry about that." But I wasn't and he knew it.

"Come here." He pulled me close to his side and whispered, "Have only sweet dreams, darling."

"You, too, love. No supermarket chases."

He groaned. "You're doing it again."

I laughed and snuggled closer to him. And fell asleep within minutes.

When my alarm went off, I sighed, then reached blindly for my phone. "It can't be time to get up," I mumbled. "I don't even remember setting the alarm."

"It's not your alarm," Derek muttered. "Someone is ringing you."

He was right. The room was still dark without even a hint of sunlight beginning to creep across the windowsill. So naturally I went into worry mode. A phone call this late at night could not be happy news.

I struggled to hit the right button, then whispered, "Hello?"

"Brooklyn, sweetie."

"Mom." Worry jumped to panic. "What's wrong? Do you need a ride somewhere?"

"No, sweetie."

I sat up in bed. "What do you need?"

Mom sighed heavily and I could almost see her biting her bottom lip, wondering how to say what I knew was going to be hard to hear.

"Oh, sweetie. A couple of hours after you left I realized my new prescription was still in my tote bag at the town hall. I'm supposed to start taking the pills first thing in the morning."

I felt a chill run down my spine. "You didn't go there alone, did you?"

"Oh, no. Of course not. Meg drove me here."

I grimaced while I blinked blindly at the light Derek had flipped on. He was watching me, worry etched on his face as well.

"Are you and Meg still there?"

Derek was out of bed, already reaching for his clothes.

Honestly, my husband was the absolute best in a crisis. Always coolheaded, clear thinking, and ready for anything. But when he heard me say his mother's name, he came to a dead stop. "Put it on speaker."

I did so. "You're on speaker, Mom, so Derek can hear, too."

"Oh, isn't that nice. Hi, Derek."

I rolled my eyes. "Go ahead, Mom."

"Right. Meg's here and, really, we're both fine so we don't want either of you to worry. But Brooklyn, we have a situation and I think we need your expertise. Yours, too, Derek."

I was sliding into my jeans. "What kind of situation, Mom?"

"Oh, sweetie," she said, and now her voice dropped to a hush as if she were reluctant to say it. Which made me reluctant to hear it. Then she did. "Well, it seems we've found a dead body."

My gaze snapped to Derek. "Okay, Mom. We'll be right there."

"Oh, thank God." She breathed out a sigh of relief, then hung up.

Derek and I stared at each other. "I forgot to ask who died," I said. "Any guesses?"

"Too many," Derek said, tugging his shoes on. "And not enough information."

"Right. Let's go save our mothers."

Chapter 5

We raced outside, jumped into the Bentley, and Derek took off like a racecar driver. At the bottom of the hill, he came to a sudden stop and swore. "With all the excitement tonight, I forgot to get Gabriel's thoughts on the local police."

I already had my phone in my hand. "I was about to call the police. Maybe I should call Gabriel first."

"Yes."

We had dealt with the local Sonoma police once before and they had been respectful, friendly, and helpful. But Dharma's population had grown so much that it now had its own police force. It was a whole new ball game and an exciting change for our small community, but I was still nervous because Derek and I had no idea who we were going to be dealing with.

Over the last few years we had gotten to know two of the San Francisco homicide detectives pretty well. Nathan Jaglow was semi-retired now, but Inspector Janice Lee was still on the job and had become a good friend of ours. That didn't mean she couldn't be bad-tempered and snarky when she came onto a crime scene and saw me standing there. She was just as liable to give me grief as to sit down and have a glass of wine with us.

I hasten to add that she rarely gave Derek grief, of course. She treated him with respect and always called him Commander, his rank when he served in the British Royal Navy. But then, he was Derek Stone, security expert and international man of mystery. And there was that whole tall-dark-and-dangerous aspect of him to consider.

And what did it say about Derek and me that we both had Inspector Lee's number on speed dial?

But Inspector Lee can't help us now, I thought with some dismay. So I tapped Gabriel's name in my contacts and switched the speaker on. He answered on the first ring.

"Hey," he muttered.

"It's Brooklyn and Derek. We're sorry to wake you."

"Who's dead?" he asked first thing.

It took me by surprise and I blinked at Derek.

"Um, good question," I said with a sinking realization that we hadn't even asked Mom who the victim was.

"Not important right now," Derek said briskly.

"Our mothers found a dead body at the town hall," I hurried to explain.

"Whoa." He paused for only a moment, as if soaking it in, then said, "I'll be there in ten minutes."

"Wait!"

"What?" he asked.

"We're about to call the local police," I said. "Have you dealt with them? Any advice? Is there anyone we should try to avoid or . . ."

"I'll take care of it," he said, and hung up.

I stared at the phone, then looked at Derek. "Guess that about covers it."

"Not yet," Derek said. "Call your father. And I'll call mine."

"Oh shoot." I winced. "You're right. They'll flip if we don't let them know what happened." I started to call Dad, then stopped. "Don't you think Mom called him already?"

He gazed at me steadily. "No."

I rolled my eyes. "Of course not." I pressed my parents' number and waited for Dad to answer. Hearing his groggy voice, I went through my apologies, then told him where we were going and why.

His response was nearly as instantaneous as Gabriel's. "I'll meet you there." And he hung up.

The police probably wouldn't appreciate all the people who'd be showing up at the crime scene, but it couldn't be helped. Dad would want to be there for Mom. Likewise, Derek's father would want to support Meg.

When Derek finished the call to his father, I stared out the window and worried. I had literally been stumbling over dead bodies for years now. But this was different.

"I can hear your brain working, love," Derek said, and reached for my hand. "What's going on?"

"It's this dead body, thing," I started, then had to take a few deep breaths. "I'll never get used to it."

"Darling, if you were ever to get used to it, you would be miserable."

"True." I squeezed his hand. "It's always a shock, and sometimes I can barely hold it together. But now that it's happening to our mothers, I feel even worse. I'm sick and sad and frightened for them."

"So am I, love." He stopped at a light and leaned over to kiss me. "I'm trying to remind myself that they're both strong women."

He was right, of course. Mom was a total rock. She
had raised six kids plus Robin. She had taken Annie
under her wing, too, along with any number of strays
over the years. Heck, she had nursed Gabriel back to
health when someone tried to shoot his head off. She
was smart, funny, talented, capable, and totally in charge.
And Meg was right up there with Mom.

But hey, I considered myself strong, too. I'd faced
down more than a few vicious killers and lived to talk
about it. And yet, it was humbling to admit that I was
liable to faint dead away—pardon the pun—at the sight
of a dead body. Especially if there was blood involved. I
had a thing about blood, even after all these years. One
of these days I would really have to do something about
it. I'd thought about hypnosis, but I wasn't sure that
would work for me.

"Yes, my mother is very strong," I said finally. "But
she's also really sensitive. She often feels things on a
different level than some of us. Like, I don't know, some
astral plane that only the true weirdos ever reach."

Derek stifled a laugh. "True."

"Right. So for her to have to deal with a dead body
and, you know, all the vibes and spectral auras and negative sensations that go along with that, it could be a
little overwhelming."

Was I starting to sound like a wingnut? Seriously.
Vibes? Spectral auras? Oh yeah, wingnut city. Because
I was my mother's daughter, after all.

I waved the words away. "Never mind."

"I won't discount your feelings, darling. I feel the
same way. After all, my mother is right there with yours,
having traveled an astral path or two as well."

"Oh boy," I muttered. Yes, Meg was just as much of
a hippie-dippie wingnut as Mom. It was one of the rea-

sons they had bonded so nicely from the start. And only one of the reasons why both women were so completely loved.

"To be honest," he added, "I find that a comfort."

"What do you mean?"

"They're going through it together," he said. "They're good friends. I think they'll bring even more strength to each other because of it."

I lifted his hand and kissed it. "I didn't think of that, but you're right. Thanks."

Still, there were a hundred different scenarios whirling around in my brain. I just had to hope that Derek really was right, that Meg and Mom were feeling more secure because they were experiencing this horrible event together.

I frowned. Actually, knowing the two of them, they might even consider it an adventure. They had probably opened a bottle of champagne by now.

Derek expertly maneuvered the car up and down the roads until we reached the Lane. Three blocks later, he turned right onto Berkeley Circle and came to a stop in front of the town hall.

"No police cars yet," I said, glancing every which way. "And no Gabriel."

"We beat them all here."

"That might be a good thing."

"It is. I want a chance to talk to my mother and yours before the police take over the scene."

"I just hope the dead person isn't Jacob Banyan," I murmured.

"Honestly?" Derek wondered as we jumped out of the car. "I can think of no one more deserving. And it seems that almost everyone in town would like to see him dead."

"I'll admit I wouldn't be too sad to find out that the victim is Banyan," I explained. "But if it is him, I'm afraid Mom will be the number one suspect."

He threw his arm across my shoulders and pulled me close. "Good point. Although, try to remember that the man doesn't have many friends in Dharma."

"Don't get me wrong," I said quickly. "I don't want it to be anyone else, either."

"Of course not."

"But jeez, Banyan and Mom had that huge argument in front of the entire festival committee. And then there was that confrontation on the Lane just a few hours ago. There had to be a bunch of people watching that happen."

"Plenty of witnesses," Derek murmured.

"Exactly." I instantly recalled the entire ugly scene. "And some of those witnesses aren't going to keep their mouth shut, if you know what I mean."

"Unfortunately, I do."

I didn't say the name Saffron Bergeron, but we both knew who I was talking about. Even though she hadn't been around when Banyan confronted Mom on the street, I knew Saffron would hear about it through the small-town grapevine and be perfectly happy to spread the gossip. She might even go so far as to accuse Mom of the crime.

We dashed from the car into the building.

Despite what I was wishing for, I had to prepare myself for the inevitability that the dead body in the conference room simply had to be Jacob Banyan. He was so horrible to so many people, it was a wonder he hadn't been murdered long before this. Someone had clearly decided that his time had come. He had to be stopped.

I wouldn't say that he deserved to die, necessarily, but Banyan had pushed and pushed until someone had pushed back, to deadly effect.

And again, I couldn't be sorry he was dead, except for the fact that my own mother and Meg had stumbled over his body and that the police might believe that my mom was involved in his death.

I shivered once more at that dreary thought and had to rub my arms.

"Are you cold?"

"No, just freaking out a little."

"I don't blame you." Derek stroked my back as we moved quickly across the wide main hall of the building. He grabbed my hand. "Let's get in there and see what we can do."

We ran to the hallway and saw the door of the festival-committee conference room wide open. Other doors were open, as well, and I wondered where Mom and Meg were waiting.

"Oh God." Something else I didn't want to think about. "They wouldn't still be waiting inside the same room as the body, would they?"

"They would've moved to another room," Derek said, sounding sure of himself.

"I hope you're right."

"Mother," Derek shouted. "Rebecca. Where are you?"

"Mom? Meg?" I called.

"Here," my mom cried. I spun around to see her run out of another room farther down the hall. She dashed toward us and grabbed me in a tight hug.

"Are you all right?" I asked, leaning back to take a good look at her. She looked . . . hmm. Excited? No, that would be weird. Maybe overstimulated was a better way to say it. Her cheeks were red and her eyes were almost twinkling. Was she pretending to be okay for my sake?

"We're fine," she insisted, but she was breathless. "Really, we're good. Meg and me, I mean. Super good. Holy moly, Brooklyn. This is crazy. Insane. Can you believe it?"

She was blathering, I realized. She must've been beside herself with fear and had worked herself into a near panic.

"Are you sure you're okay?"

"Absolutely, sweetie."

This was not the reaction I'd expected. Yes, Mom was strong, but finding a dead body wasn't an easy thing, as I knew all too well. I'd thought that I would have to console her, and here she was looking as if she'd scored front row seats to a Grateful Dead concert.

She smiled to reassure me, but how could I trust anything she was saying? She had to be in shock.

Meg had followed Mom up the hall and Derek wrapped his arms around her. She patted his back as if she were the one soothing him. "We're quite fine, dear. No need to worry."

I noted that Meg's cheeks were flushed and her face looked a bit clammy. Oh God. Did Meg have high blood pressure? I hoped she hadn't passed out.

"Good heavens," she said, pressing her hands to her chest. "I had no idea."

"No idea about what?" I asked.

"Well, about finding a dead body. It's so . . ." Meg scratched her head, clearly searching for words.

"It's okay," I said, rubbing her arm. "I know what you're going through."

"Of course you do," she said, then her eyes widened

and she laughed. "Yes, of course, Brooklyn. That's why we called you."

"I'm glad you did."

"But I must admit that while we were waiting," she said, "we got so involved in trying to figure it all out, that it slipped my mind that this sort of thing happens to you on a regular basis."

"Brooklyn's an old hand at this murder game," Mom said, winking at me.

I stared at both of them, then looked at Derek. He looked as flummoxed as I felt, because I was pretty sure that they were enjoying themselves.

"Where's the body?" he asked. "The police will be here any minute and I'd like to see where it happened before they get here."

"Oh, good point," Mom said, and turned to Meg. "Derek is so smart."

"I couldn't be prouder," Meg said, reaching up to pat his cheek.

Mom turned back to Derek and me. "The body's here in the committee room."

We followed them back up the hall. Despite the initial shock, the two of them were handling themselves pretty well, all things considered. It made me even more convinced that it was Jacob Banyan who was dead, mainly because Mom wasn't overwrought about it.

Of course, she might've been feeling relieved now, but she would have to deal with the horror later. She would probably relive that moment of discovering the dead body many times over the next few days, and maybe even longer than that. I hated to think that could be the case.

"It's just so sad," Mom said, and took my arm as we

approached the room. "I never really knew what you went through when you found all those poor dead people. But now that I've been through it myself, I have more respect for you than ever, if that's possible."

"Thanks, Mom." *I think.*

"Here we go," Mom said, and swung her arm out as if she were introducing a new guest on a talk show. Good grief.

"Yes, indeed," Meg added jovially. "There's your body. Oh, and you two should know, we didn't touch it."

"I hope not," Derek muttered.

All I could think was that our mothers made a great team.

Yes, indeed. I stared at the body sprawled on the floor. He was a large man wearing a gray hoodie and baggy black jeans. His arms were extended straight out as if he had been making a swan dive. The thought of that—and the reality of it—was grotesque and awful. There was so much blood.

Why did there always have to be blood? Couldn't we stumble across a poisoning once in a while? My head began to pound, and I had to breathe slowly and deeply as my eyelids fluttered and I groaned. "Oh no."

Derek grabbed me. "No, you don't. Just look away, love. You'll be all right."

Clearly I wasn't going to be okay because my head was spinning and I was starting to falter on my feet. I hated myself for being so weak. I wish I could say that it was the dreaded knowledge that my mother and Meg had been the ones to see the body that was causing my stomach to do backflips. But no, it was just me. And I had to wonder what had happened to that strong woman I had just been calling myself.

"Sit down," Derek ordered, and basically pushed me down into a chair.

"Okay, okay," I whispered.

"Close your eyes."

I closed my eyes. "I'm not going to faint, I promise." At least, that was what I mentally told myself in a very sternly worded speech. But really, why did there have to be blood?

"Wait here, love." Derek kissed the top of my head as if I were a well-behaved four-year-old. I opened my eyes and watched him walk toward the body, being careful of where he stepped. He wouldn't want to destroy any evidence, I knew, but definitely wanted to see how Banyan had died. As he got closer, he bent down to get a good look at the dead man's face.

In an instant he turned and stared at me.

"What?" I said. "What is it?"

"It's not Banyan," he said flatly. "It's Lawson Schmidt."

Derek had closed the committee room door and shepherded us down the hall to a room where there were no dead bodies. And that was where we waited for the police to arrive. Instead of a businesslike conference room, this room was furnished with several couches and chairs arranged around a coffee table. Bookshelves lined two walls and magazines were neatly fanned out across the end tables.

The room was clearly intended to be used as a quiet reading room. I thought it was lovely that we had such a pleasant spot in which to wait until the police were ready to grill us.

My stomach and I were doing much better, now that I wasn't in the same room with poor, dead Lawson. And thinking of him, I turned to my mother. "Mom, why didn't you tell us the victim was Lawson?"

"Didn't I mention it?" She looked at Meg and they both frowned. "Isn't that odd?"

"We were a little flustered at the time," Meg explained.

"Of course you were," I hastened to say, not wanting to upset them. "It's just that it was such a shock to see Lawson lying there."

"Oh, it was a shock to us, too," Mom said.

"To be honest," I said quietly, "I had just assumed the victim would be Jacob Banyan."

"That would make more sense, wouldn't it?" Mom said. "Funny, though. I have Banyan pegged as the killer."

Mom sure had the lingo down, if nothing else.

We heard heavy footsteps approaching in the hallway.

"We're down here," Mom called out.

The first one to walk into the room was Gabriel. He saw me and said, "Babe."

"Gabriel." Still a little wobbly, I stood and wrapped my arms around him. "Thanks for being here."

"Where else would I be?" he said simply.

Following close behind him were two uniformed officers, a man and a woman, plus another man in street clothes.

In a strategic move, Gabriel shot a meaningful look at Derek and said, "Commander Stone, I'd like to introduce you to Detective Steve Willoughby. And these are Officers Kristin Jenkins and Matthew Steuben."

"How do you do?" Derek said, his voice going into full James Bond mode as he first shook the detective's hand, then turned to shake hands with both officers.

"Commander," the detective murmured.

I blinked. "Stevie?"

The detective frowned, then his eyes widened. "Brooklyn?"

"Look at you," I said softly. "All grown up and wearing a tie."

"And you look . . . great," he said. "Wow. What are the chances?"

Stevie had no way of knowing, but the chances were pretty good when it came to me showing up around a dead body. It was sad but true.

"I thought you moved back east," I said.

"Minneapolis," he corrected. "I was on the force for ten years before moving back home to take this job."

"I hear it gets cold in Minneapolis," I said lamely.

He grinned. "You have no idea."

Even as far back as grade school, Stevie had been the all-American boy next door, friendly and blond and cute as could be. He was tall and muscular, a natural athlete. My mother always liked him because he was so polite. I hoped that was still the case. He was still blond and cute, for sure. And he was tall, though not as tall as Derek. Or as muscular. Not that I was comparing the two men, because there was no comparison when it came to Derek.

I turned to Derek. "Stevie—I mean—Detective Willoughby, and I went to grammar school together."

"Good to know," Derek said.

"Commander Stone is my husband," I said quickly.

"Well, well," Stevie said. "Congratulations to you both."

I smiled. "Thanks."

I glanced at Gabriel, who was grinning broadly. And that was when I remembered why we were all here. *Good grief. That concludes tonight's session of crime scene chitchat*, I thought.

"Commander," Gabriel said. "Will you show Detective Willoughby and the officers where the body is?"

"Certainly." Derek caught my gaze and winked, then ushered them out of the room and down the hall.

At the door, Stevie glanced back. "If you'll all remain here until we can get your statements, I would appreciate it."

"Of course," I said.

Then he disappeared down the hall.

"Well, that was strange," I muttered.

"Not at all, dear." Mom smiled. "Stevie Willoughby grew up quite nicely, didn't he?"

I could barely keep from rolling my eyes. And yet I had been thinking the same thing. "Yeah, he did, Mom."

"I wonder if he's married."

"Mom!"

"We could introduce him to Annie," she said innocently.

"She's dating Presley, remember?"

"Oh, that's right. Well, we'll think of someone for him."

"He might be married, Mom."

"We'll find out."

"I'm sure we will." Because Becky Wainwright was on the case.

My dad and John arrived a couple minutes later and joined us in the waiting room. While the parents talked quietly, I was thinking. I hated to admit that I was very nearly disappointed to find that Banyan wasn't the victim. *And what*, I wondered, *does that say about me?* That, though, was a question for a different time. The one we needed answers to now was "So why was Lawson killed?"

Dad and John had gone down the hall to the kitchen to make a pot of coffee, so my question was aimed at the moms.

I thought it was helpful that Gabriel knew the cops well enough that they allowed him to hang out on the periphery of the crime scene. It was also really nice that Stevie and the officers were showing the same sort of respect for Derek as the San Francisco cops had always shown him.

I, on the other hand, got bupkes, even though I'd been Detective Stevie Willoughby's fourth-grade crush. And lest they forgot, I was married to the *Commander*! Clearly, those important points had no bearing on my status around here and my chances of being in on their assessment of the crime scene.

"I have no idea why anyone would want to hurt poor old Lawson," Mom said softly. "It doesn't seem fair."

"Not fair at all," Meg said. "He seemed like a congenial sort of fellow."

"He is," Mom insisted. "I mean, he *was*. He's been in the Fellowship forever, so that counts for something." She suddenly glanced at me and I knew she was thinking of a certain Fellowship member who had proven herself capable of cold-blooded murder. So membership didn't necessarily count for anything, unfortunately. But I refused to think about that right now.

"Of course," Mom continued, "Lawson wasn't the best cochair in the world, but he wasn't terrible. At least he wasn't a bully like Jacob Banyan or a mean witch like Saffron Bergeron. He was just . . . Lawson."

"If that's true, then his death doesn't make any sense." I kept going back to what I'd heard Banyan say to Lawson yesterday. Good grief, was it only yesterday? *You're nothing but a thief and a liar.* What did that mean? What did Banyan think Lawson had stolen? What did he think Lawson had lied about?

And now I had to ask myself the burning question: Did Jacob Banyan kill Lawson?

"Mom, you said that Lawson handled all the money for the festival."

"Yes, and he seemed to be doing a decent job, as far as I know."

"As far as you know?" I repeated, truly confused now. "What do you mean? Why wouldn't you know what kind of job he's doing?"

"Because, sweetie, we're handling two distinctly separate parts of the festival. I'm taking care of speakers and schedules and those sorts of things. Who gets which booth and where each booth should be situated, you know. I've booked all the authors and speakers and vintners, and let's see, I've ordered books for anyone who's speaking or signing during the three days of the festival. I'm also supervising the other committee members who are handling the schedules and the details of publicity and marketing and all the banners and flyers. There's so much that goes into an event like this. Oh, and all the food and beverage vendors, too."

"Wow, that's a lot," I said, impressed that Mom had taken on so much. "And what was Lawson handling?"

"He was taking care of all the rest of it. Supplies and equipment, mainly. He had to order the booths themselves, of course, and the chairs and tables that go inside the booths. And there are the porta-potties, the trash cans, the benches and chairs that we'll line up around the perimeter to allow for seating. Plus linens, tablecloths, all those sorts of things. He was supervising a number of committee members himself, too."

"So why would Banyan call him a thief and a liar?"

"Oh, honey," she said with a sigh. "That didn't mean anything. Banyan is simply an awful person with an ugly mind."

"So you didn't hear any complaints from anyone about their bills not being paid on time?"

"No complaints at all. But then again, I'm not dealing with the same people that Lawson was dealing with."

"I see."

We sat with our own thoughts for a few minutes, then I remembered something else. "Mom, the police will be back to ask questions pretty soon and they'll probably want to hear all about your relationship with Lawson and the committee and everything else. The fact that Lawson was killed right in the committee meeting room means that there's got to be a connection."

"Oh gosh, sweetie, you're right." She gave my arm a squeeze, then turned to Meg. "See, that's why I wanted to call Brooklyn first thing."

"She did," Meg assured me. "Because you've been there, done that, and you think of all these things that would never have occurred to us."

Mom wrapped her arms around my waist and rested her head on my shoulder. "Oh, Brooklyn. I'm so proud of you and am so glad you're here."

"I'm proud of you, too." I held on to her for a long moment, then reached out to Meg. "Proud of both of you."

I sat back on the cushion, anxious to prepare them for what would happen when the police came back in here. "One thing I've learned is that when you're answering any question the police ask you, you should first of all be totally honest, naturally. If you try to sneak in a little white lie, they'll find out and it'll make things a lot worse."

"It's just like we've always taught our kids, right, Meg?"

Meg held up her hand as if she were pledging in court. "Absolutely. Tell the truth and shame the devil."

I couldn't help but smile. "Right. But I have one other word of advice and I think it's important, too. Please try not to overshare, if you know what I mean."

"I know exactly what you mean, sweetie." She winked at me. "You don't want me to start jabbering like a fool, right?"

"Well, sort of. Except you're not a fool, Mom. No way. I only mention the oversharing thing because I've done it myself and it never seems to work out well. Just answer their questions honestly and don't volunteer information they didn't ask for."

"You're too cute." She patted my knee. "Thank you, sweetie. We'll get through this."

"Yes, dear," Meg added. "Don't worry."

I smiled wearily. "Too late."

Chapter 6

A half hour later, Stevie walked into our waiting room, followed by Officer Jenkins and Derek. "We're waiting for the crime scene techs to arrive from Sonoma so we'll be here awhile longer. Which means we're sending you all home for now."

Mom grabbed Meg's hand. "But don't you want to talk to Meg and me? We're the ones who found Lawson's body."

"We can tell you everything we saw," Meg added.

"That will be very helpful, ma'am," he said. "We definitely want to talk to both of you, but we can do it tomorrow."

Mom's shoulders slumped a bit at the disappointment of not being "grilled."

"That's fine, then," she said.

His eyes narrowed. "You're not planning on leaving town, are you?"

"What? No. We— Oh, dear." Flustered, Mom patted her cheeks. "You're joking."

"Yes, ma'am." Stevie grinned, and his beautiful white teeth gleamed. "A little levity. Probably not appreciated at two in the morning."

Probably not, I thought. But I appreciated the fact that Stevie was being gentle with Mom and Meg.

Mom smiled weakly. "I admit the events of the night have taken their toll on my sense of humor."

"Understandable." He glanced around the room. "It would be helpful if all of you would make yourselves available to be interviewed at some point during the day, preferably in the morning. Our officers will call each of you to set up appointments."

"We'll be available," I said, stifling a yawn as I spoke for the group. At this point, I was no longer very lucid, but I managed a few sentences. "Do you need our phone numbers? Derek and I are staying at a different address than my parents'. Do you need that info?"

He held up a small leather notebook. "I already have everyone's information, thanks to Commander Stone."

"Okay, then." I pushed myself up off the couch while Dad and John extended their arms to help Mom and Meg do the same. I stretched my back and neck, and rolled my shoulders, feeling stiff from sitting on that overstuffed couch. It felt like we'd been there for days.

"There's a half pot of coffee in the kitchen at the end of the hallway," Dad said. "Please help yourselves."

"Appreciate it, Mr. Wainwright," Stevie said.

Derek walked over and slipped his arm around my waist. "Let's go home, shall we?"

"Absolutely, Commander," I murmured.

He gave me a light pinch and I tried not to squirm as I turned to Stevie. "It's so good to see you again, Stevie. I mean, Detective." I gave him a hug. "And welcome back."

"Thanks." He nodded to Derek. "Good night, Commander. See you later, Brooklyn." Stevie wished everyone else a good night as well, and I appreciated that. Mom was right. Stevie had always been very polite.

Outside, the first thing I noticed was the medical examiner's black van parked on Berkeley Circle. So Lawson's body was still inside the committee room. I felt an instant chill and wondered if it was due to the cold night air or the sudden image of that poor guy laid out on the hardwood floor, waiting to be carried out and delivered to the morgue.

My Dad and John had their arms around their wives and were steering them toward the street where all of our cars were parked. I checked both women with quick glances and, of course, they looked much better than I was feeling. Seriously, I wanted to be them when I was their age. Nothing seemed to stop them. Not even murder.

I zipped my jacket up to my neck, shook myself out of my morbid thoughts, and gave quick hugs all around. Then we all got into our cars and drove home.

Derek and I didn't speak for the first few minutes of the drive. Then he turned and glanced at me. "Darling, I would appreciate if you would address me as Commander from now on."

I choked out a laugh. "You're going to be sorry for that."

"I don't see why," he said, pretending to be affronted. "But to be serious for a moment, even though it was a bit ridiculous, I'm pleased that Gabriel addressed me as if I were important, because I was able to find out some information that I otherwise wouldn't have learned."

I shifted in my seat to face him. "First of all, you *are* important. And second, what'd you find out? How did Lawson die?"

He frowned at me. "Are you telling me you didn't notice?"

I grimaced. "I was a little too queasy to notice much of anything at the time. Except for all that blood."

He reached over and patted my hand. "I'm sorry, love."

"Yeah, me too." I shook my head. "I've really got to do something about that stupid little phobia. But never mind. What happened?"

Derek stared at the road ahead. "Lawson was stabbed in the neck with the sharp, broken edge of a wine bottle. The glass hit his carotid artery and he bled out. Death occurred within minutes."

Well, I asked for that, I thought. Now I was queasy all over again. "That's disgusting. Poor Lawson. No wonder there was so much blood."

"Yes."

I shook my head. "There must've been a fight, but who breaks a wine bottle and shoves it into someone's neck? Seriously, what is wrong with people?"

"That's a very good question, love." He shook his head and squeezed my hand again. "One we don't have an answer to. But I'm actually glad you didn't see Lawson. It was rather ghastly."

My imagination was now working overtime, painting vivid impressions of what the murder scene had actually looked like. My stomach turned at my own thoughts, so imagine if I'd gotten a better look.

"I probably would've lost my dinner," I muttered.

"And I wouldn't have blamed you. I do hope our mothers didn't get too good a look at what caused Lawson's death."

The thought of that possibility made my stomach

swirl. "If they had, I doubt they would've been so cheerful about it."

"I'm going to hold on to that thought," he said, and frowned. "Because their excitement level was a bit over the top, wouldn't you say?"

"They were downright giddy about it." I was wide awake now as I pondered that. The moms were usually cheerful and upbeat, and normally that was a good thing. But at a murder scene, it seemed a little out of place. "I have so many questions."

"I'm ready whenever you are."

"I'm not sure where to start."

"Dealer's choice, darling. You get to choose wherever you want to begin."

"Okay." I took a breath and let it out. "You said it was a wine bottle. Was the rest of the bottle still in the room? Was it empty? Had Lawson and his killer been drinking the wine?" I frowned. "I guess the medical examiner will have to do an autopsy to answer that one."

"Yes," he said. "Although there were two empty wineglasses on the table. And yes, the bottle was still there. Broken into several pieces."

"Could you tell what kind of wine it was?"

"The glass was dark so it was most certainly a red wine of some kind."

"Did you happen to see the label?"

"No." He scowled. "The label was completely obscured by all that blood. But the crime scene techs will surely be able to discern which winery it came from."

"I hope so." The more I thought about it, the more anxious I was to find out. "That could be important."

"I agree."

"Or not." I sighed. I knew both of us were thinking

of all of our friends—not to mention my parents—with their own wineries. If one of their bottles had been used to kill Lawson . . .

"Was any of the wine spilled on the floor?"

He frowned thoughtfully and steered the car around a curve, headlights slashing through the darkness. "I thought I saw some drops of wine spilled on the floor, but again, there was so much blood, it was hard to tell for certain which was which."

I should've thought of that. "Did the police say if they found any fingerprints on the bottle? Or the wineglasses? Any footprints on the floor?"

"Gabriel and I saw fingerprints on one of the glasses, but the other one had been wiped clean. And there were fingerprints on the bottle as well. Willoughby confirmed it. He explained that he could've pulled the prints himself, but decided to wait for the techs to arrive from Sonoma. They'll be able to gather all the evidence at one time and put together a more complete picture."

I half turned in my seat to stare at him. "What other evidence was there?"

"There was a dirty footprint on the wood floor. I'd like to think it came from either the killer or the victim, as the room appeared to have been cleaned earlier. But it could've come from our mothers' shoes. Or any of ours, for that matter. We'll have to wait and see for sure."

I frowned. "They didn't take any of our shoes into evidence."

"No." He glanced at me. "Strictly speaking, they should have. But, they'll probably check shoes during their interviews tomorrow. That is, later today."

"Right. Strange that they didn't take our shoes," I mused. I could remember handing my shoes over to Inspector Lee on more than one occasion when I'd stepped onto a crime scene. "I guess small-town detectives work differently than the big-city cops."

"Yes." He smiled. "Oh, and Gabriel found a button in the corner of the room, but we're not sure where it came from."

"A button." I frowned again. "But if the room was cleaned earlier, I would hope that the cleaners would've found a button. Which means it would've come from either Lawson's or the killer's clothing."

"Perhaps," he mused, unwilling to put too much faith in the cleaning service or in the possibility that a button might be a major clue. "Also, there were a few pages of a spreadsheet left on the conference table."

"Seriously? I didn't see any of that when I was in there."

"You were distracted, darling." He made another turn. "You were worried about our mothers and trying to avoid looking at blood."

"True. Some detective I am."

He laughed. "You're a wonderful detective—for a bookbinder."

I laughed, too, and could have kissed him for making me smile.

"Did you get a good look at the spreadsheet? Was it festival related?"

Derek turned onto Vivaldi Way and started up the hill. "I'm afraid I didn't have time to study it."

I was ridiculously disappointed. "That's too bad."

He winked and grinned. "But I snapped a photo of it so we can both study it later today."

I beamed at him. "Oh my God, you are awesome. You're also a great detective for a Commander."

He nodded regally. "Thank you, my love. And you may call me Derek."

I snorted a laugh. "You're awfully funny for two o'clock in the morning."

"Darling, for two o'clock in the morning, I'm hilarious."

I laughed again. "Yes, you are. Any time of day, really." But then I sighed. "I wish I'd been more coherent earlier. I could've helped you look around for clues."

He pulled into the driveway of Abraham's house and came to a stop. "Don't feel too bad, darling. I think your natural abhorrence of blood was exacerbated by the fact that it was nearly two o'clock in the morning. And it didn't help that your mother and mine may be implicated, so you had your mind on that as well."

"You got that right." I yawned. "I can't believe it's two o'clock—"

"In the morning. Right." He chuckled, then unfastened my seatbelt for me. "Come on, let's go to bed."

Later that morning, we sat in the sunny breakfast room, drinking coffee and feasting on iced pumpkin scones, Brie, slices of ham, and apple chunks, when Derek's phone rang. The conversation was brief and when he ended the call, he said, "That was Detective Willoughby. He'll be here in half an hour."

"He's coming to interview us himself? Not sending one of the officers?"

"Yes, he's coming himself." Derek broke off a corner of the scone, spread a generous bit of Brie on it, and topped it with a thin slice of ham. "I'm going to bet he's coming here himself because of the little girl he loved in fourth grade."

"Oh yeah? Well, I'm going to bet he's coming himself because of . . ." I lowered my voice to add gravitas to the words, "the Commander."

Derek rolled his eyes, then took a moment to chew his scone-Brie-ham concoction. "As I mentioned, my former title was useful in the moment."

"Very useful indeed," I agreed, recalling all the juicy information Derek had been able to learn from the police at the crime scene the night before.

"I believe," Derek said, "that with all the evidence left behind in the meeting room, the police will be able to track down this killer in no time flat."

"I hope so," I said, but I was worried. "I don't want the main festival headline to read 'Murder at the Book Festival.' That's not the kind of takeaway we want for the first annual Dharma Book Festival."

Derek nodded. "Your mother would find that very upsetting."

"Everyone would, but especially Mom." I sipped my coffee. "Although I've noticed in the past that murder doesn't necessarily keep the hordes from showing up anyway."

"So true," Derek admitted. "People can be ghoulish indeed."

I nodded in grim acceptance. "For that reason alone, our festival could be the most successful event in the history of Sonoma County."

"Careful . . . if you're right, the council could want a murder every year just to keep up attendance!"

I wanted to laugh, but as we'd discovered in the past, the general public could be pretty weird. So who knew?

He laughed ruefully. "If our mothers' behavior last night is anything to go by, the subject of murder will be a big draw."

I chuckled. "Do you remember when they first met at our house?"

Derek poured both of us another cup of coffee. "How

could I forget? They practically begged us to take them on a tour of the sites where you'd discovered dead bodies."

"And they were downright giggly when you allowed them to act as a distraction while you broke into an apartment to steal a rare book."

"I must say they performed well," he murmured, shaking his head. "Almost makes me worry what the two of them could do as a team if they're determined enough."

"I know what you mean. Still, they got the job done." I held up my hands in surrender. "Okay, I won't worry anymore that they discovered the body."

"Nor will I. They've held up just fine so far."

His words made me smile, but it faded slowly. "I know Mom will hate that murder has come to Dharma."

"On that we're agreed." He rolled a slice of ham around a thick sliver of Brie. "It really is too bad. Not just the murder itself, which is horrific, don't get me wrong. But the timing, love. It couldn't be worse."

I ate my scone and thought about everything we'd gone through in just one day. "Is it wrong that I blame it all on Jacob Banyan?"

"It's not wrong because, frankly, so do I," Derek admitted. "But why do you think it's his fault?"

"I'm not necessarily accusing him of killing Lawson Schmidt. But he's such a scrooge and a buzzkill. And he's not just a miserable human being, he's mean, too. A bully. You could see his attitude affecting everyone on the festival committee. His evil vibe alone might've caused someone else to lash out." I took a bite of Brie, then muttered, "That might be a little harsh."

"Perhaps a little. Yet I must agree." Derek considered it for a moment. "We'll have to keep an eye on him. If he's our killer, he'll give himself away sooner or later."

"What if he's not our killer?"

"Then we'll have eliminated one suspect."

"Good point." Though I hoped he was the killer. Otherwise, there was someone else in Dharma as dangerous as Banyan.

I checked the clock on the wall of the breakfast room and realized that Stevie would be here in fifteen minutes. "I'll clear the dishes and tidy up."

"Thanks, love." He glanced at the clock as well. "Your Detective Stevie should be here soon. I have to make a quick phone call to the office, but I'll be finished before he arrives."

"He's really not *my* detective," I said mildly, and began stacking our dishes. "And by the way, Derek. If you call him Stevie, I'm going to have to beat you."

He laughed, clearly unimpressed with my threats. "Don't worry, darling. I won't embarrass you in front of your little friend."

Little friend? I turned and glared at him. "You're really going to get it, pal."

He was still laughing when he left the room.

Derek was finished with his phone call and back in the living room when Stevie arrived.

"I just left your parents' house." He grinned at me. "They're great. Just like I remembered them."

"Yeah, they're pretty awesome."

He glanced at Derek. "And I spoke with your parents earlier."

"Aren't they wonderful?" I gushed.

"Yeah, they are. You guys lucked out in the in-law sweepstakes."

"It's true. We are incredibly lucky," Derek said. "Have a seat, Detective."

"Would you like some water or coffee?" I asked.

"No, thanks." He sat in one of the sling-back chairs across from the couch. "It's weird, isn't it, how much alike your mothers are?"

Derek and I looked at each other, each of us smiling, before I looked at Stevie. "We've noticed. It's like they're long-lost sisters or something."

"Agreed," he said, then added, "Why don't you both sit down and we can talk for a few minutes?"

For some reason, his polite request that we sit down unnerved me. I wasn't sure why. Of course we should sit down; that wasn't the point. But I was suddenly wishing that Inspector Lee was sitting here with us. I had no idea how Stevie would run this murder investigation.

Would he listen to people like Saffron Bergeron and believe that my mother was to blame for Lawson's death? Because that was just the sort of slanderous talk Saffron would spread. I had to take a few breaths and try to calm down. I was panicking already, and that was no way to approach this.

I remembered that back in fourth grade, Stevie and I were the two smartest kids in class. That was one of the reasons why we'd been drawn to each other. I just hoped he was as smart now as he had been back then.

But meanwhile, I needed to snap out of this hyper-weird zone I was in, and quickly. I didn't need a murder detective wondering why I was sweating and stuttering like a guilty person.

I sat down. *See, that was easy*, I thought. Taking another deep breath, I tried to smile. Were my lips trembling? I stood up abruptly. "I'm sorry. Excuse me. I'll be right back."

Running down the hall to the powder room, I closed the door, stared at myself in the mirror, and scowled.

"You goofball. Settle down. No, he's not your good buddy like Inspector Lee. But that's okay. He's Stevie, your old grammar school boyfriend, and he likes you. He likes Derek, too. And he likes your mother and Derek's mother. There are no problems here. Nobody in your family is guilty. We just need to answer a few questions to help him solve this crime. So shape up and get back out there and kick butt!"

And rah-rah-rah. Go team. Sheesh. Honestly, I needed to get a grip on this kind of thing. But in my defense, if it were your mom involved in a murder investigation, wouldn't anybody turn into a babbling idiot?

After a few more deep breaths, I felt as if I could walk out and conduct myself like a normal person. I washed and dried my hands for good measure, and then walked back to the living room and quickly took a seat next to Derek on the couch.

"Sorry, I had to wash my hands." It was a lame excuse, but hey, I *had* washed my hands.

Derek looked at me with some concern. I appreciated it, because I was concerned, too. I smiled at him, hoping the smile would assuage his worry. He frowned. Okay, maybe my lips were still a little shaky. I just prayed that I didn't look as unhinged as I felt.

"So, Stevie," I began, then winced. "I mean, sorry, Detective Willoughby, I imagine you have some questions for us?"

"Sure do." His smile was a little tight. "And I appreciate you calling me Detective Willoughby when I'm working a case. Otherwise, Steve is fine. Nobody's called me Stevie in twenty years."

I no longer felt shaky. Funny. His attempt to get more professional improved my balance. "Steve it is. Except for when you're on duty."

"Thanks." He opened his notebook.

"I'd like to make a statement first," I said before I could change my mind.

His look of surprise matched Derek's, but it couldn't be helped. I'd had the realization while washing my hands.

"All right," he said.

I took a deep breath, then said, "I don't know if anyone has told you, but Jacob Banyan has made numerous threats to my mother. And Derek and I witnessed him threatening Lawson Schmidt as well."

He scanned his notebook, skipping back a few pages before glancing up. "Your mother mentioned that she heard Banyan threaten Lawson."

"But said nothing about the threats to her?" I asked.

"No."

I felt my eyes crossing.

Derek said quickly, "Banyan's a dangerous man. His threats to Mrs. Wainwright are numerous and ugly, as Brooklyn mentioned. Frankly, he's a menace and should be considered a suspect."

"I'll take care of it," Stevie said, making a note in his book before giving us both a firm nod.

"Okay, thanks," I said with some relief. "I just needed to get that off my chest. Please go ahead with your questions."

He found his place in the notebook and began. "Can you give me an idea of what happened last night when your mother called you?"

"Sure." We told him the whole story, right down to the fact that I get dizzy when I see blood.

"Do you see blood often?" he asked.

"Um." I glanced at Derek. "Sort of."

"Brooklyn has been involved in a number of crime scenes," Derek explained easily. "It's due to the fact that she works with very rare and very expensive books. For some reason, there are any number of people out there who would kill for a book."

Steve looked up from his notebook. "Well now, there's a coincidence for you. Dharma is about to have its first book festival."

"Exactly," Derek said triumphantly, as though Stevie had solved the great puzzle of the universe.

Frowning, Stevie glanced from Derek to me. "But I don't see how Lawson Schmidt could've been killed over a book."

"You have no idea," I muttered.

Derek shrugged philosophically. "We've said that same thing before and it turned out that there was often a perfectly plausible reason as to why a book was a motive for murder."

"Really," Stevie murmured.

"Yes, Detective," Derek said with authority.

"And not to nitpick," I chimed in, "but even if Lawson wasn't killed over a book, he was almost certainly killed over a book *festival*."

Derek gazed at me and I wondered if he was silently high-fiving me or just laughing on the inside. It was pretty clever if I did say so myself. But Stevie didn't look convinced.

"Anyway," I rushed on, "before you conclude that I'm a complete flake, I really have been involved in a number of homicide investigations in San Francisco. And that's where my blood phobia comes from. You can get in touch with Inspector Janice Lee of the San Francisco Police Department if you need a reference or whatever.

She's familiar with my bookbinding work and the murder investigations connected to it. I can give you her number if you'd like to consult with her."

Would he think I was overstepping here? I wasn't trying to tell him how to do his job. I just wanted him to know that, well, I wasn't a complete nutjob.

"I might consider doing that," he said, surprising me.

Okay. Good news. I was breathing a little easier as I wrote Inspector Lee's phone number on a piece of paper and handed it to Steve.

"Thanks." He slipped the paper into his pocket.

And now I had to wonder and worry just how good an idea that was. Inspector Lee could be prickly sometimes and she enjoyed giving me grief. I didn't think she would throw me under the bus in this circumstance. Just in case, though, it would be a good idea if I placed a call to her myself.

A few minutes after Detective Stevie left, Mom called to ask if Derek and I would go with her to the emergency committee meeting she'd called for that afternoon.

"Of course, Mom," I said, and glanced at Derek, since he was on the speaker phone call, too.

Derek nodded. "Absolutely."

"Meg is coming, too."

"I'll pick you both up," Derek said.

"Thank you," Mom whispered.

"Are you okay?" I asked.

"I'm fine now, but the police interrogation was a little harsh."

"Harsh?" I was outraged. Maybe I would keep calling him Stevie after all. "Why? What did he ask you?"

"Oh, it wasn't Stevie's fault," Mom said. "For the life

of me, I just couldn't remember a few details from last night. I was just so nervous. Stevie said he would probably come back to ask more questions, maybe later this afternoon or tomorrow."

So Mom had been unnerved by Stevie's presence, too. Sort of like me. Weird.

"Did you tell him about Banyan's threats and outbursts?"

"Well, no. It didn't seem to have anything to do with poor Lawson."

"But he threatened Lawson, too."

"Oh, I mentioned that."

"That's good, Mom, but in case you forgot, Banyan has threatened you a bunch of times. Stevie needs to know that."

"I suppose so. I'll give him a call."

"Never mind. Derek and I already told him."

"Oh, dear. I hope you didn't upset him."

"Upset Stevie? You're the one who's upset."

"You know what I mean."

"I do, actually."

"Then explain it to me," Derek said.

"Mom thinks that if she upsets Stevie, he might accuse her of murder."

He was taken aback. "You're joking."

I shook my head.

"After all, Derek," Mom said. "We were the first ones on the scene."

"Rebecca," Derek said, clearly trying to keep calm. "Your fears are unfounded. There's nothing to worry about, I promise you."

"Derek, you are such a sweetie," Mom said, but I could tell she was still feeling tense. Worried.

"Mother, Lawson Schmidt is over six feet tall and

weighs twice as much as you do. How does Stevie figure you could've subdued him long enough to break a wine bottle and cut his throat?"

"Well, goodness," she said, her voice sounding a little wobbly. "You make a good point."

I winced a little. I hadn't wanted to see the scene myself, yet I'd just managed to draw it for my mother in living color.

"I'm sorry to be so graphic, Mom. But I'm annoyed by this whole situation." Thankfully my irritation was quickly swamping my nerves. Why should we be nervous? None of us had done anything. Stevie should be the nervous one. He had a murder to solve.

"Who would kill Lawson?" I wondered aloud. "And why would they do it in your committee meeting room? What's really going on here?"

"Oh dear, now you're the one who's stressed." Her voice had changed. She sounded like she was soothing a wounded puppy dog. "Take a few minutes, sweetie. Do some stretching exercises and breathe deeply. You don't want to clog up your chakras, do you? Derek wouldn't be happy about that."

Derek grinned.

"Mom, I'm begging you." I pressed my hand to my forehead. "Stop. Please."

"Don't be shy, sweetie," she said pleasantly. "If you need an alignment, I'll make an appointment for you."

Alarmed, I glanced at Derek who was laughing so hard that he'd fallen back on the couch and then rolled onto his side. I scowled at him. For a dignified, dangerous security agent, it wasn't attractive.

But I couldn't blame him. One of the chakras was responsible for our sexual and creative energies—and Derek knew this because my mother had told him. That's right. She had pulled him aside the night before our wedding to fill him in on all that good woo-woo stuff. Talk about mortifying! Just the sort of heart-to-heart talk a man wanted to have with his future mother-in-law.

"Jeez, Mom. Really?"

"Or I could do an enchantment spell for you."

"Maybe you should think about doing a protection spell on yourself, Mom."

She paused to consider it. "Sweetie, that's a lovely idea. We'll do it tonight."

I blinked. Was I crazy? Why did I say that? I managed to end the call and then stared back at Derek who was still grinning like a fool.

"You're not being helpful," I said.

Which only made him start laughing again.

Chapter 7

A little before one o'clock that afternoon we picked up Mom and Meg and drove to the town hall. The police had sealed up the usual room until the crime scene techs were finished gathering evidence, so we were led down the hall to another meeting room.

Earlier I had placed a call to Inspector Lee, just to cover my bases. I had to leave a lengthy message, letting her know that she might hear from Detective Willoughby about Lawson's murder. I also invited her to come to the book festival if she wasn't busy. It had been a few months since I had seen her.

As the committee members arrived, Mom stood out in the hall to greet and direct them to the new room. This time I took a closer look at Ryan, the young man who was Shandi's personal assistant. He really was a good-looking guy.

When they all were seated around the table, Mom banged her gavel to get everyone's attention. "Most of you have probably heard the news by now that Lawson Schmidt was killed last night."

"That's terrible," Ryan said. "Is there anything we can do for his family?"

"Thank you for asking, Ryan," my mother said. "The police are still investigating, but I'll call his brother this afternoon and see what arrangements are being made."

"That's really sad," Marybeth whispered, her eyes damp with tears. This was the woman whose name I had forgotten the first day. She wasn't in the Fellowship, but she had always seemed friendly enough. I remembered seeing her in the tasting room at Misty Vineyards. Did she work there? Did she lose her job when Banyan took over?

Saffron was whimpering loudly, then she turned to my mother and screamed. "How could you?"

"Oh, for heaven's sake," Mom muttered.

"Saffron," Winston barked. "Pipe down."

Jan Yarnell rolled his eyes. "She's ridiculous."

"You killed him," Saffron shrieked, jumping to her feet and starting toward my mother with raised fists.

Derek was up and charging at Saffron before I even saw him move. He grabbed Saffron's arm and gently but forcefully led her back to her chair.

"Sit down," he said with so much deadly authority that Saffron just gaped at him.

Saffron gulped, then nodded.

Mom shot Derek a grateful look and banged her gavel several times. "We all mourn the loss of Lawson. He was our friend and neighbor, a voracious reader and an avid book collector. From day one he was instrumental in helping us turn this little festival idea into a world-class event." She paused to sniff with emotion and dab her nose with a tissue, then continued. "Lawson was adamant that the book festival be a joyful and educational experience, so we must all stick together to make sure his wishes are fulfilled."

"Hear, hear," Jan said loudly.

"And no more screaming and accusing," Penny Lewis

said, holding her hands over her ears. "That's just not helpful."

Penny was a thin, pretty woman who always appeared to be on edge. She owned three cats and called herself a swinging spinster. According to Mom, Penny was a little cranky but a wiz at contacting agents to convince them to send their authors to our festival.

Saffron stuck out her tongue at Penny, who flipped her off. It seemed like the right response.

"You should've smacked her," I muttered to Derek. I knew that wasn't his style and it wasn't my style either. But Saffron needed to be taken down.

Saffron's shoulders slumped and she idly straightened her loose linen jacket. And that was when I noticed that she was missing a button.

"I should call the police," I whispered.

Derek turned to me. "Let's see if she calms down."

"She won't," I protested. "She's out of control." *And she might be a killer*, I thought. The missing button was a glaring clue. I wanted to shout it out, but managed to hold my tongue. Maybe she had lost the button while ironing or something. But then again, her linen jacket was so wrinkled, it looked as if it had never been ironed before.

I took a few breaths. Saffron wasn't going anywhere, so I decided I would wait to mention the missing button to Derek rather than turn the entire meeting into a free-for-all.

"Put the phone away, love," he murmured.

"All right, but I don't trust her." Reluctantly I slipped the phone into my pocket.

"Nor do I."

I leaned in close to Derek and whispered, "What if she lies to the police about my mother?"

"Everyone on the committee is a witness to her behavior," he reasoned. "We won't let her get away with any lies."

Meg whispered, "She's ridiculous, isn't she?"

I smiled. "Yes, she is."

Mom had the gavel in her hand again and pounded it several times to regain order. "I want you all to be aware that the police will want to interview each of you. They'll be calling to set up interview times. The sooner you can speak to the police, the sooner this awful situation will be taken care of. I'm sorry to be the bearer of such horrible news, but I wanted to let you all know as soon as possible."

"Why didn't you just phone us?" Saffron asked, her tone subdued but still belligerent. "Why did we have to come in? I have a shop to run. I don't have time for this."

It's like she couldn't learn a lesson. Was she just stupid? Or was there something else going on? Maybe she knew who killed Lawson.

"A moment ago, you were bereft over Lawson," Mom pointed out wryly. "Now you're saying you're too busy to show up and support him?"

"I didn't say that." Saffron sniffed at invisible tears. "I just asked why we all have to be here."

"The reason we all have to be here," Mom explained, "is because in light of Lawson's death, we have some urgent matters that must be dealt with immediately."

"Whatever." Saffron sniffed with disdain.

Mom stood up and glared at Saffron.

Meg leaned in close to me. "That Saffron is so unpleasant."

"She's an idiot," I whispered.

Meg nodded. "As you say."

"*Whatever*?" Mom repeated. "Really, Saffron? Could

you be any more dismissive?" Mom waved her gavel and gave Saffron a hard glare that should have curled her hair. My mother was the most beautiful soul in the world. Calm, patient, understanding—but she had a threshold you would be wise not to cross. As kids, we'd all learned just how far we could push her. Saffron apparently had not yet learned.

"Lawson Schmidt was someone we all knew for years," Mom continued. "He was a lifelong bachelor, but he had brothers and nieces and nephews who loved him. He was a genial man with a lot of good ideas for our community. And he was met with a truly violent death in our conference room last night. And all you have to say is *whatever*?"

Saffron glanced around the room, as if looking for support from the other committee members. She didn't find any because not one person would so much as look at her.

Finally, she huffed out a breath and gave Mom a withering look. "Don't lecture me."

"Someone should. Happily that's not my job." I had no idea how Mom managed, but she shook off the comment and continued to gaze at Saffron with infinite patience. "I don't know what happened to you along the road, Saffron. But you took a wrong turn somewhere. You've become a tiresome child."

"How dare you talk to me like that! I'm not a child."

I thought Mom would respond with some snarky comment. I would've. But in that moment, nobody gave the woman any grief at all. Instead, everyone stayed silent. They probably didn't know what to say that wouldn't set Saffron off on another rant.

Mom turned away from Saffron and addressed the rest of the committee. "We have work to do."

"Then let's get to it," Jan said, casting a grim sideways glance at Saffron. "We've wasted enough time on histrionics."

"Indeed," Mom said. She pulled a notepad out of her tote bag—and that was when I realized that she had actually managed to retrieve the tote from her cubby last night before the police arrived.

I'd forgotten all about it, but retrieving her tote bag with her prescription drugs had been the reason she had returned to the town hall after midnight, only to discover Lawson's blood-soaked body.

I wasn't about to mention the tote bag to the police because I didn't think it had any significance to the murder case, other than the fact that she'd forgotten that she left her pills inside it.

"My first agenda item has to do with Lawson's assignments." Mom picked up her pen and was poised to write down some information. "How many of you were working with him on his various duties?"

Four people raised their hands: Winston, Ryan, Saffron, and Marybeth.

Nodding, Mom said, "Okay. We'll discuss each of your responsibilities, but first of all, the cochair position will need to be filled. Is someone interested in that job?"

"Not me," Marybeth said cheerfully. "I like being a worker bee."

"I'll do it," a booming voice said.

Everyone in the room turned to look at Jacob Banyan as he entered the room. Saffron beamed. Clearly Banyan had a champion on the committee.

My mother took a deep breath, seemed to settle whichever chakras were jangling, and then replied smoothly, "You aren't on this committee, Jacob."

"Maybe not, but you're short a member, so I'm here to take Lawson's place."

"Your grief is overwhelming," Mom said dryly. "But believe it or not, we can struggle through without your input."

Banyan snarled like an angry dog. "I'm pretty sick of your smart mouth."

I started to stand, but Derek put one hand on my arm to stall me. "Your mother can handle him."

"Why should she have to?" I whispered back.

"Just wait," my suddenly patient husband urged.

He was right, as I found out a moment later.

Clearly used to getting his own way, Banyan looked furious and frustrated. He swept his gaze over everyone in the room before turning back to my mother. "This fight isn't over, Rebecca."

My mother lifted her chin, met his stare, and said, "As far as I'm concerned, it is."

"Shouldn't we take a vote?" Saffron asked.

"No!" Jan shouted, before Mom could speak. "This isn't a popularity contest. We need someone in that position who knows what they're doing and who's aware of what projects Lawson had been working on and which vendors he had contacted. It should also be someone dedicated to carrying out the festival committee's goals, not just their own agenda."

"Thank you, Jan," Mom said with a grateful smile. She dismissed Saffron without a word and turned to face her committee. "Is there anyone *on the committee* who's willing to take on Lawson's duties?"

"I'll do it," Winston said, then fired one quick glance at Banyan, shaking his head as if he couldn't believe what the man had tried to pull off.

"Thank you, Winston," Mom said. Looking at Banyan, she added, "And thank you for your interest, Mr. Banyan, but the position has been filled."

Banyan bared his teeth. "Your snooty attitude is going to get you into trouble one of these days."

Mom stared at him with narrowed eyes. "I'm not sure you could be more condescending, but I know you'll keep trying."

She continued to glare at him, as if willing him to say another word. At the same time, Derek remained in his chair, but began to crack his knuckles.

Distracted by the sound, Banyan turned to see where it had come from. His lip curled in disgust. "I see you've got your henchman with you."

Derek calmly continued to crack his knuckles, something I'd never seen him do before.

Fuming with anger, Banyan turned and stomped toward the door. Whirling back around, he shook his finger at my mother. "Like I said, this isn't over."

"He does that finger-wiggling thing a lot," I whispered to Meg.

Meg shook her head. "Some people think it makes others bend to their will. Which is silly, don't you agree?"

I smothered a laugh. Her British accent made her sound so prim and proper. I loved it.

Mom sighed. "Will someone please close the door?"

Ryan started to stand, but Marybeth beat him to it.

"I'll do it," she said eagerly. Her dark ponytail bounced as she crossed to the door. We could still hear the sound of Banyan's boots as he clomped down the hall.

"Thanks, dear," Mom said.

"My pleasure." She closed the door and locked it.

Derek had been right, I thought. My mother had handled the situation beautifully. She hadn't needed me to jump up and defend her. And if I had done what I'd so wanted to do, I might have made it look as though she couldn't do the job.

"Thanks," I whispered, taking Derek's hand.

"Anytime," he said softly.

"And kudos on the knuckle-cracking."

Derek just grinned and flexed his fingers for effect.

"All righty, let's move on." Mom smiled. "First, thank you again, Winston. I really appreciate you stepping up and I know you'll do a wonderful job as cochair of the committee."

He saluted. "I'm here to serve."

"As we all are." Mom's smile included everyone seated at the table. "Now, can anyone tell me where Lawson kept the festival checkbook and the petty cash box?"

"I guess that would be me," Winston said. "He kept everything locked up in the wall safe in the office."

"Everything's in there?" Mom asked.

"Yeah. Spreadsheets and financial information, the festival checkbook, and some petty cash. Lawson usually carried some petty cash with him when he knew he would have to pay some vendor, you know?"

"You're very knowledgeable about the finances," Mom said. "I didn't realize you worked so closely with Lawson."

Winston shrugged. "I guess you could say I was his second-in-command."

"Lucky for us," Jan said.

"That's for sure," Mom agreed. She checked her agenda list and glanced back at Winston. "After the meeting, we should take everything out of the wall safe to make sure we know exactly what we have to work with. And we'll have to check our bank balance, too. The vendors will be showing up with their equipment and I want to make sure the account is fully funded."

Saffron snorted. "Are we supposed to trust you with the money?"

Mom blinked, then bristled. "Yes, you are. You all elected me to this position precisely because I can be trusted."

"What's wrong with you, Saffron?" Winston asked. "It's like you've gone insane."

"Yeah," Jan muttered. "Get over yourself."

"I just don't like her authoritarian attitude," Saffron said, sniffing.

"Don't be an idiot," Clyde muttered.

"Yeah," Jan said. "It's not authoritarian to simply want to take care of business."

Marybeth jumped in. "If you don't like it, you can always quit."

Derek leaned in to me and whispered, "Saffron, it seems, is standing alone on this issue. She's not the type of person to take that well."

I nodded. I was glad for Mom that many of the committee members were on her side, but this wasn't going to make Saffron easier to deal with.

As if she'd heard me thinking, Saffron stood and glared at my mother. "I'm as important to this committee as you are."

Jan snorted. "Really?"

Saffron raised her fists in Jan's direction. "Why don't you shove it up—"

"That's enough," Mom insisted, and slammed her gavel down hard on the table. "I'm not going to allow one person to ruin the work we're all trying to do. We

have enough problems without fighting among ourselves." She thought for a moment. "Instead of waiting,
we'll take care of this right now. Winston, you and I will
go to the office and get the cash box and anything else
that's in the safe. If anyone wants to accompany us and
witness us opening the safe, please feel free to come
along."

Saffron stood and grabbed her purse. "You can bet
I'm going along. That's for sure."

"Fine," Mom muttered. "Anyone else?"

"I trust you, Becky," Ryan said, straightening a row
of pens he'd laid out in front of him. "I'll wait here."

"Thank you, dear."

Jan said, "You guys go ahead. I've got to make a
phone call anyway."

The others in the group voiced their agreement with
Ryan.

Mom glanced over at Derek and Meg and me, and
gave a little jerk of her chin. "You're coming with us."

"Why do they get to come?" Saffron asked.

"Independent observers."

"They're hardly independent," she muttered, but let
it go, clearly recognizing a losing battle when she saw
one.

Meg tugged Derek's sleeve. "I'll wait here."

Derek looked from me to his mom. "That's a good
idea. Watch these people, will you, Mother?"

She smiled up at him. "That was my intention, dear."

So Mom, Winston, Saffron, Derek, and I traipsed
down the hall and turned left toward the Dharma town-
council offices that were connected to the town hall.

We looked like a small, not-so-festive parade as we
made our way over to the secretarial-services office.

"Hi, Melissa," Mom said when we entered the spacious office.

"Hey, Becky. What's going on?" Melissa Grant was executive secretary to the town council and basically ran things when the council wasn't in session. She had three assistants working for her, along with Hal, the IT guy and overall computer whiz. If Hal couldn't fix it, nobody could.

Both Melissa and Hal had gone to school with me and my siblings, and we'd known them forever. And since my father was on the town council, we also saw them at picnics and other events throughout the year.

"I'm so sorry to hear about Lawson," Melissa said.

"It's very sad," Mom said. "I expect that we'll have a memorial service in the near future."

"I've already discussed it with Robson and we've set up a teleconference with all of the council members this evening. Once the festival's over, I'll send out a community email with all the information."

"That's wonderful." Mom beamed at her. "Thanks, Melissa."

"Now," she said. "What can I do for you?"

"We need access to the festival checkbook, the financial spreadsheet, and the petty cash box. Lawson kept everything in the safe, and Winston knows the combination. We just need to get into the room."

"I can help you," Melissa said jovially. Pulling a ring of keys from her desk drawer, she stood and walked across the room to another door. After unlocking that door, she turned. "There you go."

"Thank you, sweetie."

"I'll stay here in the office until you're finished and lock everything up."

"I appreciate it."

The five of us crowded into the small room and Derek closed the door. The room was sparsely furnished with a credenza, several folding chairs, and some very generic artwork.

Winston approached a large framed painting of a pastoral scene and pulled it away from the wall. That was when I noticed the painting was on hinges. Fascinating.

"Not that I'm paranoid," Winston explained, "but Lawson entrusted me with the combination to the safe and I intend to keep it a secret. So don't be insulted when I shield it from you all."

"Perfectly understandable, Winston," Mom said.

"Sounds like paranoia to me," Saffron muttered.

Winston bared his teeth at Saffron and said, "Just shut up."

I snorted a laugh and got a dirty look from Saffron.

Winston put one hand over the other to block our view of the combination as he spun the dial back and forth, changing directions as each number clicked into place.

When the last number clicked, he blew out a relieved breath, pulled the handle down, and opened the safe.

"Good job," Mom said.

"Looks like everything is in here," he said, reaching inside and pulling out a small steel box that looked like it might hold fishing tackle. He handed it to my mother, then pulled out a manila envelope, the kind secured with a brass clasp. "This has the financial info and checkbook inside. It's all backed up on my computer, by the way."

"Thank goodness." Mom put the cash box on the credenza and gazed at the rest of us. "Let's see what we've got."

As she fiddled with the latch, I watched Saffron stretch her neck and lean to the left to catch a glimpse of what was inside. I had a sudden image of her snatching the money out of Mom's hands and I poised myself to catch her if she tried to run.

Mom raised the lid just enough to peek inside. She stared at the contents for what seemed like forever. Then she lifted her head, held up the open cash box, and stared directly at me and Derek. "It's empty."

There was a long moment of stunned silence.

"Is this some kind of a joke?" Saffron demanded of no one in particular.

Mom ignored the woman and instead turned directly to Winston. As shocked as everyone else, Mom's questions came tumbling out one after the other. "Is it possible that Lawson took all the cash out to purchase something or pay one of the vendors? Did he often deplete the petty cash fund? Do you know how he handled the finances?"

"I didn't know his day-to-day routine," Winston said, shaking his head, "but my understanding was that there was always some cash on hand, just in case someone had to be paid. Maybe a hundred and fifty to two hundred dollars at any one time."

I quietly moved around to get Mom's attention. I was getting a really bad feeling about this. "Mom, what's the balance in the checkbook?"

"We'd better have a look at it," she said with a nervous shake of her head. "I'm sorry, Winston and Saffron. This is quite upsetting for me."

Winston looked bleak as he nodded. "For me, too."

"There's got to be a simple explanation," Mom said. "We just have to figure out what it is." She unhooked the clasp and turned the manila envelope upside down. The checkbook and a thin stack of documents slid out onto the credenza.

"Okay, here's the checkbook." Mom flipped it open to find the latest deposit. "According to the check register, we should have seventy thousand dollars in the bank. The last deposit was made a week ago."

"Well, that's a relief," Saffron said.

"Yes," Mom agreed with a heartfelt sigh.

"So Lawson probably spent what petty cash he had on hand," Winston said, shrugging. He picked up another small notebook and thumbed through it. "This is where he noted the petty cash expenditures, but it shows that there should be a hundred and seventy dollars in there." He glanced around. "He probably planned to write down what he'd spent, but I guess he never got around to it."

Mom frowned. "I suppose that seems reasonable."

Even Saffron couldn't argue, although she grimaced intensely. "I guess so."

It did seem reasonable. Still, just because there was a huge balance in the checkbook, that didn't mean that the money was actually in the *bank*. I was jumping to the worst possible conclusion, but hey, the guy had been murdered. Why wouldn't I suspect foul play? I shot a look at Derek and could tell he was thinking the same thing I was. *Great minds*, I thought. We were both equally suspicious of the situation. Was it any wonder I was crazy about my husband?

"We really should have this discussion with the entire committee," Mom said. "And we need to verify that seventy thousand dollars is still in the bank."

"Yeah," Winston said. "I can do that."

"Then let's go back to the meeting room."

We all waited while Winston closed up the safe and swung the painting and its frame back into place.

Clutching the manila envelope and cash box to her chest, Mom led the way out of the little room. "Thank you, Melissa."

"You bet." She barely looked up from her computer. "See you guys later."

As I passed her desk, she looked up and smiled. "Brooklyn, how are you?"

"Just great."

"My little girl is really excited about making her own book with you."

"Wonderful. We'll have fun." I moved on quickly, unwilling to show how distressed I was. I had hated seeing that look on Mom's face when she realized there was no cash. I wondered if she had considered yet what Derek and I had—that the bank account could've been emptied as well.

Maybe we were just asking for trouble. The money could be safe and sound in the bank. But I saw that image of Lawson bleeding out on the conference room floor and I just couldn't paint a positive picture.

I took Derek's arm and we slowed down, leaving plenty of space between ourselves and the committee members. "What do you think?"

He leaned over to whisper in my ear. "I'm not hopeful, frankly."

"Neither am I. Am I becoming too cynical? Why am I thinking that the actual bank account may not match what was in the checkbook?"

"Because you're a brilliant woman," he assured me, leaning down to plant a quick kiss on my forehead. "And by the way, you're not cynical; you're simply astute."

Astute. I could live with that.

We were careful to keep our distance from the rest of the group as Derek continued whispering. "We're both thinking the same thing, darling. Lawson, the person in charge of the festival funds, was just murdered. There was no money in his pockets and his wallet was missing."

"How do you know that?"

He gazed at me. "I checked."

"Of course you did," I said, rolling my eyes. "And I was too freaked out over Lawson's dead body to notice."

He wrapped his arm around me in sympathy and I leaned against him.

"So, empty pockets," I said.

"And an empty cash box," he said. "Coincidence?"

But I knew very well that Derek didn't believe in coincidences. "So you think Lawson was robbed before he was killed."

"There's a very good chance."

I sighed. "Could he have been dumb enough to carry seventy thousand dollars around in his pocket?"

Derek shrugged. "It's quite possible."

"So clearly robbery was the motive for killing him."

"Possibly."

He was being cryptic so I had to ask. "Why else was he killed, if not for the money?"

"Why indeed."

I almost laughed at his enigmatic responses. "It's possible that he might've been planning to meet with the vendors and pay them for their services."

He smiled down at me. "There you go. Not cynical at all."

"Oh, sure." So why was my stomach a churning pot?

"I'm going back to the committee room, sitting on the sidelines, and thinking only good thoughts."

He gave my shoulders a light squeeze. "Your mother will appreciate it."

"I hope so." I had to think positively, or my mother would pick up on my worry vibes and suggest that she sign me up for an espresso enema or something.

We crossed into the town hall portion of the building and turned down the hallway. By the time we reached the new committee room, Mom, Winston, and Saffron were already seated in their chairs around the conference table. Derek and I slipped over to the side and sat down with Meg.

Meg slipped her arm through Derek's. "Everyone behaved while you were gone."

"Good," he whispered.

"Is everybody here?" Mom asked, gazing around the long table.

"We're all here, Becky," Sue said. Her granny glasses were tinted pink today and she wore her long gray hair braided down her back.

Mom tried to smile. "Thanks, Sue."

"So what happened?" Jan asked.

"Yeah," Ryan said. "You guys were gone a long time."

Mom checked her wristwatch. "It was only about twenty minutes, but I agree it felt like an hour. I'm sorry we kept you all waiting. I know you're anxious to hear what we found."

"Nothing," Saffron grumbled loudly. She had her arms crossed tightly over her chest. "We found nothing. The money's gone."

"Please stop talking!" Winston shouted, clearly Saffron was on his last nerve. I couldn't blame him. I could tell he was feeling the weight of responsibility that there was no money in the cash box.

"You don't have to yell," Saffron said, affronted. "That was rude."

"I said *please*," Winston muttered, then schooled his expression and spoke with infinite patience. "You all need to wait until we have some facts before jumping to conclusions."

"An excellent idea," Mom declared. "Lawson was a very good businessman, so I'm sure the money will be in the bank."

"You don't know that," Saffron said, clearly taunting her.

Despite having the exact same thoughts a few minutes ago, I wanted to beat her with a stick. I hated her for giving my mother grief. She was a whiny, griping jerk.

Nope. I didn't like her. And I obviously wasn't the only one in the room who felt that way.

I watched her for a full minute. She was so aggravating. I didn't know how she had lasted this long on the committee.

Maybe it was just me, but if I were a part of this group and had to deal with her, it would take every last bit of patience and energy I could summon to keep from transmuting into a hideous snarling werewolf and biting Saffron's head off.

But again, that was just me.

Undoubtedly there had to be a few members who secretly sided with Saffron. But except for the vote they'd taken on Banyan, it was hard to tell who Saffron's comrades were. They hadn't revealed themselves yet, at least not since I'd been there. And that was smart of them, because I was ready to lash out at any moment and I would just as soon kick their butts along with Saffron's.

Mom began to speak. "As Saffron said, the cash box was empty. But Winston thinks that Lawson may have had a habit of letting the funds dwindle and then going to the bank to replenish them."

"So somebody needs to go to the bank," Marybeth said.

"We could do that," Mom said. "But it would probably be easier, if it's agreeable to the group, to have Winston check our balance online."

Sue nodded. "Let's do it."

"Yes, let's." Mom nodded to Winston. "I assume you can access the account online?"

"Sure."

"Great. Can you do it right here and now?"

"Yeah, no problem." He pointed to the manila folder on the table in front of my mother. "Can you hand me the folder? It's got all the account info inside."

"Of course." She slid it across to him.

"Thanks." He stared at his computer screen and punched a bunch of keys, then sort of zoned out for a few minutes while the computer warmed up and he accessed the bank website. He continued typing and I assumed he was plugging in the user name and password.

"Isn't modern technology wonderful?" Mom beamed with pleasure. "We'll have all the information we need in just a few seconds."

She sounded so calm, and maybe she really was. Maybe her aura had been fluffed and buffed, and all of her chakras and meridians were tuned and aligned up the wazoo. But I had a feeling that she wasn't really all that cheerful deep inside and she was putting on the show for everyone else. However she'd managed to accomplish that impression of pure serenity, I wanted to know her secret.

I scanned the room, looking at the faces of the people sitting around the table. I studied their expressions and whether or not they made eye contact with others at the table. Were they nervous? Happy? Suspicious?

I wondered, because it occurred to me once again that if Jacob Banyan didn't kill Lawson Schmidt, then someone in this room must have done it. There was no doubt that the murder was connected to the book festival. Why else would Lawson have been murdered inside the committee's own meeting room?

Had someone on the committee made promises to Banyan that they weren't able to keep? Had Lawson himself tried to make a deal to include Banyan and then had to back out of it when my mother adamantly refused to let him participate?

It was possible. And if so, then that same person had probably stolen Lawson's money and his wallet.

If it wasn't a straightforward robbery, then maybe Lawson was being threatened. Or blackmailed. But why? There were too many possibilities and not enough answers.

"Hmm," Winston muttered, bringing me out of my doomsday reverie. I seriously hoped they found all the money in the bank because I really didn't want my mother to be confronted with the ugly facts as I saw them.

Winston continued to stare at the computer screen and was tapping the keys so quickly, it was impossible to follow the keystrokes.

I held my breath as I watched my mother. I knew she was trying to cling to that calm facade, but I could see her jaw begin to tighten as she stared at the computer screen.

I was too nervous to sit still so I stood up. Derek joined me, and then Meg stood and grabbed my hand. I knew she was worried about my mom. We all felt the same way.

Everyone at the table had begun to move and within seconds they all stood behind my mother and Winston, trying to get a look at the computer screen. Nobody was talking—*a miracle*, I thought. They were just staring, watching, and wondering what Winston and my mother had discovered. *They are so quiet, it can't be good*, I thought. But Mom kept staring at the screen, and Winston kept clicking those keys.

"Sorry it's taking so long," Winston said. "I've never accessed the account from this computer so the bank had to send my email a code to verify that I'm the person I say I am."

Mom's throat had to have dried up because I was having the same problem with mine. I pulled my water bottle from my bag and carried it over to her.

"Drink this," I murmured.

Her eyes were filled with apprehension, but she tried to smile. "Thanks, sweetie."

Up close I could see a pale vein pulsing along the side of her forehead. She had to be completely stressed out. She took a couple of sips of water and handed the bottle back to me. "Thank you."

Winston pointed to a number on the screen. "Do you see this?"

Mom nodded. "Yes."

"See what?" Jan asked finally. "What's going on? How's it looking?"

I tore my gaze from the computer screen to look up at Derek. As it turned out, I wasn't cynical. I was psychic.

Mom took another deep breath, rolled her shoulders, and shook her hair back, trying to regain some of that cool, calm composure of a few minutes ago. Still gazing at the screen, she murmured, "The festival account appears to have been emptied."

Then she turned and faced everyone who'd been waiting anxiously behind her. "To put it bluntly, we've been robbed."

Chapter 8

"Maybe it's just a mistake in the online system," Jan said, always the optimist.

Sue frowned at Winston. "Are you sure you have the right password and account number?"

"Yeah, I'm sure." Winston glanced up, and his face was a study in fear and misery. "We got into the account just fine. You can see for yourself."

"Show me," Sue said.

Winston moved the computer over a few inches and angled it toward Sue, who bent over, blinked a few times, and then squinted at the computer screen. The account name was right there and easy enough to read. There was no mistake.

After a few seconds, she straightened up and gulped. Her eyes were wide with incredulity. "I can't believe it. It shows a zero balance."

"Right," Winston said. He clicked on one of the pull-down menus. "And if you go into the account and look up the daily transactions," he clicked on the screen again, then pointed for everyone to see, "you'll find that there was seventy thousand dollars in the account just four days ago."

There were shocked cries and groans as everyone moved closer to check for themselves.

"Then you go up to the next day," Winston continued, still pointing with his cursor. "Here. And there's a withdrawal of six thousand dollars."

"Right," Mom said. She touched the screen on the next line. "And here's another withdrawal of twenty thousand the day after that."

"Oh my God," Jan whispered. "It's a nightmare."

"Yeah," Winston said as he scrolled down. "Day after that, there's a twelve-thousand-dollar withdrawal."

"Jeez Louise," Ryan said.

Winston turned around and met the gazes of everyone standing behind him. "Finally, yesterday, they withdrew the rest of the money." He looked back at the screen. "Thirty-two thousand dollars."

"Nooo," Marybeth moaned.

"But Winston," Jan said, hoping against hope. "Don't you think there could be a mistake somewhere? That kind of thing happens, right?"

Winston shrugged. "Sure."

But everyone knew he was just placating us.

"Of course it happens," Mom said, her voice remaining calm even though she kept sneaking glances at Derek and Meg and me. I wasn't sure why. Did she want us to grab her and whisk her out of there? Or explain why the computer screen could be wrong? Or stand guard around her? I would be happy to do any of those things, but I doubted she needed that. What she needed were some answers. And none of us had any.

But I decided to give it a try. "Did you take a look at the spreadsheet, Mom? Does that give any clues?"

Winston glanced from me to Mom. "It might help. It's supposed to list every single expenditure we've made since we first started. Maybe it'll show that Lawson paid off a bunch of vendors at one time. That's the only explanation I can think of."

"Let's take a look, Winston," Mom said, willing to try anything at this point.

He reached for the manila envelope and pulled out the stapled sheet of papers. "Do you want me to read the whole thing or pass it around or what?"

"We should all have a copy," Jan said.

"I agree." Mom checked her watch. "When the meeting's over, I'll take it over to Melissa and get enough copies made for everyone. We can all look through it tonight and meet back here tomorrow to discuss our options."

"What options?" Saffron demanded. "We're out of money. We're screwed. We'll have to cancel the festival."

"Wow, Debbie Downer strikes again," Sue said.

Marybeth scowled at Saffron. "Yeah, stop being such a—a negative Nelly. We'll simply find another underwriter and keep going."

That couldn't be as easy as she made it sound.

Saffron seemed to agree. "There's seventy thousand dollars missing. I'm not negative; I'm just realistic."

"You can be both," Winston muttered under his breath.

"There's also a chance that we can recover the money," Mom said, still trying for positivity. "Maybe the money was transferred to another account. Maybe Lawson used it to pay off some suppliers as Winston suggested, but . . ." That was a stretch. If Lawson had been writing checks, it would be there on the account record. But cheers to Mom for trying.

Mom sighed then. "I'll call the police when I get home and see if they'll help us track down the funds."

Saffron threw up her hands. "But what if Lawson stole the money and just spent it all?"

"That's certainly a possibility," Mom allowed. "But meanwhile, let's all try not to freak out. We'll find a way to fix this."

"I'm so glad you're in charge, Becky," Sue said, patting Mom on the back. "You're always so cool and calm, while I'm just about to blow a gasket."

"I don't know, Sue." Jan grinned. "You're pretty laid-back yourself."

"Yeah," she said, with a giggle. "But my vibe is from the drugs. Becky's on a natural high."

Everyone laughed, relieving some of the intense stress. For the moment anyway.

"I know it's getting late," Mom said, "but I have one more short agenda item to go over."

There was some minor grousing, but everyone scrambled back to their seats, anxious to finish up the meeting and get home.

"It concerns our Louisa May Alcott scholar," Mom said. "She'll be here in a few days and I know Lawson wouldn't want us to upset her, so I would appreciate if none of us would mention the murder to her. She's a special guest in our town."

"She's going to hear about it one way or another," Winston said dolefully.

"And Lawson was her contact, right?" Marybeth said. "We won't be able to hide the facts."

"Plus, she's an academic," Jan said. "They soak up information like a damn sponge."

Mom nodded. "True. We can't do anything about it if she reads it in the newspaper or hears it out on the street. But I don't want our committee members feeding the fear. Agreed?"

"Sure," Ryan said.

Sue nodded. "Yeah, okay. Let's not be the ones to blow her mind from the get-go."

Mom suggested that they go around the table to hear everyone's feelings on the subject. The rest of the group agreed that the committee should only spread joy and happiness—except for Saffron who didn't bother to weigh in. She just scowled at everyone else's comments. The woman had no joy to spread anyway so her opinion didn't matter. But I didn't know how the rest of the committee could take her crappy attitude in stride.

"We done here?" Winston asked.

"Yes." Mom banged the gavel. "We'll meet back here tomorrow at two thirty."

Winston held up the pages of the spreadsheet. "I'll go get those copies made."

Mom's shoulders sagged in relief and I knew she'd forgotten about the spreadsheet. "Thanks, Win."

"I'm going to take off now," Jan said, "but I'll stop by Win's house later tonight and get my copy."

"Whatever works for you," Mom said.

A couple of others decided to do the same and the room began to clear. When the rest of the group had left, Ryan gathered his belongings and approached Mom. He looked like a college kid in a polo shirt and khakis, carrying his books. *The guy was born to wear khakis*, I thought, and then noticed the wiry muscles of his arms. I hadn't realized how ripped he was. But then, he worked as Shandi's bodyguard, so it made sense.

I glanced back at Derek and Meg. "I'm going to wait for Mom. I can meet you outside."

"We'll wait with you," Meg said, and sat down again.

"Mrs. Wainwright," Ryan said. "I was hoping I could talk to you for just a moment. It's personal."

I noticed he was the only committee member who addressed my mother that way. Was it because he was so much younger than her? Or was it just the way he was raised? It was sort of charming, either way.

Mom gave him a sweet smile. "Of course, Ryan. What's going on?"

"I know it's getting close to festival time, but I wanted to ask if you could appeal to your daughter London to recast the musical and put Shandi in another role."

Mom stared at him for a long moment as if she didn't comprehend what he was asking.

Frankly, I was a little mystified myself.

Mom considered for a moment. "But Shandi is playing Marmee, isn't she?"

"Yeah," he said, clearly disheartened.

Hmm. Was this because the beautiful Shandi was annoyed that she'd been relegated to the role of *mother* to four teenaged girls? I remembered when Annie first told me about the casting, I'd wondered if the Diva would hate playing that role. Looked like I was right.

"But Marmee is a wonderful role," Mom said brightly. "She's one of the great characters in American literature. She's highly principled, a good worker, and strong. She's cheerful in the face of adversity and she's unconventional in a wonderfully enlightened way."

"Yes, yes," Ryan said impatiently, "but she's old."

"She's a . . . mother," Mom said carefully.

He shook his head. "You don't understand." He took a deep breath and seemed to gather strength to continue his argument. "Shandi is practically an ingenue. She has a reputation to uphold and a huge fan base, many of whom will show up to spend money at the festival. They're going to want to see her in a much larger role."

"Marmee is one of the stars of the show."

He waved off that fact. "Shandi wants to play Jo."

Mom frowned. "Jo? I thought in the beginning she was interested in playing Meg."

He made a sour face. "After reading the script we realized that Meg is too boring. She's always following the rules and is just too goody-goody for Shandi. Whereas Jo is more fun! More full of life. And that's Shandi to a T."

I heard someone gasp. Turning, I saw our Meg, Derek's mom, looking apoplectic. Was she choking? But Derek took her hand and she seemed to recover.

"I'm sorry, Ryan," Mom said gently. "But none of the four girls would be a suitable role for Shandi. She's a lovely woman and a delightful actress, but let's be honest. I mean no offense, but she's no spring chicken. And she's definitely not an ingenue."

He gasped. "That's simply not true, Mrs. Wainwright," he said quietly. "Shandi is an accomplished actress of stage and screen. She can play any role you throw at her. I know it's late notice, but she's a very quick study and a tremendous talent. She's been working in movies for years."

Mom winced. "I'm sorry, sweetie, but you've just made my point. She's been around for years, which makes her simply too old to play a teenager."

"That's just mean," Ryan said.

"No, that's reality. And it's life." Mom reached out and touched his arm. "I truly don't want to hurt any feelings. I'm just being honest."

"But it's not fair," he said, almost desperate now. "She can play anything. She's a transformational talent. And besides, she's a whiz with makeup. She can make it work."

"Of course she can," Mom said, smiling as she tried to soothe his injured spirit. "Shandi really is a wonderful talent. But on a practical note, the show opens in less than a week and it only runs for one night. I'm fairly certain London won't be willing or able to make a change at this late date. And honestly, Shandi's a professional. She'll understand. And she'll get over it."

He looked miserable. *Poor guy*, I thought. I hoped Shandi wasn't going to punish him for failing to wrangle the role of Jo from my mother or London.

"Tell you what," Mom said. "If Shandi would like to talk about it, I'll be happy to explain why we can't make changes this late in the game. I'm sure she understands how complicated it would be. She's a professional, so I think she'll be fine. My hope is that the musical will be the joyous high note to close the festival. Any hurt feelings would ruin that moment."

He blew out a breath. "I'll see what Shandi wants to do."

"All right, dear." Mom patted his shoulder. "I must say, you're a wonderful advocate for Shandi. I hope she appreciates all you do for her."

"She's very good to me," he said earnestly. "Thank you, Mrs. Wainwright."

But as he walked away, I could see that he was still troubled. Would Shandi give him grief over this silly issue?

As soon as Ryan left the room, Meg walked over to the table. "What nerve!"

Mom looked at her, bewildered. "What's wrong, Meg? What happened?"

I stared up at Derek who shrugged, clearly clueless.

"That young man said horrible things about a beloved character in a wonderful book."

Mom patted Meg's hand. "I know just how you feel. Marmee truly is beloved in literature."

Meg was still frowning though, so I stepped a little closer to Mom. "I think our Meg is steamed that Ryan dumped on the *Little Women* Meg."

Did that make any sense at all? I had to wonder.

"Oh, sweetie." Mom laughed and grabbed Meg in a tight hug. "Oh, my dear friend. Please don't be offended. He's a silly boy who doesn't know his ass from his elbow. You mustn't take it personally."

"Well, I did," she groused.

Mom held her at arm's length, met her gaze, and smiled. "They're all crazy, didn't you know?"

After a long moment, Meg nodded solemnly. "Ah yes. They're all crazy, 'except for thee and me.'"

They laughed together, tickled by the fact that they both recognized the quote. Then they hugged again and my heart skipped a little. They were truly sisters of the heart and I was so happy they'd found each other.

And I was extra happy that the crisis was over.

Well, except for the part where Ryan might get fired for failing to get Shandi the part. He'd tried hard, but it was a losing proposition. And why was Shandi forcing Ryan to fix the casting problem for her? Why was she pushing for this role? What was the big deal? That was what I wanted to know.

But more than that, I wanted to get out of there. I leaned into Derek and whispered, "Let's go home and have a margarita."

"Darling, that's the best idea you've had all day."

We waited with Mom until Winston came back with the copies of the spreadsheet. A quick glance told us that Lawson hadn't listed any expenditures that totaled seventy thousand dollars. So Mom and the committee were back where they started.

After dropping off the moms, Derek and I both concluded that, sadly, it was a little too early in the day to start drinking. He had some phone calls to make and I decided it was time for me to get to work on the copy of *Little Women* that Clyde had asked me to fix.

I found the book where I'd left it on the end of the breakfast bar. Then I gathered up my tools and equipment in the large plastic file box and tucked my phone into my pocket.

"I've got my phone if you need me," I called to Derek. Then I walked out the back door, past the lovely patio and pool, and stopped when I reached the door of Abraham's workshop. Setting down the file box, I pulled out the key and unlocked the door.

I hadn't been inside Abraham's workshop in almost two years and I had no idea what I would find in there. Cobwebs? A family of rodents? Would it look the same as the last time I'd seen it? Or had Annie taken the plunge and had the entire workshop cleaned out?

"Guess I'll find out," I murmured to myself. Taking a deep, fortifying breath, I pushed the door open and stepped inside. And in an instant, I was eight years old again, tingling with excitement and awe as I prepared to explore the wondrous mysteries of the master bookbinder's lair.

The room was almost exactly as I'd remembered it when Abraham was alive, except for the fact that, to my utter amazement, it was pristine. Annie must've hired a battalion of housecleaners to work in here, dusting, mopping, waxing, and straightening every inch of workspace until the entire place was fresh smelling and sparkling clean.

All of Abraham's tools, equipment, supplies, and,

yes, even his tchotchkes, were basically where he'd left them, except that now they were all dust free, laid out on spotless surfaces in neat rows, and all color coordinated.

I had to laugh. Abraham had always given me a load of grief when I tried to clean or straighten his workspace at the end of the day. "Why bother," he'd say, "when we're just going to mess everything up again tomorrow?"

If Abraham hadn't been dead already, he would've had a heart attack to see this place now. And I thought that with supreme affection for my old mentor and friend.

"Thank you, Annie," I whispered out loud. I couldn't wait to get to work and set my file box on the floor next to the waist-high worktable in the middle of the room. The first thing I pulled out of the box was a bag of chocolate caramel Kisses and a smaller bag of candy corn. I rarely indulged in candy corn because it was basically pure sugar. But I liked to say that unto everything there was a season. And since it was fall, this was the season for candy corn.

Chocolate caramel Kisses, on the other hand, were appropriate eating any time of the year. They were loaded with nutrients, like milk and chocolate and caramel and, well, other nutrients. I was sticking to that story and would fight anyone who said otherwise.

Next I pulled out my handy new magnifying glasses that I'd discovered at my dentist's office a few months ago. They made it so much easier for me to check out things using both hands instead of having to clutch the magnifying glass with one hand and joggle the book with my other.

Next, I reached for my camera to document my work. I always used my digital camera to photograph every step of the process when I was working with a rare or antiquarian book, or with any book where I needed to demonstrate my due diligence to the book's owner.

To be honest, Abraham hadn't often cared one way or the other about documenting the work. "I do the work," he would say. "I don't take pictures of the work."

I used to tease him for being old school. "Like eighteenth-century old school," I'd add. He usually laughed, because it was true.

But I had found that photography improved my work. It helped to go back through those pictures to learn where I'd made mistakes or, alternatively, where I'd done something particularly well.

Just thinking of Abraham conjured up a picture in my mind of him standing at his workbench, his shirt-sleeves rolled up to his elbows and his black leather apron tied loosely around his waist. He was a big man and a tough teacher, sometimes instructing me to take a book apart and put it back together again, over and over and over. He might have been strict, but boy, did I learn a lot.

I felt something on my cheek and realized that it was a tear. It happened sometimes when I thought of him after he died in my arms a few years ago.

"Okay, that's enough of that," I muttered, and grabbed a tissue to sop up my tears. "Get back to work."

With a heavy sigh, I laid a large white cotton cloth onto the table and unwrapped the book. I always used a soft white cloth to lay out the pieces of an old book because it kept everything clean and because I found it easier to keep track of each piece that way.

I snipped the last few bits of cloth and carefully pulled the book cover from the textblock. Setting the textblock aside, I studied the front cover for a few minutes. The picture of the four girls was more vivid and multifaceted than I remembered from the previous day, when I saw it for the first time. The different shades of green in the grass and leaves, the charmingly unique hairstyles of each girl, the intricate patterns of the knitted shawls, all stood out in loving detail. I wondered who the artist was and hoped I would find him or her credited somewhere inside.

I took a dozen photos of the cover from different angles and then another dozen close-up shots before I moved on to the next step. The book was so damaged that I knew I would have to take the entire thing apart and fix it in stages, then put it all back together again.

I opened the book and spread the front and back covers out, spine side up, to gauge what would have to be done to the outside. The corners and edges of the book were badly frayed, and both the front and back joints were torn and almost completely separated from the spine. All of the gilding on the spine had rubbed off to the extent that the title and author name were nonexistent.

Cautiously I turned the front and back cover over, spine side down now, and once again spread everything out to study the interior. The endpapers were badly faded and the pastedown side was partly torn away from the front board. Along the front hinge, the endpaper was ripped away completely.

The back endpapers were in slightly better condition overall, which was typical because, in general, the front cover of a book was opened and closed and touched and used more than the back. Despite that fact, the back inside cover of this book was also in terrible shape, the hinge barely held together by a worn-out bit of paper.

I set the cover aside and pulled the textblock closer.

Turning to the title page, I checked the publication date: 1868.

"That can't be right," I muttered, but I still felt a tingle run up my spine at the outside possibility.

My preliminary research had shown me that copies of *Little Women* dated 1868 were the first printing, first issue. But my favorite research website had also warned me that forged title pages of the book did exist. They had also explained that the first edition version of the novel had been published in two parts. The second part was known as *Little Women, Part the Second*.

Clyde hadn't given me *Part the Second*, so that was a drag. Still, I would be happy to refurbish this copy for Clyde and maybe someday he would come into possession of *Part the Second*.

But now I had to wonder about the pretty illustrated cover. The first edition copies I'd found online were shown with plain green book cloth. Obviously some well-meaning bookbinder had spruced up the cover of this book at some point in its history. The cover was now much prettier even though it might not have increased the book's value.

Of course, it was still a first edition, so that counted for something. Once I transformed it from its sad and shabby condition into a beautifully rejuvenated version, it would shine again and hopefully go on to make lots of money for the literacy organization.

Staring at the title and publication page, I had a moment of doubt as to whether this could actually be considered a first edition. I could believe that the interior of the book was part of the original first edition, but with the cover being altered, I had to wonder if the title page had been forged. I had dealt with forgeries several times in the past and knew what signs to look for. So I looked for them now, first studying the gutter—the inside margin of the book where the pages were sewn together. An unscrupulous bookseller would simply fit the fraudulent publication page into the gutter and glue it well enough to keep it in place.

I felt the paper itself, running my fingers over the edges and the text. I noted that the title page had the same feel, same texture, thickness, and weight as the other pages in the book. Then I held it up to the light to check that it was the same color as the other pages. It was.

Still, this couldn't possibly be a first edition, could it? First of all, it was a mess. Anyone who had ever owned this book would've kept it in perfect condition. Or so I wanted to believe. But I knew that people could be awful when it came to taking care of books.

And second, if this were a first edition, Clyde wouldn't have been so blasé about handing the book over to me without an explanation. On the other hand, he had seemed awfully nervous and hadn't been too forthcoming when I'd asked him where he'd found it. Finally he'd mumbled the answer.

"A used bookstore in Grass Valley," he'd said. "Paid almost nothing for it."

Seriously?

I stared long and hard at the title page, then put on my magnifying glasses and checked the gutter again. It was clean. This page was real.

I turned to my computer and consulted my rare-book online research guide—otherwise known as Google—and typed in "rare copy of Little Women," and found an amazing first edition that was priced at twenty-five thousand dollars.

I almost laughed. There was no way this book would ever sell for that amount. First, because it was only one volume of two, and second, because I only had a few days to work a miracle. But I was an optimist and good at my job, so if I fixed it up well enough, I knew it would be worth a lot more than I had originally thought.

I popped several chocolate caramels to keep up my strength and considered my next move. I figured I would have to talk to Clyde and find out if he knew how much the book was worth. I would go ahead and repair it anyway, of course, but I had a weird feeling that he hadn't told me the whole story. He had seemed nervous and evasive when he'd given me the book and I had to wonder why.

What was he trying to hide?

Clyde and I had always been close, or as close as anyone could get to Clyde, otherwise known as the original grumpy old man. Growing up, I had spent long hours inside his wonderful little bookstore on the Lane, and while he would yell at other customers or grouse about people who lingered too long, he was always kind to me and always seemed to appreciate that I was a true booklover.

"So what's really going on here?" I wondered out loud.

I would figure out the answers later, maybe with a little help from Derek—and a margarita or two. For now, though, I wanted to finish up my initial examination of the book, clean up my mess, and go back to the house. I was getting thirsty. And after all, it was five o'clock somewhere.

Chapter 9

The last rays of sunlight were slipping behind the tallest vine-covered hill as I walked back into the kitchen. I had worked longer this afternoon than I'd realized, but that meant that it was definitely time for cocktails.

"Derek, I'm home," I called, and set the large plastic box on the floor under the kitchen table. I had folded the white cloth around the copy of *Little Women* to hold all the pieces together, then tucked it inside the box. I would have to find a better, more secure place for the book since it now seemed to be worth a lot more than I'd originally thought.

"Perfect timing," Derek called from the other room. Accompanying his voice was the melodious sound of the cocktail shaker and I knew what that meant.

"Your margarita awaits you, darling."

"My hero! I'll be right there." I ran to the powder room to wash my hands. A minute later, I walked into the family room and spied Derek hard at work behind the fully stocked bar. The room was spacious and warm with a high coffered ceiling and rich, dark wood walls. The couch and loveseat were covered in a subtle plaid while the two club chairs were an opulent shade of forest green.

The room had the manly feel of a Scottish hunting lodge and I knew Abraham had loved it in here.

It took me a few seconds to realize that Derek was not alone.

"Gabriel." I met him halfway across the room and gave him a big hug. "What a nice surprise."

"I brought a friend," he said, glancing over my shoulder.

I turned. "Alex!" I grabbed her in a tight hug. "Are you staying for a while?"

"I wish I was, but I'm just here for a quick visit. I'll be back this weekend for the festival, though. I promise."

"Oh, good." I gave her another hug. Alex was our down-the-hall neighbor in the city and she was simply perfect in so many ways. She was a successful high-powered businesswoman who wore the most awesome clothes and baked fantastic cupcakes as a way of relaxing after a hard day's work. She had taught me some amazing martial arts moves that had saved my life on more than one occasion. She was tall and gorgeous with long dark hair—currently pulled back in a ponytail—and she was in love with our dear friend Gabriel, so I cherished her friendship on every level. "It's great to see you."

"You, too." She casually reached up and brushed my hair back from my forehead, a move that reminded me of my mother and made me smile. "I understand you've had a little trouble up here."

"You heard?" I shot a look at Gabriel. "Of course you heard."

"That's why I'm here," she said lightly.

I glanced from Alex to Gabriel. "You guys are the best. I really appreciate it."

Derek handed me a margarita and gave me a warm,

slow kiss. "There," he murmured. "Sit and relax and take a few sips of your drink."

"Mm, thanks." In the last few months, Derek had perfected his margarita recipe and I couldn't be prouder. It was icy and delicious, potent and sweet yet tart, with just enough salt around the rim to give my taste buds a little kick.

I sat at one end of the couch and gazed at my gorgeous husband and two of my favorite friends. "What a wonderful way to finish off this day."

"Let's have a toast," said Alex, holding up her glass. "To margaritas with friends at the end of a long, hard day."

"I'll drink to that," Gabriel said, winking at Alex as he walked around to clink glasses with each of us. "Cheers."

After we'd all had a chance to take a few sips, Gabriel slipped into the seat next to Alex on the loveseat facing me.

"So what happened, Brooklyn?" Alex asked.

I knew what she was asking and I had to take a few more fortifying sips before I could answer. "You heard there was a murder."

"Yeah."

"Okay. I want to make it clear that I wasn't the one who found the body this time." I winced. "That was my mother."

"And mine," Derek added, and sat down next to me on the couch.

"Yes, Meg and Mom," I said. "Can you imagine? I'm just glad they were together and not alone, but still."

"But still, they're your mothers," Alex said, frowning. "That's awful."

"It was," I said. "I saw the body and I still get chills

thinking about the two of them walking into that horrible scene. The guy's throat had been cut with a broken wine bottle. He bled out on the floor of Mom's committee meeting room." My own throat was suddenly dry and I had to gulp down more of my drink.

Alex grimaced. "Sounds like a bloody mess."

"That's exactly what it was," I said, rubbing my stomach.

"How did you handle that?"

I took another slow sip, then gazed at her. "Not well, thanks for asking. Our mothers, on the other hand, were totally psyched. I mean, they were exhilarated." Shaking my head, I had to laugh a little. "It was weird." I glanced at Derek, who nodded.

"Truly bizarre," Derek agreed, frowning. "They treated it as though they were on some fascinating new adventure."

"Wow," Alex said with a reluctant smile. "I'm sort of impressed."

"I know I was," Gabriel said. "They were champions."

"Especially compared to me," I said woefully. "All that blood made my stomach spin and left me feeling like a giant weenie."

She and Gabriel gave me consoling looks as Derek stood and walked into the kitchen. He came back a minute later with a basket of chips and a bowl of salsa, and set everything down on the coffee table between us.

"Wow." I smiled at him. "I feel better already."

"When Gabriel called, I thought I'd better prepare something to munch on."

"Brilliant."

I watched Derek settle back on the couch next to me.

He patted my leg and changed the subject. "Brooklyn worked on a new book all afternoon. How did it go, darling?"

I flashed him an appreciative smile. *No more talk of blood for a while, thanks.* "It went well. I studied pieces of *Little Women* all afternoon." I stopped and blinked. "Did that sound weird to you all?"

"Yeah," Gabriel said.

Derek grinned at me. "It does sound a bit ominous, and yet I completely understood what you meant."

"Me, too," Alex said, "having read the book a few hundred times when I was younger."

"I did, too." I smiled at her. "I know my work sometimes sounds completely dull, but the story behind this book is actually pretty interesting. The bookseller in town, who I've known my entire life, gave me the book to refurbish before the festival begins. He plans to auction it off at the silent auction. The festival committee chose to celebrate *Little Women* as the official book of the festival. So obviously, the book Clyde gave me is *Little Women.*"

"Obviously," Gabriel said.

"It's in terrible condition, falling apart," I said. "And I've only got the first volume. But according to several online sources, if I were able to restore this one really well, and if I were lucky enough to get hold of the second volume, the two books would be worth about twenty-five thousand dollars."

"Wow," Alex said. "That's unbelievable."

"Unfortunately, the copy I'm working on will be worth less than half of that."

"Less than half of that is still at least twelve thousand dollars," Alex reasoned.

"That's a lot more than I thought it would be worth at first, but I doubt we'll get that much for it in the silent auction."

Gabriel's eyes narrowed. "So Clyde actually gave you the book?"

I frowned. "Do you know Clyde?" But then I remembered that Gabriel lived in Dharma now. And Gabriel was a book collector—or maybe he was a book thief. Sometimes it was hard to tell. "Wait. Sorry. Of course you know Clyde."

"Yeah, we're buddies." In a casual move, Gabriel rested his ankle on the opposite knee. "I'm kind of surprised he didn't show me the book first. Is he the one who told you how much it's worth?"

"No." I considered it for a moment. "Actually, I don't think Clyde knows how much it could be worth. Otherwise, don't you think he would've said something?"

"Yeah, probably," Gabriel mused. "Where'd he get it?"

"He said he found it in a used bookstore in Grass Valley, but I'm starting to think he was fibbing."

"I know Grass Valley," Gabriel said. "There's a book co-op, but I'm not sure any of the sellers carry any really pricey books like this one."

"Well, like I said, it looks really funky and it's falling apart, so maybe the shop owner didn't know what they had."

He studied my face. "But you don't think so."

"No. I think he didn't want to tell me where he got it."

"That's a concern," Derek murmured, and exchanged a look with Gabriel.

"Do you think it could be stolen?" Gabriel asked.

"Do you?" Derek asked, being cryptic again.

"I've already admitted that it looks awful," I said.

"But a knowledgeable book collector would recognize a diamond in the rough. Some might even consider it priceless."

"Which means there's a possibility that it was stolen," Derek said.

"By a knowledgeable book collector," Gabriel mused, then narrowed his eyes. "Maybe I'll pay Clyde a visit tomorrow."

"I was going to stop by there tomorrow, too," I said. "Maybe we can go together."

He gave me a lopsided grin. "Sure, babe. We'll double-team him."

"I'll go with you as well," Derek said.

"A triple-team is even better." Changing to another subject, I turned to Gabriel. "Have you talked to Detective Willoughby today?"

"I have."

"Any word on anything? Did they figure out what winery that wine bottle came from? Did they identify the fingerprints?"

One of Gabriel's eyebrows lifted. That always impressed me. "He's not real forthcoming with info, but I learned a thing or two."

Alex grabbed a chip and pointed it at me. "I'll bet you're missing Inspector Lee right about now."

"Oh yeah," I said. "We would have a lot more information by now."

"Inspector Lee hasn't always been that willing to share," Derek reminded me.

"She's tough," I said, and smiled, thinking of the hard-as-nails inspector. "But even if she won't tell me stuff, she'll usually tell you."

Derek's lips twisted into a grin. "True. But you and

she have become pretty good friends, so that's starting to change."

"Thank goodness. At least she's not trying to arrest me anymore." I looked at Gabriel. "So what did they tell you? Did they find Jacob Banyan's prints all over everything, I hope?"

"Nothing that specific," Gabriel admitted. "They've got somewhat of a timeline, but no suspects yet."

"Rats." I sipped my margarita. "Maybe you could nudge them in the direction of Banyan?"

Gabriel raised an eyebrow. "Good luck with that."

I sighed. "He's just so awful. I would love to see him thrown in jail for a good long time."

I gave Alex a brief rundown of what Banyan had done to my mother. "I'm scared to death that he might make good on his threats to hurt her."

"He sounds like a real jerk," Alex said.

"That's putting it mildly," I groused. "He talks like he's some kind of mob boss."

"He's not," Gabriel put in. "Just a bully with a big mouth."

Alex patted his knee as she gave me a considering look. "So, are you practicing your self-defense moves?"

"Ah." I winced. "Um, I guess it's been a few weeks."

"Brooklyn," she said. "You need to practice. You never know when you'll need to defend yourself."

"That's the thing. I never believe it'll happen to me again. And then suddenly something awful happens and I have to spring into action."

"So far you've been lucky," she said.

She was right, of course. With the number of times I'd stumbled onto murder scenes it was mind-boggling that I hadn't been attacked more often.

"I'm very lucky. The few times I've needed to put

your lessons to use lately, I was able to remember enough of what you taught me to save myself."

"Darling," Derek said, reaching for my hand. "The fact that you just basically admitted that you've had to defend yourself a few times lately? As if it were nothing? That scares me to death."

"Me, too," Alex said. She stood up and paced the room. Finally she turned and focused on me. "Okay, as soon as you get home, we're going back to work. I want those self-defense moves to become second nature to you."

I nodded. "I want that, too."

"And Brooklyn," she added, "if you have any hope of protecting your mother, you need to practice while you're here."

"Ah, the mother guilt." I shook my head in defeat. "Works every time. You're good."

"I go with my strengths," she said with a grin.

"I know, and you're right. I'll sign up for a class at the Dharma Dojo tomorrow."

"Great idea. I know Keith, the owner," she said. "I'll call him in the morning and let him know you're coming. He might give you a deal on his two-week introductory course."

"Sounds great." With a laugh, I rolled my eyes. Now Keith would be expecting me and I would have to show up. Which was just what Alex had had in mind.

"Perhaps I'll go with you," Derek said.

Suddenly I was much more interested. "I would love that."

"You know what they say," Alex said, smiling. "The family that fights together, um . . . huh. Can't think of anything that rhymes with *fights*."

I glanced at Derek. "Spends their *nights* together?"

"Poetry," he said with a sexy chuckle that made me laugh.

His cell phone buzzed just then and he answered. "Stone." He pushed himself up off the couch and listened for thirty seconds, grim faced, then said, "We'll be right there."

"What is it?" I asked. "What happened?"

"That was your father."

My heart dropped. "Mom?"

"She's fine. But just barely." He reached down to help me up from the couch.

"We'll go, too," Gabriel said, jumping up from his chair. Alex was on her feet as well.

Derek gave Gabriel the pertinent information— Sonoma hospital, emergency entrance—and within a minute the four of us ran out to our cars.

Once Derek was driving down the hill, I turned to him. "Tell me."

He reached for my hand. "Your parents went to an early dinner at Arugula. They were crossing the street afterward and your father heard someone gunning their car engine. The car came barreling up the Lane toward your mother. Jim says he practically threw her onto the sidewalk to get her out of the way and then came crashing down on top of her."

"She's hurt," I whispered. My heart was pounding, tears stung my eyes and all I could seem to manage were short, sharp breaths.

He squeezed my hand. "I know what you're feeling, love. But according to your father, your mother was just a bit scuffed and bruised."

I pressed my other hand against my mouth. "But they're at the hospital?"

"Yes. They're in the ER."

"Okay," I whispered, and took a few more deep breaths in and out. "Okay."

He gave my hand another squeeze. "Everything will be all right."

I nodded. "Did anyone see the car?"

"He's not sure. But one of Savannah's bartenders came running out and offered to call the police while your father took your mum to the hospital. We'll find out more when we get there."

I sat in silence for a long moment, then said, "This is Jacob Banyan's work."

Derek tightened his jaw as he turned onto Montana Ridge Road and headed for the hospital in Sonoma. "I would have to agree."

Derek, Gabriel, and Alex sat in the waiting area out front while I went into the curtained examination room where a doctor was evaluating my mother's injuries. Dad sat in a chair right next to her, looking emotionally drained.

"I'm not staying overnight in the hospital," my mother argued, then saw me walk in. "Oh, sweetie, it's just a little bump and a skinned knee. I want to go home."

"You've suffered a mild concussion, Mrs. Wainwright," the on-call doctor said. His name badge read DR. SHARMA, EMERGENCY MEDICINE. "And you have multiple scrapes and contusions up and down your legs."

"Well, of course I do," Mom said reasonably. "I got slammed onto the sidewalk." She winked at Dad and reached out for him. "Thank God. You saved my life, Jimmy."

He squeezed her hand. "You cushioned my fall, sweetie pie."

Tears began to stream down my cheeks as I listened to my parents' good-natured teasing. *She could've been hurt so much worse*, I thought, and swore that Jacob Banyan would pay.

When I could finally speak, I asked, "How bad are the contusions, doctor?"

"There was a lot of bruising and quite a bit of blood from the scrapes she received falling on the sidewalk. We had to dig some bits of gravel out of her left knee." Dr. Sharma sighed. "But we've cleaned her up and covered everything in antibiotic ointment." He smiled at me, then my mother. "We'll send you home with extra bandages and ointment. I would recommend using an ice pack on the bruises every hour or so, as long as you keep the bandages dry." He smiled wider. "She'll live."

"And what about the concussion?" I asked.

"I'll stay up with her," my father said. "I'll wake her up every two hours and check her pupils and her vital signs."

I turned to the doctor. "Is that enough?"

"It was a mild concussion and she shows no symptoms that indicate anything worse."

"What are those symptoms?" I pressed.

"Dizziness, slurred speech, confusion, nausea, ringing in the ears. Among others."

I stared at my mother. "Is any of that happening to you?"

"No, sweetie," she said. "I'm just tired."

I turned back to Dr. Sharma. "She's tired. Is that a bad sign?"

"Only if she wants to go dancing all night."

I was still sniffling, but I managed a weak smile. "So you're a comedian."

"Just trying to keep it light."

"I appreciate that. Thanks." I shook his hand as my father helped my mother to her feet.

I walked out to the hall just as Detective Willoughby and Officer Jenkins approached. Derek and Gabriel stood up to greet them.

"I'm glad you're here, Detective," I said.

"I'm sorry about your mom," he said. "How's she doing?"

"She's okay. She's going home. She's pretty shaken up so she won't be able to talk to you tonight."

Just then, Mom and Dad walked slowly out of the examination room.

"Well, hello, Stevie—oops." Mom shook her head and the movement caused her to wince. "I mean, Detective Willoughby. I'm sorry. I'm not doing too well, but I'm sure I'll be able to answer your questions tomorrow."

"That's all right, Mrs. Wainwright. I'm glad you're doing a little better."

"I'll be much better by tomorrow."

"That's good news. We'll stop by tomorrow morning around ten a.m., if that's not too early for you."

"That's just dandy." She turned and smiled vaguely at everyone around her. "Okay, we're going home now."

I grabbed Dad's arm. "Are you all right?"

He blew out a nervous breath and lowered his voice. "Honey, I've never been so scared in all my life. It was like my whole life passed before my eyes."

I wrapped my arms around him and felt the tears burning again. "She's going to be fine, Dad. And don't forget, you saved her life. So thank you."

He kissed my cheek and gazed at me. And I could see the unshed tears in his eyes. "I'll cry like a baby later, but right now I've got to be strong for Becky."

"Are you okay to drive?"

"I'll be fine," he said, patting my arm. "It's just a few miles."

"Okay. But if you don't mind, Derek and I will come by for a few minutes, just to check in."

He nodded. "I would really appreciate it."

I gave him another hug, and then leaned over and lightly kissed my mom. "I love you, Mom. You do everything Dad tells you, okay?"

"Oh, honey. I always do."

I snorted lightly. "That's funny, Mom."

She managed to grin. "I still got it."

I watched them walk slowly down the hall and out the door to the parking lot. And I wondered why they both suddenly looked so fragile when for all my life, those two had been towers of sheer rock.

I looked around, met Derek's gaze, and heaved out a breath. "Oh God."

He pulled me into his arms. "She'll be fine."

"I know, but now I really want to kill Jacob Banyan."

He rubbed my back. "Let's not say that too loudly with Detective Willoughby standing nearby."

"Oh, yeah." I almost laughed, just as Stevie approached us again. I turned and nodded to him. "Were you able to find anyone who saw what happened?"

Stevie pulled out his notebook, read a few lines, and frowned. "We spoke to several people who said they saw a car speed up and race through the crosswalk. One person described it as an SUV. Another thought it looked like a little sports car."

"What? Wait." Maybe I was the one with a concussion because I was totally confused. "Those are totally opposite vehicles."

"Yeah." He shook his head in disgust. "Eyewitnesses aren't generally too useful. Everyone sees something different."

"You should find out what kind of car Jacob Banyan drives. Like we told you, he's been threatening her for a while now. He tried it again today at the festival committee meeting. I think he's getting worse."

"I'll talk to him." Stevie wrote it all down, then nodded. "Thanks, Brooklyn."

"Is there anything else we can do?" I asked.

"Not just now. We'll be in touch."

"You'll talk to more shop owners on the Lane? Someone must've seen something."

"Yes, we will. And there are several businesses on the Lane that have exterior cameras installed so we'll be viewing those tonight to see what we can find."

That was something at least. I felt so damn helpless and it wasn't a feeling I cared for. "It would be great if you found something."

"We'll let you know what happens." He shoved his notebook into his jacket pocket. "But yeah, I'm hopeful."

In the parking lot we said goodnight to Gabriel and Alex.

Gabriel hugged me. "You okay?"

"Sure."

He leaned down to make eye contact with me. "Your mom will be fine."

"I know." I sniffled. "Thanks."

"I'll stop by tomorrow," he said.

"Okay, thanks for that."

He said something to Derek while I turned and gave

Alex a hug. "I'm so glad you were here. Do you really have to leave?"

"I do," she said, and pouted. "I need to get back and prep my team for a big meeting day after tomorrow."

"Sounds very high powered and important."

"That's me."

I laughed. "I'll miss you."

"I'll see you in a few days and I plan to stay all weekend."

"Oh, good. I'm so glad."

Gabriel came over and wrapped his arm around her. They started to walk away, but then she turned. "By the way, Brooklyn. I'll be checking in with Keith at the dojo. Don't blow him off or I'll track you down and hurt you."

She was smiling as she said it, but there was a glimmer of danger in her eyes.

"You're scaring me."

She grinned. "Then my work here is done."

Derek and I made it home within minutes and walked up the hill to check on my mom and dad. Mom was already in bed, fast asleep. Dad had the alarm set for midnight and planned to get up, as promised, every two hours to check on Mom. I told him to call me if he needed anything.

"I'm right down the street, remember? I can walk up here in less than two minutes."

"I wish you were always there," he said sentimentally.

I hugged him. "Me too, Dad," I whispered.

Derek and I walked down the hill to Abraham's house and were greeted at the kitchen door by Charlie who wound her way in and out and around our ankles.

"She missed us," I said, and stooped down to pet her

soft fur and give her scratches between her ears. She purred and rubbed her head against my hands, wanting more. I loved this special little cat so much, especially because she'd been a gift from Derek.

"We were gone quite a while." Derek picked her up in his arms and carried her up to bed with us.

Once in bed, Derek asked me what I planned to do tomorrow. "I've done the preliminary examination of Clyde's book and tomorrow I'll get started on repair." But the uncertainty around the book's ownership caused me to frown. "And the three of us were going to go talk to Clyde at some point, too. But now there's Mom to worry about so I don't know." I sighed. "But I'll still try and start the actual work on the book tomorrow."

"Do you think your mother will be up for another committee meeting tomorrow?"

"Absolutely," I said with certainty. "With so much going on, she won't miss it. And that means that someone needs to go with her." I thought about it. "Preferably two people."

"I agree," Derek said, rearranging his pillow so he could sit up in bed. "She's somehow become the target of someone's rage."

"I'm looking at Jacob Banyan, but whoever it is, they're ruthless and desperate." I felt those familiar chills returning to my spine. "And that describes him perfectly. I think it describes Saffron Bergeron, too, but that's only because she's so cranky and stupid." I blew out a breath. "Anyway, if Mom is going to the meeting tomorrow, I'm going with her."

"And I'll be with you, too," Derek said.

"Oh, I almost forgot to tell you. Saffron has a missing button on that jacket she wore today."

"A missing button," he mused. "Remind me to take a look at the jacket the next time she wears it. I'll be able to tell if the button we found is hers."

"Okay, good."

He thought for a moment. "They're going to have to decide what to do about the missing money."

I leaned my head against his arm. "There are a lot of wealthy people here in the valley. Someone will have to step up and cover the cash that Lawson stole."

"You do think he stole the money."

"Don't you?"

He nodded. "I don't see how it could be anyone else. Lawson was in complete charge of the finances—which was clearly a mistake."

"I know Mom blames herself, but it's not her fault for believing that Lawson was trustworthy. And she was in charge of a thousand other agenda items. She should've been able to count on him."

"I don't want to forget anything," Derek said, "so tomorrow morning over breakfast, let's write out this agenda of ours."

"Okay. I need to work on the book and someone needs to stick close to Mom." I frowned. "I would prefer if it were you and me. Or Gabriel. Or my brothers. I know our dads are willing, but I worry about them, too. And Robin is out of the question for now. I don't want anything to upset her."

He sighed. "And my mother would put up a fight if we told her she wasn't up to the task."

"So we won't say anything to anyone. We'll just make sure that Mom is well protected while there's a vicious maniac out to kill her." I reached for my purse and pulled out a small notepad and a pen.

"What are you doing?"

"We might as well start writing it down now." I jotted down the items we'd already covered. "Oh. I want to stop by Clyde's tomorrow and find out where he really got that book." I added a new item to our list.

"Your mother is our first priority," Derek said. "But we can try to stop by Clyde's at some point."

"Sounds good. Her meeting doesn't start until two thirty."

"That'll work."

I rested my head back on his shoulder. "I love you."

He leaned against me. "And I love you, darling."

"Thank you for caring about the people I love."

"It isn't difficult. I love them, too."

"I know, and it's the best thing about you."

He frowned at me. "Have you forgotten my manly arms?"

"Never. Those are right at the top of my list."

"I'd like to take a look at *that* list."

I laughed. "Oh, I just remembered, I want to stop by and watch the play rehearsal one of these nights. I'd like to get a look at Shandi Patrick and see how she interacts with the others."

Derek nodded. "Let's do that tomorrow night."

"You want to go with me?"

"Of course."

I beamed at him. "You're the best. Maybe we could have dinner at Umbria afterward."

"That's a lovely idea."

"I know," I said. "Because pasta."

"Exactly."

I started to make a note to call the restaurant, but suddenly stopped. "Oh wow. We haven't even been by to see your parents' new home."

He smacked his forehead. "I knew we forgot something. And I'm guilt ridden now that you've reminded me."

"They'll understand, won't they?"

"Of course," he said. "But they'll be happier if we make it over there sometime soon. Let's do it tomorrow after we see Clyde."

"Good idea." I wrote it down. "And after your parents, we can swing by and pick up Mom for her committee meeting."

"The timing should work out perfectly."

I gazed at him. "Aren't you going into San Francisco this week?"

"I'll work by phone," he said. "I don't want to leave you alone while your mom is in trouble and a murderer is running loose."

"Will your office be all right without you?"

"I'm the boss," he said in his tough-guy voice. "I say it's all right."

I grinned at him. "Corinne runs the place anyway, doesn't she?"

Both eyebrows arched and he got that very-British-so-insulted expression that I was so crazy about. "That's harsh, darling."

I laughed. "I was just teasing."

"So was I," he said with an easy shrug, then kissed the top of my head. "But it's the truth. Corinne is invaluable."

"In more ways than one," I added.

Derek's administrative assistant, Corinne Sterling, was definitely worth her weight in gold. She was truly invaluable, as Derek said, and not just in the office. Only a few months ago, Corinne had been a key player in a real-life spy story when she'd helped unmask a very scary killer who was out to get me.

Disconcerted by the memory, I mumbled, "Let's take one killer at a time. Sheesh." I put my notepad and pen on the nightstand, turned off the lamp, and rolled over to give Derek a soft, warm kiss. "Good night, my love."

He pulled me close to him. "Good night, sweetheart. We'll make everything work tomorrow. And you're not to worry about your mother. Rebecca will be safe. We'll see to it."

Chapter 10

Early the next morning, I called my father to make sure Mom was feeling all right.

"Hey, Punkin'," Dad said, using the childhood nickname I hated. It had to do with a youthful pumpkin-pie obsession, and I was long over it—sort of. But this moment wasn't about me. I was actually pleased by the fact that Dad had called me that because it meant he was in an upbeat mood this morning. For that reason alone, I was hopeful.

"We didn't get a lot of sleep last night," he continued, "but your mom's doing great."

"Is she awake yet?"

"She's still dozing, but I'm about to wake her up and feed her some breakfast."

"You're the best, Dad."

"Yeah. I thought she would need lots of protein to power through the day, so I'm making a breakfast grain bowl."

"What in the world?"

"It's got a little bit of everything. Quinoa, bacon, some onion, tomato, and kale, then a thick slice of avocado and topped off with a fried egg."

"Whoa, that sounds crazy."

"It's good."

"Tell Mom we're sending our love."

"You bet, sweetie."

"Will you call us if you need anything?"

"I will. Thank you, honey." He paused for a moment. "I know she'd love it if you and Derek came over for a visit. I would, too."

"We will, absolutely. And I know she's going to want to go to her meeting this afternoon, so Derek and I can take her and stay with her."

"That would be awesome, kiddo."

"It's no problem."

He gave a short laugh. "I'd like her to stay home and rest, but you know your mother. So I appreciate you watching out for her." He sighed. "I'm supposed to be at a meeting out at the winery this afternoon, but I'm going to cancel and go with you guys."

"Absolutely not." It was my mother's voice, and I could just picture her, standing in the doorway glaring at Dad.

"Guess I'm busted," Dad said, and put the phone on speaker.

Then Mom said, "You need to be there to go over the last-minute details of the harvest. We're only about six days out."

"Your safety means more than some meeting," Dad insisted. "Austin and Jackson can handle everything. They don't need me there."

"Yes, they do," Mom said. "You're the boss."

Dad gave a helpless sigh. "The real boss has spoken."

"That's fine, Jim," Derek said. "We'll take good care of Rebecca."

"We'll be there around two o'clock to pick you up, Mom," I said.

"I'll be ready."

We hung up and I stared at the phone for a long moment. Until Mom interrupted the conversation, Dad had sounded pretty jovial for someone who hadn't slept well. But that was my dad. He was the most optimistic, loving man I'd ever known and I was so thankful that he was taking care of Mom. Even when she was cantankerous.

I couldn't blame her for being grouchy though. I would feel the same way.

I sniffed and dashed a few tears away, then tried to think good thoughts about Mom's miraculous escape from what could have been a tragedy while I started the coffee.

Over a hearty plate of breakfast tacos in the sunny breakfast room, Derek and I revised and refined our agenda items for the day.

Did we know how to have fun or what?

"While I was making coffee, I remembered something we need to put on the list."

Derek looked up from his tablet where the stock market reports were streaming. "What's that?"

"We have to stop by the dojo and sign up for a class or two. Otherwise, Alex will hunt me down."

He chuckled. "We can't have that."

"No way. She scares me. In a happy, nonthreatening way, of course." I took a quick bite of toast, added the dojo sign-up to the agenda, then gave our very full list one more read-through. "You know how we talked last night about Corinne? Well, I kind of wish she was here right now to help us organize our lives."

"Don't be silly, darling. You're one of the most organized people I know."

I smiled. "That's true. And you're not too shabby, either."

"Ah, but that's because I have Corinne."

"Lucky," I grumbled.

"I am, indeed." He grinned at me, took a sip of coffee, and switched off his tablet. "Not that it wouldn't be lovely to see Corinne anytime," he added. "But I know you, and I can handle this. It's just a matter of scheduling."

"That reminds me, did you mention the book festival to her?"

"The entire office is aware of it," he said. "And a number of people have confirmed that they're planning to be here."

"That's so nice. I'll look forward to seeing them."

Most of the people who worked for Derek were terrific and I'd gotten really close to some of them since he and I had been together. I hated to say it, but in the past there had been a few bad apples. Happily, they were gone now. For good.

"And a couple of them said they'd be bringing books for you to appraise."

"That's fantastic! This is going to be fun." Part of the reason I'd been given a booth at the festival—ignoring the fact that my mother was cochair of the event—was my promise to appraise any old books that people brought with them. It was something I'd done before, and I always found it interesting and challenging, especially to do it on the fly, so to speak, since all I would have for research was my tablet and a few reference books.

I nibbled on a piece of bacon and stared at our list. "We have to switch your parents' visit with Clyde because he doesn't open the bookshop until ten."

"Ah. Good thinking. Unless you'd rather stay home and work on your book for a few hours this morning. We can always swing by my parents' place later on."

I thought about it, but my mind was pretty much already set. "I'd rather talk to Clyde before I do any more work on the book." I didn't say out loud what I was afraid I'd hear from Clyde: that the book had been stolen or had come to him through some other illegal manner. If it was connected to something illegal, it would be evidence. And in that case, I didn't want to get in the middle of a criminal investigation.

Besides, I really did want to see Meg and John's new home and I knew they were anxious to show it off to Derek.

Derek nodded. "I see your point. So we'll go by Mum and Dad's first thing. Let me give them a call."

I glanced at the clock on the wall. "It's awfully early."

"It's already seven thirty. They're usually up at dawn."

"I guess you would know best." I smiled, though the thought of getting up before dawn was a hideous one. Yes, I know. Sunrises are beautiful. Well, so are sunsets and they were more my speed. "My folks are usually up that early, too. Horrifying, isn't it?"

He chuckled. "Both of our parents had five or six children to wrangle first thing, so they're used to those early hours."

Derek called his folks, and even though I couldn't hear the conversation on their side, Derek's reaction told me that they were clearly thrilled we were coming by.

"All right, Mum. See you then," Derek said, and ended the call. He glanced at me. "I'm afraid they might want to feed us."

"Oh dear, it would be rude to refuse them." Because when had I ever in my life refused food? Never. So I stared at my plate. "I'll just finish my coffee and wrap up this taco. It'll keep for a while."

I moved into the kitchen and began to open drawers, looking for plastic baggies to pack up the food.

"Probably for the best," Derek said, mournfully giving up his savory taco.

"Otherwise we'll be stuffed."

"Undoubtedly. I know she'll have scones, at least."

"I love scones," I said dreamily. "And butter. And jam."

"She'll have all of that. And Devonshire cream, no doubt."

I grinned. "Oh boy. I love your parents."

"I do, too, but I had to talk her out of serving a full English breakfast. Guess we'll find out soon enough if I was successful or not."

I groaned. "There's no way I can scarf down more eggs, along with baked beans and roasted tomatoes and mushrooms and blood sausage and God knows what else."

He laughed. "It wouldn't be quite that bad."

"It would be worse," I muttered. I took another sip of coffee and began to load the dishwasher. "I'm excited to see their house."

"Me, too."

I turned and looked at him. "You know, we could always stay with them when we come up here."

He paused. "Darling, you know how you love your parents but don't always want to stay in their house with them?"

I frowned. "Yes."

"That's exactly how I feel about mine."

"Oh." I frowned. "But your parents are awesome and you hardly ever get to see them."

"Your parents are awesome, too."

"True." I laughed. "All right, all right. No parents."

"On the other hand," he said, "my parents will only be in Dharma for a few months at a time. We can always stay at their house when they're not here."

"That would be wonderful." I winced. "Not that I wouldn't love it if they were here, but . . . do you think they would mind?"

"I think they would love it." He drained his coffee mug and stuck it in the dishwasher. "I'll bring up the subject sometime this week."

Half an hour later, we were dressed and ready to hit the road. I had my list in hand and was looking forward to checking things off.

Meg and John's new home in Dharma was only a few blocks away, down our hill, then one block over, and up the next hill.

It was barely five minutes before Derek was pulling to the curb and turning off the engine.

"Their view is spectacular," I said, gazing at the grapevines and olive trees that dotted the rolling green hills in the distance. Much like my parents' house, Meg and John's place was the last house at the top of the road, with no other houses to block the view.

I knew from experience that at the bottom of the canyon below was the picturesque Dharma Creek where my brothers and sisters and I used to go swimming and fishing when we were young.

From up here you could see Triad Island in the middle of the Creek where all the kids went camping in the summer. I hadn't thought about Triad Island in a long time and realized I would have to take Derek there one of these days. Not for camping, of course. Those days were over. But it would be fun to explore the small island and have a picnic lunch.

We walked down the long walkway that led to the front door. Colorful autumn flowers lined the way and flowerpots on the porch were bursting with vibrant roses, lavender, and tumbling vines. Pine trees and quaking aspens grew along the property line, and a healthy green lawn spread across the entire lot from the house to the edge of the street.

"Are you ready for this?" Derek asked, grabbing hold of my hand.

"Of course. Let's go."

The house was an adorable two-story classic Craftsman home with all the wonderful characteristics that went along with that style. There was a wide porch that wrapped around the entire house and looked big enough to accommodate plenty of seating areas, including a comfy swing covered in pillows near the front door.

The house was painted a soft sage green with pale yellow trim, and four square white columns set on a river rock base graced the front of the house. The heavy oak front door was painted red.

I stared at the red door and then checked the direction it was facing. South. Naturally.

"I'm seeing my mother's influence here," I said.

"How?"

"The red door. It's a feng shui thing. I think I told you about it before. Your parents painted their south-facing front door red because the color red is associated with the element of fire, and fire governs the southerly direction. You want your front door to nourish your own personal energy and also strengthen the feng shui energy coming into your home. Anyone entering the house from this direction will bring good chi, or life energy, with them and provide a harmonious space within."

"Sounds like your mother, indeed." Derek gave me a slow, delighted smile. "And you're far more like her than you think."

I had to laugh. "That thought no longer freaks me out."

"I'm happy to hear it," Derek said. "But I happen to believe that the only reason this door is red is because my mother likes that color."

"However it came to be, it looks wonderful."

He stared at me for a long moment. "I love you." Then he wrapped his arms around me and kissed me soundly.

"What was that for?"

"Do I need a reason?"

"No." I smiled. "Just asking."

"It's for having such a beautiful spirit."

I narrowed my eyes. "Now you're making fun of me."

He kissed my nose. "I'm madly in love with you."

I leaned against him and simply breathed him in. I knew for a fact that Derek didn't wear scented cologne or aftershave, but I could always catch a hint of something wonderful when I was this close to him. At this moment I had an image of a redwood forest turned all misty with springtime rain.

Clean and woodsy. And ridiculously appealing.

He rang the doorbell and we watched it swing open within a millisecond. It was almost as if his mother had been standing on the other side of the door, just waiting for us to ring the bell.

"You're here!" Meg pulled us both inside and threw her arms around Derek and then me. "Welcome, welcome! Come in."

"What a beautiful home," I said. "I love your red door."

Meg smiled. "Did you know, Brooklyn, that when your front door faces south, the color red helps usher in lots of good energy?"

I looked up at Derek and smiled innocently, then turned to Meg. "I've heard that. And it must be working because your home is filled with wonderful energy."

"You're such a sweet girl," she said, squeezing my hand affectionately. "And your mother is a genius."

"I think so, too."

"Hello!" John said as he walked into the room. "Welcome to our Dharma home."

"Thanks, Dad," Derek said, and they gave each other manly hugs with plenty of back slaps. "It's great to finally see the place."

John gave me a hug as Meg began to point out her favorite parts of the room.

"Isn't this floor wonderful?" Meg said. "This is the original wood. They kept it in such good condition."

"It's beautiful."

"And look at this wainscoting," she said, running her hand along the beautiful wood-paneled wall.

"Lovely," Derek murmured.

"The original owners were contractors," John explained. "They did a bang-up job with everything."

"It's charming," I said, looking around. "The windows are so big, and I love this vaulted ceiling. It really opens up the room, doesn't it?"

"Did you hear that, John? Brooklyn knows that this is a vaulted ceiling."

"Clever girl," he said, winking at me.

I beamed at him. "It's because both of my brothers built their own homes and Jackson's has a vaulted ceiling. Then Austin decided on a cathedral ceiling, so I learned the difference between the two."

Meg gazed around at the different features of the room. "This reminds me very much of the traditional cottages in the area of England where we live. Mainly the countryside around Oxford and the Cotswolds."

"Except that this house is much more modern," John added. "Thank goodness. And not built for tiny people. In the old village homes, the ceilings are so low I'm forever walking hunched over."

"True," Derek said with a laugh as he turned in a slow circle to take in the room. "My brothers and I were constantly banging our foreheads on the doorframes."

I laughed because I could just see Derek and his brothers clomping through a tiny village cottage.

We made our way out to the terrace and back lawn that overlooked the rolling hills of Dharma. As we stared at the stunning views, I turned to Derek's parents. "I hate to bring up unhappy news, but I have to tell you what happened last night."

"What?" Meg demanded, her cheerful expression shifting to real concern as she caught the look on my face. "What happened?"

"Rebecca and Jim were involved in an accident last night," Derek said.

"Oh, good heavens, no!" Meg cried. She pressed her hand to her forehead and closed her eyes. "Oh dear. I had a feeling . . . well, never mind." Her eyes flew open. "Tell me what happened."

I explained the entire incident, including the extent of her injuries and everything the doctor said.

John's eyes narrowed in on me. "But that sounds like someone deliberately tried to hit her with their car."

"That's exactly what happened," I said irately. "If Dad hadn't literally thrown her out of the way . . ." I had to catch my breath. "Well, she got some bumps and bruises, but he saved her life, thank God, and she'll be fine."

"That's a bit too close for comfort, I'd say." Meg also had to take a few deep breaths in and out. "And for myself, I would blame that brute, Banyan."

"That's exactly who I blame," I said through clenched teeth.

"Derek, are you going with Brooklyn and Becky to the meeting this afternoon?" John asked.

"Absolutely," he said. "Rebecca won't be going anywhere alone. We want two able-bodied adults with her at all times until that man, or whoever did this, is in jail."

John gave a firm nod. "Good, son. That's good. If you need my help, just call." He frowned. "And I'll give Jim a call in a few minutes."

"Thank you, John," I said, knowing my father would appreciate hearing from him.

With that subject closed, our conversation deliberately lightened, bouncing back and forth from the weather to all the newest restaurants in town, to other family matters, to the upcoming grape harvest.

After a tour of the entire house and yard, we sat down to a lovely spread of tea and scones with butter, three flavors of jam and marmalade, and a pot of Devonshire cream. There was also a plate of cookies with little chocolates scattered around, just in case we hadn't yet received our daily intake of sugar. And to mix things up, Meg brought out a traditional Spanish tortilla, which had more in common with a quiche than it did with a Mexican tortilla. Jim explained that before buying their place in Dharma, the Stones had traditionally holidayed on the coast of Spain.

"Everything looks so beautiful," I said as I scooped

up jam and put it on my plate. We chatted about a dozen more topics, including my sister Savannah and their son Dalton and how happy they were. We talked about the brutal murder of Lawson Schmidt and my mother and Meg finding the body. And we even discussed the insulting words Meg had overheard yesterday from Ryan, concerning Shandi Patrick wanting to play the role of Jo and trashing the character of poor Meg in the *Little Women* musical.

It was clear that our Meg was much more traumatized over Ryan dissing the character Meg than she had been about coming face-to-face with a bloody dead body. But we all cared about different things, so who was I to judge?

Finally John changed the subject. "So what else are you kids doing today?"

I spoke up. "We're stopping by the bookshop to talk to Clyde about the book I'm working on for him. And then we're taking Mom to the meeting, as I mentioned earlier."

"You're such a good girl, Brooklyn," Meg said, as she poured more tea for each of us. "I do hope the committee will resolve their money issues."

"That will have to be addressed immediately today."

John tapped his fingers against the table. "What do you think they'll do?"

"Well, they could try to find another underwriter or some wealthy benefactor, of course." I took a quick sip of tea to give myself a few seconds to think about it. "I presume the festival itself is insured, so hopefully they can replace the money that was stolen. But it won't happen soon enough, and I don't think there's any way they can raise that much in individual donations again in such a short time, so they'll have to come up with another plan in the meantime."

And I suddenly had an idea. I glanced at Derek, who gave me a questioning look. But I didn't want to say anything just now. This wasn't the time to talk about money.

It was getting close to ten so we helped clear the dishes and straighten the dining room and left a short while later.

Derek found a parking spot on the Lane two blocks down from the Good Book. It was a gorgeous day for walking and we strolled hand in hand past the beautiful shops along the tree-lined Lane.

"I love this town," I said.

"It really is picturesque," Derek said. "The most beautiful part of the wine country."

I leaned against him, absurdly pleased that he loved my hometown as much as I did.

When we reached Warped, my sister China's yarn and weaving shop, I poked my head inside the door.

"Hey, you," I said.

"Brooks!" China cried. "And Derek. What a nice surprise." She came over and gave us both hugs. "Are you out shopping? What's going on?"

"We're on our way to the bookshop, but I wanted to stop and let you know that we plan to watch the musical rehearsal tonight. Will you be there?"

"You know I will. I'm there every night. We're doing final run-throughs and dress rehearsals this week."

"That's exciting."

She beamed. "It's thrilling. Everyone looks so good and the singing is really amazing. I think you'll be impressed."

"I'm sure we will be," I said. "So we'll see you around seven?"

"Perfect."

I finally got to the topic that had been on my mind all morning. "Hey, have you talked to Dad today?"

"No." She frowned, instantly alarmed. "Why?"

"Give him a call." I had to take a deep breath. "He and Mom were in a little accident last night. Mom's kind of bruised and Dad's taking care of her."

She grabbed my arm. "Oh my God. What do you mean, *bruised*?"

"She's got some bruises and scrapes from when Dad threw her on the sidewalk to get her out of the way of the driver who was deliberately aiming for her." *Okay, not such a "little" accident*, I thought.

Derek gave her the thirty-second history of the Banyan debacle.

"That creep," she said, seething with anger. "I'll call Dad right now."

"Can you call Savannah and London and tell them, too?"

"Sure. I'll call them after I talk to Dad."

"Okay," I said. "I'm sorry to bring you the bad news, but Mom will be okay. I promise."

"I believe you, but I still want to talk to them."

"They'll be happy you called." We both gave her quick hugs. "We'll see you tonight."

"Can't wait."

We closed the shop door and Derek took my hand again as we continued walking to the Good Book. Apparently, Dad hadn't spread the word about last night's incident, and I wondered if China was going to call everyone else or if I should do it.

On the way to Clyde's, I began to take notice of which stores had security cameras and which way they were pointed. Most had them angled toward the front door of the shop, but a few of the larger shops had two or even three cameras mounted and some of those were pointed toward the street.

I knew Detective Willoughby was diligent, so I hoped he had already collected the videos from the owners. I figured most of the shops only held on to the recordings for forty-eight hours or so.

We walked into the Good Book and I was instantly assailed by my favorite scents of rich leather and musty vellum and the lovely sight of all those stacks and rows of books. It was amazing how quickly those sensations brought back memories, some wonderful, others bitter-sweet, of my life around books.

I had always been a reader. I remembered spending long hours curled up in one of Clyde's comfy chairs, getting lost in a good story. From my earliest childhood days, I couldn't get enough of books. Historical fiction and mysteries and romance and biographies. When I was twelve I went through a World War II phase and had to read every last story of D-Day and the Nazis' rise to power and the bombings and the heroic resistance fighters in France.

Then I went through a phase where I was reading books about different occupations. I must've glommed onto a couple dozen books about nursing.

After those books, I switched to fictional stories about nurses. I read them all. From Sue Barton to Cherry Ames to evil Nurse Ratched in *One Flew Over the Cuckoo's Nest*. And then there were the real-life stories of Florence Nightingale and Clara Barton.

It was a real miracle that I didn't go into nursing. But given my phobia of blood, I wouldn't have made it through the first day.

"Good morning, Clyde," I called when I saw him working at the back counter. "It's me, Brooklyn."

"Oh hey, Brooklyn. Good to see you." He frowned. "Wait a minute." He shuffled toward us carrying a stiff broom, and came up to pat my shoulder. "I heard about your mom. It happened just down the block from here. How's she doing?"

"She's much better today, Clyde. Thanks for asking. It was pretty scary."

"An eyewitness claims it was a deliberate attempt to hurt her, to run her down," Derek added.

I could tell by the way Derek said those words that he was looking to elicit a more emotional response from Clyde. Not that he suspected that Clyde had been behind the wheel of the car, but the old man knew everyone in town, including Banyan. He was also on the festival committee, so maybe he knew some dark secret about one of the members. Or maybe he'd overheard something.

"What? No!" Clyde's eyes clouded over. "Oh no. That kind of stuff shouldn't happen here in Dharma."

"No, it shouldn't," I murmured, and grimaced at the reality that in fact, it *did* happen here. "But Lawson Schmidt was brutally killed the other night, so unfortunately it looks like that stuff *does* happen here. Someone in the area is trying to hurt people."

Clyde looked ready to cry. "I'm so sorry your mom was injured."

"Thanks, Clyde. She'll be okay. In fact, she's determined to go to the festival meeting this afternoon."

He made a face. "I guess if she can take it, I can, too."

"What do you mean?"

"Some of those people drive me crazy."

"I feel your pain," I said with sincerity.

"Yeah, thanks." He gave the broom a couple of sweeps. "It's not so bad when I'm just working with my own people, ordering books and stuff for the authors coming to the festival. But when I've got to meet with the rest of the committee heads, it can get ugly."

"I hear you." Feeling a little awkward, I coughed to clear my throat. "Look, what I really wanted to talk to you about is the book you gave me. *Little Women*."

He glanced up from his broom. "Not sure what you want to know. Tell you the truth, I just saw the book, noticed what kind of shape it was in, and thought that if you could fix it, I'd give it away at the auction. Didn't really look at the inside pages."

I couldn't believe that. Clyde was a book buyer and a booklover. How could he not be curious? "It was published in 1868, which makes it a first edition, but I think the cover has been updated. That might diminish its value slightly, but I still think it could be worth thousands of dollars if I do a good enough job on it. Oh, and it's supposed to have a second volume. Did you see one in that Grass Valley bookshop?"

"Nope."

Okay, that reaction sounded truthful.

"Did you pay a lot for it?"

"Nope."

"How much was it?"

"Rather not say." He suddenly got real busy staring at the floor. It was a wonder he had anything to sweep up since he kept his shop so clean. He was clearly avoiding eye contact with me. Which led me to believe, once again, that he had lied about where he got the book.

And I was shocked that he wouldn't tell me how much he'd paid for it.

"Clyde, what's up? I know you're not paying me to trace the provenance, but when I see a book like this one, I get curious. Like, where did it come from? Who owned it last? I want to know these things. Because I'm a book nerd, just like you."

The door opened and another customer walked in. Clyde looked relieved and immediately called out, "Be right with you!"

I exchanged a glance with Derek. Would Clyde take the opportunity to blow us off and go help the new customer?

"Hey, Clyde, it's just me," a voice said from behind us.

Derek and I both turned and I almost sagged with relief. "Gabriel."

"Hey, babe," he said. "Derek. You looking for books?"

"All the time," Derek said.

I smiled, happy that Gabriel was here to help us triple-team Clyde.

"We were just asking Clyde about the *Little Women* book he asked me to refurbish."

"Oh yeah. Neat book. Interesting story." He gazed at Clyde. "Brooklyn told me you got that book at the co-op in Grass Valley. Man, I would love to find a book like that in some out of the way place. How'd you get so lucky?"

Clyde shrugged. "It happens."

"Yeah." Gabriel's tone implied that asteroids also plowed into the earth, but it didn't happen often. "I plan to go back and take a closer look at their inventory. Which of the sellers did you get the book from?"

Clyde gave Gabriel a dirty look, then glared at me. "You people are nothing but trouble."

Feeling a twinge of guilt, I said, "I don't mean to trouble you, Clyde. I've always treasured your shop because I know you love books as much as I do. So that's why I was wondering about the copy of *Little Women*. But if you don't want to tell me, it's fine. I'll still fix it up nicely and it'll get a decent price at the silent auction."

"That's all I want," he muttered.

"I don't really believe that's all you want. You know as well as I do that if you want to get your money's worth, you'd be better off selling it to a rare-book expert or the Covington Library. They'll pay you what it's worth. Maybe ten or twelve thousand dollars, or even more after it's repaired."

Gabriel leaned against the counter and studied his nails. "So what's the deal, Clyde?"

He threw up his hands. "Aargh! You'll all be the death of me."

"It's just me, Clyde." I smiled at him and added, "And I definitely don't want to be the death of you."

"Humph," he grunted.

Gabriel took one step toward Clyde. "Who do I have to kick around to get an honest answer from you?"

Clyde's eyeballs widened. "Don't you go all tough guy on me."

"Gabriel," I said, slapping one hand out in front of him to stop him. "Cut it out."

He chuckled. "Come on, babe. Sometimes you gotta fight dirty."

"No we don't. Just forget we asked." I looked at Derek. "We should go."

"Chill, babe," Gabriel said. "This is just the way Clyde and I negotiate."

I blinked. "Really? By haranguing and threatening each other?"

"Works for us, right, Clyde? So where'd you get that book?"

"Yes," I said. "Please tell us where it came from."

Clyde let go of a huge sigh. "Fine. If it's any of your business, I got it from Lawson."

Well, that shut everyone up for a full minute. Maybe longer. I stared up at Derek, then shot a look at Gabriel. He didn't look as shocked as I felt, but he'd definitely been taken by surprise, I could tell.

I'd had enough of the stunned silence. "I hate to state the obvious, but Lawson is dead."

"Tell me about it," Clyde grumbled.

I still felt as though I'd been sucker punched. "Clyde, did you kill Lawson?"

"Aw, come on! Brooklyn, you know me better than that!"

"Just checking," I said. "When did he give you the book?"

"Right after the meeting," Clyde confessed. "You know, after Banyan threatened your mom. Lawson was freaking out because Banyan had attacked him, too."

You're nothing but a thief and a liar.

Was Banyan talking about the book or the festival funds? Or was there something else going on? I wondered. "I remember," I said.

"Yeah, well." Clyde leaned his elbow on the broom. "Lawson was really nervous, which was understandable. So after the meeting, he pulled me aside to show me the book and asked me to keep it."

I stared up at the ceiling for a moment, because I was seriously wondering what in the world was going on. Finally I asked, "When he said 'keep it,' did he mean 'keep it safe for him,' or did he mean, 'keep it, it's yours'?"

"He wanted me to hang onto it for a few days," Clyde insisted. "He was nervous. He knew it was worth a lot of money and he was worried that it might get stolen."

"Why would he think that?"

Clyde's cheeks puffed out as he exhaled heavily. "I don't know but somebody was trying to freak him out."

"Freak him out how?"

Clyde shrugged. "Calling his phone, and then hanging up. Throwing rocks through his window. Little stuff that was really putting him on edge."

I looked from Derek to Gabriel, and then frowned at Clyde. A rock thrown through a window hardly counted as *little stuff*, but that was just me. And who was to say those attacks had anything to do with the book?

"Was it Banyan?" Derek asked.

Clyde used his hands to emphasize his words. "I don't know!"

"Okay," I said calmly. "So he was being harassed. But why would he think it was connected with the book? I mean, we now know that he stole all of the festival funds. Maybe his harasser knew that he'd done that."

"He didn't say anything about the money," Clyde said. "He just wanted to make sure the book was safe."

"But then you gave it to me to refurbish. Did he know you were going to do that?"

"No, but he wouldn't have minded. You'd make it look a lot better than it did."

While that was true, I felt a little weird that Lawson hadn't known.

"Did he tell the police about the harassment?" Derek asked.

"I doubt it."

Gabriel shrugged. "Sounds like he didn't want the police to dig too deeply into his activities."

Clyde pointed at Gabriel. "Exactly."

"When you got the book, weren't you frightened?"

"Why would I be? Nobody knew I had it. I figured I'd give it to you to clean up and then I'd give it back to Lawson. But then they killed him, so I don't want it back. Bad juju. So I'll sell it in the silent auction. Get rid of it. Figured whoever was scaring the pants off of Lawson could maybe bid on it during the auction."

That might be one way to lure the killer into the light, I realized. Assuming that the killer actually cared about the book. He might've been after the festival funds and didn't know anything about the book. "So when you gave the book to me the other afternoon, Lawson was still alive."

"Yeah." He pressed his lips together in a tight frown. He looked downright miserable about losing his old friend.

"Are you sure nobody knows that Lawson gave the book to you?"

"Positive."

I carefully watched his every movement and expression as I asked the next question. "Do you think somebody knows that I have the book now?"

He shrugged. "I didn't tell anybody. Look, it's not that big of a deal."

I believed the part about him not telling anyone. But he was totally wrong about the part where it wasn't that big of a deal. Because to me it was a really big, really bad deal.

But thank God he hadn't told anyone else. That was something, I thought with relief. But another glance at Derek told me he wasn't feeling the same. No. In fact, he was getting more and more furious by the second, because he knew that having this book in my possession was putting me in jeopardy.

I'd been here before. In jeopardy, that is. My husband still hated it and, frankly, I wasn't really thrilled about it, either. I sighed. "Clyde, I have to ask you one more question. Was Lawson killed because of that book you gave me?"

"Huh?" Clyde just gawked at me for a really long moment, and then frowned deeply. "You crazy? No way. Lawson's dead because he stole the money from the festival committee. I gotta believe that." He glanced at Gabriel as if looking for corroboration, then turned to Derek for the same. Finally he stared at me like I was certifiably psycho-screwball-cuckoo crazy.

"I mean, come on," he continued. "We're talking about seventy thousand *smackaroos*! You said yourself the book's only worth twelve grand at most. So doesn't it make sense that he was killed over the committee money? Why would you think that a book, no matter how fancy it might be, would have anything to do with Lawson's death?"

I stared at Derek, who was still beyond angry, then gazed at Gabriel, who was chuckling at the sheer wacked-out absurdity of the situation.

I had to just shake my head. Right? Because anyone who knew me knew without a doubt that every time I'd ever been involved in a murder investigation, it *always* had to do with a book.

Chapter 11

Out on the street, we said goodbye to Gabriel.

"Call me if you need me," he said, then waved and walked off, his black leather duster brushing against his black leather boots, like a cowboy heading into the sunset.

I gazed up at Derek. "That went well."

He choked on a laugh. "Bad enough that your mother was being threatened, but now you're both in danger." He raked his hand through his hair, a sure sign that he was thoroughly frustrated.

"On the upside, we don't know for sure that I'm in danger this time."

He gave me one of those endearing looks that clearly said, *Brooklyn, my love, I'm not an idiot.*

"I'm so sorry." I laid one hand on his arm. "I really hate this."

"None of this is your fault, love."

It was sweet of him to say it, but I didn't really believe it. No matter what, somehow I always ended up in the middle of a mess. Good thing I was a bookbinder. Imagine what would have happened if I'd been something more dangerous. Like a hair stylist or something.

We started walking down the Lane, but something

made me stop. I stared at the crosswalk and realized we were standing directly across the street from where my mother had almost been killed.

"Let's cross the street," I said, and took a step toward the curb.

Derek grabbed my arm and pulled me back. "That's not a good idea."

I gazed up at him. "I know you would check out the scene if I wasn't with you, so let's just go and get it over with."

Derek knew it was useless to fight me so we crossed the street. He kept my arm firmly tucked in his, and when we reached the other side, I was really glad to have his support.

"There's blood," I whispered.

"Yes. She must've fallen right here." He pointed. "And this is where her knee scraped the surface."

I had to force myself to breathe steadily. This time it wasn't at the mere sight of blood, but because it was my mother's. Right there on the sidewalk.

There wasn't a lot of blood and I knew she hadn't been badly injured, but at that moment I wanted to kill Jacob Banyan.

"Let's go, sweetheart," Derek said quietly. "This won't help you."

"Yes, it will," I said, gazing up at him and nodding. "Really. I want to remember everything I see here because it'll give me the strength to fight this guy with all that's inside me. Knowing she was hurt . . . knowing that she was meant to be killed . . ." I took a deep breath and reached inside for the balance Mom was always talking about.

But it wouldn't come.

He stared at me and then nodded. "Then let's take

some time here. And I'll ask Gabriel to keep tabs on the police investigation."

"Good. But don't tell them about the book. They might take it."

I took a few minutes to imagine the scene. Stooping down, I touched the place on the sidewalk where my mother had scraped herself. And I counted the drops of blood. Six. It didn't seem like that many, but those drops ripped away at my heart. And I pictured my father, angry and frightened and helpless as my mother cried out in pain.

Everything in me yearned for payback. I knew it wasn't very civilized of me, but I didn't care. Someone had hurt my mom and they were going to pay.

After another moment, I looked up at Derek. "Thanks. We can go now."

We crossed the street and started walking toward the car. But when we reached the bakery, Derek stopped and checked his wristwatch.

I felt like I'd been sleepwalking. "What time is it?"

"Barely eleven. We've got plenty of time before we need to pick up your mother."

"Can we go home for a little while?" I asked. "Talking to Clyde wore me out."

"We have an agenda, darling," he said with purpose. "Let's go check out the dojo."

I'd frankly forgotten all about the dojo, but didn't say a word to Derek since he seemed to have figured that out already. I just hoped he wouldn't say anything to Alex about my little lapse in memory. She would kick my butt.

We walked past Warped and a few more shops, then turned on a side street. Three doors down from the corner was the Dharma Dojo.

I liked the place immediately. It was smaller than Alex's place in the city, but just as clean and organized as hers.

As we were looking around, a man walked out of an interior office and headed straight for us. He was about my height, five foot eight, with dark hair and an olive complexion. And while he didn't look like a bodybuilder, he was lean and muscular and solid. "Can I help you?"

"I sure hope so," I said.

"We'd like to sign up for a couple of self-defense classes," Derek said. "Refresher classes, actually."

"You're Alex's friends," he said.

"Right," I said with some relief. "You're Keith?"

"Yes."

I reached out to shake his hand. "I'm Brooklyn and this is Derek."

Derek shook Keith's hand. "Derek Stone."

"And you're Brooklyn Wainwright," Keith said, smiling now.

"I guess Alex already gave you our full names."

"No, she just said to be on the lookout for Brooklyn and Derek. But I recognized you as a Wainwright because of your sister China. She's one of my students. You look just like her."

I felt my eyes widen. "China takes classes here?"

"Yes. She's a green belt in tae kwon do."

I opened my mouth to respond, but I couldn't speak, I was so shocked. My younger sister was a *green* belt? I knew there were a bunch of different degrees and levels of proficiency within each color, but still, green was only two below a black belt. Holy moly. I clearly had some catching up to do. And I wanted to talk to China about this. Why hadn't she ever said anything to me?

China was good at so many things, I had to wonder if she had knitted her own green belt.

"That's lovely to hear, isn't it?" Derek said to me, and slipped his arm securely around my waist as if he expected me to slither to the floor in a dead faint. "Perhaps she can teach you a few moves."

"Uh, yeah." I shook my head to clear my brain. "Sure. Wow. I'm amazed. That's . . . fantastic."

I let Derek take care of the paperwork with Keith, setting up a schedule of classes every other day for the next week. By the time we were ready to leave the dojo, I had my act together, sort of.

Of course by this point, Keith probably thought I had taken a vow of silence or something. So I would have to make up for lost time.

"I really appreciate you fitting us into your schedule," I said brightly. "I'm looking forward to learning some new moves."

He gave a brief bow, as he would have if we'd just finished a session. "I look forward to having both of you in my dojo. And soon, Brooklyn, we'll have practiced enough simple moves that you'll be confident to defend yourself in any situation."

"That's our goal," Derek said, and bowed in the same way Keith had.

"Thank you so much, Keith," I said with a smile. "We'll see you tomorrow."

We walked in silence back to the Bentley. When we were sitting inside the car, I turned to Derek. "I can't believe my little sister is a green belt. I'm sort of blown away—as if you couldn't tell from my practically comatose behavior in there."

"It's quite an accomplishment," he said mildly.

"I know." I shook my head, still feeling a little bewildered. As far as I knew, China had never been interested in self-defense. What else was going on in her life that I was clueless about? I'd have to find out. "And I just now realized I'm jealous of her."

"You could get there, too," he said. "If that's what you want, you can have it. I've never known anyone as determined and talented as you."

I gave him a smile for that. Honestly, he was the best husband ever.

"I always thought I just wanted to learn enough to be able to kick someone's butt." I laughed sheepishly. "But now I want to learn more. I want to be as good as China." I thought about it for another few seconds and realized that I meant every word. "But also, I guess I want her to be proud of me." I gazed at him. "And you, too. Is that weird?"

"Not at all. It's natural. But darling, I *am* proud of you. So proud. Still, anything that motivates you to improve yourself is a good thing."

"You sound like Keith."

He smiled. "I'll take that as a compliment. I liked his philosophy."

"It was definitely a compliment," I assured him.

"Brooklyn, dearest," he said, his fingers softly stroking my cheek. "I want you to be able to kick someone's butt if they're a danger to you. But I also will support you if you want to keep going toward a green belt. Even if you simply want to rub your sister's nose in it."

I laughed. "That would be a definite side benefit."

He started the engine. "Let's go see how your mother is doing."

My mother was just fine. More than fine, really, if you didn't count the ugly bruises underneath her sweater and long pants. She was antsy and ready to get out of the house.

"How are you doing, Dad?" I asked, and gave him a hug.

"I'm groovy," he said. "I'm just glad that your mom's feeling better. It was a little scary there for a while."

"You can say that again," I murmured, and hugged him once more for good measure.

"But I'm fine now," Mom insisted, and glanced up at the clock. "We should get going."

"All right." I looked at my father. "We're taking off. You're going to your meeting at the winery soon?"

"Yeah. I'll be there all afternoon." He gave Mom a gentle kiss on the cheek. "I'll see you later, baby."

"I'm not fragile," she said, pulled Dad back, and kissed him on the lips with a resounding smack.

"All righty then," I said, and started for the door. "See you later, Dad."

"Take care of your mother."

I raised my hand in acknowledgment. "We'll watch her like a hawk."

I forced my mother to sit in the front seat again and climbed into the back, taking her tote bag with me.

"Thank you, Derek, for driving with me."

"Of course, Rebecca."

I spoke up. "You know, Mom, you might think about going back to the scene of your accident later."

"Oh, sweetie, I'm not sure I can face it."

"It might not be easy for you. I did it just a while ago and it was hard. But it's right out in front of Savannah's restaurant, Mom. I think we should wave a little white sage around to clean up the negative vibes."

She didn't say anything for a moment, then I heard a sniffle.

"Mom? You okay?"

"I'm just so proud of you for suggesting that," she said. "And yes, if we have time after the meeting, I would love to go and banish all of that negativity. It's important. I should've thought of it myself."

"You've had a few things on your mind."

She laughed lightly. "I suppose I have."

In the rearview mirror, Derek met my gaze and nodded in approval. And that made me very happy, even though I was still a little amazed that I'd been the one to bring up the subject of banishment spells to my mother.

Good grief. Since when had I ever suggested sage waving and wacko spellcasting? Since never. No, I was simply nervous about her safety and knew how to make her feel better. Yeah. That was it. Nothing more to see here.

"I'm just so worried about the festival," Mom confessed as we drove up the Lane toward the town hall.

"Because of the money?"

"Yes." She shook her head and let go of a heavy sigh. "I heard from the porta-potty company."

"That sounds like a fun conversation."

"It wasn't," she said flatly. "Our check bounced and they won't deliver any porta-potties if we don't pay up."

"That's serious," I murmured.

"You bet your sweet bippy it's serious. We're expecting at least five thousand people to show up in a few days and we can't have them wandering into the woods to drop trou."

"Whoa, Mom!"

Derek laughed out loud.

They were both having a good laugh at my reaction, but what could I say? My mom was never boring.

*   *   *

We parked outside of the town hall and Mom turned and smiled at us. "I have a quick surprise for both of you."

Derek and I exchanged a look. "I'm not sure I can take any more surprises."

"You'll like this one, sweetie."

"Okay. Lead the way."

"It's right over here," she said, and walked across the street to the small park situated in the middle of Berkeley Circle. The festival booths were starting to be erected along the Circle drive itself and they looked so pretty and festive in their alternating pastel shades of blue, pink, yellow, and white. Each booth held two utility tables and several folding chairs, and I couldn't wait to get started decorating my booth with colorful tablecloths and posters. And lots of books, naturally.

The booths faced the central park where the pretty gazebo in the middle of the Green would act as the children's stage where musicians, magicians, and characters would perform.

There were dozens of chairs and benches already set up along the periphery for any visitors who needed to take a break from the festivities. If we could figure out the financing, the porta-potties would be set up in a long line along the northern edge of the Circle.

Mom checked her watch. "We may need to move your car if the meeting lasts longer than two hours."

"I'll take care of it," Derek said amiably.

"It's kind of exciting, watching everything get set up," I said, weaving my arm through my mother's.

"Yes," she said, sounding wistful. "Almost two years of planning and it all begins in a matter of days."

Mom kept walking.

"So where are we headed?" I asked again.

"Just over here," she pointed. "By the festival entrance."

But before we reached the entrance, I heard a familiar voice.

"Yoo-hoo! Brooklyn! Derek!"

"Oh!" My eyes lit up at the sound. And that's when I saw them. I looked up at Derek and he grinned. We would recognize that lovely Indian accent anywhere.

"It's Vinnie and Suzie!" I jogged over and grabbed them both in a group hug. "It's so good to see you."

Derek came up right behind me and wrapped all of us in his arms. "Wonderful to see you both." He looked down at Lily sitting in the baby stroller. "I mean, all three of you."

They had officially adopted the little girl almost two years ago, after their best friends, Lily's parents, were killed in a traffic accident.

"Hey, kiddo," Suzie said, punching my arm. "How you doin'?"

"Oh, Brooklyn," Vinnie said in her delightful lilting accent. "You look so good. And Derek, what a delight."

Then she straightened up and smiled and nodded to my mother. "Hello, Mrs. Wainwright. What a pleasure to see you again."

"So formal, Vinnie." Mom laughed and grabbed her in a hug. "It's wonderful to see you, too."

Suzie swung her arm around Mom's shoulders. "Sorry, you won't get much formality from me. How's things, Mrs. Wainwright?"

"Couldn't be better." Mom was still laughing as she gave Suzie a hug. "I'm so glad you're here."

"We are, too." The two women both wore their signature outfits of torn jeans, leather vests, chains, and black boots.

Derek knelt down to get eye to eye with little Lily. No leather and chains for her; she wore a frilly pink dress with pink leggings and pink tennis shoes. Derek glanced up. "She is gorgeous."

"Yes, she is," Vinnie murmured.

Derek rubbed Lily's chubby cheek with his knuckles and the little girl simply stared, mesmerized by his handsome face.

"Dak," she said on a sigh. It was close to "Derek."

I understood completely. Lily was already half in love with Derek and who wouldn't be?

Suzie laughed. "You have a fan, Derek."

I smiled. What female wouldn't love it when a man like Derek Stone touched her cheek that way?

I stooped down in front of Lily. "Hello, angel."

"Book!" Lily squealed, giving me a grin. I loved her nickname for me. She couldn't quite manage "Brooklyn," so she called me "Book." And that was way appropriate, I thought.

"My Lily girl," I said. "You look beautiful!"

Lily patted her pink hair ribbon and preened a bit. "Tankoo."

"You're welcome."

Then I listened to an incomprehensible list of news items from the tiny girl before I finally stood up, smiling.

Vinnie hugged me again. "The two of you have such a special relationship."

I loved their adopted daughter to pieces. "We relate on a whole different plane."

Suzie snickered. "That's one way to put it."

"So where are they putting your sculpture?" I asked.

Suzie pointed. "Over there. They're using it right at the main entrance. It's up on a pedestal." Her voice held a ring of pride, and who could blame her? As incredibly talented chainsaw artists, Suzie and Vinnie had created some of the most beautiful pieces I'd ever seen. This one was no exception.

I stared at the large piece of sculpted burl wood in the shape of an open book. The thing was massive; at least ten feet across and five or six feet high. "Wow. It's fantastic."

"Let's go get a better look at it," Mom said, and once again led the way to the festival entrance where Berkeley Circle began.

The sculpture depicted a huge open book with pages fluttering like a fan. The pages were each as thin as an actual piece of paper and I could see words carved into them.

"It's ingenious," I whispered, circling the imposing piece, admiring their skill. How they managed to create something so beautiful out of wood with a chainsaw was simply impossible for me to comprehend. "And it's huge. I love that they put it right out front."

"I'm just thrilled," Mom said after a long moment of studying the piece. "It makes such a wonderful statement for our very first book festival."

"Hey, it's a book," Suzie said, grinning. "And it's at a book festival. Makes sense."

"It sure does," Mom said, laughing as she touched Suzie's arm. "But it's so much more than just a book."

In the last few years, Vinnie and Suzie's work had won awards and acclaim at art shows around the country. They billed themselves as the chainsaw-wielding lesbians, and one reason their style was so unique and revelatory was because even though they sculpted in heavy burl wood, they had the talent to turn the massive rustic chunks into the most delicate pieces imaginable.

I could still picture their last significant piece: a ten-foot-tall woman, whose hair billowed in the wind. Each strand of hair was only as thick as actual human hair. It was stunning.

"It's simply brilliant," Derek said. "Your genius grows with every new work."

Vinnie sniffed. "It is so touching to hear you say it, Derek. You bring tears to my eyes."

Suzie tugged Vinnie over to her side for a hard hug. "Everything brings on the waterworks lately."

"Why is that, Vinnie?" I asked, concerned that she might be sick.

"Because Lily is no longer a baby," Vinnie explained. "She's almost three years old and a big girl now. She starts preschool after the New Year."

"Wow," I said. "She's growing up so fast."

"We will be empty nesters in a few months," Vinnie cried. "What will we do? How will we live?"

"Empty nesters for three hours a day, Vin," Suzie corrected.

"How will we fill our time?" Vinnie was practically wailing.

Suzie shrugged. "We can always play bingo at the senior center."

Vinnie moaned and we all laughed.

"Come on you guys," I said. "You're younger than I am."

"Still, the time passes." Vinnie sniffed again, then waved her hand. "I'd rather not talk about it."

Suzie gave Vinnie a quick kiss. "She gets emotional."

"You do, too, Suzie. But you hide it better in public."

Suzie winked at me. "Gotta maintain my tough-chick persona." She flexed her muscles and we all laughed some more.

"It's really good to see you guys." I glanced at my mother. "But we have to get my mom to her meeting."

"We will be here all weekend," Vinnie said. "Perhaps we can get together for a meal."

"We would love that," I said. "I'll give you a call."

Mom had barely called the committee meeting to order when Saffron began to wail. "We'll have to cancel everything!"

"Calm down, Saffron," Mom said, pounding the gavel on the table. "We have a lot to talk about today and we can't do it if people start freaking out."

As if on cue, everyone began to speak and Mom banged the gavel a few more times. Then she rubbed her head and it was obvious that she was getting a headache.

If this continues, I thought, *I'll grab that gavel and cancel the damn meeting myself.* As it was now, Mom wouldn't get anything done if everyone kept blathering over each other. *She's so fragile right now*, I thought. But I would never say so to her face, knowing she would fight me.

Derek leaned up close to me and whispered, "I can see every muscle in your body on red alert. Are you all right?"

"I want to help her."

"I do, too. But honestly, she's handling it quite well. And we don't want to diminish her authority."

He was right, darn it. I watched Mom for another half minute, then said, "Okay, I won't charge the table just yet."

"Good girl. If you feel that you might need to, let me know and I'll make the charge with you."

I squeezed his hand, so grateful that he was mine.

"Winston," Mom said, "Did you speak with the bank?"

"I did."

"Can you give us a report?"

Winston gave a summary of his conversation with the vice president of the bank. "The money is definitely gone, and since the person who withdrew it was the same person that was listed on the account, namely Lawson, there's nothing the bank can do for us."

"Thank you," Mom said. "Sue, did you talk to any of our underwriters?"

"I spoke with the president of the Friends of the Library. She's devastated by our loss, but she also told me that their forty-thousand-dollar contribution was insured by their insurance company."

"What?" Saffron sounded like she didn't believe what she'd just heard.

"But that's great news," Jan said.

Marybeth pounded on the table. "Fantastic!"

"Yeah, so that's the good news," Sue said. "The bad news is that they can't give us any more money until their insurance company pays them the funds. And that'll take a while. So we're out of luck there."

"The Friends of the Library has a booth at the festival," Saffron said. "Can't we threaten to cancel their booth if they don't give us more money?"

"Oh dear lord," Jan said, turning to look at Saffron as if she had two heads. A shame she didn't, really, since one of them might have had some sense. "Are you insane?"

"Criminally insane is more like it," Clyde grumbled.

Despite our strange discussion earlier that morning, I was happy to see Clyde and gave him a thumbs-up. He grinned back at me and it was a rare but welcome sight.

"Saffron, please," Mom said with infinite patience. "We're not going to threaten anyone in order to obtain the money. I think that's called bribery, or maybe extortion."

"Good gravy," Jan muttered loudly, shaking his head.

"Besides," Mom continued. "This is a *book* festival. The Friends of the Library organization supports books and reading. Why would we want to do that to them? They weren't the ones who lost the money."

I leaned over and whispered to Derek. "What would you think about offering to give the festival the money they need?"

He simply stared at me, clearly stunned.

I gulped, frankly surprised at his reaction. "I take it you're not thrilled by the idea."

"I'm simply surprised. I didn't realize you were thinking along those lines."

I shrugged. "I thought about it earlier, but then got distracted and forgot to mention it. But now that we're here and listening to everyone and worrying about Mom and the fate of the festival . . . And well, I'll talk to the lawyers, but it could be considered a business expense, right? Because it's all about books. So what do you think? It's not a completely horrible idea, is it?"

"Not at all." He slowly smiled. "It's lovely. And by the way, it's not up to me. You have plenty of your own funds at your disposal."

I squeezed his hand. "I know. But we're a team."

He grinned and wrapped his arms around me. He kissed my cheek and said, "Yes we are. And I think it's a brilliant idea."

"Okay, when there's a break in the conversation, I'll bring it up."

"Bring it up now," he suggested. "Your mother can use an infusion of good news."

I grinned at him, then stood. "Excuse me, I'd like to speak to the committee."

Mom turned and stared, looking almost as shocked as Derek had been a minute ago. "What is it, sweetie?"

"I wish to submit an idea or a proposal or whatever you want to call it."

"Don't call it anything, just say it," Clyde said.

I laughed self-consciously. "I'm new at this. So okay, here's the deal. Derek and I want to contribute seventy thousand dollars to the festival fund."

There was complete silence in the room. Mom blinked and stammered, and I thought she might faint. But she finally managed to get the words out. "Sweetie, that's very generous but you can't do that. It's too much money."

"Mom, remember Abraham?"

She blinked again, and then suddenly she whispered, "Oh."

I smiled. I guess she had forgotten that my bookbinding mentor Abraham had left his entire estate to me when he died.

Needless to say, seventy thousand was a mere drop in the bucket. Okay, not really. It was a lot of money for almost anyone. Most days, I forgot that I had that kind of money in the bank. And I certainly didn't make frivolous expenditures, like a fancy sports car or a pied-à-terre on the Boulevard Saint-Germain.

Last year, Derek and I had purchased the charming three-story Victorian building across the street from our apartment. It was known as the Courtyard Shops and it contained eight lovely shops and restaurants as well as apartments on the two upper floors. Our lawyers had considered it a wise investment since the building would've been torn down and replaced by soulless condos that would've diminished our property values and destroyed the spirt of the neighborhood.

But other than the Courtyard Shops, I hadn't spent a dime of Abraham's money. The money sat in an investment fund and made more money for me. It was weird.

"So, it's settled," I said. "Call the porta-potty guy and get those things rolling."

Mom sniffed and smiled. "I'll call them as soon as we take a break."

"Thank you, Brooklyn," Winston said quietly.

Sue grinned. "You're a peach, girl."

Clyde gave me a thumbs-up and nodded proudly.

There was a commotion in the hall and the door suddenly banged open. And Jacob Banyan walked in.

I jumped up, ready to accuse him of attempted murder. Derek grabbed my hand and I managed to resist pouncing, but just barely.

"Mr. Banyan," Mom said calmly, "you're disrupting our meeting, as usual. Please leave now or I'll call the police."

"You won't call anyone." His voice was low and sinister. "I hear your little festival is broke. No money. I'd help you out, but I would need a little something in return."

Mom played it cool. "And what would that be?"

I seriously wondered how she could be so calm. Was it all that deep breathing she did?

"It's simple," Banyan said. "I'll give the festival one hundred thousand dollars, and all I want is a booth." He tucked his hands into his pants pockets and rocked on his heels, obviously enjoying being in what he thought was the driver's seat. "See? It won't cost you a thing."

Mom snorted. "Except our reputation, our pride, our honor, our dignity, our self-respect, our—"

"All right, all right!" he shouted, frustration dripping from every word. "That's enough. I can pay for this festival without breaking a sweat. You need my money."

"No, we don't," Mom said calmly, and her lips curved in a beautiful, delighted smile.

His eyes narrowed in on her, and he ignored her words and just said, "Now that I think about it, I do want one more thing."

He swaggered over to my mother and pointed his finger right in her face. "I want *you* off this committee."

My mother smacked his finger out of her face and seemed to enjoy his frustrated expression.

I happened to catch a glimpse of Saffron. She sat on the edge of her chair, almost shaking with . . . what? Excitement? Fear? Had she been the one to tell Banyan that the money had been stolen? How had he found out? Did Lawson tell him? Was that why Banyan had said what he said?

You're nothing but a thief and a liar.

Had Saffron told Banyan to make his money offer conditional on getting rid of my mother so she could take over? Did she really think the rest of the committee would put up with her constant whining and inability to concentrate for more than ten seconds?

Clearly, Saffron hadn't expected me to make my offer. And certainly not before her man Banyan had a chance to impress everyone with his generous proposition.

After another minute of chaos, Mom banged the gavel and called the meeting back to order.

She looked directly at the blowhard standing in front of her in his fancy dark suit and power tie and spoke clearly so everyone in the room would hear. "I want to thank Mr. Banyan for his generous offer, but we won't need your money, sir. We already received an offer before yours and I accepted it on behalf of the committee."

He was stunned into silence for half a second, then he exploded. "That's a bunch of crap. You're lying."

"That's not acceptable language here, sir," Mom said in that edgy schoolmarm voice I was so familiar with.

"Do I care?"

"No more than I do for you," she countered, taking the wind out of his sails. "Look, Mr. Banyan," she tried again, her voice even. "Dharma is a small town. We all love it here and we welcome newcomers with open arms—unless they prove themselves to be unpleasant or even dangerous to others. You, sir, are a dangerous man with evil intentions."

"You ain't seen nothin' yet," he muttered.

"So you admit you attempted to kill me?"

"What? You're out of your mind." His eyes narrowed. "But it's not such a bad idea."

"You're a big jerk," Sue said.

"Who asked you?" Banyan said, practically growling the words.

"You're mean and you're a bully," Mom said. "And frankly, Mr. Banyan, you're a distraction. We just don't have time to deal with you and your nastiness. We've only got a few more days before we put on a major book festival and a full-scale musical production."

"I don't give a hoot about that stupid musical." He gave a harsh laugh. "A bunch of amateurs and one pathetic over-the-hill actress who couldn't sing her way out of a paper bag."

"That's uncalled for," Winston said.

I caught a quick glimpse of poor Ryan, who looked devastated. He pushed away from the table and shakily got to his feet. Was he going to faint? Had anyone ever said something like that about Shandi in front of him? I hoped he knew Banyan was full of hot air. The man had a need to lash out at anything standing in his way.

"How dare you, sir!" Ryan said, sounding like Dudley Do-Right protecting his fair lady.

"Buzz off," Banyan snarled, and turned back to face Mom. "Look, all I want is a booth at the damn festival to sell my wine."

"Dude, what you're selling isn't wine," Jan argued.

Banyan rounded on Jan. "Who asked you?"

"That's enough." Mom stepped forward and pointed to the door. "You need to go. Now. Thank you and have a good day."

Mom's attempt to be pleasant was lost on Banyan. Everyone in the room watched and wondered what he would do now. Clearly, he didn't intend to go anywhere.

I watched his jaw clenching tighter and tighter, and it reminded me of a torque wrench my father once used to tighten a bolt on his tire. He pushed it one click too far and the bolt cracked and the threads were stripped.

Banyan was about to crack.

I gave Derek a quick glance. We both knew that Banyan wouldn't leave voluntarily and I was starting to worry that he might actually try to hurt my mother, right here in front of witnesses.

He moved even closer and bared his teeth at her. "I warned you more than once that your smart mouth would get you in trouble."

"And you'd be smart to back off," Mom said. "The police already suspect you of attacking me."

"They're barking up the wrong tree."

My mother stared at him, not backing down. "Are you married, Mr. Banyan?"

"What?" His scowl grew even darker. "No, you idiot."

She nodded. "I'm not surprised."

"You . . ." He raised his fist and everyone gasped.

There was a blur of movement and Derek was across the room and gripping Banyan by the back of his shirt before anyone else could move. "That's the last time you threaten a member of my family," Derek said.

"Hey!" Banyan howled, twisting and squirming to get away from Derek. "Leggo of me!"

Derek said nothing else and just shoved him toward the door and out of the room. We heard Banyan's shouts and cursing until Derek shut the door and locked it.

For five full seconds there was complete silence. Then nearly everyone stood and applauded. It was the shock of seeing someone physically confront the worst bully in town that did it.

Derek calmly brushed his shirt back into place and walked over to stand next to me. I grabbed his hand and squeezed it.

"Wow," Jan said breathlessly. "Amazing job. You're a real hero."

"You rock!" Sue cried.

Ryan stayed seated, looking dazed. I wondered if he was pleased by Derek's actions or jealous that he hadn't been the one brave enough to kick the guy out of the room.

I watched Clyde stand and raise his fist in a "power to the people" sign. Like so many others in town, he was an old hippie and now he simply grinned in triumph at the defeat of "the man."

I wanted to laugh, but gazing at other expressions around the table sobered me up real fast. Especially Saffron's. Her lips were pressed together in suppressed anger.

Mom ran over and threw her arms around Derek. "Thank you, sweetie."

He patted her warmly on the back. "It was my distinct pleasure, Rebecca."

I thought she might burst into tears so I reached for my purse to find a tissue. But instead, Mom moved her shoulders to some inner rhythm only she could hear.

I wouldn't have been surprised to see her start doing a boogie around the room, but instead, she gave a weak smile and sat down. And I was reminded that she had suffered a concussion the night before. Banyan could've made things even worse, yelling at her like that.

I started to move toward her, thinking that maybe she'd want us to take her home. But instead, she picked up her gavel, banged it on the table two times, and said, "I'm ordering the porta-potties today, people. So let's get this potty started!"

Chapter 12

On the return trip to Mom's house I sat in the back seat and called our lawyer to ask him to expedite the transfer of funds from my investment account to my bank so I could start writing checks. It sounded so official and I guess it was, but mostly I was just thankful that Abraham had gifted me with enough money to use for good things. So many of us had been pushing for a book festival for years, and now I could be a part of making it happen.

Meanwhile, Mom made the call to the rental company and told the guy that she had a new source of funds and would hand him a cashier's check when he delivered his porta-potties to Dharma.

When she ended the call, Mom made some notes in her book, then said cautiously, "I'll need a check for ten thousand dollars. Are you still up for doing that?"

I smiled. "Mom, I'm doing this." *But wow, porta-potties aren't cheap, are they?* For that kind of money they should at least come with air fresheners.

"Oh, sweetie, you have saved our lives. I'll never be able to thank you enough."

"Hey, I'm part of this festival, too, right?"

"A very important part," she said firmly. "You always were."

I leaned forward in the seat and patted her arm. "Our lawyer said it was a great idea to give you guys the money because I'll be investing in my hometown, supporting literacy, and getting an excellent tax write-off for my business."

"Wow. You're a triple threat." She laughed. "Well, then, I guess we're back on track."

"You bet we are." I gave her shoulder a light squeeze, and then sat back in the seat. "So let's get this potty started."

Mom giggled. "That was a good one, wasn't it?"

"Superior," Derek said. At a stop sign, he turned to look at Mom. "Would you like to stop by Arugula and take care of those negative vibes now?"

I had to smile. Derek rarely mentioned the word *vibes*, and never spoke of auras and enchantment spells and such. But for my mother, he was willing to get into the groove. It choked me up and made me love him all over again.

She laid her hand on Derek's arm. "Don't think too badly of me, sweetie, but I really just want to go home and rest. I promise I'll do it tomorrow."

"Rebecca, it is impossible to think badly of you. I'll drive you home now."

I leaned forward again. "Honestly, Mom, I'm surprised you're still standing after putting up with Saffron shooting daggers out of her eyes, and then that horrible Jacob Banyan threatening you for the tenth time. And let's not forget Lawson's murder, and then there's the pilfering of seventy thousand dollars. No big deal."

She shook her head and made a *tsk-tsk* sound. "When you put it all together, it sounds so awful."

"It *is* awful. Really awful. Especially Jacob Banyan. I'm sure he's responsible for your injuries last night. And good grief, he almost assaulted you this afternoon."

"Thank goodness for Derek," Mom whispered.

I patted Mom's arm. "I say that ten times a day."

Derek snorted. "Only ten times, darling?"

Mom laughed and it was a wonderful sound.

"Make that eleven," I said, grateful that he'd made Mom laugh.

Derek turned and gazed at me, his lips twisted in an almost sheepish smile. "That's quite enough."

"I'm just going to close my eyes for a few minutes," Mom murmured, and turned toward the passenger side window.

I leaned in close and whispered in Derek's ear, "Thank you for protecting my mother."

"She's mine, too," he said, low enough that only I heard him. My heart was almost too full to handle his words, so I just stroked his arm until the light turned green and he had to go back to concentrating on driving.

Unbidden, I had a sudden image of Jacob Banyan raising his fist at my mother and Derek rushing with lightning speed to stop him. I would never forget that moment.

But it brought home the stark fact that Banyan was a menace and Mom was in real danger.

And she wasn't the only one, I realized all over again. If Clyde was wrong and Banyan had killed Lawson Schmidt over the *Little Women* book, it meant that I might be in mortal danger, too.

Again.

Still, I couldn't see that oversized knucklehead Banyan wanting anything to do with an old, beat-up copy of *Little Women*. But maybe he knew how much Lawson had wanted the book and what he'd done to obtain it. Thievery? Lying? Had Banyan tried to blackmail him? Was that why Lawson had stolen the festival money?

The only thing I knew for sure was that I was spinning around in circles with more questions than answers.

After making sure that Dad was home from his meeting, we dropped Mom off and drove down to our place to check on Charlie, give her some hugs, and freshen her food and water. We warmed up our breakfast tacos— which were even yummier than they'd been that morning—and had a glass of wine before changing into warmer clothes for the evening. I grabbed my down vest and Derek pulled on his worn leather jacket, and then we drove back to the Lane and walked three blocks to the theater next door to the town hall.

The actors were mid-rehearsal when we arrived so we walked quietly down the red-carpeted aisle and sat in the third row from the stage. There were a few people scattered throughout the audience who were dressed in vintage costumes so I figured they were cast members who weren't in this scene.

I looked around for my sister London but didn't see her anywhere.

"London must be backstage," I whispered to Derek.

"She's sitting in the back row, love," he said. "There are two men with her."

"She is?" It was so dark back there that I had to squint to see anything. Sure enough, I spied my youngest sister sitting with two others in the very last row. "You are so much more observant than I am."

Of course he was, I thought. Derek had been with MI6, the British version of the CIA. If he didn't notice people sitting behind him in the dark, it could mean his life.

I wondered if London, as the play's director, was checking to make sure that the actors on stage were projecting their voices well enough to be heard in the farthest back rows.

Or maybe she was just back there gossiping without being overheard by anyone else.

I turned back to watch the action on stage, just as Annie walked out and began to sing. "Oh goodie, I think this is where she dies."

Derek leaned over and whispered, "She has a lovely voice."

I grinned, ridiculously proud. "She really does."

When the song ended and Annie lay down on the couch, pulled the thick blanket up, and fell asleep—and died?—I couldn't help but applaud loudly. I was so impressed!

Annie sat up in her death bed and grinned.

From the back of the theater, London said, "Brooklyn, stop disrupting the actors."

"Yes, ma'am." I could tell she wasn't really angry with me. At least I hoped not. My baby sister had a tyrannical streak—which probably made her an excellent director.

"That sounded good from back here, Annie," London yelled as she walked down the aisle toward the stage. "Let's take five, everybody."

I stood up as London approached. She looked beautiful, as always. She wasn't capable of looking bad. It was an impossibility. She wore her hair in silly pigtails and she still looked amazing. She had always been adorable, which made her the perfect foil for our jokes and ridicule growing up. It was for a good cause, my sisters and I had argued, because we'd helped her develop a spine. And a sense of humor.

I loved her to death.

Halfway down the aisle she took off running and grabbed me in a powerful hug.

"It's so good to see you," she whispered, then turned and gave Derek a hug. "Hi, Derek."

"Hello, London," he said. "Everything looks fantastic."

"Thanks. It's amazing how much talent we have around here."

I watched the two men from the back row amble over to the stage. "Who are those two guys you were sitting with?"

"Sound and lighting. We're checking the view and the sound from different spots in the audience."

"You're so smart," I said. "It's always a shock."

"Very funny. A bookbinder comedian." She grabbed my hands and squeezed. "So how are you, really? We were so worried when your college friend was killed. And then those horrible people showed up at your wedding."

I waved off her concerns. "We haven't thought about that in months." I wasn't about to fill her in on the three murders we'd dealt with since then. "We're doing fine and we're so happy, aren't we, Derek?"

Derek kissed my hand. "Blissfully happy, my love."

"That's so sweet," London said, pressing her hands to her heart. But then she frowned. "Oh, we heard about that person who was killing Derek's friends."

"That's old news, and we weren't in any danger," I lied. Patting her cheeks, I changed the subject, saying, "You look awful, as usual."

She laughed, automatically assuming I was kidding.

I was, of course, but it was so annoying that she knew how beautiful she was. But then, London was beautiful on the inside, too, and thought the same of all her sisters and brothers. But she was still fun to tease.

"How are the twins?" I asked. More proof that London was an overachiever was the fact that she'd given birth to beautiful twins, Chloe and Connor. We had to give her grief for that, of course.

"They're adorable," she said softly. "They're learning Japanese."

"But they're only four years old."

"That's the best time to learn. Anyway, I'm going to miss them terribly because I'll be staying at Mom and Dad's for the next few days so I don't have to drive back and forth from Calistoga every night. Trevor's bringing the kids into Dharma on Friday for the festival."

"They'll love that. So how's the play going?" I asked. "Annie sounds great. And the costumes are fabulous."

"Everyone's doing so well, and it's so much fun working with Shandi. She's such a pro."

"Really?" I asked, and glanced up at Derek. "Well, that's good to hear. I'm glad."

"You sound surprised. Why would you doubt it?"

"You hear stories." I shrugged. "You know, the Diva throwing her weight around. Stuff like that."

"Oh, no. She's a pussycat."

"Okay. Good to know." I glanced around. "Have you met Ryan?"

She practically cooed with pleasure. "Isn't he a cutie-pie? So attentive to Shandi. She was super lucky to find that one."

I smiled. "You make it sound like he's her boyfriend."

She laughed. "Oh, gosh no, he's much too young for her. I just mean that he's a really good assistant."

"I think so, too. We've seen him at Mom's committee meetings."

"He's a true advocate for Shandi," Derek said.

I nodded, then glanced around some more. "I thought we'd see him here tonight."

"Oh, he's around here somewhere. Probably in Shandi's dressing room. He's always taking notes and making lists for her."

"Is Shandi here?" I asked. "We would love to meet her."

"She'll be here later. She had to run out to meet someone. Apparently it was important because she's never missed a rehearsal."

"That's too bad." I lowered my voice. "I don't know if Mom told you, but Ryan asked Mom to try and talk you into recasting Shandi in the role of Jo."

"Oh, that would never happen," London insisted. "Shandi's perfect as Marmee. It's like she was made for that role."

"Really? Ryan said that Shandi felt the character was too old for her. He said it's not a big enough role for her fans. And, you know, she doesn't like playing the mother of four girls."

"I have no clue where Ryan got that idea."

Probably from Shandi, I thought, but didn't say so.

London looked around to make sure they weren't overheard. "I'm sure Shandi's vanity would prefer that she play a younger character, but she's just right to play the mother. And honestly, she's never said a word to me about it."

"Maybe she didn't want to complain to the director so she asked Ryan to work out the problem without getting her involved."

"Maybe." London shook her head. "But aside from

all that, I don't see why she would want to change roles at this point. Everyone's comfortable with each other and, honestly, it's a really great role. She gets to sing the most beautiful, heartbreaking song in the show. And she looks gorgeous in her costumes."

"I'm glad to hear that." I touched her arm. "And I'm sorry if I worried you."

"Hey, no worries." She grinned. "Besides, what would I do at this point? I'm not going to switch things around less than a week before the performance."

I smiled. "That's what I figured." I glanced around again. "Really, everything looks so fabulous. Who knew you could pull off something like this?"

"It's a shocker to me, too."

We both laughed. It was fun to hear her goof on herself.

"We're looking forward to opening night," Derek said.

She grinned. "Me, too."

"I know you need to get back to work," I said. "We'll just sit and enjoy the show for a few more minutes, if that's okay."

"Stay as long as you want," she said, and gave us both hugs. "Hey, I can't wait to hear your wine and book pairings this weekend."

"I'm pretty excited about that, too." Before she left us, I asked, "If you're staying with Mom and Dad, I guess you heard about their accident."

"Yes. But it doesn't sound like an accident, does it?"

I frowned. "No."

She sighed. "They seem to be doing pretty well in spite of their bumps and bruises. But I'll keep an eye on them."

"Good. I'm glad you're staying there."

"Me, too. Ciao," she said with a smile, and hurried away, up the steps to the stage, where she disappeared behind the side curtain.

A minute later, China appeared from behind the curtain and shielded her eyes from the bright stage lights. "Brooks?"

"Here we are," I said, and waved.

My siblings and I had all been named for the various towns and places where my dedicated Deadhead parents had conceived or given birth to each of us. China was named after China Lake, where my parents attended a protest march at the Naval Air Weapons Station.

China walked downstage and took the steps. "I'm glad you guys made it."

"We wouldn't miss it." We jumped up and met her halfway, and there were hugs all around.

"The costumes are lovely, China," Derek said.

"Aw, thanks, Derek." She squeezed his arm affectionately. "I can't take all the credit. I've got some of my most talented customers helping me with them."

"That was smart of you," I said. "It must mean that you're pretty talented yourself."

She smiled and fanned herself. "I do try."

I laughed, then changed the subject. "Have you seen Mom and Dad?"

"I talked to Mom on the phone and I went to see Dad." She took a deep breath and let it out. "He's feeling much better about Mom's prognosis."

"Yeah, she's pretty tough." I gazed at her. "So, Derek and I signed up to take some classes with Keith at the Dharma Dojo."

Her eyes widened. "You met Keith? Did you know he's my teacher?"

"Not until he told us." I narrowed my eyes at her and

China grinned. "How long have you been studying there? And why didn't you ever tell me you were a green belt?"

She shrugged. "I've been studying for about five years and got my green belt in May. It wasn't a secret or anything," she said. "It just never came up, you know?"

Whoa. Five years. I had some catching up to do.

"I had no idea," I said. "And I'm really jealous. So I'm warning you, I'm going to beef up my training and one day I'll come after you and take you down."

She snorted. "You can try." Then she laughed and grabbed both of my arms. "Seriously, I hope you do it. There's no better feeling than knowing that you can protect yourself. It's a huge confidence builder. That's why I started taking the classes in the first place."

"What do you mean?" I frowned. "Did someone try to hurt you?"

"Oh, it was nothing," She waved her hand dismissively. "Happened years ago. I was walking to my car one night and someone came out of the shadows and tried to rob me." She grimaced. "Well, more than just *rob* me, but I don't want to go into that."

"That's not *nothing*," I whispered. It didn't matter how many times I'd been in danger myself. This was my sister and someone had tried to hurt her. And I'd never even known about it.

"Did they find the person?" Derek asked immediately.

"Yes." She looked at both of us. "And he's still in jail."

"Good," I said. "Oh my God, China. I never knew that."

She took a deep breath. "I didn't talk about it for a long time."

"So what happened, exactly?"

"Well, like I said, the guy came out of nowhere." She

crossed her arms over her chest in a self-protective move. "He grabbed me and I fought back, but he was too strong. But luckily, I was parked right by the dojo and Keith walked out at that very moment and took care of the guy. You know, Keith doesn't look that big, so the jerk thought he could beat him up, too." China actually chuckled at the memory. "Let's just say that Keith changed his mind. Forcefully."

"I hope he sent him to the hospital," I said through clenched teeth.

"He sent him to the hospital and I helped send him to jail. Turns out I wasn't the only one he'd attacked." China shook her head. "There was a whole string of victims in San Francisco ready to testify against him. Apparently he was just in Dharma for the weekend and saw me as an easy victim. Some of the others were hurt pretty badly so I guess I got off easy. But it didn't feel that way at the time. I was never so scared in my entire life."

I had to take in a breath and let it out slowly. Nothing about her story was good, but I had to admit I was glad the guy hadn't been stalking the streets of Dharma all that time. "I'm so grateful that Keith walked out when he did."

"You and me both." She smiled determinedly. "Anyway, the next day I walked into the dojo and asked Keith to teach me everything he'd done to that guy the night before. And I've been studying with him ever since."

I threw my arms around her in a fierce hug. "I'm so incredibly proud of you."

"Thanks, Brooks."

"And so am I," Derek said, and joined the hug.

China laughed. "I love you guys."

"We love you, too." I gave her arm another squeeze. "But I'm still going to kick your butt someday."

She laughed again. "I notice you aren't willing to give it a try right now."

"No, because right now you could knock me over with a feather." I bunched up my fists. "But someday, watch out."

"Yeah, yeah." She was still laughing. "I'm so scared."

We stayed and watched the rehearsal for another half hour, then took off. We had talked about having dinner at Umbria, but changed our minds. After such a long day, I didn't want to sit in an elegant restaurant and behave myself. Derek agreed, so we ordered a pizza and salad to take home.

Walking over to the Lane, we ran into Clyde who was just coming out of El Diablo, the best Mexican restaurant in town.

"Hey, Clyde," I said. "Are you on your way home?"

"Not yet. I'm going back to the store for a few minutes, just to clean up. We're having a very special author visit tomorrow night and I need to get everything ready."

My ears perked up. "Author visit? I would love to come to that. Is there still room?"

"I'll put your name on the list. Your mother will be there, too."

"Oh." I exchanged a look with Derek. "Then that settles it. I'll definitely be there." No way would I let her walk around town at night while Jacob Banyan was still out there looking to gun her down.

Clyde glanced at Derek. "Your mother's coming, too."

Derek frowned. "My mother?"

He nodded. "Her name's on the reservation list. She and Becky are tight, you know."

"I'm aware," Derek murmured. "And who's your featured author?"

"You might find this lineup interesting," Clyde said. "We've got an outstanding trio of British authors."

Derek looked mildly impressed. "I might enjoy that, indeed. Who are they?"

"Agatha Christie, Margery Allingham, and Dorothy L. Sayers. They'll be discussing the 'Golden Age of Detective Fiction.'"

Derek did a double take. "Beg your pardon?"

I laughed. "Derek, Clyde only has author signings with dead authors."

"Fascinating," Derek muttered.

I almost giggled at his droll tone. "I guess the proper term for the event would be a séance."

"Hey," Clyde grumbled. "I had authors coming out here for years and finally I said, 'No more.' I couldn't stand all that snooty author crap. So I changed my speaker format."

"I see," Derek said.

"Love their books," Clyde admitted. "Hate their egos."

I wondered if Derek was rolling his eyes.

We walked in amiable silence until we reached the door of the Good Book.

"We'll wait until you're safely inside," I said.

"That's nice of you," he said, as he pulled out his keys to unlock the door. "Huh. Weird."

"What is it?" Derek asked, always alert.

Clyde looked at me and grimaced. "I must've forgotten to lock it."

"I don't believe that." For as long as I'd known Clyde, he had been super security conscious. Both his front and back doors had two dead bolts each and he was also hooked up to the local alarm company.

"Do you forget to lock the door often?" Derek asked.

"Never." He frowned. "This is the first time."

"Were you distracted when you left earlier?"

"No. In fact, I distinctly remember locking the door." He started to push the door open.

"Don't step inside," Derek cautioned.

"What do you mean? I've gotta see if anything's been stolen."

"Wait." Derek's tone caused Clyde to stop instantly. "I'll go in first, if you don't mind."

"Derek owns his own security firm," I explained quickly. "He's an expert at this stuff and he's really strong." *And he usually carries a gun, too*, I thought, but didn't mention it.

"Okay, okay." Clyde stepped aside to let Derek take the lead. "You go ahead."

My first thought was that maybe someone had broken into Clyde's shop to search for the *Little Women* book. But then, nobody knew that Clyde had it. Or that he'd given it to me, I hoped. So who would break into the bookshop and risk being caught and arrested?

Who was I kidding? I'd worked with rare books long enough to know that there was always someone willing to break the law or kill for them. I wondered again if the book was the reason Lawson was murdered.

Unless, of course, Clyde had simply forgotten to lock the front door. It was unheard of in the past, but then, Clyde wasn't getting any younger.

I felt immediately guilty for having that thought. He might've been getting older, but he still had all his faculties and he was still a fighter.

But as soon as Derek pushed the door open, all of those thoughts melted away to nothing.

In the dim light cast by the desk lamp at the far end of the shop, I could tell that the bookshelves were untouched. Everything was neat and tidy, as always. Nothing was disturbed, at least as far as we could tell. Except that there, on the carpeted floor, was a body.

It lay between the door and the first row of book-shelves, and his back was turned toward us. It was definitely a man, given the size of those big brown shoes he was wearing.

"Oh my God," I whispered.

Derek stood at the threshold, studying the room. He pulled out his phone and used the flashlight app to examine the area surrounding the body. "Don't come inside. There's blood seeping into the carpet."

And there went my stomach. I really had to look into hypnosis.

"Jeez Louise," Clyde muttered. "Who is that?"

Derek looked beyond Clyde and met my gaze directly. "Brooklyn love, call the police."

"Is he dead?" Clyde asked.

Derek's grim expression answered that question.

"Who is it?" I whispered.

He reached out and grabbed my hand. "It's Jacob Banyan."

Chapter 13

I didn't even like the guy. In fact, I hated him. He had threatened my mother and maybe even tried to kill her, and for that, there was zero forgiveness. I was glad he wouldn't be around to torment my mother ever again. But it didn't make my stomach feel any better to see the jerk's blood oozing out of him and into the oriental carpet on the floor of Clyde's shop.

Poor Clyde. Poor bookshop. The Good Book had been a landmark in Dharma for over twenty years. I loved this place, but now the shop would always be a murder scene. It might bring more tourists in, but I had to wonder if I'd ever be completely comfortable here again.

So many happy memories were all wrapped up in Clyde's charming shop. But now they were clouded after finding the bloody body of creepy Jacob Banyan lying dead on the floor.

Banyan ruined everything, I grumbled under my breath. But I wouldn't let him ruin Clyde's Good Book for me.

Within minutes, Stevie—I mean Detective Willoughby—arrived with two officers. After confirming that Banyan was indeed dead, they began to question

Derek and me. They wanted to know how and when we had run into Clyde and why we had walked with him to the bookshop where we found Banyan's body.

I told Stevie everything that had occurred at the committee meeting earlier that afternoon and how Banyan had once again threatened my mother and insulted almost everyone else on the committee. I made a point of telling him how Derek had thrown the big jerk out of the room. I reiterated my suspicions about Banyan trying to run Mom down. I wasn't sure that mattered anymore, but I was compelled to mention it anyway.

It was clear from Stevie's line of questioning that the police were suspicious of Clyde. After all, the body was found in his bookshop. I told Stevie that he was barking up the wrong tree and should look elsewhere because there was no way that Clyde could've killed Banyan.

"First of all," I said, "the timing is all wrong. Clyde was having dinner at El Diablo at the same time that Banyan was killed."

"Are you sure about that?" he asked.

Well of course not! I thought, but didn't say it. Instead, I just shrugged. "Not entirely, but I know you'll interview the restaurant staff to make sure."

"Yes, we will," he said tightly, although I thought I caught a gleam of amusement in his eyes. I hoped it was amusement, anyway. I occasionally saw the same glimmer in Inspector Lee's eyes, but that usually meant she was getting ready to lampoon me. I couldn't be sure if Stevie had reached that level of mockery yet, but time would tell.

"And second," I continued, picking up where I left off. "Banyan was so much bigger and more powerful than Clyde. How could Clyde possibly overpower Banyan enough to shove a knife in his throat?"

"How do you know it was a knife?" Stevie asked.

I opened my mouth to speak, but then had to close it quickly. Was this a trick question? Frankly, I had no idea whether he'd been killed with a knife or not.

"I don't know exactly," I admitted. "But it's, you know, an educated guess since there was lots of blood around his throat." I ran my fingers along my neck, just in case he was unclear on the concept. I frowned. "Was it another broken wine bottle?"

Stevie flipped to a new page in his notebook. "Did you see anyone else on the street as you were walking toward the bookshop?"

I closed my eyes and tried to picture our walk down the Lane earlier that evening. With a sigh, I opened my eyes. "There were people walking up and down the Lane, but I didn't see anyone I knew."

He jotted something down and thought about it for a minute. Then he closed the notebook and slipped it into his jacket pocket. "Okay, that's it for now. We'll probably have some follow-up questions in the next day or so."

"Call me anytime," I said. "I want to get to the bottom of this as much as you do." I hesitated, then added, "I just hate that there's a murderer roaming the streets of Dharma. It's shocking and frightening. I hate that it's happening right before the festival. It's all so wrong."

"Yeah, it's wrong," he said flatly. "And we intend to catch him before anyone else gets hurt."

I nodded. "Good."

He raised his hand and gave me a casual salute. "Good night, Brooklyn."

So Jacob Banyan was dead. Even though his death meant that there was still a vicious killer roaming the streets of Dharma, I felt a keen sense of relief. Because, you know, that big brutish bully Jacob Banyan was gone and we were safe.

But that was just a lie. We weren't safe. My mother wasn't safe. Someone had tried to kill her and now we didn't know if the driver had been Banyan or the even more vicious person who had killed him. Either way, we would still be sticking to Mom like superglue for the foreseeable future.

"I think we need to make a list," I said, taking a sip of wine.

Derek and I had made it home and had settled down in the comfortable family room with our mushroom and sausage pizza, antipasto salad, and the lovely Cabernet Sauvignon that my father had handed Derek when we stopped by to give them the news about Banyan a little while ago. Mom had been completely shocked and expressed her sorrow that he was dead. But I sensed some relief from her, too.

I had hated to spoil the moment by reminding both Mom and Dad that there was still a killer out there who may have also targeted my mother.

"A list, you say," Derek said, and sipped his wine.

"Yes. A list of murder suspects, now that our best suspect is dead."

Charlie must have sensed our somber mood because she jumped up onto the couch and squeezed between us, rubbing her soft, furry body against both of us. Then she cuddled up in the middle, allowing us to take turns giving her strokes and soft scratches and nonsensical murmurs, calling her silly names like "my little peanut" and "punky-wunky."

I'll confess that Derek doesn't call her silly names. That would be me.

"Our prime suspect is dead," Derek lamented, picking up on my last comment. "It tends to spoil all of our best laid plans."

"Yeah, I hate it when the prime suspect dies."

I bit off a small chunk of the delicious Italian sausage and savored it. "I especially hate that we still have to worry that there's someone out there who wants to kill my mother."

Derek frowned. "We don't know that someone else is trying to kill your mother. Now that Banyan's dead, the threat to her may be over."

I pressed my hands to my stomach. "I hope so. Because the thought of her still being in danger makes my stomach twist itself into a pretzel."

"I know, love, and I'm sorry. It's not a good situation." Derek frowned thoughtfully. "We've got to find this killer before he tries anything again."

"Or *she*," I added.

His eyes narrowed. "Yes, there is definitely that possibility."

"So back to my list." I took another quick sip of wine, then picked up my pen. "Saffron Bergeron."

"She belongs at the top of the list," Derek agreed. "She's quite bitter and seems to have it in for your mother. I watched her when Banyan lost his chance to fund the festival. She was as angry as he was."

"And that's just stupid, because my mother is a wonderful person."

"She is indeed. And that's one more reason why Saffron can't understand her."

"What a contrary muggle she is," I muttered.

Derek grinned, but said nothing for a long moment. Then he asked, "But why would she kill Banyan?"

"Oh heck. I have no idea." I took a big sip of wine.

"Let's move on. Number two on my list is Shandi Patrick."

He gazed at me. "That's quite a leap since we've never even met the woman. Why do you think she belongs on the list?"

"Remember when Mom told us that she had stormed into the bank looking for Banyan?"

"Yes. She was angry that he was attempting to foreclose on her winery."

"Right. Glenmaron Winery. Of course, she doesn't have to worry about the winery now that he's dead."

"And you think she might've killed him to prevent him from going through with that plan."

"Yes."

"It makes sense. Isn't she also trying to make a Hollywood comeback?"

"That's the rumor." I shrugged and reached for a cherry tomato.

"I'm not certain her wanting to make a Hollywood comeback is relevant. But I would agree that there's something going on with her. It's too bad we couldn't meet her tonight."

"Yeah, it would've been good to get a feel for her personality and attitude."

Derek stared at his wineglass, obviously thinking about something. "She had to run out to meet someone, your sister said."

"Right. And then Jacob Banyan winds up dead. Coincidence?"

"You know my answer to that."

"Jacob Banyan said something snarky about Shandi during the committee meeting. I wonder if Ryan reported that to her."

"He could have, and I imagine it would've enraged

her. But it's also possible that he didn't say anything, not wanting to hurt her feelings."

"Yeah, that's probably more likely." I thought for a minute. "There are plenty of suspects when it comes to Banyan's death, but who would want to come after my mother?"

"And who among those suspects would also want to kill Lawson Schmidt?" I set my wineglass on the table. "This is getting too complicated."

"Let's not throw in the towel yet," he said. "How do you feel about the other committee members?"

I closed my eyes and pictured the meeting room. "There's Mom, Winston, Jan, Sue Flanders, Mary-beth Novak, Professor Dinkins, Clyde, Ryan, Saffron Bergeron." I opened my eyes and frowned. "I remember counting ten committee members that first day. So who am I missing?"

He gave my arm a light squeeze. "You're missing Lawson, darling."

"Oh dear. Sorry. Of course." I picked up a slice of pizza and took a bite. "I don't know who to put on the suspect list because if anyone didn't like my mom or Lawson, they invariably liked Jacob Banyan. So who would kill both of them?"

"I haven't a clue. But I do have other questions. For instance, why would Ryan urge your mother to fix things for Shandi?"

"I don't know. He was destined to fail. Which makes him come off as a fool while Shandi comes across as conciliatory and willing to go along with whatever is asked of her."

"At least, that's how London made her sound," I said. "London seems to love her. And funny how Shandi never asked to be cast in a different role."

"Because she cleverly plays up to her director," he guessed.

"Pretty smart, since London's in charge of the entire production." I took another bite of pizza.

"Do you think Ryan would kill for her?"

I almost choked on my pizza but managed to swallow. "What?"

"It's something to think about."

"I guess. But I hate to think he's that malleable." I put the rest of my pizza down on the plate and shook my head. "Of course, he's so mild mannered, he's practically invisible."

"Beware of the quiet ones," he murmured, sipping his wine.

"I suppose you're right. But do you really think he could've faced down Banyan?"

"I have no idea. And for all we know, the killer surprised Banyan with no facing down involved. I suppose if she pays him enough, Ryan will do whatever she says."

I thought about it. "I don't really believe he's our prime suspect because he has no reason to kill anyone."

"I agree," Derek said. "But Shandi does. And so does Saffron. And when it comes to Banyan, the entire committee does, too. So for now, they all stay on the list." He took a bite of pizza and chewed it thoughtfully. "So what about Lawson? We haven't really discussed who might've had it in for him."

"True, but any one of those committee members might've come after him, seeing as how he stole all of their money."

"In that case, your mother would be a suspect."

"Oh, she would love to hear us say that," I said with a laugh.

Derek swirled his wine. "Our biggest problem is still that whoever went after your mother would never go after Banyan."

"But Lawson is another problem altogether. There are too many suspects in his case." I reached for my own wineglass. "I'm getting confused."

"I'm going to go out on a limb," Derek said. "The same person who killed Lawson and Banyan also went after your mother. And that person is a member of the festival committee."

"I'll agree to that."

"And the most prominent suspects, in my humble opinion, are Saffron, Clyde, that professor fellow, and Ryan, simply because of his connection to Shandi."

"You're gunning for Ryan."

He smiled. "I'm not, honestly. But I do remember him casting that 'no' vote. Along with Saffron and the professor and someone else I can't recall."

"Professor Dinkins works at the Sonoma Institute of the Arts."

"Do you know him well?"

"I always got along with him when I was teaching at the Institute, but we weren't close."

I had a sudden flashback to my days at the Institute and how awful some of the professors turned out to be. I hesitated to remind Derek of what we went through back then, but I knew I had to say something. "I'm wondering if Dinkins was a friend of Solomon's."

Solomon—he only went by the one name—was a professor who loved to have students fawn over him. He collected sycophants and was very creepy.

Derek's jaw clenched. "That man was a psychopath."

"Oh, for sure. But even psychos have friends."

Derek swirled his wine, the casual move belying the tension he had to be feeling. *Those were dark days*, I thought.

"If Dinkins was close to Solomon," I finally said, "I wonder if he knew how truly screwed up he was."

"More importantly," he countered, "does he know of Solomon's connection to you and me?"

"And to my mother," I added, and felt a chill crawl up my arms and gather in my shoulders. "I don't even want to consider that possibility."

He took a deep breath and exhaled slowly. "I don't either. But we won't discount Dinkins altogether just yet."

I munched on another bite of salad as I studied the names. "Who are we forgetting?"

Derek gazed at me. "Clyde."

"No."

"Excuse me?" Derek said, surprised at my vehemence. "You said that very quickly."

"I know I should put him on the list." I thought maybe I should be wringing my hands, I felt so guilty. "After all, Banyan was killed inside his shop and he could've been faking that whole unlocked door scene."

"Yes, he could've made that up on the spot. And let's not forget that Clyde had the book that once belonged to Lawson."

"But he gave the book to me. Look, I've known him most of my life. And sure, he comes across as an old grump, but once you get to know him, he's . . . well, he's still grumpy. But he's smart and funny and charming. And don't forget, Gabriel likes him."

"Gabriel's opinion weighs a lot," Derek said, squeezing my shoulder fondly. "But not as much as yours. If you'd rather not add him to the list, we won't. For now."

I breathed out a sigh. Could the man be any more perfect for me? I didn't think so. Especially when we could enjoy pizza and wine, and consider murder suspects all at the same time. "Thank you. I love you."

He began to laugh. "I love you, too, darling. But I can see that you're stressing out over this list. But it's *our* list. We can make it up as we go along. We make the decisions, isn't that so?"

"Yes." I grabbed my wineglass and sucked down a healthy sip. "We're the deciders."

"Hear, hear," he said, and clinked his glass to mine. "So read me the names on the list."

I set down my wineglass. "Saffron, Shandi, Ryan, Professor Dinkins, and everyone else on the committee, including Clyde, but not really Clyde."

"So, not Clyde," Derek said. "Which leaves us only four real suspects. I was expecting several dozen."

"There could be people we aren't even aware of. Like some friend of Banyan's. Or someone who was blackmailing Lawson. Or—"

"We can search the entire valley for suspects and motives, love, but I think we should stick to the committee. Otherwise, we'll drive ourselves insane."

"Okay, you're right," I admitted. "But I'll just add that blackmail is a very good motive. Specifically with Lawson."

"And I agree. But now let's change the subject to the fact that you could be in danger because of that book."

I could feel my stomach begin to tighten all over again. "I've been so concerned about my mother that I keep forgetting that other little issue."

"Well, I haven't," he said. "And as long as we're sticking close to your mother for safety's sake, I'll also be sticking close to you."

"Despite the possibility of mortal danger, I'm happy to have you close by."

"You can't get rid of me so easily."

"Don't want to." I gazed at the names and wondered. "So any last word on motives?"

"For Lawson's killer, it could have been about the money. Someone stole the money that he stole from the festival. Or someone was blackmailing him for taking the money in the first place so he handed over the money."

"I thought it had to be Banyan who killed Lawson," I said. "All along, I've been thinking that all Banyan wanted was his own festival booth. I suppose he thought it would bring him some respectability, which is kind of ludicrous when you think about it. I mean, the guy was making box wine in the midst of the Sonoma wine country. He was never going to be considered respectable."

"He might not have realized that."

"No," I murmured. "He was too vain, too far into himself to see the reality."

"What other reasons would he insist on being part of the festival?"

I thought about it. "Prestige? Connections? Acceptance? Visibility? Was he trying to impress someone?"

"We might never know," Derek said.

"Well, that's not very satisfying."

He chuckled. "We'll do our best to find out."

"I hope so."

Derek finished the last of his wine. "Could Banyan have been working with Lawson behind your mother's back?"

"I suppose so. To tell the truth, I never really trusted Lawson all that much."

"Perhaps they had a falling out when Lawson couldn't work out a way to get him a booth at the festival."

"So Banyan killed Lawson? And then someone killed Banyan?" I frowned, then yawned. "Could we really have that many murderers wandering through Dharma?"

"It's possible."

"So what was the motive for killing Banyan?"

Derek smiled. "I believe we need to cut this discussion short and go to bed."

"Good idea." I stretched my arms over my head. "I'm so tired all of a sudden. There are too many players and I'm getting confused about motives and I'm worried about my mother."

"Let's go to sleep. We'll think more clearly in the morning."

We straightened up the room and packed up the food. Then Derek picked up Charlie and we went upstairs to bed.

The next morning my phone rang, and it was my mother. "You won't believe who called me."

"Who?" I asked

"Saffron. She called a few minutes ago, hysterical about Jacob Banyan. She accused me of killing him!"

"She's insane," I said, and suddenly this morning's delicious avocado toast formed a ball of anxiety in my stomach. "You need to get rid of her."

"I can't get rid of her. She's in charge of the festival promotion, and to be honest, she does a good job. She's just a miserable person."

"Okay. But you should call Stevie and report her phone call. She could come after you if she honestly thinks you had anything to do with Banyan's death."

"I'll call him right now."

"And, Mom, I don't want you to go anywhere today."

"I can't stay home! I have far too much to do."

"Derek and I will take care of all your book-festival errands. You do everything you can on the phone and the computer, and then just text us with directions on anything that needs to be done in person."

She protested but finally acquiesced. But as extra insurance, Derek called Gabriel to ask him to contact Stevie to see how the murder investigations were proceeding.

"And ask him what's happening with those surveillance cameras on the Lane," I said.

"I'll take care of it," Gabriel said.

The rest of the day flew by in a flurry of activity. Derek had several hours of conference calls with his office and with clients, and I got lost in the pages of *Little Women*. We didn't slow down until it was close to midnight and we finally went to bed.

The next day I had to spend more time working on the book rehab, but I knew Mom had work to do at the festival and I didn't want Derek to be her only protector. He solved the problem by calling Gabriel who agreed to meet them at the town hall.

I knew that Mom's first priority was to make sure that the booths were being set up in the correct pattern around Berkeley Circle. She was also going to meet up with the porta-potty dude and give him my cashier's check for ten thousand dollars, which meant that she and Derek would have to walk over to my bank on the Lane and get a cashier's check from my checking account, on which Derek was a signatory. They promised to call me if there were any problems. But there weren't, thank goodness.

My personal priority was to work on the book for

four hours in the morning. Then Derek would pick me up and we would attend the committee's tea party to welcome the Louisa May Alcott scholar.

It was a pretty sure bet that Gabriel wanted nothing to do with the Alcott tea party. But then, neither did Derek. He had insisted that he was looking forward to it, of course, and I was pitifully grateful to him for lying.

Meanwhile, I had a moment of sheer panic when I didn't see the *Little Women* book inside my plastic book-binding crate.

"Oh God." I had meant to find a more secure place to hide it, but had completely forgotten in all the chaos surrounding the two murders and my mother's attack.

"This isn't happening," I muttered. I definitely re-membered wrapping it in the soft white cloth and put-ting it right on top of the crate. And I couldn't remember taking it out again. So it had to be here.

Unless it had been stolen.

But who knew I had the book? Clyde had sworn he didn't tell anyone and I believed him. Not only was he grumpy, but he didn't talk about his business much.

I wondered how anyone could've broken into Annie's house. I knew it had a state-of-the-art alarm system comparable to Gabriel's, because he was the one who had installed it. Still, there were ways. Maybe the book thief was a friend of Annie's. Maybe he knew the code or had talked her into letting him come inside at some point.

"Search the whole box," I said to myself. It could be stuck between something. I went ahead and started by removing my canvas traveling bag of tools, then my pint container of Polyvinyl Acetate or PVA, which was the archival glue I used most often for bookbinding.

And that's when I saw the bit of white cloth pressed

against the lower side of the crate. The book must have slipped down when I carried it from Abraham's workshop back to the house.

I had to take a minute and breathe. All that panic for nothing, but seriously, I wasn't sure what I would've done if that book had been stolen. Maybe I was kidding myself and maybe it wasn't as valuable as I hoped it would be, but I had a feeling that the book could be the key to everything.

I put my tools and glue jars back into the box, placed *Little Women* on top, and carried everything out to Abraham's workshop.

As before, I put the box down next to the worktable and pulled out the bag of chocolate caramel Kisses to keep up my strength. Then I grabbed my magnifying glasses and my camera. I laid out the white cloth and placed the book on top of it. I studied it as though it were the first time, admiring the illustration of the four sisters, then checking the front and back.

I had to finish sweeping each page and each gutter with my short, stiff brush, and check for foxing all through the book. The paper itself was of good quality, not thin and weak, and I thought I might be able to get away with using a soft gum eraser on any smudges. Yesterday I had cut new endpapers, a new cover, new headbands, and new pastedowns.

I was happy that the book had a cloth cover rather than leather, so I would simply replace it with a high-quality bookcloth. I didn't mind working in leather, but it was a much more time-consuming job. And the one thing I didn't have was much time to complete this job. I had already decided to carefully remove the cover illustration and insert it into a cutout within the new bookcloth. I envisioned a beveled edge that would improve the look of the cover, and I hoped that Clyde would be happy with it. Not that he cared, I supposed, but I would be happy.

I would also have to gild the titles and add a touch of decoration onto the spine. That would take some extra time and I planned to save that job until the end.

For now, I splayed the book open on the white cloth and used my X-Acto knife to cut along the front hinge, separating the front cover from the textblock—this consisted of the actual sewn pages that made up the book's interior content. I did the same with the back cover, cutting along the hinge until the entire cover and spine were separated from the rest. I set the cover aside and took hold of the textblock. I gripped it with the spine facing me and tore off the original headbands, those small, decorative fabric bands attached to the head and foot of the spine. The headbands, besides being pretty, served to cover up any remnants of loose threads and glue that might otherwise be visible after binding. Ideally, they also add strength to the spine itself.

I carefully picked a few bits of old glue from the spine and from the super, which is a very stiff strip of woven cotton that also adds strength to the spine.

Books from this era were invariably held together with animal glue and, sure enough, that was what I found on the surface of the spine. Animal glue was derived from animal protein, and while it had its uses, it tended to turn brittle on paper and darken and shrink with age.

Of course, if the book's owner had kept the book in pristine condition, it wouldn't have been an issue. But since I had to take the entire book apart, I would go ahead and get rid of this glue and replace it with good old archival PVA.

I pushed away from the table and walked over to what Abraham had always called his glue cupboard, where he kept his myriad containers of every type of glue known to man. I found an unopened bag of methyl cellulose powder and poured two-and-a-half table-spoons into the large glass mixing cup that he kept in the cupboard. At the sink, I turned on the hot water and waited for it to warm up, then added one-quarter cup to the powder. I stirred it quickly to keep any lumps from forming, and when it was a nice consistency, I carried it over to the worktable.

Once again holding the textblock with the spine facing me, I began to brush on the mixture. This would help loosen and break down the old animal-based adhesive and allow it to be more easily removed.

While the methyl cellulose did its thing, I started work on the front cover. I had to peel away the book-cloth from the cover boards, but since I wanted to keep the charming illustration intact, I had to carefully pry it away instead of just tearing it.

I rolled out my canvas tool kit and found my micro spatula, a paper-thin stainless steel tool that's exactly what its name implies: an eensy-weensy spatula. I slid the tool in between the interior endsheet and the cloth turnover and used it as a wedge to separate the two, inching ever so slightly forward from the outer edges to the center of the board, until the entire cover was loosened.

Later, I would trim the edges of the pretty illustration and fit it into a beveled space in the bookcloth that would give the effect of a picture frame. But that would happen tomorrow.

For now, I returned to the textblock spine and began to scrape off the softened animal glue with another micro spatula. Since I had discovered this tool in a catalog last year, it had become one of my favorites. I had a feeling it was originally created to be used by surgeons in hospitals, but I didn't want to think about that too much because blood.

Eventually I would have to sand the surface of the boards to make them smooth before laying down the new bookcloth and endpapers. I wanted to avoid the bubbles and ripples that could ruin a pretty new cover.

Removing the old cloth was a painstaking job that took more time than I realized. When the alarm on my phone beeped, I was surprised that four hours had passed.

I stood and stretched, and wondered where the time had gone. It seemed to fly by when I was immersed in my bookbinding work.

Knowing Derek would be home any minute to pick me up, I quickly packed up my equipment and supplies, wrapped up the book in the white cloth, and carried everything back to the house.

I changed out of my jeans and into a slightly dressier pair of brown plaid pants, a pretty mocha-colored sweater, and black booties. I carried a jacket and scarf with me downstairs and sat and played with Charlie until I heard Derek's car drive up.

"You have a good day, Charlie," I murmured, stroking the fluffy, soft fur of her back and scratching her ears. "I love you, funny face."

I gave a quick glance around to make sure there was nobody listening to my ridiculous conversation with my cat. Then I locked up the house and set the alarm. Before I could even turn around, Derek was standing beside me.

"Hello, darling," he murmured, and kissed me.

"Hi, you." I smiled up at him. "Everything okay with Mom?"

"Gabriel is with her and so is my mother."

"Meg is at the town hall?"

"Your mother invited her to attend the tea party."

"How nice. That'll be fun for both of them." I batted my eyelashes at him. "And for us, of course."

"Oh yes," he said somberly. "Tea parties are my life."

I laughed. "Gabriel will be there and there are other men on the committee."

"Fun for all of us."

I touched his cheek. "You can slip out with Gabriel and have a beer."

His eyes narrowed. "I'm not going anywhere unless you and your mother are there with me."

I sighed. "Thank you."

He glanced down at the plastic crate I'd carried out of the house. "What's this?"

"My bookbinding tools are in there, but more importantly, it contains the copy of *Little Women* that I'm working on."

"The expensive one?"

"Yes. I didn't know where to hide it safely inside the house, so I was wondering if we could just put it in the trunk of your car."

"Good thinking," he said, easily lifting the crate. "My car is fairly safe."

I smiled. "I know."

I watched while he stowed the book and my tools in the trunk and shut the lid with a heavy thud. His Bentley was built like an armored tank inside a beautiful, classy exterior, and his alarm system was, like everything else he did, one step beyond state-of-the-art.

We got in the car and Derek leaned over to kiss me

again. Then he deftly reached into the glove compartment and pulled out his very deadly looking gun.

I shivered at the sight of the weapon. "Do you think you'll need that?"

"I hope not," he said lightly, "but I won't take chances with our mothers."

"I appreciate that."

As we drove off, I stared at the glove compartment in front of me. I realized I had the truly convenient facility for forgetting there was a deadly weapon just inside that box, waiting for the next time Derek called it into action.

I truly hoped today wasn't one of those days.

Chapter 14

The tea party was in full swing when Derek and I walked into the town hall conference room. There were two long utility tables covered with pretty lace tablecloths, and six wide platters were spread out across the space. They were filled with a variety of finger sandwiches, bite-sized pastries, and dozens of fancy cookies. At one end of each table was an industrial-sized hot water dispenser and three teapots per table. These contained loose tea, ready to be filled with steaming hot water.

Two dozen elegant teacups with saucers were placed next to the tea service, with spoons and napkins spread in neat rows.

My mother stood in a circle with some of the other women on the committee and a stranger I guessed to be the visiting scholar.

I did my daughterly duty and went over to meet her. My mother grabbed my arm and gave me a harried smile. "Professor Trimble, I'd like you to meet my daughter Brooklyn. You might be interested to know that she's a bookbinder who specializes in rare-book restoration."

"It's nice to meet you, Professor," I said, reaching out to shake her hand.

"Nice to meet you, too." She wore a severe navy suit with a skirt hanging well below her knees and a wrinkled white blouse, with what my mother would call sensible heels. She wasn't much for smiling, I noticed. It was a trait I'd seen in other academics through the years. They took their jobs very seriously. Nothing wrong with that, I supposed, but this was a tea party. Maybe she would lighten up as we all got to know her better, or maybe she was simply a permanent frowny face.

"So. You're the bookbinder." Why did she sound so suspicious?

I gave her a smile. "That's me."

"Lawson told me about you."

Now that was a surprise. "Did he?"

"Yes."

"How did you and Lawson know each other?"

"We went to college together." She leaned in closer. "I heard that he was killed."

"Yes, I'm sorry."

"Before he died, did he show you the exquisite copy of *Little Women* I sent him?"

"I did see it," I said carefully, not wanting to say too much. Maybe it wasn't fair, but I thought she seemed cold. I didn't trust her. "You sent him the book?"

"Well, not for free," she was quick to explain. "It was a business transaction."

"Of course. Would you mind telling me how much he paid for it?"

"Didn't he tell you?"

"No."

She scowled. "The money shouldn't matter."

"I don't mean to pry," I said, not certain what tack to

take with her. She was so unpleasant, but since I wanted information, I kept going. "It's simply an intellectual question. In working with rare books, I'm often asked to track the provenance of a book. Where was it made, who owned it first, what their occupation was, where they lived, who they gave it to next, and down the line. For me, the cost of a book plays a part as well in creating an overall picture of a book's life."

"Well," she said. She seemed mollified, if not completely sold on my explanation. "For Lawson, the cost truly didn't matter. He was willing to pay any amount, so I quoted him what I thought was an extremely reasonable price of ten thousand dollars. As soon as I received his check, I sent him the book."

I nodded. "He certainly was a big fan of *Little Women.*"

"I should say so. He literally begged me to sell it to him." She frowned again. "He's always been a bit obsessive."

"A bit," I agreed.

"And he was truly obsessed with obtaining the book. Wanted it for his mother. He called her Marmee, you know." She rolled her eyes at that. "Apparently she was a big fan, too."

"That's nice," I said weakly. Marmee? Who knew? But still, Trimble didn't have to be so rude!

She continued, "He was quite proud that he'd convinced the festival committee to honor Louisa May Alcott and *Little Women.*"

"I did hear that the choice of *Little Women* was his idea." I tried a smile. "So can you tell me more about the book?"

"If you've seen it, you know." She huffed impatiently.

"But all right. It's very old, a first edition, with a delightful illustration of the four sisters on the cover. The paper is good quality and with a few nips and tucks, it could be worth even more. I happen to believe that Lawson got quite a bargain."

"It will take more than a few nips and tucks," I said. "The book was in very poor condition."

"I wouldn't call it *poor*," she said, with a disapproving sniff. "It might need a few pieces of tape here and there, but that's the sign of a well-read book."

I stifled a gasp. "Yes. Well, enjoy your visit." I walked away in a daze. A few pieces of *tape*? The woman was a barbarian! *She might know all about Louisa May*, I thought, *but she knows very little about caring for books*.

But now I knew where Lawson had found that book. I also knew that Lawson didn't have a lot of money. In fact, he lived on social security. But if his obsession had kicked in and he absolutely had to have the book, as Professor Trimble claimed, he certainly might've stolen the festival funds to buy it. Except he only would've needed ten thousand dollars, so why was the entire amount of seventy thousand dollars missing?

I crossed the room and slipped my arm through Derek's. I couldn't wait to tell him what I'd found out, but I couldn't do it here.

"Have a nice chat with the guest of honor?" he asked.

"It was enlightening," I murmured. "Isn't this a nice party?"

"I don't see any beer," Derek whispered.

I laughed, just as Gabriel walked up and shook hands with Derek. He turned and gave me a warm hug. "Babe," he said.

"Hi, Gabriel. Thanks for watching out for Mom."

"Not a problem. Your mom's a kick in the pants."

"She likes you, too." I pulled him off to the side of the room and Derek followed. "Have you talked to the police about Jacob Banyan's death?"

"We had a conversation," he said cryptically.

"Well? How was he killed?"

"Why do you ask?" he responded, his tone suspicious. Then he grinned. "Just kidding, Babe. Banyan was killed by a knife across the throat. He bled out."

"Sounds familiar," Derek said cynically.

"Yeah," Gabriel muttered. "There's a pattern for sure."

"Was it a different kind of knife?" I looked at Derek and frowned. "Because I told Detective Willoughby that I thought Banyan was killed with a knife to the throat and he gave me grief. So what gives?"

"Perhaps he doesn't enjoy having civilians come up with their own theories," Derek surmised.

"I don't see why not," I said. "Inspector Lee always enjoys my input."

Both men laughed until I had to elbow them. "People are staring."

"Can't help it, babe," Gabriel said. "You're a laugh riot."

"Did they leave the knife at the scene?" I asked, ignoring the comment.

Gabriel grinned. "Not very proper tea party conversation."

"That's okay."

"No knife was found at the scene."

I nodded. "Okay."

Gabriel looked at Derek. "You want a beer?"

"Why, yes." He shot me a look. "But not right now."

"I can't believe you aren't excited about Darjeeling," I said.

"Be right back," Gabriel said, giving us another glance. "You guys stay here and watch your mom."

I knew Derek was dying to go with him, but he made the heroic sacrifice to stay with me and my mother.

"Let us know what you find," I whispered, knowing he was actually going to go out and do a perimeter check.

He gave a quick lift of his chin in agreement. "Be back soon. Enjoy the crumpets."

I laughed as he dashed out of the room. Slipping my arm through Derek's, I leaned my head against his shoulder. "My hero. Thanks for hanging in."

"Darling, I wouldn't want to hang anywhere else."

"Sure." I had to laugh. "So. You want a crumpet?"

Now it was his turn to laugh.

"I have something to tell you," I murmured.

Derek was still smiling. "Is it related to that woman I saw you talking with?"

"Yes. I found out that she sold Lawson the book for ten thousand dollars."

"What?" he almost yelled.

I would've told him the details but his mother walked in at that moment and we greeted her with happy hugs.

"I'm so glad you're here," I whispered. "Mom will be thrilled to see you."

"I'm thrilled as well," Meg said. "I'll just pop over to say hello."

After everyone had mingled and had their fill of finger food, cookies, and tea, Mom stepped to the head of the table. With one deep breath in and out to center herself, she spoke, "I'm so pleased to introduce Bettina

Trimble, our very special guest from New Jersey. As most of you know, Professor Trimble is a distinguished professor of American literature at Princeton and a renowned scholar of Louisa May Alcott's life and literary works. She is the current president of the Alcott Collective and travels the country on its behalf."

Mom extended her arm toward the visitor. "Professor Trimble, would you say a few words? Let's give her a warm welcome." Mom began to applaud and everyone joined her as Bettina Trimble walked over to stand by my mother.

Professor Trimble stood with her hands clasped together tightly as she peered out at the crowd. Her short hair was a nondescript shade of brown and she wore no makeup. She frankly looked worn out, as though she'd been traveling across the country for the past month in a covered wagon. But who was I to judge her appearance, just because she didn't know how to take care of books?

Yes, I was holding a grudge.

I thought she looked a bit like one of Louisa May Alcott's war-weary characters from *Little Women*. Perhaps that was the world she aspired to live in.

"Thank you, Mrs. Wainwright, for the warm welcome," she said, bowing slightly toward my mother. "I'm so pleased to be here in your wine country."

"And we're so pleased to have you," Mom said. "I hope you've had a chance to look over the short list of festival events we've scheduled for you."

"Yes, of course. The panels and workshop subjects sound fascinating. I hope to do them justice."

"Of course you will," Mom said jovially. "And we can't wait for you to see our musical production based on Louisa May Alcott's major work, *Little Women*."

The crowd burst into spontaneous applause and Professor Trimble was taken aback. "Oh my." She patted her chest nervously.

"I do think you'll enjoy the musical," Mom said with even more than her usual perkiness in order to cover up the professor's awkward reaction to our excitement. "I've seen the rehearsals and they are doing a wonderful job."

I moved a little closer to the woman. "Are you all right, Professor? Can I get you some water?"

"I-I was just a bit thrown off," she said. "I hadn't heard that you were performing a musical version of Louisa's master work."

"I'm sure you'll enjoy it," I said quickly.

"It's very clever," Mom added. "The costumes are authentic to the time period and the cast is so talented. I believe their work would make Louisa May Alcott proud."

"Oh please." The woman sniffed again, then made a *tsk-tsk* sound of disapproval. "Ever since they performed the work on Broadway, we've had nothing but problems with these backwoods small-town performances."

There was utter silence in the room.

"I'm not sure I understand your point," Mom said, though it sounded as if she understood all too well.

The professor twisted her lips into a tight frown of annoyance. "The Alcott Collective has set up very strict guidelines for the theatrical use of Ms. Alcott's works. I'm going to have to view your musical presentation of *Little Women* to make sure it is deemed acceptable by the Collective. I'll let you know my findings."

I exchanged a look of concern with Mom, then glanced up at Derek, who was obviously irritated by the woman. A quick scan of the room showed me that almost everyone was feeling the same.

Mom cleared her throat. "I don't quite get what you're talking about, Professor."

"It's very simple, really." Her tone implied that as simple as it might be, we wouldn't understand because we were all too dumb to breathe. "Unless supervised by a member of a scholarly organization such as mine, the common person will rarely give the work the proper respect and reverence it deserves. A small town like this, with your little community-theater types cast in the roles of Ms. Alcott's beloved characters?" She threw up her hands. "It simply never ends well."

Mom straightened her shoulders and smiled at the professor. "You're right. This won't end well."

"But—"

"Nevertheless," Mom continued quickly, "we would love to have you view our small-town performance. However, we have no interest in hearing your opinion of our quaint little theater group, nor do we wish to win your organization's acceptance. Frankly, we're all just here to have a good time and maybe learn a little something. If you'd like to be a part of that, you're more than welcome to stay. But if you're here to critique and judge us—which, I must admit, it's pretty obvious that you are—then you should probably call a cab and head on back home."

The room was silent again, except for the professor's loud "Harrumph!"

I started to laugh. I couldn't help it. Suddenly the entire room joined me, laughing and applauding Mom's words as she gently took hold of the woman's arm and led her out the door and down the hall.

Naturally, Derek and I followed them out of the building, not knowing what might happen out there.

Standing out in front of the town hall, Mom pointed toward the Lane and Professor Trimble clomped away.

"Mom?" I said. "Where is she going?"

"She's going back to her hotel, packing up and leaving."

"Didn't you pay for her flight out here and her hotel room?"

"Sure did," she said bluntly. "Don't care."

I frowned at the uptight professor and her sensible shoes as she hobbled down the brick sidewalk toward the Lane. "Did she just expect to show up and automatically be put in charge of everything?"

"Apparently so." Mom shrugged. "And I just couldn't let that happen. I know I'm going to have to apologize to the committee, but I'm over it. They'll just have to deal."

"Yay, Mom," I said. "But I really don't think they'll mind."

"No." She sighed. "And I sure don't care. Maybe it's because someone tried to kill me the other day, but I figure life's too short to put up with overbearing people like that."

"You've got the right of it, Rebecca," Derek said.

Meg had followed us out and now she wrapped her arms around my mother in a tight hug. "I'm so proud of you."

"Oh, sweetie," Mom said. "Don't you know I'm just a country bumpkin?"

"Then so are we all," Derek said, using his most erudite tone.

Our moms laughed and, suddenly aware of the target

we all made, I said, "Let's go back inside where it's a little less wide open."

"Excellent idea," Derek said.

"Besides," Meg said, locking arms with Mom. "I want another biscuit."

Back in the conference room, Mom made the announcement that the Alcott scholar wouldn't be attending the festival.

"She was right," Clyde grumbled. "That did not end well."

"Well, hip hip hooray," Winston Laurie said.

"Right on!" Sue yelled.

And once again, most of the group began to cheer and applaud.

"She was dreadful," Derek whispered, "but at least her presence served some purpose. We now know where Lawson got the book."

"And we also know why he stole the festival money," I said. "At least, part of the money. I'm guessing that someone found out about it and blackmailed him for the rest."

"It's quite possible," he murmured. "Perhaps we should look more closely at the committee members who assisted Lawson with the finances. They would be first to notice that the funds had been depleted."

"Are you thinking that Winston might be involved?"

"Or the others." He thought for a moment. "There were four hands raised when your mother asked who else had helped Lawson with his various duties."

"Yes." I stared at him. "Winston, Ryan, Saffron, and Marybeth. Guess we'll move them all up on the suspect list."

"Indeed."

Derek and I watched the way everyone in the group interacted with my mother and Meg as well as one another. We had talked about how anyone could kill under the right circumstance, but I couldn't see how these committee meetings and the book festival were the right circumstance.

Saffron was avoiding my mother, a good thing since I was ready to punch her if she said one word against her.

The woman was definitely capable of murder and the most likely suspect, simply because she hated everybody and everything. It was ironic that she had accused my mother of murder, but maybe that was just a ruse. We had to figure out what her motives were and how she, as a woman of about five feet four inches tall, had managed to cut the throats of two much taller, very heavyset men. I didn't see how she could've done it, but stranger things had happened.

"Who's in charge here?" a woman's voice demanded from the doorway.

Ryan perked up. "Shandi!"

Mom looked at me with wide eyes, but recovered quickly. "Come in, Shandi. Help yourself to a cup of tea and a snack."

Derek and I exchanged looks, and then I turned to study the woman walking into the room.

From across the room, Shandi Patrick looked beautiful, with a clear peaches-and-cream complexion and thick blond hair with lustrous waves tumbling over her shoulders and down her back. She wore a lovely formfitting black jacket over tan stretch pants fitted into knee-high brown boots.

She was stunning. But as she walked closer, I started to see the flaws. Not that I minded flaws, personally. But

Shandi knew how to work a room just the right way so that people didn't notice the imperfections. She knew where every lamp and light was and how to angle her face to show off her best attributes. It was amazing to watch. She'd had a nose job somewhere along the line and probably some augmentation here and there. Not that I cared about that, either. She was simply fascinating and a little bizarre.

She didn't lead with her left side, I noticed, instead keeping her right side toward the crowd. I strolled over to the tea kettle to fill up my cup and that's when I saw why she turned her left side away.

Her left cheek had a barely discernable vertical scar from her eye to the curve of her mouth, but you had to be in the right light to see it. And her left eye was slightly droopy. I wondered if she had been in an accident or if she had always been able to work it out so that only her best features were accentuated.

"It's nice to see you again, Shandi," Mom said. "Can I introduce you to some people?"

"I'm not here to socialize," she said sharply.

Mom didn't flinch despite the woman's rudeness. And now I knew I could happily hate her. She was definitely on the suspect list because she had a mean streak and I didn't like it. It didn't seem fair that Mom had had to deal with a frumpy know-it-all and now, a glamorous one.

Shandi strutted farther into the room. "I want to know what happened to Lawson Schmidt."

"Lawson was murdered the other night," Mom said candidly. "His throat was sliced with the broken edge of a wine bottle."

Shandi cringed at the picture Mom had painted and I was glad to see it. Who did she think she was, coming in here and making demands? This wasn't a Hollywood soundstage. How dare she try to throw her weight around and diss my mother!

"Do they have a suspect yet?" she asked.

"Maybe," was all Mom would say.

"Everyone's a suspect," Winston said.

Shandi looked horrified. "Are we all suspects?"

"Did you know Lawson?" Jan asked.

"Yes."

He grinned. "Then chances are, you're a suspect."

"Don't be rude to Shandi," Ryan said.

"Hey, kid," Jan said. "I'm just telling it like it is."

Shandi gave an amused smile. "Ryan's my protector. He'll beat you up if you're mean to me. He's a lot stronger than he looks."

"Yeah, we got that," I muttered.

Shandi whirled around and stared at me. "Who are you?"

"Nobody."

"Shandi, this is Brooklyn Wainwright," Ryan said. "She's London's sister."

She scanned me—with her good right eye—from my toes to the top of my head. Was she trying to intimidate me? Or was that just how she got to know people?

"So that makes you China's sister, too."

I nodded. "That's right."

"You have two very talented sisters," she said, almost grudgingly, and shook my hand. That's when I realized that the woman might've been fifty years old, but her grip was solid and I could tell that she was strong.

"Thanks. I think so, too."

Mom took a step forward. "Brooklyn's also very talented. She's a bookbinder."

"Ah." Shandi seemed to be considering this information. "Do you know anything about a book Lawson was holding for me?"

I caught a glimpse of Clyde. He looked suddenly panic-stricken and I took the hint. I gazed back at Shandi and said, "I don't know anything about any of Lawson's books. Sorry."

"Too bad. It's supposed to be a beauty."

It would be when I was finished with it, I thought. "Do you collect books?"

"Not really." She waved one hand regally. "This one sounded interesting though, because it's *Little Women* and that's the musical we're doing. Lawson told me about it and said he'd sell it to me." She shrugged. "I thought it would be a fun takeaway."

"That's a nice idea," I said. *A ten-thousand-dollar takeaway?*

If she was trying to raise money for a Hollywood comeback, would she really pay ten thousand dollars for an old copy of *Little Women*?

"Yeah." She ambled toward the door. "Well, see you all at the festival."

"See you, Shandi," Saffron said, and it was the first time I'd heard her sound happy.

Were they friends? I didn't believe it. What an odd woman Shandi was. She had swept in furious, then left as if she were the queen.

As soon as Shandi left, someone else walked into the room.

"Robson!" I said, completely shocked to see him.

"Hello, gracious," he said, taking both of my hands in his and squeezing lightly. "It is so good to see you."

"It's wonderful to see you."

"Are you working with your mother?"

"Not really working. I just like spending time with her."

"That is a lovely thing to hear." He turned to Derek and the two men shook hands. "And you will stay close by Brooklyn and her mother?"

"Absolutely," Derek said quietly.

I was amazed as always that Robson had his finger on the pulse of everything that occurred in Dharma, from the major losses of life down to the smallest disruptions.

Robson nodded his approval and smiled at Derek. "I am glad to see your mother is here."

"Yes, so am I." Derek grinned, and moved aside so that his mother could come closer.

"Hello, Margaret," Robson said. "I met you at the wedding of Derek and Brooklyn."

"Yes. What a lovely day that was." She held out her hand and he shook it gently. "My friends call me Meg."

"Then I shall be honored to call you Meg," he said. "It is so nice to see you again."

"Lovely to see you too, Robson."

"Derek is a fine man."

"Oh." She touched her heart. "Thank you. I think so, too."

He glanced toward my mother then and extended his hand. "Rebecca, gracious."

She grabbed his hand as though it were a lifeline. And maybe it was. He had been her teacher and mentor and guru and friend for over twenty-five years and being in his presence was always special for her. And for many of us, too.

Robson was the person my parents had followed from San Francisco to Sonoma all those years ago. He was the head of the Fellowship for Spiritual Enlightenment and Higher Artistic Consciousness. He was Guru Bob. And just seeing him here made me angry all over again that Saffron had dared to call our group a cult. Robson was just a man, but he was highly spiritual and kind, and he had devoted his life to helping others.

He was the one person I had gone to when I had started finding dead bodies. I thought of his words all the time because the dead bodies kept on coming.

He'd said, "Have you not considered the possibility that the dead seek you out? In each of the instances of which you speak, even when the victim was not your friend, you have been compassionate, as well as passionate, in leading the charge for justice. Do you not think the universe recognizes this?"

"Wait a sec," I had protested. "The police are pretty good at this, you know."

"Ah, but in many of these situations, it is my understanding that you have led them to several clues they might not have otherwise uncovered."

Guru Bob had helped me out, and remembering everything he had said to me kept me sane, mostly, in the middle of murder investigations.

"Robson," Mom said, interrupting my memories. "Would you like a cup of tea or a pastry?"

"No thank you, gracious." He smiled and gazed around the room. "I simply wanted to see you all and thank you for generously giving your time and energy toward making this book festival a wonderful experience for everyone who visits."

"Thank you, Robson," Mom said. The others chimed in their thanks, too, and Robson waved and left the room.

"Wow," I whispered.

"A powerful force," Derek murmured.

"I'll say."

Mom found her tote bag and pulled out her gavel. She probably hadn't thought she would need it at a tea party, but apparently she did. Banging on the table, she brought the room to order. "As some of you may have guessed, our Louisa May Alcott scholar has decided to go home early."

"Aw, such a shame," Clyde muttered, and the rest of the committee clearly felt the same.

Mom smiled and said, "With that done then, as the last official act of the committee today, I would like us to have a moment of silence for Lawson."

"Good idea," Sue said.

"B-but what if he stole that money?" Saffron said in her usual whining tone.

"He's dead," Clyde said in a flash of anger. "Show some respect."

"Yeah," Sue said. "We'll do the same for you when somebody knocks you off."

Outside on the Green, Derek and I walked on either side of my mother and Meg while they chatted together.

We scanned the workers who were setting up the booths, watching for odd behavior of any kind. Nothing seemed out of line.

The four of us walked over to the north end of the Circle where the porta-potties were being set up. We had a fascinating conversation with Buck, the self-proclaimed "porta-potty king," and learned all about the workings of those handy contraptions. Mom had ordered twenty deluxe toilets—"deluxe," meaning that they flushed. Woo-hoo. Two of those were ADA-compliant and actually quite large. Buck showed us how all of them worked. It was a revelation.

After that, we ran into Gabriel by the festival entrance where the sculpture still stood, thank goodness. He had some news for us.

"Derek, dear," Meg said. "Becky and I are going to have a sit-down on the bench right here and chitchat for a few minutes."

"All right, Mum," Derek said, noting that the bench was barely ten feet away. "We'll be right here."

I pounced on Gabriel. "You were gone forever. Did something happen?"

"Babe," he said, amused by my enthusiasm. "No, I was just checking things out."

I was almost disappointed. I wanted something to happen. I wanted answers.

Glancing over at Meg and my mom, I was pleased to see them giggling about something Mom was holding in her hand. Happy to have a distraction, I left the men to commiserate and walked over to talk to the ladies.

"What's going on with you two?" I asked.

"Oh, sweetie. We both picked a card from the tarot deck. Meg drew the Sun."

I'd learned a bit about tarot a few years ago. "Doesn't the Sun indicate joy and happiness, among other things?"

"Yes, it does," Meg said with a big smile. "Isn't that lovely?"

"Yes," I said, "and it suits you, Meg."

"Aren't you sweet to say so?" Meg sniffed a little and Mom patted her shoulder.

"Your Brooklyn is such a dear," Meg whispered.

Mom beamed at me and reached for my hand. "She certainly is."

I grinned. "What's your card, Mom?"

"I drew the World."

"Wow," I said, nodding. "Success and balance. Wholeness and achievement."

"The beginning of one cycle and the start of another," Meg added.

"Both of you drew Major Arcana cards. That's huge. Mom, I'm sure all that success and achievement is referring to your work with the festival. It's going to be tremendously successful."

"And there will be great success in your personal life as well," Meg added.

"Well, our Robin is having a baby," Mom said.

"That's right," I said, and laughed. "So many changes. So many cycles."

"Isn't it marvelous?" Meg said.

"That was great fun." Mom slipped the cards back into the box and leaned down to put them into her tote bag.

Just then, something whizzed past Mom and hit the side of one of the booths that had just been erected. The pretty yellow cloth lining that draped down the side of the booth recoiled from the impact, but managed to bounce back and stay upright.

"Derek!" I shouted.

"I'm here," he said. "Get down!"

He'd already drawn his gun and Gabriel had taken off running across the green lawn.

I grabbed Mom and Meg and shoved them toward the booth behind us. *The cloth hanging down on the sides won't protect us from a bullet*, I thought. *Still, we'll be hidden, which is better than remaining out in the open like sitting targets.*

"Let's hunker down here for a minute," I said, trying to keep my tone level.

"Yes, this is a good place to hide," Meg said agreeably.

"It couldn't have been a bullet," Mom said decidedly. "The cloth on that booth didn't tear."

It figured Mom would be reasonable even under attack.

"No, it didn't." Meg pursed her lips in thought. "Perhaps it was a rock or something like that. I wonder where it came from."

"Both Derek and Gabriel have quick reaction times, don't they?" Mom commented.

"Yes, they're both excellent," Meg agreed. "Very well trained. I feel quite safe with them nearby." She patted my knee. "You, too, Brooklyn. Thank you for whisking us out of harm's way."

Once again, Mom and Meg had come out of this fiasco with their nerves and sensibilities intact. I imagined I would've been shaking and whimpering if I'd been here by myself. But these two had nerves of steel, calmly discussing reaction times and whether or not it had been a bullet or a rock. But then, they'd both survived raising multiple children. That made them plenty tough. They would be pretty good companions in a foxhole.

"We're clear," Derek announced, having slipped his gun back under his jacket.

"Thank you, dear." Meg grinned at Mom. "Well, wasn't that exciting?"

"Very. I'm all out of breath."

Gabriel came running up, gave Derek a pointed look, and shook his head. Which meant that they hadn't caught the guy.

Meg looked up at Derek. "What was it exactly that was flung at us?"

"It was a good-sized rock," Derek said, opening his

hand to reveal a rock only slightly smaller than a golf ball. "And it was indeed flung. Probably by a slingshot."

That size rock coupled with its speed was enough to kill, I thought.

"I knew it couldn't be a bullet," Meg said. "Becky and I were just guessing that it had been a rock."

"That's right, Derek. Your mom thought of it first." My mom said with pride in her voice.

"Well done, Mum," Derek said, looking a little flustered, and who could blame him?

"Didn't anyone out here notice a person flinging a rock from a slingshot?" I asked.

Derek pointed to the roof of the town hall directly across the Circle from where Mom and Meg were sitting. "He was probably perched right there on the roof. Then he likely dashed behind the clock tower to avoid being seen."

"There's easy access from the roof down into the kitchen," Gabriel explained. "Then out the door on the other side and he disappears into the crowd."

"He has pretty good aim," I mused.

"Yeah," Gabriel said. "Maybe we should be looking for a major league pitcher."

I shook my head in wonder. "How can anyone send a rock that size so far and so accurately?"

Gabriel shrugged. "The right person using a good slingshot can shoot the distance of more than four football fields at a speed up to one hundred miles an hour."

"How do you know this stuff?" I asked.

"I'm a man of many talents." He just grinned and I realized that Gabriel was probably one of those people who could achieve that distance and speed. And that same accuracy. Whew. And looking at Derek, I figured he couldn't be far behind in those skills.

"Never mind," I muttered. "Hey, Gabriel, did you get a chance to ask Detective Willoughby about the security cameras on the Lane?"

"Yeah," he said, and grimaced. "They got nothing. Plenty of sidewalk action, but very little of the street itself. Sorry, babe."

"That's okay. I guess I wasn't expecting much." But I had been hoping. "Oh, and did anything ever come of that missing button you guys found in the meeting room?"

He chuckled. "It belongs to one of the housecleaners."

"Ah. Well, okay." So much for my top-notch investigative skills. I sighed and turned to my mother. "Are you all right, Mom?"

She had to have been shaken up, even though the rock hadn't made contact with her. And seeing the way Derek had whipped out his gun and I had shoved them back behind the booth, it couldn't have been easy for her or Meg.

"I'm fine," she said. "I didn't even know what was happening, until you got us up and out of there."

I gazed at Derek and he put his arm around my shoulder. "I think you're more shaken up than our mothers, darling."

I blew out a breath. "I heard that rock whizz by. It sounded like a missile."

"I heard it, too, dear," Meg said. "But since it quickly became clear that none of us was hurt, I refused to worry." She glanced at the booth. "I suppose that booth got a bit shaken up, though."

"The booth will be fine," I said with a smile.

Gabriel said, "I'm going to call Steve Willoughby and report this."

"But no one was hurt, dear," Meg said.

"No, but somebody might've noticed a person carrying a slingshot."

"That's something you don't see every day," Mom observed. "So you'd probably remember if you did."

"That's the hope." Gabriel grinned. "I'll have the cops check it out."

Chapter 15

The four of us ran into Clyde on the way back to the car and he gave us the bad news.

"My author event has been cancelled due to the Good Book having been turned into a crime scene."

I groaned with disappointment. Was that callous of me? Caring more about the Dead Author event than I did about Banyan's death? Maybe, but in my defense, Banyan hadn't given me many reasons to care about him, while Clyde had.

"Oh dear, Clyde," Mom said. "Will you reschedule?"

"Yeah, I'll figure out a date as soon as the cops let me back into the store. I'll post the new date on the website but it should be sometime in the next two weeks."

"What a shame," Meg said. "But we'll do it again."

"Yes, I'm dying to see Agatha Christie," Mom said.

"And she's dying to see you, too." I snickered. "Get it?"

"Well done, Brooklyn," Meg said cheerfully, but my mother just rolled her eyes.

"It was a cheap joke," I admitted. "But worth saying, don't you think?"

"Get in the car, love," Derek said, ending the discussion.

As soon as we got home, Derek pulled the plastic crate from his trunk and I took it out to Abraham's workshop to continue my work on *Little Women*.

I was disappointed that Clyde's author visit had been cancelled tonight, mainly because I had relished the thought of dragging Derek to a séance. Derek, on the other hand, was pleased to have a quiet night to ourselves.

Who was he kidding?

Through no particular planning on our part, we ended up with a houseful of people that night, along with a massive amount of food. I called it our prefestival festival. We had chicken, spicy wings, more pizza, and six different side salads. There was more wine than I could have ever thought of drinking in a lifetime, but that was normal.

We had invited Vinnie and Suzie, who put Lily to bed in the nearest guest bedroom off the kitchen; Gabriel and Alex, who had returned for the weekend; Austin and Robin, who had concocted her own "signature cocktail" for her pregnancy, something with fancy soda water, lime juice, and a splash of bitters over ice; Presley and Annie, who was just happy she wasn't going to have to clean up this mess; and Jackson and his new love Elizabeth, although they'd known each other for years. And her name was actually Elisheba, aka Elise. It was a long story.

I had invited China and London, too, but my sisters were both too busy to attend, what with last-minute play rehearsals and costume changes. Our parents had been

invited but they had chosen to spend the evening playing cards at my parents' house. I knew they would probably have a better time with just the four of them. They
could talk about their kids.

My work on the book was almost finished so I put it
away and joined my friends and family members. Most
of these were people I didn't get to see very often, like
Elizabeth who had saved Annie's life last year. And
Robin. And Vinnie and Suzie, too, even though they
lived across the hall from us in San Francisco. These
days we only waved at each other when we passed in the
hall on our way to the elevator. We were all so busy, so
this was the perfect time to catch up on all of our lives.

I moved from group to group, refilling wineglasses—
and one soda water—and joining in on conversations.
Robin had pinned down Vinnie and Suzie to pick their
brains about child-proofing their home.

"But how do you manage to keep Lily safe with all
your deadly chainsaws and flying wood splinters?"
Robin wondered. She was a sculptor herself, with a big
studio off the kitchen where she kept a lot of potentially
dangerous tools and equipment.

"We have child-proofed the entire house," Vinnie
assured her. "And we clean up everything at the end of
each day."

"We thought about renting a studio," Suzie said, "but
we would've brought Lily with us every day anyway, so
what was the point?"

"So we soundproofed the living room and continue
to work there, and we've turned Lily's bedroom into a
little girl's fantasy playroom." Vinnie beamed. "She can
spend hours in there and she knows that we are nearby."

"And that works?" Robin asked.

"Oh yes," Vinnie said.

Suzie added with a grin, "And then there's the gate we installed across her door."

Vinnie nodded. "The gate is most essential."

I laughed and moved on to another group, then noticed Alex and Elizabeth standing alone by the fireplace. I wandered over and was surprised to hear the two women quietly sharing tales of their exploits as intelligence agents in the most dangerous parts of the world.

I stopped to listen to their fascinating stories. After a minute or so, they realized I was close by. They exchanged a look, then said in unison, "Now we'll have to kill you."

I held up the bottle. "But I have wine."

"Then you may live," Elizabeth said, and held out her glass.

I rolled my eyes and filled their wineglasses. The two women were always a lot more circumspect when discussing the details of their old covert operations, so I stared from one to the other with suspicion. "What were you really talking about before I walked over here?"

"Sorry, Brooklyn." Alex smiled. "We saw you coming."

Elizabeth grinned. "Alex was sharing her latest cupcake recipes with me. Listen to these." She pulled a piece of notepaper from her pocket. "The first is a lemon meringue cupcake with lemon curd and real meringue on top."

"Oh my," I whispered reverently. "Lemon meringue pie is a favorite of mine."

"Mine, too," Alex said. "So these are like eating lemon meringue pie cake."

"My mouth is watering."

Elizabeth nodded. "The other recipe is for pumpkin spice latte cupcakes."

I turned an accusing glare to Alex. "You've never made those for me."

She laughed. "I'm still experimenting."

The evening broke up shortly after that, but I was not surprised to learn that there were other cupcake fanatics in my circle of friends. As everyone was slipping into their coats and pulling on warm hats, I overheard Annie offering Alex a contract to make cupcakes every week for her kitchen store.

That would be one way to get Alex to visit Dharma more often, I thought. And it would sure make Gabriel happy. I was too tired to join in the conversation, but I made a mental note to encourage Alex to say yes tomorrow.

I went to bed way too late, but very happy.

The next day, the festival participants were invited to decorate their booths. I spent a few hours hanging posters of rare books and enlarged photos of the books I'd made in the past. In one corner I hung a replica of the large kite I had created for the Covington Library Children's Museum display. For the book festival version, I had used handmade paper that resembled tie-dyed cloth, and hung it from the steel pole that ran across the top of the booth. It made a fun statement, for sure.

I laid two colorful tablecloths over the utility table and set up a mini-bookshelf on top with some of my reference books that I'd be using for my book appraisals and for my book and wine pairings presentation.

Under the utility table I had three plastic bins that held all of my bookbinding supplies for the children's book arts demonstration. Any child that participated would take home a really cute accordion book that they'd made themselves. It was easy to do and a good way for parents to take a break while their kids were having some paper art fun.

Tucked inside the plastic bins were also six different bottles of wine that I would use during the Friday book and wine pairings for visitors to sample. Since I was scheduled to do one of these presentations each day, I still had twelve more bottles waiting back at the house for Saturday and Sunday.

Besides the Dharma police officers patrolling the festival grounds, Robson had hired ten extra security guards from the Fellowship to help with crowd control during the day and to keep everything safe and secure overnight. I hadn't left anything of real value in the booth, except the wine, of course. But I wasn't too concerned, since a number of booths were being used by vendors from the local wineries who had boxes and wine refrigerators filled with bottles that they would be pouring from all weekend. My little stash was nothing compared to those guys.

I went home to finish the *Little Women* book with time to spare. I had completed all the work on the interior of the book and only had to clean up the cover.

If the cover had been leather, I would've been able to use a light leather cleaner or a leather consolidant that would improve hardness and eliminate cracks. But since this book had a cloth cover, all I could do was use a short, stiff, dry brush, working it into the joints and along the edges of the illustration to scrub away the years of dust and grime. It was surprisingly effective.

The colorful illustration of the four sisters had been done on thick, coated vellum, and to this I applied a very thin oil that brightened it nicely. And when I placed it behind the beveled frame of the book cloth, it looked absolutely brand-new.

Thrilled with my efforts, I brought the book and supplies back to the house and readied everything for my big festival adventure.

With nothing else planned that night, Derek finally got the quiet evening he had wanted. We had a blissfully uneventful night watching TV while we finished the leftovers from last night's party and played with Charlie before going to bed.

The night passed without a panicked phone call waking us up, thank goodness, and we woke up early to a glorious sunny day in the wine country. The air was cold and clear, but the sun was bright with the promise of a warm afternoon. Festival days were finally here!

I awoke with a feeling akin to Christmas morning—despite the memory of two grisly murders in the last few days. I knew it was book-geeky of me, but I was really excited to get out to the festival and get that potty started.

Derek had made coffee and warmed up some scones from his mother, so we ate lightly—if you didn't count two scones each and all that butter and jam and the mock Devonshire cream that I whipped up. Delicious!

Then we headed out to the festival grounds to get ready for the onslaught. They were predicting at least five thousand visitors this weekend. It helped that it was almost time for the grape harvest and the leaves on the trees were turning every wonderful, warm, rustic shade of autumn. It was a beautiful time to be in Dharma.

Mom would be driving with Dad and Robin and Austin, so for once, Derek and I weren't playing security guard for her. I knew she was just as relieved as we were.

Still, there was a killer on the loose, so once we got to Berkeley Circle, Derek planned to keep a watchful eye on her. We had alerted Austin and Gabriel as well.

Mom and Meg had dressed up their psychic booth with colorful posters of Tarot cards and a palm reading chart. Silk material hung from each corner to the center of the booth, giving the space a lush, romantic feeling. Happily their booth was directly across the Green from my own, so I would be able to keep an eye on them. The rest of my family planned to stop by often, too.

I settled into my booth and laid out the supplies for the children's accordion books. I had room at the table to teach five kids at a time, and since I had already cut and folded the paper, cardboard, and ribbon, I estimated that each group would only need about twenty minutes to make their little books.

I was pleased to see that the Dharma Winery booth was close by, as well. I waved to Dad and Austin and promised I would stop by if I could get away. Likewise, Robin promised to take over booth duties for a half hour each day so I could check out the other vendors and maybe do some shopping. She also assured me that she would bring me sips and snacks once in a while. I had a feeling I would need the fortification.

For all the preparations that Mom and her committee had gone through to make the festival a success, I couldn't believe that we pulled it off—and still managed to have a wonderful time. Friday was a madhouse and Saturday was even busier. But I loved it. For three days we welcomed thousands of visitors who wandered the festival grounds, chatting with booksellers and authors and vendors. They bought books and goodies and paraphernalia, drank wine and nibbled on snacks, and occasionally just sat and enjoyed the wonderful weather. They partied and listened and walked and laughed and learned a few things.

Each day I had a few dozen kids making little accordion books in my booth. They loved these cute little books that expanded like an accordion when the ribbon was untied. Adults loved them, too, and they were remarkably easy to make.

I appraised ten to twelve books a day and many of the book owners went away happy. I had to disappoint a few, though, who thought that their beloved books might be a rare and wondrous find. Too often their treasured leather-bound book club editions were not as valuable as they'd hoped. I assured them that the book's real worth was in its sentimental value. There were some unhappy faces, but most of my visitors took the news with good humor.

But there was one book that caught my eye and piqued my interest. It was a pristine copy of *Harry Potter and the Philosopher's Stone*, the British version of J. K. Rowling's first book in the series.

"Where did you get this?" I asked the young man who had pulled it out of a small brown shopping bag.

He grinned. "My father was on a business trip to England and heard about this book, so he bought it for me. He always used to bring me a little gift when he was on one of his business trips." He chuckled. "He traveled a lot, so I figure he was feeling the guilt."

"That's a nice dad you have."

"He's pretty cool," he admitted. "He's retired now and he lives with me so I get to see him all the time." He glanced across the Green. "He's checking out the kitchenware booth. He likes to cook."

"You're lucky."

"Yeah. Especially since I can't cook to save my life."

Welcome to my world, I thought. I opened the book to the title page and verified that this was a first edition copy. I checked the strength of the inside hinges and carefully glanced at a few pages to see how well the paper had aged.

"You must've been pretty young when he brought this home," I said. "How did it stay in such good shape?" Children were notoriously hazardous to the health of books.

"Dad used to read a few pages to me each night, then he'd put it away on a shelf. He's a real booklover, so he wouldn't let me get my hands on it."

Smart dad, I thought. "Have you had this book appraised before?"

"No. I would never sell it, but I heard that you'd be doing these book appraisals so I thought I'd check it out."

I knew the book was valuable but I wasn't sure how much it might be worth so I took a quick look online. A minute later I glanced up at him. "Are you ready?"

"Yeah." He grinned. "Should I sit down?"

"Maybe. Because it's in such good condition, it could be worth at least fifty thousand dollars and maybe even as much as a hundred thousand."

"Whoa." He blinked, muttered his thanks, and stumbled away to find his dad.

Another satisfied customer, I thought with a smile.

A lot of the people who stopped by my booth were quick to comment on Vinnie and Suzie's giant book sculpture. I was so happy that Mom had commissioned them to create something so perfect for our first annual festival and I knew she would make sure it was stored properly so that we could use it every year.

From my booth, I could hear the childish laughter and applause for the acts performing on the children's stage in the middle of the Green. Robin finally came by to relieve me for a few minutes and I was able to stroll around and enjoy the energy of the crowd. I checked out Annie's kitchenware booth and bought a book called *Cooking for Dummies*. Perfect for my level of expertise.

When I returned to my booth, Robin jumped up. "I'm going to run over to Becky and Meg's booth to get my palm read."

"Okay, but no running. Not in your condition."

"Yes, ma'am." With a smile, she saluted and took off.

I watched her cross the Green and that was when I noticed the line of people streaming out from Mom and Meg's psychic booth. There had to be at least thirty people waiting to get their fortunes told!

Our moms' booth was ridiculously popular. Mom deserved all the success she could get after what she'd been through lately. And I gave myself a little pat on the back because I had predicted that the psychic booth would be a real crowd pleaser. It helped that my mother and Meg were such delightful psychics in their flowing robes and with such positive energy. I would have to ask for a private palm reading next week.

Meanwhile, back at my booth, I jumped right into my book and wine pairings. It was fun to see the reactions of the people who listened as I read a paragraph from a selected book and then tasted the wine I'd paired it with. Most were simply astonished at how well the wine went with the literary passage. I had to laugh because my choices were completely subjective and whimsical— for instance, I paired a chilled Viognier, with its soft start and sweet-citrusy notes, with Jane Austen's *Emma*.

Why not? It had to be the power of suggestion that made my choices seem fitting and reasonable. Or maybe I was really onto something. *Um, no. It was just fun.*

I'd had postcards made up that listed the books and wines I'd paired together, and I handed them out to anyone who wanted them. Not so coincidentally, all of the wines I'd chosen were from Dharma Winery. I mentioned this to my father who thought that was a brilliant ploy, but when I told him I expected a kickback, he laughed himself silly.

Saturday night in the town hall gallery room, we held the official festival cocktail party and silent auction. I walked from item to item, checking out the lists of names of all the people anxious to bid on the items.

Many of the items were book related, of course. There were a number of baskets of books by the same authors and a few baskets that included things like a pretty bookmark and tea and cookies and warm socks or a snugly blanket for cozying up with a good book. Some baskets combined wine and books, which appealed to me, naturally. I added my name to a few of those lists.

There were several copies of *Little Women* being auctioned off. I looked at the numerous names on the bidding sheets and figured a lot of people wanted a nice copy of the official festival book to take home. One of the copies was nicely bound in leather with lots of gilding on the spine. It looked expensive, but it actually wasn't. This was another one of those book club editions I'd had to deal with in a few of my appraisals earlier that day. They were pretty and nicely bound, though not particularly rare or aged. I hoped the new book owners would be happy when they learned that they'd won.

Clyde's copy of *Little Women* was placed on a sturdy wooden bookstand with a sign that said "please do not touch." I smiled, knowing that plenty of people would try to touch it anyway. There were only a few names on the bidding list and the bids they'd offered were very low. Without thinking too much, I added my name to the list with a bid of forty dollars. I knew it was worth a lot more, so I promised myself I would make out a check to the literacy organization later. But I didn't want to write down too much money on the bidding list in case someone was looking for Lawson's copy.

On the other hand, if the book had any connection to the murders, this might be the perfect way to lure our killer out of hiding. I checked the names of my fellow bidders and didn't recognize them, but the evening was still young.

I had noticed that Shandi's name was listed on the other shinier book club edition, but not this one. Didn't she know that this was the book that Lawson had told her about? Had he shown her the book? Apparently not. That was okay with me.

An hour later, the auctioneer began calling out the winners, and when it came to the copy of *Little Women* that I'd refurbished, the speaker called my name.

"I won!" I cried, and Derek grinned. The very book that Bettina Trimble had sold to Lawson Schmidt for ten thousand dollars had barely received six bids. And while I'd listed a higher amount than anyone else on the list, I'd still figured there would be more bidders after me.

But no. I was thrilled to hear my name called as the winner. A silent auction could be a cutthroat experience, with people glancing over your shoulder waiting for you to add your bid and leave, then slithering up to add their own higher bid. I was amazed that I didn't have a serious competitor for this lovingly refurbished rare book. And again I had to ask myself, why hadn't Shandi bid on it? Clearly she hadn't connected the dots to realize that the book Lawson had told her about would be older and perhaps slightly less shiny than the one she had bid on. *But most people like shiny objects*, I supposed.

I was especially amazed that I'd only had to pay forty dollars for the book that was arguably worth ten thousand. When I told Clyde I'd won it, he gave me his blessing. Especially when I confided that I planned to write my own check to the literacy organization and that I intended to give the book to Lawson's mother—"Marmee"— as he would've wanted. I might've been mistaken, but I thought I spied a mist of tears in Clyde's curmudgeonly eyes when he heard the news. And that was worth more than anything I might've gained by selling the book to someone else.

By four o'clock Sunday afternoon, everyone had started packing up their booths and clearing out. I had already packed most of my books and tools and decorations back in the three bins. Derek had taken the posters, the photos, and the kite to the car, and Gabriel and Alex helped us cart the rest of the bins to the car, too.

The workers had begun breaking down some of the booths and packing them up in the massive truck that would take them back to the rental company until next year.

As we dragged ourselves to our cars, I suddenly realized that the last night of the festival probably hadn't been the best evening to schedule a performance of a big musical production.

"I'm so tired," Alex said.

I nodded. "I can barely stay awake. But we've got to rally somehow. We've got to summon enough energy to enjoy the musical."

"I'll make a pot of coffee when we get home," Derek said.

"You're a lifesaver."

We took a thirty-minute nap when we got home, then woke up and took a quick shower. The shower helped revive us both, and the two cups of strong coffee made my eyes pop. I also chewed on peppermint candies to keep me awake through the performance. I was pretty sure we would make it through to the end—and sleep like the dead later tonight.

We sat on the left side of the second row surrounded by family and friends, including Mom and Dad sitting in the center of the first row next to Meg and John. Alex and Gabriel sat next to us on the aisle and we chatted quietly until the orchestra struck the first notes and the curtain slowly rose.

It was thrilling to see my family members and friends walking on stage and delivering lines as if they'd been performing forever. Where did all this talent come from? I was so impressed and enjoyed every minute of the first act.

I began to notice that from where we sat, I could see a partial section backstage on the left side where most of the actors entered and exited. It was a bit of a thrill to get a glimpse of the behind-the-scenes action every few minutes.

I was ridiculously proud of China's work on the costumes. They added so much to the production value and I couldn't wait to celebrate with her. I still planned to kick her butt someday, but for now I couldn't be prouder.

The singing was wonderful, and as London said, Shandi's voice was remarkably good. She was clearly a professional talent, but the big shocker was that her acting was surprisingly inclusive and generous. I had worried that she would try to upstage the others, but she was supportive and aware of all the other characters on stage at the same time she was performing. I wondered if London had had a hand in directing her to be that way.

Halfway through the first act, I watched one of the actors exit stage left, her heavy costume brushing the curtain back enough that I could see Ryan standing on the sidelines. Had he been there the whole time? Was he there to personally support Shandi? I wouldn't be surprised. Like a prizefighter's manager in between the rounds, I could imagine Ryan feeding her sips of water and giving her pep talks.

His adoration of the Diva was almost embarrassing sometimes. I thought back to Shandi's visit to the conference room a few days ago and how Ryan had watched in awe as she mingled and spoke to the "little people."

That memory reminded me of the day Ryan had begged my Mom to convince London to recast the play. I shook my head, recalling Mom's words. *She's no spring chicken.* I frowned as I realized that it was later that evening that Mom was almost killed by the hit-and-run driver.

Because I couldn't help myself, I tried to connect the other moments when someone had said something that wasn't quite complimentary enough about Shandi.

Jacob Banyan had told Mom that he "didn't give a hoot about that stupid musical. A bunch of amateurs and one pathetic over-the-hill actress who couldn't sing her way out of a paper bag."

Jacob Banyan was killed that night.

Oh my God, I thought, and had to catch my breath at the realization that we had a motive, as crazy as it seemed. Was I nuts or was there really a link?

And Mom's attacker hadn't given up yet. That rock that was flung from a slingshot a few days ago had been meant for her. Anybody who could shoot a slingshot that far would've also been accurate enough to hit their target—unless, at that precise moment, Mom bent over to stick those cards into her tote bag.

But then, what was Lawson's crime against Shandi? Clyde thought Lawson was killed because he had stolen the festival money. I had assumed—as I often did—that it was all about the book. So which of us was right? Or was it something else?

Shandi had come looking for the book Lawson had told her about. Was she behind all of the killings? That was a stretch, but it still made sense. But if it was all about the book, then why hadn't she bid on the valuable edition of *Little Women*? And another thing: I refused to believe that Shandi was proficient with a slingshot.

But maybe I was being sexist. An actor had to have skills in all sorts of areas. Horseback riding, shooting, different languages. So why wouldn't Shandi have learned to shoot a slingshot somewhere in her career? Maybe she'd played a role in a rural comedy or a desert island adventure. Slingshot skills would be useful in those locales, depending on the script. I made a mental note to look up her acting roles and see if anything slingshot-related jumped out at me.

Shandi had her admirers and minions, though, and I

wondered if one of them might have gone to bat on her behalf. Saffron, for instance, had been living in this rural area of the wine country for years. She might've found a slingshot useful now and then when taking down wildlife critters.

I almost cracked myself up at the image of snooty Saffron Bergeron taking down critters. So where was I going with all of this slingshot theory? I sobered up, knowing it really wasn't a laughing matter. Someone had tried to attack my mother with a big honking rock and a slingshot. I imagined it was that same person who'd tried to run her down that first night. Actors needed driving skills, too.

The curtain wafted out again. And staring at Ryan, I suddenly realized that he might know how to use a slingshot, too.

He's so quiet, I thought. Almost invisible. Never making waves. Was that part of his appeal to Shandi? He wouldn't be noticed when he took care of something she had directed him to do. Like kill her enemies, for instance.

Maybe he'd been after anyone who'd spoken ill of Shandi. But what about Lawson? I'd never heard him say anything about the woman. Was it simply about wanting the book? That didn't make sense. But then, I had learned over the years that when it came to books, some people could go a little crazy.

I was going way out on a limb with this Ryan-as-killer theory and I had no way to prove any of it. Not yet anyway. But I continued to watch the young man on the sidelines and wondered. And worried. My mother was in the audience tonight, in the first row. From where he stood, Ryan probably had a direct visual line to her. Was he staring at her right now? Would he try something tonight? In front of three hundred audience members, a good-sized cast of characters, and a full orchestra?

I picked up the program to give my antsy hands something to do. In the dim light I could barely read the synopsis of the play and the various biographies, but my eyes quickly became accustomed to the dimness and I scanned the words as the actors continued performing on the stage. I was surprised to read that Ryan was listed as an understudy for the role of Laurie, the boy who lived next door to the girls and who was in love with Jo through most of the play. So he was an actor, too? Was that how he and Shandi met?

Ryan's biography listed his other credits as well as his accomplishments and educational background. He had served in the military, and he spoke French and Spanish and Cockney English. Who knew? He rode horseback. He sailed. And he was proficient with weaponry, particularly knives, handguns, rifles, crossbows, and even vintage weaponry such as catapults and slingshots.

Oh my God. Was this for real? Did they teach all of that in the military?

I grabbed Derek's arm. "Read this," I whispered, and shoved the program in his hand.

He gave me a look that told me he thought I'd gone nuts, and maybe he was right. But he went ahead and read it, holding the program at an angle so that he could get the maximum light to shine on it.

And then he whipped around and stared at me. "No way," he whispered.

"Way!" I whispered back, still shaking with nerves.

Alex elbowed me and I could see her smiling. "What's going on with you two?"

I handed her the program and leaned in close to

whisper, "Have Gabriel read this. Right now." I pointed to Ryan's bio.

She gave me the same doubtful look, but leaned over to Gabriel and asked him to do what I'd said.

A minute later, Gabriel leaned forward and looked down the row at Derek. He made two hand signals, and Derek nodded, then pointed to his wristwatch and sent two other signals back.

These guys, I thought, and had to smile. Their inner spies were gearing up for a fight.

Gabriel nodded and went back to watching the play.

I sat back and enjoyed the show, knowing that the game was afoot.

Chapter 16

During intermission, Alex and I went to the bar to get two small glasses of wine to share with our guys. We found them in a dark corner of the patio, discussing a plan of action.

I told them everything I'd put together in my head about Ryan, even before I'd read the program.

"He's standing backstage left," I said. "He was there for the whole first act."

"I noticed that, too," Gabriel said. "But he slipped outside just as intermission was starting. The stage manager told me that Shandi sent him off to the drugstore because she didn't like the brand of water they had backstage."

Alex rolled her eyes. "Prima donna."

"They call her the Diva."

"Suits her," she said.

I scowled. "And I'm pretty sure Ryan had his eye on Mom most of the time he was standing backstage."

"Someone's out to get her," Derek murmured. "It could be him."

"But I don't think he would do anything until after Shandi's solo in the second act." I took a quick look at the program. "It's Marmee's big moment. No way would he ruin it for her."

"Good point," Gabriel said.

I nodded. "I say we enter on the right side, make our way backstage, and sneak around to the left side, going behind the back curtains, behind the scrim, and grab him."

Gabriel and Derek exchanged a look, then Gabriel said, "We have to get him before he can utter a sound."

"Otherwise, we'll disrupt the play," Derek noted. "The less commotion, the better."

Alex looked at the two men. "Do you want me to take care of it?"

Gabriel shot a look at Derek and shrugged. "She's better than both of us."

Derek nodded. "I'm good with it."

"You can take him, Alex," I whispered. "He's ex-military, but there's no way he has your skills. And once he's out cold, I can help you drag him around to the back."

Alex looked at me, then stared directly at Derek. "I'm not going to tell her."

Derek shook his head. "I'm not going to tell her."

Gabriel laughed shortly. "I'll tell her." He looked at me. "Babe, you're staying in your seat."

"No." I bristled. "I'm the one who busted him. I'm the one who showed you the program."

"Darling," Derek said.

My shoulders sagged. "Come on. I want to go with you guys."

"Babe," Gabriel said.

I held up my hand. "Fine. I played my part. Now I'll stay behind and make sure Mom is safe."

"Darling, we're not going off to war."

I scowled. "You know what I'm saying."

Gabriel saluted with a wink. "Read you loud and clear, babe."

"Just don't forget." I shook the program in their faces. "I'm the mastermind. You're the muscle."

Derek threw his head back and laughed out loud. "I love you, Brooklyn."

Gabriel chuckled. "Babe, you're a riot."

"Okay, we got this," Alex said, and gave me a friendly punch in the arm. "Thanks to you."

I smiled, then sobered. "I hate to interrupt my sisters' fabulous presentation, but I think you should do it before the play is over. Because if he stays where he is, he's got a clear sightline to my mother."

Derek looked through the program and found the page he wanted. "There's only one act left. We'll wait until we hear this song, 'The Fire within Me,' and that's when we'll move up the right stairs." He tapped the program page again. "By the time we hear 'Small Umbrella in the Rain,' we'll be in position to attack. Alex, you'll render him unconscious, and Gabriel and I will carry him out of here."

"Just try not to make too much noise," I said, wincing. "I'd really love it if the audience doesn't catch on."

"We'll be quiet," Gabriel said. "But even if there's a scuffle or a few screams, people in the audience will think it's part of the play."

"Screams?" I said. "Clearly you've never read *Little Women*. There's no screaming."

Alex snorted.

"We'll be quick," Derek said brusquely. "The point is to render him helpless and get him out of there."

"Should we call the police?" I asked.

"Cops?" Gabriel said.

Derek grinned. "Where's your sense of adventure?"

"You guys sound like our mothers," I said, but I was smiling, sort of. "I'll call the cops as soon as I see you carrying him away. And don't feel guilty that I don't get to go on an adventure."

They gave each other remorseful looks, as if they were almost about to change their minds and bring me along.

I smiled hopefully.

Then Alex said, "Nice try, snookums."

"No guilt here," Derek said.

"Yeah, forget it, babe," Gabriel said.

Alex stood, then leaned down and whispered, "Get that green belt, Brooks. Then we'll talk."

The bell rang three times, signaling the end of intermission.

"Here goes nothing," I muttered as we walked back to our seats.

Someone in the audience must have noticed those three well-dressed people tiptoeing up the stage right stairs, but nobody said anything. The show's climax was about to begin and the music was stirring everyone's hearts.

My three spymasters disappeared behind the curtain and I held my breath for what felt like several long minutes. The action on stage continued. Annie, playing the youngest sister Beth, had died and was laid out lovingly on one of the couches.

I kept checking the backstage area and didn't see Ryan. Was he still at the store picking up water? I was getting really nervous.

When Jo revealed to her sisters that she had written a book, I knew we had reached the climax of the story.

The first chords of the song gave me chills, not only because it was an emotional moment on stage, but because Ryan had returned to his position offstage. And now I could see Alex, standing ten feet back from Ryan. He didn't notice her because he was staring into the audience, even though Shandi was performing on stage.

I tried to follow his sightline and realized with horror that he was staring at my mother, just as I'd feared. He couldn't get away with this.

But then I watched him reach into his jacket pocket and pull something out. He let his hand drop to his side and I saw what he was surreptitiously holding in his hand.

Oh my God.

Had Ryan seen Alex creeping up from behind? Did he know he'd been caught? Or had he simply lost his mind?

Without another thought, I stood and shouted, "He has a gun!" Then I launched myself across the row of people in front of me and grabbed my mother, dragging her to the ground.

Alex reacted instantly, tackling Ryan and wrestling the gun away from him. They tumbled onto the stage and the audience went bonkers. There were screams and laughter—did they think it was part of the show?

Shandi stared at Ryan and screamed, "Why are you ruining the climax of the play?"

Sara, the girl playing Jo, continued singing and scuttling out of the way as the fighting moved across the stage. Finally she stopped and shrieked, "Who are you? What are you doing in my song?"

And then she burst into tears.

The dead sister, Beth—our Annie—finally sat up and looked around, thoroughly confused. Someone in the audience shouted, "It's a miracle!"

Most of the audience laughed. And that's when I remembered to call 911 and report that someone had a gun at the theater.

Alex and Ryan were now the stars of the show. The orchestra conductor finally realized it and signaled the musicians to stop. Until that moment, none of them had heard anything but the music. Now they all stood and watched Alex straddling Ryan, who was still trying to grab the gun. Everyone was shouting and cheering on the good guys, although it was hard to tell who the good guys were versus the bad ones.

"Sweetie, are you all right?" my mom asked.

"I hope I didn't hurt you, but Ryan had a gun pointed at you."

We pulled each other up to a sitting position. "I'm fine," she said. "Isn't this crazy? But fun."

"Oh yeah. Fun."

Alex finally managed to calm a squirming Ryan. No thanks to me. I had alerted him and put Alex in danger. But in my defense, the jerk had a gun! Which put everyone in danger.

Derek and Gabriel walked onto the stage and hoisted Ryan up off the floor.

The audience applauded the two hunky men, but meanwhile, Shandi and the four sisters were still screaming and shouting for everyone to shut up so the last song could be finished and the musical could end on a high note. But most in the audience couldn't care less. They were having too much fun watching the action.

So much for being a mastermind, I thought. But at least I'd managed to save my mother from imminent danger. That was how I would insist on painting it, anyway.

Derek shoved Ryan onto one of the couches. "Stay

put," he ordered, then glanced out at the audience. "Is there a representative from law enforcement in the audience?"

Were the police here yet? I had my answer when Steve Willoughby shouted, "Right here," and jogged down the side aisle. "Please remain where you are." He rushed up to the stage with two of his officers, who weren't in uniform. Had they all been in the audience?

Shandi was still yelling at Ryan. "How could you ruin it all?"

Ryan was cringing at Shandi's accusations. Finally, he shouted back, "I did it all for you. I've always been here for you."

The audience began to quiet down, as people realized there was another show to watch.

"You needed money," Ryan said in a rush, "and I tried to get it for you."

"I don't need it that badly."

"Well, I wanted to help. But then a lot of people were saying mean things about you and I tried to make them stop."

"People's words don't bother me," she insisted.

"But you said you wanted to make a big Hollywood comeback. If people believed those bad things about you, they might not want to produce a movie for you."

"I was going to do that myself."

"Right," Ryan said agreeably, "and you needed money to do it, you said. So I got you some money. And then you said you wanted Lawson's book so I went looking for it. It's my job to get you everything you ask for."

Did they know they had the audience's full attention? Except for Shandi, I didn't think so.

"But why?" Shandi cried. "Why did you do all that?"

Ryan's eyes bugged out, clearly incredulous that she had to ask the question. "Because I love you!"

Shandi stopped in her tracks. She turned to the audience, striking a pose as if she were about to make a speech, but she only wanted us to see her astonished reaction. Always the Diva. It was so contrived, the audience burst into laughter.

I had to admit she knew how to put her best foot forward.

"I didn't know any of this," she said, her tone sorrowful.

Derek turned to Ryan, "You killed Lawson Schmidt for the money?"

"Yes."

"You killed Lawson?" Shandi said, shock in her tone.

"He had the book you wanted," he said, exasperated. "And he'd used the festival money to get it. So I warned him that I would reveal what he'd done unless he gave me the rest of the money."

"That's blackmail," Shandi said.

"So what?" he said. "It was working. I was getting the money for you. But then Lawson said he was going to tell the police, so I had to, you know, kill him."

"Who are you?" she whispered.

He just shrugged.

"How did you find out about Lawson's book?" I shouted.

Ryan shielded his eyes from the bright stage lights, focused on me, and said, "I overheard Lawson telling Clyde about it. Said he paid ten thousand dollars for it. They didn't notice me listening. Nobody notices me. I'm quiet."

"He *is* quiet," Mom admitted.

She and I moved closer to the foot of the stage to hear the details. Ryan was completely without remorse. It was sickening, but fascinating all the same, and I wanted to catch every word he said.

"Lawson was going to give you all the money?" Derek said.

"Not at first," Ryan said. "But I'd heard him talk about the book and how he'd pilfered some of the money, so I threatened to tell Becky and he offered to give me a portion if I would keep my mouth shut."

"But you wanted it all," Mom said.

"You bet your ass."

"So you met him that night in the conference room?" I asked.

"Yeah. I offered to share a bottle of wine with him so of course he came willingly. You wine people are easily led to slaughter."

I snorted. This guy had killed or attempted to kill at least three people and he was disparaging *us*?

Clyde shouted from the side aisle, "Once Lawson was dead, did you try to work a deal with Banyan to get him into the festival?"

"Sure. Why not? He has money. I figured he could pay me as much as he'd been willing to pay to get a seat on the committee, right?"

Someone knelt down next to me. "Talkative little creep, isn't he?"

I turned and did a double take. "Inspector Lee!" I grabbed her in a tight hug. "I'm so glad you're here."

The San Francisco homicide detective looked as beautiful and chic as ever in a black cashmere sweater, silk slacks, and high-heeled booties.

"I was at the festival earlier but didn't get over to

your booth." She grinned. "Never a dull moment around you, Brooklyn."

Clyde wasn't finished with Ryan. "Why did you break into my bookshop?" he demanded.

"I knew that Lawson had given you the book, so I figured I could track you down and steal it. Not that I cared about the book that much, but I knew Shandi would like to have it." He gazed longingly in Shandi's direction. "There's nothing I wouldn't do to make you happy."

The actress was rolling her eyes, clearly fed up with her thoroughly corrupt assistant.

"Did you expect to kill me, too?" Clyde asked.

"If I had to."

Clyde sucked in a breath. "Did you lure Banyan to the bookshop?"

"No, he followed me there. He walked in and threatened me, so I pulled my knife." He grinned. "He didn't look too happy when I sliced his neck."

"A total psychopath," I muttered.

"And completely insane," Inspector Lee whispered, then shook her head. "It's always the clean-cut, boy-next-door types you've gotta look out for."

I turned my attention back to Ryan and said loudly, "But you didn't find the book."

Ryan squinted in order to see who had spoken. "Oh, it's you again. No."

Pulling the book out of my purse, I waved it in the air, taunting him. "You could've won it in the silent auction for forty or fifty bucks, but you were too stupid to recognize its value."

His eyes widened and without warning he leaped toward me, trying to get his hands on the book. Or my neck.

Gabriel and Alex both grabbed the back of his shirt and shoved him back onto the couch. "Dude, you're not going anywhere."

"Why did you attack me?" my mother shouted from the first row.

He looked at Shandi then and his bottom lip trembled. Was he finally showing some hint of emotion? "She told me you were too old to play Jo. She said you were no spring chicken."

Shandi started to laugh and it was the first honest sound I'd heard her utter.

Ryan looked incensed. "Don't laugh! It was awful. She had to pay."

"But Ryan, honey. It's true. I'm no spring chicken. But I've got plenty of years left to strut my stuff."

"I just wanted to make sure you could return to Hollywood in style. In fact, I'm glad I ruined this whole musical. You'll get more publicity than ever and you'll return to A-list status. You'll be in demand. I don't mind if I go to jail."

"No worries, he's definitely going to jail," Inspector Lee whispered.

Ryan scanned the stage and the audience looking for sympathy. "My only concern is for Shandi."

Shandi glanced out into the audience and held out her hands in mock surrender. "What can I say? People love me."

And the crowd went wild.

Chapter 17

Maybe that wild reaction of the audience could be blamed on the anxiety and stress we'd all been suffering. After weeks of preparation and then three days of festival frenzy along with two murders and several attempts at a third, maybe things had simply caught up with all of us.

Not only that, but we had all just watched a vicious killer get taken down, live on stage at the grand finale of a lighthearted musical. It was operatic, for goodness' sake!

So yeah, everyone in the crowd just sort of lost their minds.

The police had taken Ryan away and had finally managed to calm the crowd down. But before they could get everyone out of the theater, Shandi came to the edge of the stage and shouted for attention. "The police have a job to do, but so do we. We want to finish the show."

"The show must go on," London yelled from the side of the stage.

Stevie wasn't about to make everyone in town hate him, so he gave a big wave to Shandi. "Nobody leaves until we see that big final number."

With a flourish, the orchestra struck up the chords to the big finale and the entire cast joined in to sing "Sometimes When You Dream."

And there wasn't a dry eye in the place.

The police instructed everyone to leave the theater in a single-file line. It was slow going, but the authorities had to get names and contact information from each person before they were allowed to go home.

Unfortunately, that didn't include me. Or Mom. Or anyone else who was still on stage, including all of the actors and Derek, Alex, and Gabriel. Stevie assured us all that we weren't leaving anytime soon.

I noticed that Saffron Bergeron had slithered out with the rest of the audience. I really wanted to know what schemes she had been running with Banyan and Ryan and anyone else who was willing to sabotage the festival and my mother. But those questions would have to wait.

I sat in the first row with Mom. Inspector Lee had disappeared a while ago to commiserate with the local police detectives, but now she strolled toward me, shaking her head and rolling her eyes. "Jeez, Brooklyn, we really can't take you anywhere."

I let out a heavy breath. "I know."

"So, let's talk motives," she said. "Was it all about the book this time?"

"The book definitely complicated things," I admitted. "But mostly it was all about obsessive love and greed."

"Two of my favorites." She sat down next to me. "So I guess you kind of saved the day."

"Would you mind mentioning that fact to Stevie?"

The Inspector's lips twisted in a wry smile. "Stevie?"

I winced. "I mean, Detective Willoughby. He and I

were in grammar school together. Back then he was known as Stevie."

"That's sweet." She watched the goings on up on stage for a minute, then gave me a sideways glance. "Nice vault, by the way."

I remembered how I'd hurdled over the heads of several people to get to my mom.

"I wasn't even thinking," I admitted. "I just did what I needed to do."

"You stopped the show, kid." She gave me a light elbow jab. "And probably saved your mother's life."

Her warm words shocked me so much that I felt my eyes burn. I had to breathe in and out for a few seconds. I refused to break down and cry in front of Inspector Lee, but my heart was full. I guess she was right about saving my mother's life, but it hadn't been a conscious decision. It was simply an instinctive reaction in the moment. *Gun. Mom. No!*

Four days later, the grape harvest began. Each night Derek and I went home exhausted but happy. We dined at Arugula one night, spending a few minutes in the kitchen chatting with my talented chef sister Savannah and Derek's brother Dalton.

I had breakfast with Robin finally—pancakes with the most decadent banana whipped cream and drizzled with chocolate sauce—and we talked about nothing but babies. I was so thrilled for her and Austin, and laughed a lot, especially when she lamented the inevitable loss of her cute figure.

I spent two days working my butt off with Keith at the Dharma Dojo and he pronounced me "not bad." I couldn't wait to tell Alex how much he had gushed over my progress. And I seriously couldn't wait to get back to

Alex's studio and really start pushing toward my very own green belt. I dreamed of the day when I could finally match moves with my sister China.

Gabriel filled us in on the latest happenings in Ryan's double homicide case. Apparently Shandi was happy to spill everything she knew about Ryan and his machinations on her behalf. She admitted that she'd ignored most of what he did because she was the beneficiary of his actions. But when it came to murder, she refused to condone his behavior.

Which made her okay in my book.

After the last long day of the harvest, we all gathered at Mom and Dad's house to celebrate another fantastic season. As Dad poured drinks for everyone, Mom pulled me aside.

"You'll never guess what I found out this afternoon."

I smiled. "You're right, I'll never guess. Tell me."

"Saffron's house is up for sale."

I blinked in surprise. "What does that mean? Is she moving away, I hope?"

"Yes," Mom said. "Far, far away, I imagine. She has no more friends here and her flower shop is going under."

I frowned. "I hate to wish bad luck on anyone, so I won't. But darn it, Mom, that woman was evil."

"She was definitely constipated," Mom said, nodding.

I had to laugh. "Okay, good enough."

"I have more news," she said.

"You're full of news, aren't you?"

"All I have to do is walk down the Lane and people talk to me."

"So what else did you hear?"

"Misty got her winery back. She threatened to sue

the bank for selling her deed to Banyan and they re-scinded the foreclosure notice."

"Now, that's wonderful news," I said, and gave Mom an enthusiastic hug. It was the perfect ending to a long, painful period in the young history of our beloved Dharma.

On our last day in Dharma, Derek wanted to take a ride around the hills and enjoy the views. I jumped into the car, happy to be with him as we meandered through the valley. We drove past both of our parents' homes, then crossed over Dharma Creek toward the winery. Derek turned on Vineyard View and headed for Red Mountain Highway.

"It's so pretty up here," I said, as we drove toward my two brothers' homes in the hills overlooking the vine-yards.

Before we reached the top of Red Mountain, he turned on a smaller road and followed the mild twists and turns until we reached an overlook. He edged off the road and stopped.

"I've never been up here," I said, gazing out at the green hills with their terraced rows of rustic grapevines. "It's beautiful, isn't it?"

"It is." He smiled and unbuckled his seatbelt. "Let's have a look around."

"Okay."

I joined him on the narrow path and held hands as we took another long look at the spectacular view. Then he walked toward a narrower road a few yards up the hill.

"Where are we going?"

"Just up here." He turned down the narrow road and we walked for another forty or fifty yards. Then he stopped in the middle of a wide swatch of land that stretched from the narrow road all the way to the edge of a shallow gorge a few hundred yards away. "What do you think?"

I smiled at him, mystified. "About what?"

He spread his arms out. "About building a second home here."

I opened my mouth, but no words came out.

"Is that a yes?" he said, laughing.

"You've managed to stun me into silence," I admitted.

"A moment for the history books." Still laughing, he wrapped his arms around me. "We need a more permanent home here, darling. We visit often enough and it's fine to be able to stay in the houses of our friends and family. But there's a baby on the way and I know you're going to want to be here for Robin. And with my parents visiting more regularly, I'd like to see them as well. What do you say?"

"This land is for sale?" I asked, my voice sounding tremulous.

"Yes. Robson owns it and is willing to sell it to us for a good price."

"Okay, you've shocked me again." I blinked away tears of happiness and looked around again, loving what I saw from every angle. I knew that Derek had probably checked out every square inch of dirt on this large, lovely plot of land so I wasn't worried there would be too many flaws to consider. And not only did it have views for miles, but it was also ten minutes away from our parents' homes and five minutes away from Robin and my brothers. A few minutes more would take us to Gabriel's house on the other side of Montana Ridge Road.

"I'm amazed and thrilled that you thought of it," I said. "I love you so much."

"And I love you back," he whispered, and stroked my hair. We turned toward the view. "So what do you say?"

I laughed and squeezed my arms around him. "I say yes."

Recipes

BREAKFAST GRAIN BOWL

2 cups cooked quinoa or rice
4 slices of bacon, diced
¼ cup onion, diced
1 tomato, diced
4 cups baby spinach, kale, arugula,
or any combination thereof
Mild vinegar
Toasted sesame oil or olive oil for drizzling
1 avocado, sliced
4 eggs
Salt and pepper

Divide grain into four bowls. Keep warm.

Heat a pan over medium heat. Add bacon and onions, and cook until bacon is browned. Toss in tomato and greens. When the greens are wilted, divide into the four bowls. Drizzle with a little vinegar and oil, then stir. Place one-quarter of the avocado in each bowl.

Return pan to heat and spray with nonstick cooking spray or add a little oil to the pan. Crack the four eggs into the pan, one at a time, keeping apart. Cover pan and turn off the heat, but leave the pan on the burner. Leave the eggs there, without flipping, until the whites are set but the yolks are still runny. Top each bowl with one egg, and salt and pepper to taste.

Tip: Use good quality fresh eggs. Cage-free, vegetarian-fed makes a difference in terms of not having the yolk break on you in the pan.

STREUSEL-TOPPED MAPLE-PUMPKIN SCONES

MAPLE SUGAR:

*1 cup granulated sugar
2 tbsp maple syrup*

Stir together maple and sugar with a fork until well combined. Set aside.

STREUSEL TOPPING:

*¼ cup flour
2 tbsp maple sugar, packed
1 tbsp butter*

Whisk the flour and sugar until well combined. Cut in the butter with a pastry blender (or two butter knives). Set aside.

SCONES:

½ cup canned pumpkin (not pumpkin pie filling)
2¼ cups flour
1 tbsp baking powder
½ tsp baking soda
½ tsp salt
1 tsp cinnamon
½ tsp nutmeg
½ cup maple sugar, packed
½ cup cold butter, cut into ¼-inch chunks
1 egg
¼ cup + 1 tbsp cream, divided
1 tsp vanilla

Place pumpkin in a sieve over a bowl so the pumpkin will drain. If possible, do this the night before and put the sieve and bowl in the fridge because cold ingredients make for flaky scones.

Preheat oven to 400 degrees F. Line a baking sheet with parchment paper and put in the fridge.

Sift together the flour, baking powder, baking soda, salt, cinnamon, and nutmeg. Whisk in the sugar. Add the butter to the dry ingredients and cut in with a pastry blender until the mixture has a crumb-like texture.

In a separate bowl, whisk together the egg, pumpkin, ¼ cup of cream, and vanilla. Fold into the dry ingredients just until the mixture pulls together into a ball. If necessary, add additional cream one teaspoon at a time. Don't overwork.

Place the ball on the parchment-lined baking sheet and pat down into a 10-inch circle. Slice into 8 wedges and pull apart so each scone is separate. Brush with cream. Top with streusel. Bake until scones are brown on bottom and streusel is golden on top, about 20–25 minutes.

AVOCADO TOAST WITH CHEESE, BACON, FRIED EGG, AND ONIONS

2 slices of bacon
2 small or 1 large ripe avocado
2 tbsp olive oil
2 slices of a large onion
2 thick pieces of bread—whatever bread you find most delicious
2 eggs
2 very thin slices of the cheese of your choice
Salt and pepper

Cook the bacon in a skillet. Meanwhile, mash the avocado flesh with a pinch of salt. When the bacon is done, drain on paper towels and set aside, but keep warm. Drain the bacon grease and wipe out the pan. Add the olive oil. Once it's shimmery, caramelize the onions over low heat. While the onions are cooking, toast the bread.

Set onions aside and keep warm. Crack the eggs into the pan, breaking the yolks immediately and spreading the yolk across as much of the egg's surface as possible (to get that flavor in every bite). While eggs are cooking, top each slice of toast with half the avocado and half the bacon.

Flip the eggs over, top with cheese and the caramelized onions, then turn off the pan and cover. Let sit until the cheese is melted, about a minute. Put one egg atop the toast-avocado-bacon base. Season with salt and pepper.

PANCAKES WITH BANANA WHIPPED CREAM

BANANA WHIPPED CREAM:

1 cup heavy whipping cream
1 tsp granulated sugar
½ tsp vanilla
Yellow food coloring (optional)
1 banana, ripe but not discolored

If possible, refrigerate the empty bowl for an hour or more before making the whipped cream. The cream sets up better in a cold bowl. Put cream, sugar, vanilla, and if using, a few dashes of food coloring into the cold bowl. With the whisk attachment on a mixer, whisk on low speed. Gradually increase speed until you reach the maximum. Be careful not to let the cream spill over. Continue to whisk until whipped cream reaches the desired consistency. Mash the banana in a separate bowl, then add to the whipped cream. Whisk until thoroughly incorporated.

PANCAKES:

1 cup all-purpose flour
1 tbsp baking powder
1 tbsp granulated sugar
1 tsp salt
¾ cup milk

1 egg
2 tbsp melted butter, plus butter for the pan

Sift together the dry ingredients. Whisk together the milk, egg, and melted butter. Add to the dry ingredients and stir gently just until combined. The batter should be lumpy.

Heat a griddle over medium heat. Add a thin slice of butter to the pan. When melted, spread it out with the spatula. Pour ¼ cup of batter at a time to make four-inch pancakes. When you start to see bubbles form around the edges, check carefully to see if the pancake is ready to flip. Keep warm until ready to serve.

MEG'S SPANISH-STYLE TORTILLA

The Spanish-style tortilla has more in common with a quiche or an omelet than it does with a Mexican tortilla. This is not something you use to wrap other ingredients. Rather, it can be a meal on its own.

¼ cup of good quality extra virgin olive oil
3 medium-sized red potatoes, peeled or unpeeled, cut
into ½-inch chunks
1 medium onion, diced
Salt and pepper
6 eggs

In a 10-inch nonstick skillet, heat the olive oil over medium. When the oil is shimmering, add the chopped potatoes and onions. Sprinkle with salt and pepper. Cook, stirring occasionally, until the potatoes are cooked.

Whisk the eggs and pour them over the potatoes and onions in the pan. Let them cook without stirring until the eggs are nearly set. To help the process, you can gently lift the edges of the cooked egg so that uncooked egg slips under that section.

When nearly set, slide the whole pie-shaped mixture onto a plate or the lid of the pan. Then invert the pan on top of the eggs and flip the pan, the eggs, and the plate so that the uncooked side of the tortilla is now on the heat. Cook all the way through.

To serve, cut into wedges.

MOCK DEVONSHIRE CREAM

There really is no substitute for Devonshire cream. But since it's not easy to find in the United States, this may be the best you can do.

8 oz mascarpone cheese*
½ cup heavy whipping cream
1 tsp sugar
½ tsp lemon juice
½ tsp vanilla

Using a mixer with a whisk attachment on high speed, whip together the cheese and cream in a cold bowl until soft peaks start to form. Add the sugar, lemon juice, and vanilla, and whip until thoroughly combined. Serve alongside fruit jam with traditional scones.

*If you can't find mascarpone cheese, you can use cream cheese.

TRADITIONAL BRITISH SCONES

2 cups of all-purpose flour
2 tbsp sugar
1 tbsp baking powder
½ tsp baking soda
½ tsp salt
3 tbsp cold butter, cut into ¼-inch chunks
¾ cup milk
1 egg, separated

Sift together the dry ingredients. Cut in the butter with a pastry blender or two butter knives until the mixture resembles coarse crumbs. In a separate bowl, whisk the milk and egg white. Pour over the dry ingredients and stir very gently, just until moistened.

Turn dough, which will be quite sticky, onto a lightly floured surface. Dust with more flour and add some flour to your hands, and knead gently 5–10 times. Pat into a 10-inch circle or, for smaller scones, into two five-inch circles. Cut into wedges.

Bake on a pan lined with parchment paper at 350 degrees F until golden brown, about 25 minutes. Serve with jam and Devonshire cream.

BREAKFAST TACOS
WITH HOMEMADE SALSA

HOMEMADE SALSA:

1 14-oz can of diced tomatoes with juices
2 tsp ground cumin
*½ of a jalapeno (with seeds for spicy, without seeds for
mild), cut into ½-inch chunks*
1 clove of garlic
¼ cup fresh cilantro leaves
½ tsp salt

Put all ingredients into a food processor. Pulse 4–5
times.

BREAKFAST TACOS:

Mexican tortillas—flour or corn
Scrambled eggs
Sausage or bacon
Shredded cheese
Diced onions
Diced tomatoes
Diced potatoes or hash browns, cooked

Warm the tortillas. Top with any or all of the suggested
ingredients, plus salsa. No amounts are provided because it depends on how many people are being served—
and how hungry they may be.

THE GRIM READER

Kate Carlisle

Book Group Discussion Questions

MENU SUGGESTION FOR BOOK GROUP:
Breakfast smorgasbord, using recipes found in this book

Note: These questions may contain spoilers. It's recommended that you finish reading the book before you read any of the questions.

1. Who were the suspects in the murder? What were the clues that made you suspect each one? Did you figure out the killer before the end of the book? How?

2. What were the red herrings in this book? (A red herring is a false clue that leads you to suspect the wrong person.)

3. Were you surprised when one of the main suspects was killed partway through the book? Why or why not?

4. In each Bibliophile Mystery, the modern-day mystery centers on a rare book in Brooklyn Wainwright's care. In this case, *Little Women*. What interesting facts did you learn about *Little Women* by reading *The Grim Reader*?

5. *Little Women* is very much a story about a close family, and so is *The Grim Reader*. Describe how the closeness of Brooklyn's and Derek's families were revealed throughout the book.

6. Have you read any or all of the previous Bibliophile Mysteries? (You'll find a full list on the Books page at KateCarlisle.com.) How do you think that impacted your reading experience?

7. At the book festival, bookbinder Brooklyn Wainwright hosted several activities.

   • *Accordion bookmaking for children*. Share an early childhood book-related memory with the group.

   • *Book and wine pairings*. Name one of your favorite books and suggest a wine that would pair well with it.

   • *Book appraisals*. Do you personally own any rare or antique books? Tell the group an interesting anecdote about a book in your collection. For example, how did you acquire it? Have you had it appraised?

8. What did you learn about bookbinding after reading *The Grim Reader*? Have you ever taken a book arts class?

9. Brooklyn and Derek spend most of their time in San Francisco, but this book took place entirely in Dharma. How did the setting of Dharma impact the storyline? For next year's Bibliophile Mystery, do you hope it will take place in Dharma or in the city—or neither or both? Based on the ending of *The Grim Reader*, where do you think the next book will take place?

10. Suggest other rare books you'd like to see featured in a future Bibliophile Mystery. If you'd like to come up with a list as a group, Kate Carlisle would love to hear from you. You can contact her at KateCarlisle.com. While you're there, visit the Secret Room to find fun bonus content such as puzzles, word games, maps of Dharma and Brooklyn's San Francisco, contests, and more.

Keep reading for a sneak peek of

Little Black Book

The next Bibliophile Mystery by Kate Carlisle!

The black book arrived in the mail on a quiet Saturday afternoon.

My husband Derek walked into my workshop balancing a large bundle of letters and parcels in his arms. "We've quite a backlog of mail, darling."

I glanced up and smiled at him. We had been married less than a year, so I could forgive myself for wanting to sigh dreamily. I would never grow tired of looking at his ruggedly handsome face, with those dark blue eyes and his dangerous smile. I simply loved everything about him, even the way he occasionally aimed one inquisitive, raised eyebrow in my direction—how did he do that?—or the way his voice could go all cold and upper-class Brit when dealing with some knucklehead trying to pull a fast one over on him. Of course, that same voice turned rich and warm when he was talking only to me. He was tall and lean and tough and sexy. And he made me laugh every day, which made him even sexier in my book. He was just plain perfect for me.

And somehow, he felt the same way about me.

"Darling?"

I blinked. "Oh." *Whew, what brought that on?* "Um, yeah, looks like the mail really piled up while we were gone."

Late last night Derek and I returned home to San Francisco from Dharma, where we had spent the last ten days enjoying the wine country, visiting our parents and friends, and checking on the final phase of construction on our new home away from home. It was no wonder we had so much mail.

And so much work to catch up on, I added mentally, staring at the fractured copy of *The Adventures of Tom Sawyer* spread out in pieces in front of me.

He was still staring at me, his lips twisted in a wry grin. "Are you sure you're all right?"

"Oh yeah, I'm dandy." But I had to take a quick breath and let it out slowly. Sometimes it hit me just how much I loved this guy. And what made it even better was that he loved me right back. I'd probably get used to it in a few hundred years or so. "I guess I'm still a little tired from the trip. And now I've got to finish this book before I do anything else."

"You'll get it done." He kissed the top of my head, and we leaned into each other for a brief moment. Then he stepped away, and I shook my head to clear my errant thoughts. It was time to concentrate on my work.

I carefully separated the ragged covers of the old *Tom Sawyer* copy I'd been asked to restore. I planned to replace the faded cloth cover and spine with a sturdy new cloth in deep forest green, and then add new end-papers to the inside—front and back. The text block it-self was remarkably undamaged, the pages still crisp and clean. Clearly the book had been lucky enough to have escaped the ravages of any children who, in general, have an overwhelming tendency to love their favorite books to death. With a sturdy new outer shell and a little help from me, these pages might last a few hundred more years.

Derek walked around to the opposite end of my worktable and set the piles of mail down. Then he proceeded to sort them into smaller piles.

"Lots of bills," he muttered. "And plenty of junk. Ah, here's a postcard from Douglas and Delia. They're in Santorini."

"I hope they're having fun," I said. Douglas was Derek's oldest brother and a general in the British Army. His wife Delia was lovely and had a wonderful dry wit.

"It seems they are," he said, giving the card a quick scan.

"I'm glad."

"Alex is doing well, by the way," he said, speaking of our neighbor down the hall. "She promises she'll be by shortly with cupcakes in honor of our homecoming."

That got my attention. "Cupcakes? For real?"

"I saw them with my own eyes."

Alex Monroe had offered to collect our mail while we were gone and also to keep an eye on our place. As a former CIA operative, she was handy when it came to security issues. She was the high-powered head of her own company and liked to bake cupcakes to relax. She really was the best kind of neighbor in every way.

Derek set the postcard down on one of the piles he'd created and continued perusing the stack. "Someone sent you a book."

He walked around and placed the excessively taped and padded manila envelope down in front of me.

"A book for me?" I grinned. "Why would anyone send me a book?"

He chuckled because I was joking, of course. I'm a bookbinder specializing in rare-book restoration. I received books in the mail from clients all the time.

I was thankful the envelope was padded because the back was scuffed and dirty and slightly dented from traveling. I turned it over to see who it was from, but there was no individual's name on the return address. Just a company, Quinn Imports, located in Inverness, Scotland.

Scotland?

I stared at the addressee. "Derek, this isn't for me. It's addressed to you."

"Me?" It was his turn to frown. "How odd. I didn't even look. I could tell it was a book and naturally assumed it was for you."

"I did, too." I held out the package. "But it's got your name on it."

He took it and glanced around for some way to cut through the layers of packing tape.

"Scissors in the top drawer," I said helpfully, pointing toward my desk.

"Of course." Once he had it opened, he slid the book out onto the worktable. Looking at the title, he said, "Now I'm doubly sure it was meant for you."

I picked up the book. The cloth cover was a stark black. The only thing on the front of the book was the one-word title printed in faded gold and slanted in the upper left-hand corner: *Rebecca*.

"*Rebecca*." I flashed him a bright smile. "One of my favorites." I had always been a sucker for gothic novels. The plucky heroine doomed to live a life of drudgery, rescued by the handsome stranger—or is he a killer? Dark and moody, romantic and suspenseful, I had spent my preteen years gobbling them up.

I chuckled at my own thoughts, then naturally turned to the book itself to examine the condition of the front and back covers. That's my job, after all, so it was second nature for me to check out the spine, which showed the same elegantly styled title and the author's name below it in simple block letters. I ran my hand along the spine.

The cloth covers of old books had a tendency to separate and sag away from the stiff material underneath, but this spine was still firm and smooth.

I turned the book over again. "Outer corners are slightly rubbed. Spine has a bit of wear at the bottom edge." I pointed out the discoloration.

"I see," Derek murmured.

"The binding is tight, though," I added, standing the book upright on the table. "No wobbling, see?"

"I do, and it thrills me." He leaned over and kissed my cheek.

I laughed. "You need to get out more."

He picked up the book and studied the cover. "Can you fix the discoloration?"

"Of course. But I won't do anything until we find out who sent it to you and why."

"Yes." He handed the book back to me. "Why, indeed."

"Do you know anyone named Quinn?"

"I don't think so."

Opening the book to the title page, I studied the information written there. "Derek, it's a British first edition. First printing. 1938." I turned the page. "And look. It's signed by Daphne du Maurier." I looked up at him. "Wow."

"That is impressive," he said with a nod.

"I'll go through it more thoroughly later, but overall the book appears to be in very good condition. And that signature raises its value significantly." I smiled. "Someone must like you a lot."

"I'm a likeable fellow." But his eyes narrowed slightly and that wonderful mouth turned grim as he wondered where the book had come from. He pushed the sleeves of his navy sweater up to his elbows and leaned against the table. "Is there a card or something inside the book that indicates who exactly sent it? And why?"

"Good question."

While Derek studied the front of the manila envelope, I carefully leafed through the book, then held it upside down, gently fanning the pages open so that anything that might've been slipped inside would fall out. But there was nothing. "Is there anything else inside the envelope?"

He checked it thoroughly. "Nothing."

"So it's a mystery," I said.

He raised an eyebrow. "Just what we need. Another mystery."

"It's been months since the book festival," I said with a shrug. "We're about due, don't you think?"

"Bite your tongue, darling."

The Dharma Book Festival last October had been a huge success and had garnered lots of publicity, no thanks to the two murders that had taken place only days before it all began. Happily, though, the killer had been caught before he could complete a third, and eventually all of our lives had settled back down to normal. Or as normal as we could ever be, given my tendency to attract evil killers and their ilk.

So yes, mysteries and murderous intentions did seem to follow us wherever we went, but it wasn't all my fault. My dear husband was one of the world's top security experts and, after all, the book had been sent to him. So for once, this little puzzle was on him. Which was, no doubt, why he was staring at the mysterious book with such a thoughtful expression.

The doorbell rang and we stared at each other.

"Cupcakes?" I wondered.

"Let's hope so."

He took my hand and we walked over to the door.

"Welcome home," Alex declared, and strolled in carrying a large sturdy plastic cupcake carrier. She looked ridiculously elegant in simple black leggings, white sneakers, and a sage green tunic. Setting the carrier on the kitchen island, she turned and grabbed me in a fierce hug. "So glad you guys are home."

"We are, too," I said. "Thanks so much for taking care of Charlie and for holding our mail. And for the cupcakes and for everything else you always do. We really appreciate it."

"It's no prob." She glanced around. "Charlie was right behind me."

"Charlie?" I called.

Hearing her name, our little beast dashed through the door and immediately began winding herself around my ankles and mewing loudly.

"Aww. Hello, sweetie," I said, and picked up the cat. Charlie gave my cheek a light head butt. "So good to see you."

Alex smiled. "I think she missed you."

"I missed her, too." I rubbed my cheek against her soft fur, enjoying the sound of her contented purring. After another minute of cuddling, I set Charlie on the floor and got down to business. "Now about these cupcakes."

She laughed. "Twelve of them. Three different flavors."

Derek joined us. Reaching down, he lifted the pretty white and orange cat into his arms, much to Charlie's delight. "Alex, honestly. We should be the ones bringing you cupcakes. We owe you."

"Don't be silly." She reached over to scratch Charlie's neck. "I got to play with Charlie for ten whole days, so that's more than a fair trade. Besides, you know I'm compelled to bake. I can't seem to help myself. So if I didn't give some of them to you, I'd have to eat them all by myself."

"So we're doing you a favor?" I said.

She grinned. "Exactly."

"Well then, how can we refuse?" I glanced up at Derek. "Guess we should have a cupcake."

"It's about time." For a sophisticated international man of mystery, he pretty much turned to putty when it came to cupcakes.

The three of us clustered around the cupcake carrier and Alex snapped off the lid.

"Wow," I said.

"My thoughts exactly," Derek said.

I recognized her red velvet cakes with their tall swirl of cream-cheese frosting. The chocolate-chip cupcakes were slathered in glistening white icing with tiny chocolate chips scattered on top. The third row looked like a yellow cake with white frosting of some kind. I desperately wanted them all, but didn't say it out loud.

Pointing to each row of cupcakes, Alex said, "You've had the red velvet and the chocolate chip before, but this one is something I've been experimenting with. I think you'll love it."

"Of course we will," Derek said, examining the new treat. "What is it? Some sort of yellow cake?"

"It's a lemon meringue cupcake."

"Oh," I whispered in awe. "I've heard you talk about this."

"I didn't want anyone to try it until I'd perfected it." She wiggled her eyebrows gleefully. "And now I have."

"They're so pretty." The frosting was a tall swirl of

shiny white, with tiny sprigs of lemon and lime zest sprinkled on top.

"They taste even better than they look," she assured us.

I glanced at Derek. "We could split one. For starters, I mean."

"That works for me."

We both took a bite and discovered a surprise. Inside the cake was a pocket of rich, lemony curd, sweet and slightly tart. The meringue icing was light and fluffy and melted in my mouth.

"This is heavenly," I said, when I could speak again. "It's like eating lemon meringue pie."

"Only it's cake. Moist and delicious." Derek surreptitiously brushed a crumb off his sweater. "I believe your talents are wasted running that silly corporation of yours."

Delighted, Alex laughed and tossed back her long, dark, silky hair. "Thanks."

"It's true," I insisted. "Why sell your soul to high finance when you could be selling cupcakes out on the street?"

The three of us spent a few more minutes laughing and talking and gossiping. After she'd agreed to come over for dinner the next night, Alex headed back home.

Derek went to his office to return some phone calls and I went back to work on the *Tom Sawyer*. Even knowing that Derek was just down the hall, it was easy for me to become consumed by my work. Books—especially old, decrepit books—had always been a major part of my life, and I looked at each one like a dedicated surgeon looked at a suffering patient. *How can I make you whole again? How can I improve your life?*

The interior pages of the *Tom Sawyer* were actually in pretty good shape, except for some tears and mild foxing in various sections of the book. I went ahead and separated the cover from the text block in order to clean the gutters thoroughly and eventually resew the pages with a new, stronger thread. I wanted this book to last another few hundred years.

As usual, I got lost in my work, and it wasn't until several hours later that I emerged, ready to call it a day. I straightened my work space and laid a white cloth over the separated sections of the old book.

I hadn't realized that Derek left the copy of *Rebecca* on my worktable, but now I saw it and a dozen questions popped into my head. Who had sent it to Derek? And why? Why no return address? What was this all about? Was it from someone who simply wanted their book to be refurbished? Maybe they knew that Derek's wife was a bookbinder but didn't know my name.

But things were never that simple, were they? Then again, was I making too much of this little mystery? I had been involved in so many bigger mysteries over the past few years that I might've been letting my imagination run away with me. But just in case, I figured it would be smart to slip the *Rebecca* into our safe, just to be cautious.

I headed for the old dumbwaiter in our hallway and opened it up to reveal a seriously well-built, steel-lined fireproof safe where I kept my most valuable books, along with some extra cash and a few important documents. Whatever its background story was, the *Rebecca* was safe and secure for now.

I joined Derek in the kitchen where he had just poured two glasses of red wine.

"You read my mind," I said, and pulled a box of crackers from the pantry. I found a round of cheese in the cooler drawer and remembered the little jar of fig-and-apple compote that my mother had given us, which would be perfect for spreading on the cheese and crackers. Then I filled a small bowl with olives and another with almonds and placed everything on a serving tray.

Derek handed me a glass and touched his to mine. "Cheers, darling. Welcome home."

"It's good to be home." I studied the rich color of the estate-bottled Cabernet Sauvignon that we had brought back from Dharma. "We were smart to bring all these goodies back from Dharma."

He wisely hid a grin. "Now we won't have to settle for takeaway on our first official night back in town."

It was a well-known fact that I didn't cook. Although, to be fair, lately I had been experimenting with a few simple meals. And since neither of us had come down with food poisoning yet, I considered that a real accomplishment.

I'd started to take a sip when the doorbell rang. I checked the kitchen clock and saw that it was just after five o'clock. It was still light outside, but not for long. "That's the downstairs doorbell."

"Yes. Let's see who it is." Derek's voice was calm. His posture was deceptively relaxed, but I knew he had gone on full alert. As the owner of a multinational security firm and former MI6 operative, it was pretty close to his natural state.

We walked together into the kitchen where our nifty television monitor and security system was set up. After surviving several disturbing break-ins in the past, our building security had been upgraded last year. The monitor screen would give us a good view of whoever was standing outside our building's front door, six floors down from our apartment.

An attractive woman stood on the sidewalk. She had dark red hair and I guessed she was in her early thirties. She wore a navy blue anorak over a thick cable-knit sweater with faded jeans and sturdy ankle boots, an outfit similar to that worn by thousands of women in the chilly month of May. Her shoulders were hunched and she held her arms tightly across her chest, as though she were freezing from the cold.

And she looked vaguely familiar.

"Yes, hello?" Derek spoke into the microphone.

The woman glanced around as if she might be trying to figure out where that voice was coming from.

"Hello, good afternoon?" Her own voice held a hint of a British accent—or was it a brogue? She continued looking around, then noticed the camera up above the door. "Oh, right. Hello. My name is Claire Quinn. I apologize for interrupting your afternoon, but I wonder—if you wouldn't mind, that is—can you tell me please: Are you Derek Stone? And did you recently receive a package from Scotland?"

Derek and I turned and stared at each other. Then I glanced back at the woman on the monitor. I moved closer to the screen and took a good, long look. Gazing at Derek, I pressed my finger over my lips in the universal symbol to be quiet.

He leaned into the microphone and said clearly, "Just a moment, please, Ms. Quinn." He pushed the mute button so the woman wouldn't be able to hear our conversation.

"I know her," I said in a hushed tone.

"I thought she looked familiar as well."

"She and I worked together on *This Old Attic*. Do you remember her?"

"Ah, yes." He nodded, connecting the dots.

The popular television show traveled around the country and invited local people to bring their treasured family heirlooms and antiques in to be appraised on camera. When the production company came to San Francisco two years ago, I was hired to be their book expert for two weeks. I recognized the woman on the monitor as one of the other experts on the show.

"Claire," I said. "We were friendly. Do you remember her?"

It was Derek's turn to study the screen more carefully. "Wasn't she the weapons expert?"

I beamed. "Good memory. Yes, she specialized in antique weaponry. But she was also a big reader, so she and I bonded over books. She brought in some of her favorite old books and asked me if they might be worth anything."

"Were they?"

"Oh, yeah." They were mostly gothic novels, I thought. How very interesting. "I remember an amazing copy of *The Castle of Otranto* that was published in 1765. She could've easily sold it for ten thousand dollars, but apparently it had sentimental value." I waved my hands impatiently. "But that's not important. The package she's referring to is obviously the *Rebecca*."

"Yes." He frowned. "And apparently she has no idea that you live here."

"That hit me, too." I frowned. "She asked for you. Weird, don't you think?"

"I do indeed. Have you any idea where she's from?"

"I'm not sure. I always thought she was English, but since she mentioned Scotland, I'm going to bet she's from Inverness."

Derek's eyes narrowed. "Like the package."

"We shouldn't leave her standing out there in the cold. Let's buzz her in and find out what this mysterious book is all about."

"I'd rather not buzz her in," Derek said. "I'll go down and bring her up."

He knew his security stuff. Instead of allowing Claire to wander upstairs on her own, he would escort her from the lobby straight to our front door. "Much better idea."

Derek gave me a nod and a quick hug. "And then we'll figure out what in blazes is going on."

He switched off the mute button and said into the microphone, "Sorry to keep you waiting, Ms. Quinn. Did you send the package?"

She pressed her lips together and her eyes narrowed. In frustration? Anger?

I studied the woman for a few long seconds. She wore her thick red hair pulled back in a ponytail and she was very pretty, with a rosy complexion and clear blue eyes. Her leather bag had extra straps that she'd fashioned into a backpack. And despite her warm clothing, she looked chilled to the bone.

I noticed that her shoulders were stiff and her arms were tightly crossed. She was more than just cold. She glanced around nervously, and I wondered if she thought someone might be watching her. Or worse. Did she have a partner out of camera range who would attempt to jump Derek? Was this a setup? Would the two of them attack him and rush into our building lobby? Would they race upstairs and break into our apartment?

I confess I have an active imagination. It comes from being confronted one too many times by vicious killers. And if I were thinking more clearly, I would've remembered that it was next to impossible for anyone to get the jump on Derek.

After a long moment, Claire admitted, "No, I didn't send it. I believe my aunt sent it. And now she's missing."

Derek and I exchanged a speculative glance and then nodded in unison. He said into the mic, "Please wait a moment. I'll be right there to let you in."

He jogged down the hall to his office. A minute later he returned wearing his black leather bomber jacket. He stopped at the console table by the front door to grab his keys, and when he turned, I caught sight of him tucking a deadly looking gun into his inside jacket pocket.

"I'm going with you," I said, pulling on the sweater I'd draped over a dining room chair. It was springtime in San Francisco, and with the sun going down, it was growing colder. But that had nothing to do with the chills I felt running up and down my spine.

He eyed me warily. "I'd prefer you to stay here."

"No way." I followed him as he hurried across the living room, through the alcove, and into my office workshop, where he took a quick glance out the front window. This room had the only street view to the south.

"It looks safe enough out there," he reasoned. "I'll only be gone a few minutes."

"I'm still going with you."

He gave me a half smile. "Are you worried about me?"

"After everything we've been through? You're darn right I'm worried."

"And you think you can protect me?"

"I always do."

With a quick, fierce laugh, he grabbed my hand. "Then let's go."

Ready to find
your next great read?

Let us help.

Visit prh.com/nextread